the Risky way Home

The Risky Way Home
Published by Even Before Publishing; Christian books by Wombat Books.
P. O. Box 1519, Capalaba Qld 4157
www.evenbeforepublishing.com
www.wombatbooks.com.au

© Paula Vince 2012
Second Edition
Original edition published by Apple Leaf Books, SA
ISBN: 978-0-9581257-4-1

Design and layout by Even Before Publishing

ISBN: 978-1-922074-10-2
Kindle Ebook ISBN: 978-1-922074-12-6
Epub Ebook ISBN: 978-1-922074-11-9

Paula Vince

Even Before Publishing

Australia

Chapter 1

Casey climbed a flight of steps paved with slate. The studio was on the second storey of a complex built in the old colonial style. It was a beautiful area to work.

Well, I'm here now. She attempted to bolster herself up. *'I might as well go through with it. I suppose I have nothing to lose.'*

Asking her old school friend for a job was the last thing Casey ever expected to do. Suzanne had been loads of fun but Casey remembered her old way of drawing her friends into trouble with the teachers. She'd been so popular the other girls had considered it a privilege rather than a problem. Scandal seemed to surround Suzanne like an aura from her earliest childhood. She used to tell Casey that she'd been the victim of a kidnapping. Her mother had stolen Suzanne and her brother away from their father. But that had been 'top secret'.

Casey cleared her throat and a bell tinkled over the door as she walked in. Behind a counter sat a handsome young man with cropped, blonde-tinted hair. 'Good afternoon. Can I help you?'

'I'm looking for Suzanne Bowman.'

'I'll get her.' He called, 'Suze, there's someone here to see you.'

Casey studied the gleaming hardwood floorboards. She looked at the plump blue leather couches in the waiting area. Suzanne knew how to land on her feet. She'd done hardly a scrap of work at school but always got by on sheer audacity.

'Casey Miller! Great to see you!' Suzanne rushed over and enveloped Casey in a cloud of overpowering perfume. The wavy black mane of hair still flowed down her back like a lustrous cloud. 'Well, what have you been up to since we left school? Mum told me you'd been to University.'

'Yeah, I finished a degree in History.' Casey couldn't help flushing. She knew this was not the sort of accomplishment Suzanne would admire.

'History, that's right. You always were the brainy one. So what's next?'

Casey sighed. 'That's the problem. I started a teaching diploma but quit. I'm not cut out for teaching.'

Suzanne giggled and patted Casey's shoulder. Rings gleamed on every slender finger.

'I don't blame you. Do you remember when we used to bombard poor old Mr Bell with little paper bombs during science?'

'I know how it feels from Mr Bell's side of the desk now. I was hopeless at discipline and keeping lessons on track. I felt like a pigeon in a pack of vultures. But Dad is upset with me for not hanging in there for longer than one term. I know he'll be angry unless I come up with another job quick smart.'

'Gee, that's too bad,' Suzanne said. 'What can we do for you today? Can we cheer you up with a lovely photo of yourself?'

'Actually, I saw your ad in the paper. You're looking for somebody to help with make-up and clothes for your clients, aren't you? I thought I'd come and apply.' Casey fumbled with the clasps of her handbag. 'I have some references. I did a few make-up and accessory courses last year during my holidays.'

For the first time, Suzanne was serious. 'Thanks Casey. We put that ad in the classifieds a few days ago and there's been a great response but we haven't chosen anyone yet. By the way, this is my partner, Eric Adams. Eric, Casey and I went to school together. I haven't seen her for five years.'

'Pleased to meet you, Casey.' His bold gaze lingered over her. 'Most of the other applicants have had at least some experience in the industry.'

Casey flushed. 'I understand. I didn't really expect to get the job... I just thought I had nothing to lose and... it's been good to see Suzanne again, anyway.'

'Listen, leave your references here. Eric and I will look at them. I promise I'll contact you as soon as I can. Where are you living?'

'At home with my parents.' Casey wished she hadn't come.

'You're joking. Do you mean to tell me that you drove all the way from Victor Harbor to Adelaide when you were at uni? That's more than fifty kilometres!'

'No, I lived in one of the boarding colleges then.'

Another young lady stepped through the door. 'Hello, I'm here for my two o'clock appointment.'

'Yes, you must be Kylie? Step through here.' Suzanne peered over her client's shoulder at Casey. 'I'll be in touch.'

'Thanks.'

Casey stepped into the warm air outside. She leaned against the rough stone wall and let her breath out in a long stream. *Why did I ever think I had a chance? They made it clear that other applicants are more experienced. Suzanne was just being too polite to tell me on the spot.* Asking scatterbrained Suzanne Bowman for a job had been as awkward as Casey had anticipated.

'I felt like the prize idiot,' Casey sat with her mother sharing hot chocolate. 'I had a nerve to think she'd hire me. I have no experience in the glamour business at all. I'll bet Suzanne was just stalling for time by telling me she'd get back to me. I haven't even *seen* her for five years.' She buried her face in her hands.

'At least you've caught up with an old friend,' Helen Miller said. 'I'm sure she feels flattered that you applied. I remember when Suzanne would come here to get you and you'd whiz off on your bikes to the beach.'

'That was a long time ago.'

At school, Suzanne Bowman had been a pivot around which other girls swarmed. She gave the impression of being ravishingly beautiful but a closer look revealed that she was really not even particularly pretty. *Striking* was the word used best to describe Suzanne. Casey would have died for Suzanne's graceful figure.

'You ought to see her boyfriend. He's gorgeous.'

'Do you mean the chap in the studio with her? I don't think he's her boyfriend. Moira says he's only her business partner.'

Casey was astonished. 'She introduced him as her partner. I assumed she meant *partner* partner.'

'Not according to Moira. She might be wrong, though. Suzanne never keeps her mother up-to-date with what's happening in her life.' Helen sighed. 'I feel sorry for Moira. She thinks the world of both her children but they don't seem to understand her. She helped Suzanne get that business up and running and I don't think she got much thanks for it.'

'Did Moira pay for Suzanne's business?'

'She lent a hand. Suzanne couldn't afford all the equipment and fancy clothes she dresses her clients in otherwise. Eric put up his share too. He's the one with the photography expertise. Moira tells me he's quite brilliant.'

Casey shook her head and sighed. 'Where did she discover him? Where does Suzanne meet all these interesting people?'

The Bowman family had always been an enigma. They had appeared in the district some twenty years earlier and bought a large family home. Before that, they lived in France. Rumours had quickly spread that Moira was a wealthy woman although she lived a simple life with her mother and two children. Since the children had left home, Moira and her elderly mother continued to live the same frugal way. Casey liked her. Moira had always been kind to Suzanne's friends. Perhaps having a rich mother explained some of Suzanne's lucky breaks. Casey had no idea if Suzanne's old kidnapping story had a grain of truth in it. Moira seemed far too timid to commit a daring crime.

Casey's father poked his head through the sitting room door. 'Casey, there's a phone call for you. I think it's that Bowman girl.'

Casey leaped out of her armchair and shot past him. Doug Miller looked at his wife and shrugged. 'What's the big deal? We haven't even seen the Bowman girl for five or six years.'

Casey snatched the receiver off the kitchen bench. 'Hello.'

'Hi Casey. You've got the job.'

Her heart jolted. Then and there, she decided that there was nobody in the world like Suzanne who deserved all the lucky breaks she ever got. 'That's fantastic. How can I thank you?' Casey's pulse raced.

'Meet me tomorrow for lunch. We'll discuss pay and all the other mouldy old details then.' Suzanne's giggle tinkled over the line. 'This is the first time Eric and I have been in the position to hire an employee. Business has been booming like you wouldn't believe.'

Casey heard a door slam in the background at Suzanne's apartment and several laughing voices urged her to get off the phone.

'Alright, gotta go. I'm off to a party with a French theme. You should see me sitting here, dressed as Marie Antoinette. This powdered wig has to come off after a few drinks. Let's make it noon tomorrow, back in the studio. Au revoir.'

Casey replaced the receiver in its hook. For some reason, the joy she felt was mingled with regret. Casey trudged upstairs to bed. She kicked off her huge fluffy slippers, sat on the edge of her bed and gazed down at her flannel pyjamas.

Wish I was going to a French party.

Casey met Suzanne at midday, as planned. Eric greeted her pleasantly and returned to work.

Suzanne grabbed Casey's wrist and gave her a whirlwind tour over the premises. Next to the viewing room was the actual photograph studio. A huge camera on a tripod and a fancy silver umbrella stood at the back and by the opposite wall was a roller blind of backdrops. Suzanne flicked them down one by one: pale mauve, violet, light blue, autumn leaf scene, toy land scene for children.

'You'll never need to come in here, though. This next room is where you'll be working.'

They stepped through to a walk-in-wardrobe room lined with beautiful clothes. One wall was for men, one for children and two for women. Behind it was a smaller, ante-room with full length mirrors from floor to ceiling. There was a sink and a small fridge against the back wall. In a corner stood a huge make-up cabinet bursting with eyeshadows, mascaras, lipsticks, blushers and pencils.

'Suzanne, I'm lost for words.'

'Great, isn't it? Let's tootle off to lunch now. Eric will hold the fort for an hour but I need to be back in time for my male model,' Suzanne winked. 'Some young guy wants a portfolio. Eric's always willing to let me handle those clients and I don't complain.'

They left the studio chuckling. Suzanne took Casey to "The Hedgehog's

Hole", her favourite café. They settled into a cosy booth for two by the window. Suzanne ordered ham, cheese and asparagus croissants dripping with butter and double cheese while Casey conscientiously chose a salad platter. Suzanne had always been able to eat whatever she pleased without gaining a scrap of weight.

'Most of the week, a mobile lunch service delivers to us,' Suzanne was saying. 'They make the most scrumptious food. But I wanted to come here today for a good natter. Will you be able to start on Monday morning?'

'Absolutely.' Casey still had no accommodation in Adelaide. She pushed an olive around with her fork and wondered if she dared ask Suzanne to help her find somewhere. Suzanne might suggest a friend who needed a new flatmate.

'You'll be bringing clients through to us, helping them to dress when they've chosen clothes to suit the image they want to present, looking after the laundry and cleaning up. And you'll be doing some bookwork and handling a bit of cash. I'm warning you, you'll find yourself having to change clients' minds whenever they choose something that would look dreadful.' Suzanne wrinkled her nose. 'I'll be happy to leave all that to you so that I can concentrate on photos and make-up.'

'Suzanne, you've helped me out of a really tight spot. I was sure you'd think I hadn't enough experience,' Casey confessed.

'Some of the applicants did have more, but I convinced Eric to let me have a go at having an old friend work with us. I like the idea much better than hiring a stranger.'

'I'm glad you talked him around.' Casey resolved to give the wonderful Eric no chance to regret the decision. 'Suzanne, do you know of any fairly cheap accommodation I could share? It's a long way to North Adelaide from Victor Harbor.'

Suzanne set her chin on her hands. 'Hmmm, I hadn't given that any thought. We'll have to organise something. You can't spend all your free time travelling. I don't think any of my friends have room just now. I'd ask you to share my apartment but my boyfriend, Tim, wouldn't like it. There's already another girl living with us and I really think he'd dig in his heels over two. I'm sorry, Casey. Wish I could…'

'Never mind. I'll find somewhere. So, your boyfriend's name is Tim? I thought Eric might be…'

Suzanne flourished her hands in a sweeping gesture of denial. 'Good heavens, no *way!* Eric and I tried to start something once but we're too alike. We see each other far too much at work for a relationship, anyway.'

Casey nodded, saying nothing. *I think it'd be great to work with a man if I loved him.*

'Tim suits me better than Eric. He's a fairly intense sort of guy. Mysterious. Eric *is* stunning to look at, though.' Suzanne's sharp features suddenly brightened. 'Hey, are you interested in him?'

Casey felt heat infuse her cheeks. 'Hang on! I've only just met him.'

Suzanne giggled. 'You were never good at hiding things. You think he's a dream. Admit it. It'll be fun working with you. I'll do the best I can for you, I promise. I'd rather see Eric with you than with the little flirt he's just split up with. She tried as hard as she could to convince him to stop working with me. She was jealous because Eric used to go out with me. She didn't give a stitch about his feelings or his career. Although I'm not his girlfriend anymore, I want to see him happy. You might be good for him.'

Casey was blushing but Suzanne didn't seem to notice. She went on, 'I've been off on a tangent. All this isn't helping you find a place to live. But I've just had a brainwave! You can stay with Piers. He's been looking for a boarder.'

Casey's heart sank. 'Your brother?'

'Yeah. He has a big old house a little way out of Mount Barker and he's always short of cash. Did you know he has a three-year-old boy?'

'Your mum mentioned something.' Casey's mind raced to think of a polite way of refusing. Suzanne's younger brother was the last person she wanted to live with. He'd been in many of Casey's classes at school but had not shared his sister's popularity. He and his two sole friends had been renowned misfits. Suzanne used to call him her greatest embarrassment. Whenever anybody referred to the 'three stooges', people knew they meant Wayne Forbes, Justin Edwards and Piers Bowman.

Piers had been smarter in lessons than either of his friends but he was judged by the company he kept. He had Suzanne's wild and woolly hair but it had looked odd on a boy. He'd generally suffered asthma attacks during P.E. lessons and had to stagger off the oval to puff his Ventolin.

Suzanne dropped her napkin on her plate and sprang to her feet. 'Come on, let's go back and strike while the iron's hot.'

'No, don't go to any trouble on my account. I can just as easily shoot back and forth.'

'Rubbish! Mount Barker is far closer than Victor Harbor. It won't be putting me out because I'll be doing you both a favour.'

Back at the studio, Suzanne made her phone call. 'Hey Piers, it's me. I've found you the perfect boarder. Do you remember Casey Miller from school...? I'm *dead* serious. She's going to work for me and Eric in the studio. She needs somewhere closer than Victor Harbor to live so I thought of you ... No, she likes the idea. It'll help you both out of a tight spot. Jerome'll like Casey too. I want her to start on Monday so we could come and move her in on Sunday afternoon... Fine. We'll see you then.'

Suzanne hung up with a satisfied beam. 'All done. Piers would be delighted to have you. Those were his very words. He just couldn't believe you'd consider going there. I can tell you, you won't find cheaper rent anywhere else.' For the first time, Suzanne studied Casey's face. 'You don't mind, do you?'

Casey pursed her lips and chose her words carefully. 'Suzanne, I'm not sure. Piers and I never had much in common you know.'

'Now, come on, Casey. You're not harking back to school days, are you? They're a long way behind us now. He's really not all that bad.'

Casey felt herself in a bind. How could she be honest about Piers without offending Suzanne? Suzanne had generously offered her a job for which she was not qualified and then organised some living quarters at Casey's own request. Casey could think of no way to stipulate, 'I don't want to live with your dopey brother,' without sounding incredibly ungrateful.

Instead, she mumbled, 'You really shouldn't have gone to all that trouble.'

'It only took two minutes. I'll meet you here at the studio on Sunday afternoon and we'll drive up to Piers' together. You'll love Jerome. He's a little doll.'

When Casey slid behind the wheel of her car half an hour later, she groaned and thumped the steering wheel with her forehead. How on earth would she come up with an acceptable way to back out of the arrangement? *Why did I open my big mouth?* A few hours drive each day would be preferable to living with Piers Bowman. Casey knew she would have to try hard to find some even closer accommodation to the city in the space of three days.

Chapter 2

Casey hoped she could count on her parents to help her out of the arrangement. Over dinner, she begged them to come up with an excuse for her. "I couldn't think of a thing to tell Suzanne on the spot but I'd hate to live with Piers."

'I don't think you should live with Piers simply because he's a young man and you're a young woman,' Helen said. 'It would be a different story if there was a third person living there.'

Casey gaped at her mother. 'I'm not *interested* in him. I can hardly stand him. Think of something else. If I told Suzanne that, she'd laugh me right out of the studio. She doesn't think the same way we do.'

'It's all the reason you need,' Doug Miller stated with his usual dogmatic attitude. 'Living with that boy would be asking for trouble. Find some girls to share a flat with. I don't care what you tell Suzanne but I don't like it. Just because she lives with men, I don't want *my* daughter to do the same.'

Casey's brother, Dale, who'd driven up from the city, hooted, 'Do you think Casey would have a fling with old Mophead, Dad?'

His sister snapped, 'Very funny. What if I stay at your place? That'd solve my problem.' The thought of sharing Dale's flat would have to be second bottom on her list of preferences. When they were younger, he'd left his litter and belongings spread across the floor of their shared cubby-house. The noise of his drum kit gave her headaches and his feet always seemed to smell, no matter how recently he'd washed them.

Dale shook his head. 'I don't know how long I'll be there myself. After one particular rowdy party we had a week ago, I doubt if my landlady would welcome a sister of mine. There's no room for you, anyway.'

'What have you been up to now?' Helen snapped at her son. 'Can't you stay out of trouble for even one month?'

Casey sighed as her parents turned their attention to her recalcitrant brother. They were no help at all. She wanted to please Suzanne to secure the job with her but she didn't want to compromise her morals either. Suzanne, with her fast lifestyle and independent outlook would not understand. She might even take back her job offer. Casey had pored over all the rentals in several newspapers and found nothing suitable. *There's no way out by Sunday.*

Was the job worth it? Suzanne had said the house was fairly large. Perhaps she would not need to talk to him beyond necessary pleasantries. Would necessary pleasantries be worth it?

The conversation turned back to her plight. 'Don't do it, Casey,' her father said. 'I know you want to work with that Bowman girl but it wouldn't be worth sacrificing your principles.'

'Dad, if I live with Piers, I won't sacrifice my principles,' Casey spoke slowly and earnestly. 'I'd never dream of what you're thinking. That's a promise. I'll only be his boarder. I don't even want to be his friend.'

'It seems you've made up your mind,' her father grumbled. 'You're over twenty-one and we can't force you to change it, but if you go, it'll be without my approval.'

'Won't you trust me and accept my promise?' Casey did not need her father's censure for going to live at a place she did not want to go with a person she didn't even like.

Helen tried to soothe her husband. 'It might work out. I've seen Piers when he visits his mother. He seems like a nice enough young man. He could certainly use the help of having a boarder and I know Moira would be relieved if it was Casey. I think being a single parent has forced him to grow up fast.' She shot her son a look. 'I wish we could trust Dale as far as Moira can trust Piers. I'm sure he's not the sort of boy who'd make trouble for a girl, dear.'

'He made trouble for the mother of his kid,' Doug shot back.

The Risky Way Home

'Well, according to Moira, that girl was the one who made trouble for Piers.'

'Moira's his mother. Of course *she'd* say so.'

'Well I have faith in Piers because his mother is one of my best friends.'

Doug snorted. 'Does that make him a saint in your books? Remember the way Suzanne used to carry on like a man-crazy fool? Moira Bowman is her mother too.'

'Piers is different to Suzanne, Dad,' Dale explained. 'She was cool and he was a nerd. Always had his nose buried in his work and wouldn't even look anyone in the eye.'

'That was years ago,' Doug said. 'Who knows what he's like now. Listen, my girl, if you go to live there, you guard yourself carefully and keep your promise.'

'I will! I'm telling you, if there was a way out, I wouldn't be going.'

'If you've made up your mind, you might as well go cheerfully,' Helen said. 'I think you'll like the little boy. He has a sweet face.'

But Casey shook her head. 'I'm not interested in little kids. I suppose it doesn't matter much where I go. I'll only have to eat and sleep there. And I'll arrange something else as soon as I can without offending Suzanne.'

———————————

Her stomach churned as she trailed Suzanne's small red Pulsar around the curves of the South Eastern Freeway. Casey was on her way to her new home and her back seat was loaded with belongings. Her portable TV seemed ready to topple at any moment so she tried to drive with care.

Suzanne had said, 'It'll be great for Piers to have you there. He's buried alive like a hermit with only little Jerome, and a three-year-old isn't much company. Someone with a spark of life might rub off on him.' While Casey had been flattered by the compliment, she didn't intend to be around Piers long enough for anything to rub off on him.

She followed Suzanne off the Mount Barker exit and eventually onto a narrower, lonelier dirt road. *I hope none of our old school friends find out that I'll be sharing a house with Old Mophead.*

Suzanne turned up a long, pebbly driveway and there was the old, red brick house, with a cute dormer window poking from the green iron roof.

A white goat stood tethered to a post near the stone verandah. It bleated as Casey and Suzanne stepped out of their cars. A cloud of tiny, smoky-grey kittens bounded out of a lavender bush, paws outstretched. Casey found it difficult to take a step without kicking them. She couldn't help smiling as she stooped to scoop one into her hand. It was light as a ball of wool and rumbled with a purr which seemed fit to burst it apart.

The screen door crashed open and a small boy rushed out. 'Hi Auntie Suze.' He had all the marks of a Bowman: unruly hair, clear complexion and large eyes with long lashes.

Suzanne caught him up and spun him round and round, close to her chest. The toddler gave a rollicking chuckle but when she set him back on his feet, he caught sight of Casey. His smile vanished.

'Jerome, this is my friend, Casey. She's going to live with you and Daddy.'

The child ducked his head and buried his face in his aunt's black skirt.

'Hi, Jerome.'

His shoulders stiffened and he shuffled behind Suzanne.

'You're a funny moppet,' Suzanne laughed. 'Jerome is shy with people he doesn't know. He'll take awhile to warm up to you but then you'll have a friend for life.'

Casey looked into the wary, inky grey eyes of Jerome and doubted that.

The door creaked open more slowly and Piers stepped out. 'Hi, Casey. Long time, no see.' His manner was bashful but once he would not even have said that much to her. Wavy tousled hair tumbled down the back of his neck.

'Hi, Piers.'

He looked at his clenched hands and stammered, 'It's good to see you. I'm really glad you've come to stay. I mean… I'm glad that if you need a place to live, you'd consider coming here.' Piers blushed.

'Thanks for agreeing to have me.' A sinking weight tugged Casey's heart to the pit of her stomach. *If this is what conversations will be like, it'll be hard going.* There was Piers, shy and uptight, on one side and Jerome, totally speechless, on the other.

Suzanne stepped inside with Jerome clinging to her neck like a pet monkey. 'Now that formalities are over, we'll help ourselves to a cup of

The Risky Way Home

tea. Where have you decided to put her?'

'Up in the top room. It's got the best view.'

Casey's eye caught a glimpse of fur beneath the table and she recognised somebody she hadn't seen for several years. 'Is that Sam?' An old, biscuit coloured Labrador slept curled in a padded basket. He raised an eyebrow when he heard his name, curved his mouth in a gummy smile and thumped his tail once before dozing off again. He had been the Bowman family's exuberant pup who'd hurtle after Suzanne's bike whenever Casey stopped by to ride with her to school.

'Mum brought him here because we all thought he'd like the space,' Piers told her, 'but he hardly ever staggers further than the verandah steps. He's a bit arthritic but I think he's happy.'

Piers had got together an odd assortment of cups. Each seemed to be cracked or chipped. Casey chose one with just a small nick in the rim and helped herself to a teabag, sugar and hot water. She felt a flash of annoyance with Suzanne for bringing her to live there. Suzanne herself would never dream of living with Piers in such a rough-and-ready house in the middle of nowhere.

Suzanne said, 'Look at this table and the kitchen dresser. Piers made them.'

Casey was impressed despite herself. The furniture was solid and finely crafted. 'They're great.'

Piers smiled. 'Thanks. People seem to like good, plain furniture.'

Suzanne stood to fetch a biscuit tin from the kitchen cupboard and there was a lapse in the conversation. Jerome still gaped at Casey as if she'd stepped out of a horror movie. Piers drew a breath, flexed his knuckles and said, 'I hope you'll enjoy working with Suzanne in the studio.'

Suzanne returned with sparkling eyes. 'I'm going to try to match her up with Eric.'

It was Casey's turn to blush. 'I've only ever seen him twice.'

"But you think he's good looking,' Suzanne prodded. 'Don't you?'

"Well, yeah, sort of.' Nobody would deny that.

'You'll be working at the right place, then,' Piers said.

Casey drained the dregs of her chipped cup and pushed back her chair. 'I'd better bring my things in.'

'I'll help and give you the grand tour,' said Suzanne.

They lugged Casey's bulging duffle bags up a short flight of steps. The dormer bedroom was spacious and clean. There was a single bed, a chest of drawers with an oval mirror and a small, free-standing wardrobe. Casey decided on the spot to bring a few paintings from home and a braided floor rug to brighten the place up. She and Suzanne returned to the car for her small TV and electric heater.

'I'll show you the rest of the place now.'

At the front of the house was a cosy lounge room with a deep stone fireplace. Directly across from it were two smaller bedrooms. One was clearly Jerome's, with a cot full of stuffed toys and posters of Sesame Street characters tacked up around the walls. The other was Piers' and his bedroom floor was strewn with clothes.

'Come outside now. I'll show you Piers' work shed.' It turned out to be a large shed full of partially completed bookcases, cabinets and small toys. The place smelled pleasantly of fresh sawdust, varnish and wood polish.

The sun had begun to hang heavily in the sky. A lone cricket already chirped somewhere.

'I'll have to fly,' Suzanne said. 'We're meeting some barrister friends of Tim's for a cocktail party. Have fun settling in, Casey, and I'll see you bright and early tomorrow.' She swept Jerome off his feet and smothered his face with playful kisses. 'See you next time.'

As Suzanne's tyres churned up gravel, Jerome squinted at Casey and his baby face crumpled. He plucked Piers' hand and lifted his arms to be picked up. 'Go home, Daddy,' he mumbled. Casey guessed that he meant, 'Send *her* home.'

I wish I could *leave.* Without Suzanne's sunny presence, there was no sound but the rustle of wind in the trees and the occasional bleating of the white goat. Casey forced a smile. 'I won't bother you,' she promised Jerome. 'I'll keep to myself. You won't know I'm here.'

Piers pushed back his thick fringe and said, 'Don't worry about him. He always acts nervous whenever a lady comes to visit. The only ones he knows well are Mum and Gran and Suzanne. You won't be in our way. Tell us if we get in yours. '

Casey escaped to her bedroom and switched on her little TV. The sky outside of her dormer window faded from golden to grey and then became black. Silence reigned beyond the noise of her TV. Turning up the

The Risky Way Home

volume made the emptiness feel thicker so she switched it off and sat by the window wondering what she'd stepped into.

————————————

The following afternoon, Casey stood in the wardrobe room, pressing some garments with a steam iron. Her ironing arm was aching because she'd used it for two hours. Before that, Suzanne had asked her to wash the front windows and mop the hardwood floors. Casey's soapy water had turned black and needed emptying ten times. The seemingly immaculate premises had really been quite grubby.

Suzanne stood in the make-up room tidying up her cabinet. Eric was in the studio room snapping photos of a mother and her two teenage daughters. The door between the studio and wardrobe room stood ajar and Casey could see his fine profile. It was already March and still his February tan was perfect.

Eric's low, pleasant voice drawled, 'Amy, rest a hand on your mum's shoulder. Place your fingers together. That's lovely. And Brooke, remember, right hand over left and don't cross your legs. That's the way. Mrs Bradley, are you ready?'

At least twenty flashes of light followed. After the session, Casey and Suzanne picked up the crumpled piles of clothes. Casey was relieved to flex her aching wrist and give the ironing a rest. The teenagers sat on the floor, giggling and tugging on their sneakers.

When the family left, Suzanne was ready to celebrate. 'That's it for today. Let's have some drinks for Casey's first day.' She opened the small fridge in the corner of the make-up room and spread champagne glasses and several chilled bottles on the table top of the cabinet. Eric stepped in and sank onto a chair.

'You take the teenagers from now on, Suze. Empty-headed little idiots, the lot of them.' He poured from one of the bottles and raised his glass. 'Cheers.'

'The only difference between them and full grown women is that teenage girls haven't learned to hide their admiration,' Suzanne teased. 'What would I do without my resident heart-throb?'

'You'd lose two thirds of our business.'

Paula Vince   19

Casey wasn't quite sure whether Eric was joking. She sat close enough to sniff his spicy aftershave. *I hope I'm good enough at hiding my admiration.* She had felt awkward all day because both Suzanne and Eric wore stylish work clothes. She was convinced that Eric, with his classical features, would look good in absolutely anything and Suzanne's navy-blue pencilled suit accentuated her tall, shapely figure. Suzanne glided wherever she walked. Casey had put on the best clothes she owned but now she realised that her staid, tailored blouse and skirt were more suitable for an office than a glamorous photograph studio.

Although she was not used to drinking alcohol, she tried to drown her uneasiness with little sips of tequila and orange. Eric stuck to bourbon, which Casey had never tasted. Suzanne stepped out to answer the phone and he gave Casey a mischievous wink. 'I hear you've moved in with Suzanne's brother.'

A sick hand clasped Casey's stomach. 'I had nowhere else to go in Adelaide,' she whispered as she twirled the pipe of her glass around in her fingers.

Eric chuckled. 'Another of Suzanne's hare-brained schemes? I suppose you couldn't think how to say no. I've only been there once, for ten minutes. A person could wilt and die there. At least you can escape to work. Ssh, here she comes.'

He straightened and looked as if he had not said a word while Casey's ears burned.

'I'd better go easy on the bubbly,' Suzanne was saying. 'Tim's taking me to one of his firm's dinners tonight. They're really ritzy affairs.'

They all left the premises and walked down to the car park. Eric climbed into a shiny red Porsche. Casey's heart sank as she unlocked her own brown Gemini. She'd never been ashamed of it before. It had seemed perfect for a university student.

She groped for the park brake unsteadily. Although Casey hadn't even finished her glass of tequila and orange, she was not used to drinking any alcohol.

'Have a safe drive home,' Suzanne said, but Casey felt light-headed and slightly queasy. *I'll have to get used to drinking a little bit, to fit in with them. I'll have a good sleep tonight.*

The Risky Way Home

Chapter 3

Casey tossed and turned for several hours. At home with her parents she was used to being lulled to sleep by the murmur of the ocean. The hush at Piers' place rang in her ears and kept her awake for the fifth night in a row. Once, Jerome shrieked in his sleep downstairs until Casey assumed Piers must have gone to settle him. Although Jerome still hadn't spoken a word to Casey, he'd been peeping into her bedroom. Earlier that evening when Casey went to clean her teeth, the toddler took the chance to jump on her mattress until she came back. Then he'd darted out like a frightened rabbit.

Just when she finally began to nod off, Ben, the goat, started bleating outside. The plaintive din droned on, far more irritating than a barking dog. She hated Piers for having a stupid goat. It was easy to hate a person at two o'clock in the morning after five nights of sleep deprivation.

Casey was reluctant to complain to Piers because she suspected that he already regretted asking her to stay. She was always tired after a day of work and headed straight for the solitude of her bedroom without bothering to talk. On the first two evenings, Piers had greeted her cheerfully and asked if she'd had a good day. Casey's polite replies were brief on her way upstairs. He seemed to have got the message. After the third attempt, he stopped asking about her day and just said 'Hi.'

I suppose he thinks I'm rude. I'd better not make too many waves on my first week. He might tell Suzanne and she'll think I'm a pain in the neck.

Casey always read novels or watched TV until her stomach growled at about seven o'clock. Her dinners were the simplest she could throw together: grilled cheese and tomato on toast, baked beans or scrambled eggs. She longed for one of her mother's good, filling casseroles but Casey never wanted to take over Piers' kitchen for too long. She often returned downstairs to nibble fruit or bread for supper and he probably thought she was eating all the time.

She craned her neck to peer at her clock radio. The time flashed 3.45am and Casey had not slept a wink since two o'clock. That was enough! She gripped the electric cord and yanked it out of the power point. The flashing numerals disappeared. Casey swung her feet out of bed and her eyes burned with tears of frustration. She ripped her quilt off the bed, wrapped it around her shoulders and stalked downstairs to huddle on the couch. A distant rooster crowed and Casey glowered toward the window. *People are already waking up to go to work and I've hardly slept!*

Something cold and wet touched Casey's hand. She almost yelled out loud. It was Sam, the Labrador, and his shiny, wet nose. Casey released her breath and scratched him behind the ears. 'You scared me, fella.' He whacked his stumpy tail twice on the floor and rested his chin on her knee. 'How can you put up with 'em?'

After watching the sun rise, she got ready for work well before necessary. There was nothing else to do. Casey arched her back beneath the shower and stretched the kinks out of her arms and legs. A magpie warbled outside. Casey stepped out of the cubicle and opened the window wider. As she inhaled steam and fresh morning air, her spirits brightened. It was Friday and that night, she'd be home with her family for the weekend.

At work, Suzanne asked Casey to collect some business cards from a printer's shop in the city. Casey placed the cardboard package on her passenger's seat and glanced at the sample card which had been pasted on the lid. Beneath small, coloured images of Eric's and Suzanne's faces, *Before and After* was embossed in gold across the centre. At the bottom of the card were the business fax and phone numbers, the email address and the names Suzanne Dupont and Eric Adams.

Casey stared. 'Suzanne *Dupont?*'

When she delivered the cards to Suzanne, she commented, 'I didn't know you'd changed your name.'

Suzanne gave a coy smile. 'That's one thing my mother couldn't have reported to yours because she doesn't know. Don't tell her. And don't tell Piers either. I don't think he'd understand. It's top secret.'

'Did you get married without telling them?' Casey blurted.

Suzanne giggled, like fizzy champagne. 'No, I didn't get married. I've never thought highly enough of any man yet to sign a lifelong prison term. I just changed my name back to what it should have been.'

'What do you mean?'

'Dupont was my father's name. Don't you remember when I talked about him at school? I haven't seen him since I was tiny. When we left Paris and came to Australia, Mum never let me mention his name. I had to obey her then but she can't stop me from using it now. His name was Jean-Michel Dupont. Doesn't it roll off your tongue?'

Casey nodded. Moira Bowman discussed almost everything under the sun with Helen Miller but Casey had never heard the name of her ex-husband cross her lips.

'I decided to use the name that should have been mine by rights for this business,' Suzanne explained. 'It's the only part of my father I'm able to hang onto. Dupont sounds classier than Bowman, don't you think? Would you rather have your photos taken by Suzanne Bowman or by Suzanne Dupont?'

'I wouldn't mind what my photographer's name was, if she was as good as you, but I see what you mean. Anything French sounds stylish.' Yet Casey had always thought the name Suzanne Bowman carried a certain allure, anyway.

'If Mum knew, she'd go off the deep end.' Suzanne's eyes narrowed. 'She'd think I was doing it just to spite her. I'm only Suzanne Dupont for my business image and I never show her my business literature anyway.'

Casey couldn't help feeling sorry for Moira, who always spoke highly of Suzanne's talent. 'Your Mum says she's proud of you.'

Suzanne began to count money from the till into bank bags. '*Proud* of me!' she snorted. 'Then why has she always heckled me and nagged me to be different than what I am? Casey, you only see the side of my mother that she wants people to see. Her warm, caring front is completely false. I'm the one who had to live with her until I could escape and I tell you, she's rigid, narrow-minded and impossible to get along with. I can't stand Gran, either. Mum always lavished more attention on that rotten old bag than she ever did on either me or Piers.'

Casey was silent. She didn't know what to say.

Suzanne looked up with a weary smile. 'Let's not talk about them. I always see red whenever somebody mentions Mum or Gran. They ruined my childhood. Gran always made nasty digs about me and Piers, and Mum always agreed with her. She should've stood up for us. I know she's your mum's friend but I can't help how I feel.' She patted Casey's shoulder as she breezed past and said, 'She did me a favour by telling you that I needed help here, anyway. You've been here only one week, but I don't know what we ever did without you. You work like a Trojan, Casey.'

Casey was glad to begin the long trip home. The first stars were twinkling when she reached her parents' house, but it was worth the drive to sniff the salty air and hear the distant crash of the surf when she stepped out of her car. She enjoyed a roast dinner and slept in her own cosy bed. Casey spent Saturday relaxing and on Sunday morning she went to church with her parents.

The house was full of noise because Dale was living there again. He had left his flat in Adelaide without telling their parents why. Now the fridge was crammed with beer cans, his drum kit filled a corner of the lounge room and football blared on TV just like old times. Casey used to hate living with her brother but it was worth it to escape spending all weekend at Piers' house.

On Sunday afternoon, Helen said, 'Let's visit the Bowmans. Henrietta has been feeling poorly and I like to give Moira a break.'

'You don't need me to come.'

'I'd like you to say hello. Moira was excited when I told her I was expecting you home so she can hear about her children.'

'OK, but I don't have all that much to tell her.'

Moira's mother had always felt poorly ever since Casey had known the Bowman family. Suzanne had never been allowed to have sleep-over parties because her grandmother was too sick to bear it. In fact, whenever Casey entered the house, Moira would greet her smiling, but whisper, 'You'll have to keep it down, girls. Suzanne's granny is not feeling up to scratch.'

Moira Bowman answered their knock and ushered them inside, beaming. 'Come and have a cup of tea and slice of chocolate cake. I have some fruit tarts too. Mother's having a nap but she'll be awake soon. She'll be so glad you called.'

Casey grinned to herself, imagining Suzanne's reaction to that. Henrietta was never glad about anything. Casey had never been certain what her ailments were but they seemed to be a combination of arthritis, angina and a hacking cough. She was never free from all three at the same time.

The delicious cooking aromas in the kitchen made Casey's mouth water. Moira put Casey in mind of a faded flower. She was an older, washed-out version of Suzanne with none of her daughter's polish and not a scrap of make-up on her face. Her once pure black hair was tinged with strands of silver.

'Casey, what do you think of the studio?' Moira asked. 'Haven't Suzanne and Eric done a wonderful job of doing it up?'

Casey swallowed a mouthful of delicious lemon tart. 'It's fantastic, Mrs Bowman.'

Moira's face glowed. 'Suzanne has always had a flair for decorating. It was obvious from the time she was a little girl. I'm so glad she's found a career that suits her so well. But you see her every day, Casey. Tell me, do you think she's truly happy?'

'She sure is! She goes to so many parties; I don't know how she keeps up with them all.'

Moira's eyes clouded over the rim of her tea cup. 'I don't remember the last time she came home to visit me. I suppose she doesn't have time.'

'Why don't you drive down to the city and visit her in the studio, Moira, when you visit Piers?' Helen Miller asked.

'I'd love to, but I can't visit either of them for some time. Mother's been very poorly. Her arthritis has been troubling her more than usual. I don't know why. It must have something to do with this unusual windy weather. She wouldn't be able to make the journey and I couldn't possibly leave her home alone for so long.' Moira refilled her cup with an unsteady hand. 'I'd love to see Suzanne. I haven't seen her beautiful face for months and it feels like years. Tell her that I think of her every moment, Casey.'

'I will.' *But I don't think she'll care.*

'Are you heading back to Adelaide tonight?'

Casey nodded. 'Straight after tea.'

'I'm delighted that you're staying with Piers. I was really concerned when he told me he wanted a boarder. He lives so far out of town and I imagined that he might get some crazy cutthroat who'd murder him and Jerome in their beds and take off with all their money. I'm so glad it's you! Thank you, love, you've put my mind at rest.'

Casey mumbled, 'That's okay,' and stared at the crumbs on her plate, wondering what Moira would say if she knew Casey hoped not to be there for long.

'This chocolate cake is for you to take back. Jerome loves it, bless his heart. How are Piers and Jerome going?'

'They seem to be fine.'

'That's good. At least Jerome doesn't get the terrible asthma that Piers used to have. That's a load off my mind. By the time Piers was Jerome's age, he'd had several such violent attacks, I thought he'd die. His face would turn blue and he'd gasp for every breath he took.' Moira set her tea cup back in its saucer with a clink. 'That's enough about that. I don't even want to think about those days. I thought *I'd* die!'

She pushed her hair back from her face. 'I'm dying to give Jerome a cuddle. I hated it when they had to leave home, but Mother couldn't live with a howling baby. Jerome used to cry a lot in those early months. He'd wake up ten times a night and scream the house down. She was too old to live with it, so they had to go. It broke my heart to say goodbye because Jerome was just a few months old and I was the only one who could rock him to sleep. I was so worried that Piers wouldn't be able to look after him properly.'

'You don't need to worry about that, anymore. Piers is great at looking after Jerome.' At least Casey had noticed enough to be able to assure Moira that.

'Do you think so? He's learned a lot these last few years. Maybe Mother is right and being alone has been good for them. I really miss them, though. She might be awake by now. Will you come and say hello?'

Although Casey would far rather not, they followed Moira through the house. At the end of the passage, the atmosphere changed. A hazy film enveloped them as they opened Henrietta's door. Casey's throat began to itch. The old lady was a chain smoker. She sat propped against two cushions with one withered hand clutching a cigarette and the other holding her TV remote control. Above her bed was a placard.

'They told me to smile because things could be worse. So I smiled and behold, things got much worse.'

'Hello Helen. Hello, girlie. What brings you here today?'

'Casey is home visiting Doug and Helen for the weekend, Mother.' Moira spoke brightly. 'She works with Suzanne now, remember.'

Henrietta stared into Casey's face. 'When is that girl going to pay us a visit? I haven't seen her face in this house for over a year.'

'I don't know.'

'Why don't you know? You work with her.'

'We don't talk much about family.'

The old lady twitched her covers. 'That'd be right. You see, Moira. You give your last drop of blood for your kids and they never even give you a thought. She's a selfish little minx.'

'Suzanne's always quite busy,' Casey blurted. She drew her eyes from Henrietta's face and looked at the side of her head. The old lady's peppery grey hair was sparse and pink scalp was visible all over her head. *I'd better just shut up. I'm probably making things worse.*

'You work there too and I see *you're* not too busy to come and see your parents.'

Casey was silent. She looked at her mother, silently asking Helen to speak instead.

'Admit the truth. Suzanne hates our guts. She always has.'

'Mother, that's not true!'

'Moira, when will you wake up to yourself? You're approaching fifty years old and still burying your head in the sand. She loathes you. You helped her to set up that posh little glamour studio but is she grateful? She seems to think you owe her every cent. Still, what can you expect when you consider who her…'

'Mother, don't say it!' The colour drained from Moira's face. Casey wondered what Henrietta had been about to say.

'Let's change the subject,' Moira went on. 'Casey told me little Jerome is good.'

'Good for nothing,' Henrietta muttered. 'That child is far too shy and Piers spoils him rotten. If he keeps him wrapped in cotton wool like a little dummy…'

'Piers doesn't deliberately keep him secluded, Mother. They can't go out much because he works from home.'

Casey quietly studied Moira. *She never loses her cool, no matter what that mean old lady says. Why does she keep putting up with it?.*

Helen Miller tried to help Moira without offending Henrietta. 'Piers must be doing wonderfully well to keep his head above water, when so many other small businesses fail. Henrietta, don't you think it's handy for him to be able to work from home and care for Jerome at the same time?'

'I think it was handy for him to be able to ask his mother to lend him money to pay for all his tools.' Henrietta puffed a cloud of smoke into their faces. 'He merrily ignores us when it suits him but when he's in hot water, he rushes to his mother to rescue him.'

'He's already paid me back just under two thirds,' Moira put in. 'I didn't mind lending him the money. He was hardly in the position to go and work full time outside the house with Jerome just a few weeks old.'

'Well he made his own bed so you should have let him lie in it. If he hadn't gone chasing that crazy girl when we warned him not to, he wouldn't have a child to support. We told him she was a no-hoper but he wouldn't listen.' She peered at Moira over the rim of her spectacles. 'Reminds me of someone else I know.'

For some reason, Moira flushed crimson.

Casey waited curiously for Henrietta to say more. She couldn't imagine what a girlfriend of Piers' would have been like.

'I hope he'll find somebody else some day,' Moira said.

Henrietta gave a wheezy laugh. 'Don't hold your breath. He'd only get some other dead-beat. What sort of self-respecting girl would latch onto a shabby hobo like Piers and his little clone, Jerome?' Her fingers trembled as she lit another cigarette.

Instead of answering, Moira said, 'Mother, remember what Dr White said about smoking too many cigarettes.'

'He said that if I tried to quit at my age, the withdrawal symptoms would probably kill me. Smoking is one of the few pleasures I've had for twenty years so I'll smoke until I'm six feet under.'

'But he also said that chain smoking too quickly might cause those faint spells in the head.'

'Stop nagging me.'

'Henrietta, we came to have a chat with you. We can stay here for awhile and let Moira pop out to the shops.'

'You're a liar, Helen Miller. Why would anybody bother to visit me? My own grand-daughter never does. Still, Moira can go to the shops if she pleases. Remember to buy me more smokes and my TV guide.'

Moira snatched her opportunity and hurried out of the room with a flustered smile of thanks for Helen.

'See, she couldn't wait to get away from me,' the old lady remarked.

'Who, Moira?'

'Who else? She hates me as much as Suzanne does. I can see it in her eyes.'

'She loves you. She does all she can to make you comfortable.'

'Do you call that love? I call it obligation.'

'What do you mean?'

Henrietta just stared up at the ceiling with a twisted smile. 'You don't know half of it, Helen Miller. When Moira has cups of tea with you, you think she's such a sweet and lovely person. You think butter wouldn't melt in her mouth. Don't you? You have no idea what I rescued her from.'

Helen straightened Henrietta's sheet and replied, 'Whatever it was doesn't concern us and must have been a long time ago.'

Henrietta muttered, 'Humph,' and leaned back against her pillows.

When Moira returned home, she saw them to the door and walked as far as the letter box with them. Casey looked back at her, a stoop-shouldered, thin figure in an old floral house dress. Helen Miller turned to Casey and said, 'I don't know why, but Moira is one of the most graceful people I know, no matter what she's wearing.'

'I can see what you mean,' Casey mused. 'Suzanne was telling me that

Moira never let her mention her father's name. Mum, who was Moira's husband? Has she ever told you?'

Helen shook her head. 'She's only let slip a few chance remarks that make me think she's been through some great tragedy. She always clams up and changes the subject whenever she mentions her past. It must be too painful for her to talk about.'

'Do you think that old kidnapping story of Suzanne's is true?'

'I'd take anything Suzanne ever said with a grain of salt.'

'I wonder if you asked Moira straight out...'

'No, I'd never do that. I'm one of the few people Moira seems to feel at home with. If she wanted me to know about her background, she'd tell me.'

Casey shrugged. 'I suppose if she hasn't spilled the beans for twenty years, she probably never will.'

'Visiting Moira makes me feel sad. She always puts a brave face on everything, but I'm convinced that inside, she's one of the loneliest people I've ever known.'

At home, Casey packed her bag to take back to Piers' place. She inhaled her mother's warm cooking odours with satisfaction. That night she would have a decent meal.

'Henrietta Bowman is an old tartar,' Helen pronounced over dinner.

'Tell us something we don't know,' Doug said dryly.

'Why do you even bother going to visit them, Mum?' Dale asked.

'Because Moira is my friend. I like to give her a breather.'

'Then you did what you went for. Hey Casey, is Suzanne still as foxy as she used to be?' Dale asked. He'd been in her year level at school.

'I think you'd say she's even more gorgeous than ever.'

He whistled. 'Can you wrangle me a date with her?'

Casey grinned and shook her head. 'She lives with a handsome barrister. Tough luck, Dale. You're not her type, anyway.'

Their father commented, 'I've never understood all the fuss about Suzanne Bowman. I never thought she was particularly attractive.'

Dale said, 'You need glasses, Dad.'

Chapter 4

By the time she'd had dinner with her family, helped wash the dishes and stashed more paintings, rugs and clothes into her car boot, it was already getting dark. Jerome was asleep in his bedroom when Casey arrived back at Piers' place and Piers was on the couch, watching TV.

'Hi, did you have a good week-end?' He turned down the volume to greet her.

'Yes, thanks.' She placed the chocolate cake on the coffee table. 'Your mother sent back a treat.'

He sat up straight. 'Good old Mum. She never trusts me to look after ourselves properly, but at times like this, I'm glad she doesn't.'

Casey stepped through to the kitchen for a drink. To hear at least one of Moira's children speak well of her was refreshing.

Piers sliced the cake and offered some to Casey. The aroma had tantalised her all the way from Victor Harbour so she accepted a slice on her way up to her bedroom. If she hadn't been afraid of waking Jerome, she would have had a shower, late as it was.

As she switched on her bedside lamp, a flash of movement caught her eye. Casey realised with a creepy chill that she was not alone. Halfway up her wall was a black spider the size of a small tea saucer. She let out a gasp and edged closer to the door. The beast skulked higher up the wall. Casey was certain she could discern a pair of eyes in its fuzz. It was watching her.

Moving slowly, she tiptoed backward. Casey's heart raced. She couldn't bring herself to whack a spider that size with her shoe but she could not possibly sleep with it in her room. There was only one other thing she could do. *I'll look like an idiot but I suppose it doesn't matter.*

She returned downstairs.

'Excuse me, Piers. Would you please help me with something in my bedroom?'

'Sure.' He followed her back up.

The spider lurked in a corner of her ceiling. Piers whistled. 'What a monster.'

'You can say that again. Will you get rid of it for me?'

'OK. I'll knock it down with the broom and sweep it into the dustpan. Might not even need to kill him. I can just shake him out your window.'

'Fine! Please be quick!'

Casey cowered at the bottom of the stairs while Piers went to the laundry for the broom and pan. She heard several thumps and scuffles. At last there was silence. 'I got him,' Piers called.

'Thanks.' Casey stepped back into her room. Now that her fear was over, she felt red and foolish.

'Don't mention it. We blokes love to rescue damsels in distress.' He was grinning.

'No need to rub it in. Do you get gigantic spiders like that very often?'

'No, that was the biggest I've seen for awhile. There was one almost that size above the hot water tap in the shower a few months ago. I was standing in there and almost touched it. Jerome heard me yell from his bedroom.'

Casey let out a laugh at the thought of it. Piers stood in his paint-stained overalls smelling like varnish. His gaze took in the bright cushion covers, the colourful braided rug on the floor and the two cheerful paintings on her wall. 'You've made it nice and cosy up here. It's never looked like this before.'

'I've just brought a few bits and pieces from home. It's nothing much really. I'm sorry to have bothered you. I never would have if I didn't think it was urgent.'

He sighed, suddenly sober. 'I'm well aware of that.' Piers looked down at his hands. 'Anytime you need a hand… just give me a call.' He loitered for a few seconds as if he would have liked to stand around for longer but

The Risky Way Home

there was no reason to. He lifted the dustpan and broom and left.

Casey took a long time to fall asleep. The silence outside of her window pressed down on her senses. She was too keyed-up to go to sleep.

Casey had her hair cut one evening after work because she was tired of her shoulder-length bob. She left the salon with a modern cropped cut and a chilly neck. Casey had not intended to have such a complete change but her stylist had been persuasive and found herself pleasantly surprised. Every part of her felt lighter and even her freckles appeared saucy instead of stark. *I wonder if Eric will notice this.* She found herself feeling flustered at the thought.

That same evening, Eliza May, an old school friend, gave her a phone-call. 'Casey, would you like to have dinner with me and Vicki tomorrow night? I haven't caught up with you girls for ages. I have some exciting news. I'm engaged.'

'That's wonderful. Congratulations. I'm free tomorrow. I'd love to meet you for dinner and find out all about your fiancé.'

'Great. Do you realise the three of us haven't seen each for three years? I'm looking forward to finding out news from you and Vicki too.'

'Yeah, it'll be great fun.' Casey was glad Eliza hadn't phoned a few weeks earlier. She would have had absolutely nothing to say. *At least now I'll be able to tell them about working for Suzanne in the studio.* At school, Casey, Eliza and Vicki Foster had always admired Suzanne Bowman and aspired to belong to her group. Sometimes Suzanne would graciously allow them to join her elite crowd, yet she preferred to shun the younger girls when it suited her.

At work the next day, Eric Adams didn't comment on the new hairstyle. Casey was preoccupied enough to be only mildly disappointed. She hurried home to shower and freshen up so she could return to the city to meet Eliza and Vicki.

On the Freeway, her car began a strange wheezing drone. When Casey pressed her foot hard on the accelerator her temperature gauge soared. *No! Keep going, little car. I* can't *have a break-down tonight. Not when I'm supposed to meet Vicki and Eliza. I really want to see them.*

She made it home. The little brown car stopped with a shudder in its spot beneath the carport. Casey opened her door and sniffed an acrid, scorched metal odour. Her heart lurched when she saw wisps of smoke drift through the crack in her bonnet.

Piers looked out of his work shed and smelled it too. He hurried over. 'What's up?'

'It's my car. It started acting funny when I passed Bridgewater. Can you fix it for me?'

He looked doubtfully at the smoking bonnet. 'I think it's something major. I'm no mechanic but I'll take a look.' He propped up the bonnet and released a hiss of steam before he leaned over to examine the mess inside. Casey's heart sank when she saw him straighten, shaking his head.

'You've cooked your engine. You should have pulled over when you first noticed it playing up at Bridgewater.'

She blinked back her tears. 'I was in a hurry to get home. I know nothing about cars.'

Piers grinned. 'It shows. Perhaps your radiator was dry. Don't worry, it's nothing that can't be fixed. I'll help you take it to a garage.'

Casey kicked her tyre hard. 'But I need it tonight. I'm supposed to meet Eliza and Vicki at a Thai restaurant! I haven't seen either of them for over three years and I've been looking forward to it. Now I'll have to cancel but Eliza was going to head down straight after work and I don't have her work number. They'll be sitting there wondering what's happened to me and there's no way I can let them know!' She turned aside to swipe her hand across her burning eyes.

Piers stood awkwardly watching her. He gazed at his sooty hands and rubbed them down the legs of his overalls. 'You can borrow my van tonight. Your car can wait. We'll take it to the garage tomorrow.'

She slumped against her bonnet. 'No I can't.'

'Why not? I won't be needing it.'

'The gears are manual and I've only learned to drive automatics,' she mumbled with a tinge of shame. 'Thanks anyway.'

He looked nonplussed for just a moment. 'I'll drive you down then, and pick you up when you tell me to.'

'You can't do that!'

'Sure I can. I'll take Jerome to look at toys. It'll be fun. You go and

The Risky Way Home

get ready.'

She hesitated for a second.

'I don't mind,' Piers insisted. 'Honestly.'

'Well okay then. Thanks. Thanks very much.' Casey dashed into the house. While she stood beneath the shower, she heard Piers round up Jerome. 'Get your shoes and socks. We're going late-night shopping. I'll buy you an ice-cream.' A high-pitched squeal told her that Jerome was happy with the idea.

It was dim and cold when the three of them climbed into the van. There was no back seat so Casey sat jammed between Piers and Jerome in his chunky infant seat. Whenever Piers changed gears, he scraped his knuckles against her right knee and whenever Jerome wriggled his legs, he kicked her left knee.

'Say hi to Eliza and Vicki from me,' Piers said after a prolonged pause.

'Okay, I will.' *No I won't! I don't want them to know that I have anything to do with him.*

'I like your new haircut,' he told her.

Her hand instinctively tucked a stray tendril behind her ear. 'Thanks.'

'It looks great. But I liked it before, too.'

She forced a smile, thinking, *He wouldn't know a decent hairstyle from a shaggy mop.*

When they drove into the restaurant car park, Piers said, 'There's Eliza May by the wall.'

Eliza stood beside a floodlight and managed to stare right in at them as they drove past. She fixed her gaze on Casey's face and waved frantically. Casey turned hot to the tips of her ears and Piers commented, 'She hasn't changed much.'

When Casey left the car and joined her friend, Eliza demanded, 'Was that Piers Bowman?'

'Yes, he gave me a lift because my car broke down. That's all. There's nothing between us or anything like...' Casey bit off her words. Eliza had asked a simple question and she'd said far more than she needed to.

Then she got the surprise of her life. Eliza gave a dreamy smile and said, 'Too bad. He's turned out cute.'

Casey studied her face. 'Are you teasing me?'

Eliza's eyes were clear and frank. 'No. He really is very good looking.'

'You never had any time for him when we were at school. We used to make such fun of him and the other two stooges.'

'He seems to have grown into that wild hair of his. It looks trendy now.'

A wave of relief swept through Casey. She'd been ashamed to admit that she lived with Piers and now she was beginning to re-examine her attitude. She drew a deep breath, inhaling the delicious odours and her stomach growled. She had already started to enjoy her evening.

'Was that *his* kid?' Eliza asked.

'Yes, his name is Jerome. He's three years old.'

'Who's his mother?'

'I've no idea. I've never asked.'

Eliza stared at her. 'Why not?'

'I never have anything to do with Piers so it's none of my business. Suzanne's the one I'm working for.'

'And I'm dying to hear more about this glamour studio. It sounds like Suzanne still weaves her old magic. Here comes Vicki.'

'Guess who dropped Casey off. Piers Bowman.'

'Old Mophead?' Vicki cried. 'You're kidding me. He was such a nerd.'

'He's changed a bit since old times.'

'What's he doing with himself these days?'

'He's started his own cabinet-making business.'

'Woodwork was his best school subject,' Vicki recalled. 'Do you know what's happened to Psycho and Giggles?' They had been the nicknames of Piers' two friends, Wayne Forbes and Justin Edwards. Justin had earned his nickname because often when he spoke to any of the girls, he'd finish his sentences with a nervous laugh, even if what he said wasn't remotely funny.

'No. I haven't asked. I don't know if Piers has kept in touch with them.'

'Maybe he hasn't, if he's as successful as you say he is. They were both so hopeless at everything. Why would he bother?'

'Who cares about Psycho and Giggles anyway? Tell us about yourself, Vicki.'

The next few hours flew as the girls caught up with each others' news and enjoyed their meals. At the end of the evening, Casey found Piers waiting in the car park at the appointed time. Jerome was fast asleep with his chin nodding on his chest and Piers leaned his head back listening to soft music.

'Are you ready?' he asked. 'Take your time if you aren't. I'm happy to wait.'

'I am ready. The others have left too.' She scrambled up in the passenger's seat, careful not to wake Jerome. Casey sneaked a glance at Piers to assess Eliza's summary of him for herself. *I suppose he is okay in his own way.* She noticed how he had tended his son with the utmost care, wrapping him in a blanket and removing his shoes for comfort. Piers *had* changed from the gauche boy she had known at school.

'We wondered what became of your friends, Justin and Wayne,' she said.

'I'm not sure about Wayne. He had some sort of break-down two years ago and had to stay in hospital for months. I went to visit him. He didn't say a word the whole time I was there. Don't know if he knew me or not.' Piers shrugged sadly. 'He's moved inter-state now and I wouldn't have a clue where he is.'

'I'm sorry to hear that.' Casey twisted her fingers in her lap. She regretted all the heartless, 'Psycho' jokes she had joined in with at school.

'But Justin's doing well. He lives in Melbourne. He and his cousin set up a carpet cleaning business and they're doing brilliantly.'

Jerome stirred in his sleep. Casey felt a sudden urge to trace his milky smooth profile with her finger.

'How was your evening?' she whispered.

'It was fun. We looked at toys and then we looked at power tools, so we were both happy.'

When they arrived home, Casey went straight up to her bedroom and sat by her window to gaze out at the clear night sky. She heard Piers carry Jerome to his bedroom and she heard the little boy's tired whines of protest. Piers' soothing voice drawled on for ten minutes and then there was the silence she was becoming accustomed to. Casey stretched her arms behind her head, listened to the whisper of wind in the trees and realised that after a social night, she welcomed the peaceful solitude of the little house in the Adelaide Hills. There was something almost otherworldly about it.

Her car took a week to be repaired and cost Casey plenty in both cash and inconvenience. Her new job paid the bill and she felt grateful to have it. That weekend, she was unable to make it home to visit her family. On Monday and Tuesday, she had to wake up extra early to catch a bus into the city. On Wednesday, Suzanne, who had stayed overnight with another set of friends in the Hills, came past to pick her up.

'I'm here!' she called as Casey finished up in the kitchen.

Jerome fairly flew down the passage and leaped into her arms. 'Hi, Auntie Suze.'

'Hello, little Pumpkin!' She spun him back to the kitchen, set him on the bench and smothered his cheek with kisses. Jerome wiped his face, giggling. Casey recognised Suzanne's billowing violet skirt as one from the studio which always took over half an hour to iron.

'I had a late night. I could do with a cup of coffee before we leave.' Suzanne flung her handbag strap carelessly at the spiked back of a kitchen chair but it missed. The bag burst open and its contents spilled onto the floor.

Piers knelt to help her retrieve them. 'You need a strong black, with such a lousy aim,' he teased, then stopped and frowned at something in his hand. 'Why are you calling yourself *that?*' He held one of the business cards bearing the name 'Suzanne Dupont'.

She gasped and snatched it back but it was too late.

'Well, why shouldn't I? You know it should have been my name by rights.'

He turned to fill the kettle at the sink. 'But what's the point of using it now? It'd only make Mum upset.'

'Why should I care if Mum gets upset?' Suzanne snapped the clasps of her handbag shut. 'She never cared when she upset me. She hasn't even seen my business card so the only way she'll find out will be if you tell her. But I'm thinking of changing my name back to Dupont, anyway.'

'Why? We've been Bowmans almost all our lives. I don't even remember being a Dupont. We know nothing about them.'

'Speak for yourself. You don't remember our father but I do. And he was fantastic! You don't know what we've missed all these years. You just spout the drivel that Mum and Gran have brainwashed you with.'

'They've told us nothing about our father so how could they have brainwashed me one way or the other?'

Suzanne sank down, visibly rattled. 'Missing our father isn't the only reason I want to change my name back to his. I want to do it because I hate her.'

'Who? Mum or Gran?'

'Both of them, but I meant Mum!'

Piers sighed as he spooned coffee into a cup. 'She isn't that bad. I mean... I know it was annoying the way she always went along with Gran...'

'Annoying?' Suzanne cried.

'Alright, it was absolutely disgusting. But I've come to see she cares about us in her own way.'

'Cares about us? You really are talking rubbish! Do you call it care when she'd fob us off, even when we pleaded with her to listen to us?'

'No, I hated it. You know I did. But she tries. She lent me money to help set up my business. And she helped you to finance your studio.'

'She told you that!' An angry red spot appeared on each of Suzanne's cheeks beneath the blusher she'd already applied. 'She said she wouldn't tell anybody. Shows what a two-faced, hypocritical cow she...'

Casey beckoned to Jerome to follow her out of the kitchen. He'd grown accustomed enough to her to obey. They crouched in a corner of the lounge room beside his plastic road map and container of Matchbox cars.

Jerome's eyes were wide. 'Is Auntie Suze mad at Daddy?'

'No,' Casey whispered. 'She's mad at somebody who isn't here and she's just letting off steam.'

Jerome cocked his head with a blank expression.

She ruffled his hair. 'Does that make any sense at all?'

'A bit,' he mumbled. 'Casey, look at this one. It's a van like Daddy's. It goes real fast.'

The voices carried from the kitchen. 'I'm telling you, she didn't tell me. Gran let it slip when I was over there one day. I know Mum cares because she supported me when I wanted to keep Jerome and everybody else was trying to talk me out of it. She didn't have to stick her neck out for me and go reason with Anna. You know she didn't.'

'But she didn't support you enough to let you live with her and Gran. She stood by and let that rotten old bag kick you out with a newborn baby.'

Casey heard Piers laugh. 'That suited me fine. Who'd want to live with 'em anyway? It was bad enough when we were kids.'

'That's not the point. She wouldn't have let you live with them if you'd wanted to. I'll tell you why I hate Mum. She's totally ruined my life.'

'What's wrong with your life?'

'I've been torn away from my native country and the family I belong to. Then my personality was crushed because Gran never stopped criticising me and Mum would just stand around agreeing with her. They've done the same to you and they've done such a thorough job that you don't even know.'

'Of course I know! Do you think I'm dense? But all that stuff doesn't matter any more because we can't change the past. We might as well just get on with our lives.'

'It does matter. Look at yourself. A bloke your age should be out partying. Not stuck with a child and no proper support from his family.'

'At least I'm happy,' he shot back.

'Are you insinuating that I'm *not* happy?' Her voice was sharp. Jerome stopped playing and winced.

'Well, are you?'

'I'm happier than you! At least I've got a life!'

'Well if you're happy, then Mum didn't ruin your life.'

Casey heard chair legs scrape across the floorboards. Suzanne's voice was muffled and choked with tears. 'You're such a smart-aleck, always trying to get the better of me. If you knew how you appear to other people, stuck here like a rat in a hole…'

Jerome pressed himself against Casey. 'I think she is mad at him.'

'Look Suzanne, I didn't mean to make you upset. You call yourself any name you like. Here's your coffee.'

Jerome tugged Casey back into the kitchen. She found Suzanne standing beside the table, staring into the cup. 'I'm too churned up to enjoy it now!' She shoved it away from her and the black liquid sloshed over the side and onto the table. 'I'll wait 'til I get to work. Thanks for nothing.' She scooped up her keys. 'Come on, Casey.'

Jerome approached with his face raised to give his aunt a kiss but Suzanne swept past him and didn't even notice.

Chapter 5

Suzanne clutched her steering wheel tight, leaned her head back on the sheepskin headrest and sighed, 'I've got a headache. I had a bit too much to drink last night and that argument came right on the heels of it. I suppose I sounded terrible.'

'No, you didn't. I argue with my brother too. All the time.'

'I'm sure you overheard the things I said, though. How could you help it? Casey, I'd like to keep venting my spleen and Piers is too close to the situation to listen objectively. Will you hear me out?'

'Of course I will.'

Suzanne turned her head slightly to give Casey a faint smile. 'Thanks. Here goes! The most unforgivable thing Mum ever did was to snatch us from our father's grip when we were too young to have any say about it. Those stories I used to tell you were true. Gran had some grudge against him, as she does against almost everyone alive. Mum has always been like putty in her hands. Gran convinced Mum to leave him without a trace, just like that! I can remember the day we left. I was five years old. They told us they were taking us shopping. They hustled us into a taxi and whisked us off to the airport. We were on a plane bound for Heathrow and before I knew it, we were on a jumbo bound for Australia! They never told us we weren't going back.

'Whenever I pleaded to go home to Papa, Mum fobbed me off with some lame excuse about how much happier we were without him. Well I sure wasn't happier!' Suzanne cleared her throat before she continued. 'I used to pray at night that Papa would come and find us. God didn't answer my prayer. I guess that was when I lost faith in Him.

'Papa was a wonderful man. He was a stock-broker. I don't remember what he looked like except that he was tall with dark hair. I *do* remember the parties he used to throw. You should have seen them, Casey! He'd have the place decked out with gold and silver streamers from top to bottom. He taught me to dance and sing so that I could show his friends at the parties. We lived in a beautiful house. It had a huge flight of stairs with marble balustrades and there was an enormous playroom full of toys. I would far rather have stayed with him than Mum.'

'But you've had good times here in Australia too. Haven't you?'

Suzanne's jaw tightened as she overtook a truck. 'I've had more bad times. Gran has filled Mum's head with all sorts of poison about me and Piers for twenty years. Our whole world was forced to revolve around her. Mum has listened to her and pampered her and given her everything she asks for. Piers and I have always had to take a back-seat. Gran is supposed to be so sick but she's been slowly dying for twenty years and never gets any worse as far as I can see.

'If I ever got sick or needed Mum's attention, Gran would put on her dying swan act and Mum would scoot up to her like a wimp. Whenever Gran said, "Jump" Mum would say, "How high?" It makes me sick. I haven't even mentioned the nagging and scolding I'd get. When we were kids, we weren't allowed out of Mum's sight for a second. I'm not kidding! She'd be right there by the school gates waiting for us, rain or shine. Even at High School I couldn't do anything without her eagle eye pinned on me. I wanted to go to France as an exchange student but that was out of the question. I never forgave her for not letting me go. And do you remember how she'd monitor the length of my school uniform?'

'Yes, and I remember how you'd hitch them up with safety pins as soon as we got to school.'

For the first time that morning, Suzanne giggled. 'At least I had that one up on her. As well as being a control freak, she was also pretty dumb.' They'd arrived at work and pulled into Suzanne's car-park but she made no move to get out. She dashed a tear from her cheek and drew a shaky breath.

'I tried to reach my father two years ago. I found his old business address listed in a French telephone directory somebody lent me. My letter was returned in another envelope with a note written in French. I took it to a friend who could translate it for me. My father's company doesn't exist anymore. The business dissolved and the partners couldn't be traced.' Suzanne raked her fingers through her hair to try to restore some semblance of order. 'Even if my father had received my letter, perhaps he wouldn't have been able to read my English.'

She pressed the palms of her hands against her eyelids. 'I can't go in like this. Eric will notice I've been upset and make a big deal of it. Let's wait for a bit longer. I won't think about all this anymore. Casey, will you change the subject to get my mind on something else?'

'I don't know if I can think of anything.'

'Of course you can. Come on, anything. '

'OK, who was Jerome's mother?' Casey was half surprised to hear the question shoot from her mouth.

Suzanne's eyelashes flickered apart. 'That'll do. Well done! She was a girl Piers met at Uni. Her name was Anna Carter. She was quite pretty but a bit eccentric. Mum and Gran couldn't stand her. I had nothing against her in the beginning, except that she was an environmental fanatic. Always campaigning to save whales or Indian tigers or the ozone layer or whatever she was into at the time. She was the sort who'd get offended if you didn't jump straight onto her band-wagon.

'I did find her annoying and pushy the more I knew her. For some reason, she decided that she liked Piers and started following him around. Perhaps she saw him as a rare species who needed her help.' Suzanne's giggle was already brighter than before. 'I don't think any other girl had ever looked his way so being chased went straight to his head. I couldn't believe what he did.'

'What did he do?'

'He defied the two dragon ladies and moved in with her. They abused him and ordered him to have nothing to do with Anna but for the first time in his life, he told them where to go.' Suzanne began to re-apply her smudged eye make-up. 'I wish it'd worked out for him, because I hate giving them any opportunities to say, "I told you so."'

'Why didn't it work? What happened?'

'Dunno really. She grew tired of him. Anna was a manic depressive.

Whenever anything didn't go her way, she'd hit rock bottom. She was addicted to her mood pills and heavier stuff, like heroin. Once, Piers got home to their flat and found that she'd smashed every single piece of dinner china.'

'You're kidding!'

Suzanne shook her head. 'Sad, isn't it? He tried all he knew to cheer her up but she got stuck into him for falling short. This all lasted for months. It was quite a saga. In the end, I'm not certain whether he left or she kicked him out. He'll never discuss it. Anyway, he moved back home with Mum and Gran.'

'And what about Jerome?'

'Well, Anna found out that she was pregnant after Piers left but it turns out she was set against abortion too. The rights of the unborn, you know.' Suzanne placed her eye-liner back into her purse with a grim laugh. 'Thinking about poor Anna reminds me that some people have had even blacker luck than me. This was a good tangent to get me off on, Casey. Back at the time, Piers thought she should have an abortion. He tried to talk her into it but she wouldn't listen. Gran used to get stuck into him.' Suzanne put on a raucous, wavering screech. *See what happens when you don't listen to me? You'll be stuck paying support for that girl's brat for the rest of your life.'*

'Was Anna going to bring Jerome up herself?'

'No way! She didn't want a baby. She could barely look after herself. She planned to put him up for adoption when he was born. Then, when he was born, for some reason, Piers decided he did want him after all. To me, that was the biggest mystery. But everybody tried to browbeat him out of it.

'Anna was afraid that Piers would start wanting her help if he kept the baby, and she didn't want a bar of either of them. She'd got an adoption agency involved and they pressured him to change his mind. They told him there was always a chronic shortage of babies for stable, loving families. When he stood his ground, they called him a selfish, naïve boy who didn't realise he was messing with a human life. Gran called him a damn fool!'

'What did you think?' Casey asked. 'Did you stick up for him?'

Suzanne shrugged her slim shoulders. 'I tried to stand aloof from the whole mess. Nothing I said would have made much difference. But now

I'm glad he stuck to his guns. Jerome is a cutie. And Piers is great with him. He surprised us all.'

'How did it finally work out?'

'Mum, of all people, managed to get through to Anna. She realised how determined Piers was and ended up taking his side. I don't think Gran ever found out. Mum managed to get Anna to agree to a meeting with her and Piers. And she talked her round to seeing that the baby would be better off with its biological father instead of strangers. She made Piers promise in front of Anna that he'd keep out of her life and never try to contact her or demand anything from her.'

'So is that the way it still stands?' Casey asked. 'Anna still wants nothing to do with her son?'

'No, you haven't heard the last part. Anna died early last year.'

Icy shock swept through Casey. 'What happened?'

'She O-D'd on heroin. It could've been suicide. Nobody knows for sure. Piers went to the funeral. He was over her by then, but it was still very sad.' Suzanne arched her back and stretched. 'That's about it.'

'Then, I guess I can understand why Piers sticks up for your mum,' Casey mused. 'She did him a wonderful favour by going to speak to Anna and helping him to get custody of Jerome.'

Suzanne tilted her pointy chin to re-apply pink lipstick through the rear vision mirror. 'Do you call that wonderful?' She stepped out and tossed her hair behind her shoulders. 'I call it the sort of favour a mother should do. She owes it to us, after messing up our lives.' On her way up the steps to the studio, Suzanne called over her shoulder, 'Pity it was an isolated event. She should've helped us out far more often than she ever did.'

'Casey, will you do me a favour?' Eric asked.

She looked up from her ironing. 'Sure.'

'Well put that iron down, for heaven's sake, and come through here so I can ask you properly.'

She set it with a clunk into its metal holder. Eric stood leaning his elbow against the doorway of the make-up room. He looked her up and down and the corners of his eyes were crinkled with smiles.

Casey must have glided across the carpet, for she found herself beside him.

'I'd like to take you out to dinner on Friday night if you're not doing anything else.'

No.' One hand made its way up to the necklace at her throat. 'I mean yes. Dinner would be great.' *I sound like an idiot!* 'I didn't mean no, I don't want to. I meant no, I'm not doing anything.' She twisted the chain.

His deep green eyes kindled with amusement. 'I understand.'

Her face burned. 'Thank you. Thank you very much.'

Eric chuckled. 'No need to thank me until Friday night. I've been thinking about doing this for some time. Especially since you changed your hair. The new style gives you a certain... shall we call it *flair* which you didn't have before. Let's just say, I like it.'

Casey struggled to come up with a suitable response. 'Well, thanks.' Dismay coursed through her. *I've already said that.*

'I'll pick you up from your place Friday night at six o'clock.'

'Great. Do you need directions to get there?'

He shook his head. 'I've been there once. And I have the address. It's on your file.'

'Of course it is. Okay. I'll look forward to it.'

'I'll surprise you with the venue, but dress up.' He winked at her. 'It isn't anywhere cheap. I've booked a good table by a balcony window.'

'Do you mean... you've already made reservations?'

'I sure have.'

Something seemed odd. In a flash, Casey realised what it was. 'How did you know I'd say yes?'

The corners of Eric's mouth tilted up. He cupped his hand beneath her chin. 'Let's just say, I had a fairly strong hunch.'

The bell above the studio door jangled. He breezed through to greet his client.

Casey found Suzanne kneeling in a corner of the wardrobe room, sorting through a pile of shoes. 'Guess what. Eric has asked me out to dinner with him.'

Suzanne gave a hushed squeal of pleasure. 'When?'

'Friday night.'

'He's finally come to his senses. I was beginning to be worried that I'd ruined your chances with him.'

'How do you mean?'

'I'd tried so hard to convince Eric to ask you out. He called me an old nag and kept saying that you weren't his type. I thought he'd set his mind against you just to prove that he doesn't listen to me. But he must've taken a good, hard look at you and decided he'd be a fool not to give you a fair go.'

Suzanne's words were salt to Casey's raw nerves. 'Well, heaven help me, maybe he's doing it as a *favour* to you. *I* don't know how to hold his attention.'

Suzanne tilted her head and surveyed Casey from head to toe. 'Have you ever dated a guy like Eric before?'

'Do you mean a good looking one?'

'He's also a very talented photographer with big ambitions to publish his own books and calendars. Has he mentioned any of that to you yet?'

'No.' Casey knew Suzanne had probably guessed the answer.

'I thought not.' She scrambled to her feet and began to whip through clothes on the hangers. 'I'd love to see you and Eric start something good together. I know you'd be perfect for him, but he's been out with a lot of women and it's made him a little... hard to please. I might as well come right out and say it. He's nit-picky. I suppose when you consider how handsome he is, you can understand. So many girls have tried to throw themselves at him. The perfect woman might be right beneath his nose and he'd be too jaded and choosy to even notice.'

Casey forced a nervous laugh. 'Why are you telling me this? Are you trying to shatter my confidence to pieces?'

'I'm trying to help you.' Suzanne finished one row of hangers and started on another. 'I'm going to give you a head-start on your date. I used to go out with Eric myself so I know what turns him on. I'll choose you something to wear. I mean this in the nicest possible way, but sometimes you pick clothes that my mother would wear.'

Casey was stung, knowing Suzanne's opinion of Moira. 'Thanks.'

Suzanne laughed and turned to pat her arm. 'No, you're not that bad. Nobody is as dowdy as her. I only meant that you tend to be conservative in your taste.' She selected a short, sleeveless dress of fine black lace with a plunging neckline. It was the sort of daring garment that Suzanne often carried off to perfection herself. 'This'll be ideal.'

Casey shook her head. 'I couldn't wear that.'

'Why? What on earth do you have against this dress?'

'I have nothing against it. It'd look gorgeous on you.'

'Then why not on you?'

Casey sighed. 'I'm not tall and willowy. I have no waist. My thighs are chunky. And I'm too broad across the bust and the back for anything sleeveless. Look Suzanne, I'd rather choose my own dress.'

'No way. I don't trust your opinion of yourself. Listen to me because I'm the professional. You are nicely proportioned. You aren't petite but you certainly aren't *too* solid. You have wonderful translucent skin but Eric never gets to see much of it because you keep your best parts covered. I know him through and through. He loves a bit of leg. Be a dare-devil. He won't be able to keep his eyes off you all night if you wear this. I can *guarantee.*'

Casey ran her finger down the soft, sheer fabric of the dress. A wistful longing swelled in her heart like yeast. The lace felt chic and decadent. She imagined herself sliding into it like a snake's skin. Wearing a dress Suzanne recommended could give her a booster shot of confidence. Could it help her to be sparkling and bold, like Suzanne herself? It would be a tactile reminder to hide her anxiety about going out with Eric Adams.

'Okay, I'll wear it. I guess I need to straighten up my image a bit.'

Suzanne's white teeth flashed. 'Good for you. By the way, you can borrow clothes from the studio any time you like. I do it all the time. If we look good, customers are more likely to want to use us.'

The thought of Eric's eyes locked on her in that dress, made Casey giddy with feelings she couldn't quite identify. Perhaps they had something to do with the fact that if a successful, stylish photographer like Eric Adams approved of her, she would be able to give herself permission to hold up her head with self-assurance she'd never felt before.

Chapter 6

The following evening, as Casey washed her dishes after tea, Jerome plucked her sleeve. 'Ben just tore your dess off the clovesline.'

Casey stared bewildered at the small boy, trying to take in what he said. Then she dropped the pot she was scouring into the sink and dashed out of the kitchen. Ben was the billy-goat and the 'dess' was the first one she'd borrowed from the studio; a sleek, fabulously delightful creation of green velvet. It had been airing out after a few hours of passive smoking from a hotel at lunch time. Casey flung open the laundry door and shot out into the dusk.

She saw the two empty pegs on the clothesline.

'Ben!' she screamed. 'Where are you?'

A flash of movement caught her eye. His white rump bounced in a strip of thistles far away near the edge of the property. A dark patch flopped from his mouth.

'Come here, you rotten goat!' She tore after him.

Ben leaped onto the old wooden gate at the bottom of the garden with the sure-footedness of a trapeze artist. The dark strip snagged on a splinter of fence post and he tore it loose with a shake of his bearded head. Casey groaned as she stopped to catch her breath. Footsteps pounded the ground behind her.

'I'll get him for you!' Piers streaked past her.

Casey saw Ben's furry face turn. With a joyful bleat, he jumped off the gate and skittered into the blackberry bushes on the other side. Piers leaped over in hot pursuit. Casey couldn't keep up. As she hunched over to nurse a sharp stitch in her side, her left foot squelched into a cold patch. There had been a steady drizzle the previous night and the ground was a quagmire.

'*Yuck!*' Mud oozed into her sneaker and through her sock. Piers and the goat were so far ahead, Casey couldn't tell where they were. She tripped over an exposed root and fell on her hands and knees. Casey scrambled up, sick to the heart, and resumed walking, slowly and carefully. The skin on her fingers felt tight and itchy but her veins pulsed with blood.

At last they returned. Piers shamefacedly dragged Ben by his collar. He handed her a sodden, torn, velvet rag. 'Casey, I can't tell you how sorry I am.'

'It isn't even my dress! I borrowed it from the studio. Suzanne has offered to let me wear them from the goodness of her heart, and now my name will be *mud!*' She looked down at her filthy feet and knees. It seemed an apt analogy.

'I'll tell her it was my fault. I let Ben escape from his tether. I'll offer to pay for the dress. She can buy a new one.'

'Do you have any idea how much a dress like this costs?'

He shook his head. 'A hundred dollars?'

Casey snorted. 'More like *four* hundred.'

Piers said nothing but his eyebrows shot up.

'Will you *still* offer to pay?'

'Of course. I said I would.'

She examined the remnant of the dress, somewhat mollified. 'I always feel nervous whenever I wear clothes this expensive, in case I spill something on them. I thought that when I took it off and hung it up, it'd be safe enough.'

'This isn't the first time Ben's pulled things off the line. He's stolen a few of my T-shirts. I should've warned you.' Piers scowled at the goat. 'That's the best quality meal you'll ever have, so I hope you enjoyed it.' He looked at Casey and managed a wry grin. 'I wonder if it was like eating truffles or caviar instead of potato chips.'

A chuckle surged up in her chest but Casey cleared her throat to get rid of it. She wasn't ready to see the funny side. 'Why do you bother keeping a silly goat?'

'Couldn't get rid of him. He was here when we moved in. The old

The Risky Way Home

owners came back a few times and tried to take him with them. He kept turning up two or three days later. So they asked me if I'd like to buy him. They promised he'd make a good lawn-mower. You're a homebody, aren't you, old Ben.' Piers absent-mindedly scratched the fuzz around Ben's short horns, then recollected himself and shoved him away. 'I mean, get home. I'm mad at you.'

Casey could no longer hold her giggle back. 'So would I be, if he cost me four hundred dollars.'

Piers heaved a sigh. 'It's far more than I paid for him.'

She touched the silky tuft on the top of Ben's head. 'I suppose it's not *his* fault. He was just doing what goats do.'

Ben's ears pricked up as he heard Jerome stamping and singing on the back verandah. With a snort, he frisked toward the square of light from the kitchen window. His cloven feet kicked clods of mud into Casey's eyes.

She gasped and wiped her face. 'Ben, you silly...'

Piers let out a laugh. 'That's just what goats do, too.'

'Well, it's okay for you to laugh. Your face is clean.' Casey bent over to scoop up a sloppy handful of mud.

'What are you going to do with that?'

'Stand still and you'll find out.'

'You wouldn't throw it.'

'What'd you do if I did?'

He laughed again. 'I'd make you regret it.'

'Is that right?' Casey let fly. The mud found its target on the front of his shirt and it was her turn to laugh. 'You and Ben are the ones to blame for this disaster so it's not fair that I should be the only one covered in mud.'

'Well this means war.' Piers reached into the mud.

'No! I was just getting you back for letting my dress get ripped to shreds and then for laughing at me. We're square now.'

'Well, seeing you're already plastered, a bit more won't matter.'

She shielded her face with her arms and squealed.

Jerome jumped down the porch steps and dashed over. 'What's happening?'

'Do you want to help me turn Casey into a mud pie?'

'No, don't do it! Help me get your daddy smack in the nose. You may never have another chance.'

'Choose sides, Jerome,' Piers cried.

Jerome cocked his head to consider. A slow smile lit up his face and he pitched a handful of mud into the middle of Piers' shirt.

'You little traitor!'

'The battle's on!' Casey hastened to form mud balls but even with Jerome's help, she wasn't fast enough. Somehow, Piers kept a steadier flow of ammunition coming. She gave up trying and simply flicked mud at him with her fingers.

'Is that the best you can do?' Piers teased. 'It's getting nowhere near me.'

Suddenly Casey's legs shot out from under her. She sat down hard in a cold patch which had been churned up by their running feet. Gazing into the sky, she tried to catch her breath. Heavy rain clouds had blended with darkness and by the light of the kitchen window, it looked as if the sky was swirling. Piers squatted beside her, uncertain whether or not to keep laughing.

'Does this mean I won?'

She drew a breath but before she could answer, Jerome crept behind his father and dumped an armload of mud onto his head. Casey shrieked with laughter.

Piers spun around. 'Hey, not fair. I wasn't looking.'

Scrambling to her feet, she spun the giggling boy around in her arms. '*We* won! My slipping over was part of the plan. And as the winner, I'm going to have the first shower.'

'Can we play this again tomorrow night?' Jerome pleaded.

'I won't be here tomorrow,' she told him.

'That's right, it'll be Friday.' Piers recalled. 'Will you be heading back to Victor Harbor for the week-end?'

'Actually, I won't be heading back until Saturday morning. Tomorrow night, I'm going out to dinner with a friend.' Casey's knees turned weak as she thought of Suzanne's black lacy dress hanging safely in her wardrobe. *I'll make certain Ben never gets his teeth into* that *one!*

The following evening, Casey squeezed herself into the black dress and found it hard to draw her next breath. Her ribs were compressed like toothpaste in a tube. She stepped back to survey herself in the mirror. The dress's plunging neckline made her appear buxom and Casey wasn't entirely comfortable with so much cleavage showing. *I love this dress... on people like Suzanne, but it highlights every ounce of flesh on my body.* Casey knew the dress would be far too revealing in her father's opinion, but Doug Miller knew nothing about fashion. *I'm just not sure.*

As she was ready, there was no reason not to go downstairs to wait for Eric. Piers sat with his legs crossed Indian fashion on the couch. She knew his asthma had been playing up. She'd heard him cough and he clutched his inhaler in one hand. He glanced at her as she entered and looked down at his shoelaces. Casey flushed, wondering if she looked too ridiculous for comment.

'Do I look okay?' She instinctively crossed her arms in front of her chest but dropped them to her sides again because she felt the fabric stretch across her back. Suzanne had forgiven the damage to the first dress Casey borrowed. Her patience would surely snap if Casey tore the second one too!

'You look nice.'

She stared out of the window. '"Nice" isn't very encouraging,' she mumbled.

Piers shuffled on the couch behind her. 'Well, it looks like something Suzanne would wear.'

She spun around. 'So what?'

His voice was low. 'I only meant that if he wanted a clone of Suzanne, he would have stayed with Suzanne.'

Casey felt stung. 'That's a mean thing to say!'

'Only if you take it that way,' he mumbled.

Her eyes burned. 'It's none of your business anyway and I don't need your opinion.'

For the first time, he raised his inky grey eyes to look at her. 'Then why did you ask for it?'

She flung a question at him in return. 'Why are you in such a bad mood?'

He quickly scrambled from his seat and strode to the kitchen. 'I'm not!'

'You had me fooled, then!' she called after him.

He was thumping tins of spaghetti onto the kitchen bench. 'Just because I didn't say what you wanted to hear, why do you assume I'm in a bad mood?'

'Suzanne's right. You are a smart-alec.' Casey strode back through the passage and brushed past Jerome as he backed out of his bedroom, tugging a container of Duplo blocks behind him. Jerome's eyes lit up when he saw her. 'Casey's dess is too small!'

She heard a smothered laugh from Piers. 'You'd better not say that. You'll get in trouble.'

Casey slammed her bedroom door. She tore ten tissues from the dispenser and pressed a wad against each eye. Tears would smudge her make-up and make her eyes red and swollen. *I won't let him ruin my night! What would* he *know? His whole life is a disaster.*

At last, she removed the tissues to inspect her reflection. Her cheeks were pink and although her eyes burned, they were dry. She peeled the black dress off like skin from a boiled hot-dog and scrambled into the creamy, cool, silky dress she'd always considered her 'best' until she'd met Suzanne again. Casey sat on her bed until she heard a light tap on her door.

'There's a Porsche coming up the driveway,' Piers called.

She stepped out. 'That's him.'

'I guessed that.' Although his normal, friendly smile was in place, Casey swept past him without another word.

'Have a good night,' Piers called after her.

She slipped downstairs and waited for the knock at the door.

⊢──╳──╵──╳──╴⊣

'Casey, you look like the dream of an angel standing here in the moonlight.' Eric opened the passenger's side of his Porsche for her to climb in.

'Thank you.' It was the nicest compliment she'd ever received but instead of relaxing, Casey's body turned tense. He slipped into the driver's seat beside her and filled her senses with his spicy aftershave. Eric's hair was gelled immaculately and in the buttonhole of his dark suit was a fresh carnation. Casey had no idea how to keep a fine, discerning man like Eric Adams interested. Already, she was floundering.

He leaned back to fetch a bouquet of fresh orchids and baby's tear drops from the seat behind him and presented them to her with a flourish.

'I've always tried to make a point of choosing flowers to suit my date.' His green eyes twinkled at her. 'You definitely put me in mind of an orchid. Modest and shy, but pure and priceless.'

'Eric, they're lovely.' Casey buried her face in the flowers. They still had dew on their petals. 'Thank you.'

He took her to a silver service restaurant high on a hill with a panoramic view over the city lights. A pretty waitress led them to a secluded table beside a window, spread napkins across their knees and took their drinks orders. Casey ordered champagne and Eric chose bourbon. He said it was the only drink that ever truly satisfied him.

When their food orders were being taken, Casey said, 'I'll try the chicken breast, please.'

'You don't need to choose that one.' Eric's tone was lightly rebuking.

'But... why not?'

'It's the cheapest dish on the menu. I'm taking you out to dinner. I can well afford it.'

'Okay.' Casey's skin prickled. She'd made a faux pas without even knowing it. Her eye skimmed down the menu over a range of exotic dishes she didn't fancy. Nothing tempted her at all but she moistened her lips and said, 'I'll have the salt and pepper squid.'

Eric smiled with no comment and ordered oysters. Casey had no idea whether or not he approved of her choice.

When the waitress disappeared, he grinned and reached out to tilt her chin. 'Lighten up. You look as if you're about to sit an exam.'

She forced a frozen smile across her face. A tension headache began to pound behind her temples.

'You have a photogenic face,' he told her. 'A good, strong chin and nice sized cheekbones.'

The only reply that came to mind was that she liked his face too, but Casey didn't think that would be appropriate. *I'm sure he already knows.* Instead, she fell back on, 'Thanks.'

He reached into his suit pocket and drew out a miniature album. 'Would you like to see one of my portfolios? These are a few of my prize-winning shots.'

Casey jumped at the opportunity. 'I'd love to.'

He was a talented photographer who honed in on the most miniscule details of his subjects. Slender honey-eaters with their beaks pushed down flower cups, spider webs shining like spun silver in early morning light, silky green tree frogs with great, bloated throats. Each image highlighted the brilliancy and intricacy of the vivid world just outside her door, which she so often walked straight past.

'You have such a gift,' she breathed. The words seemed inadequate for the skill he possessed.

He smiled as he re-filled his glass. 'I wish the people whose opinions held weight would always agree with you.'

Further into the album were snapshots of beaming women, similar to the clients' photos Eric took at work every single day. 'I enjoy taking nature photos but I don't do it much anymore. Pandering to female vanity seems to be what pays.'

'It must be because you're so good at it.' Casey turned over a photograph of Suzanne with her hair coiled lavishly on top of her head like a medieval princess. Innate refinement was evident in everything from the tilt of her chin to the sparkle in her limpid eyes.

'Isn't she gorgeous?' Eric's tone softened. 'Suzanne enchanted me when I first met her.'

'She enchants everyone,' Casey said softly.

Eric considered her comment and nodded. 'You're right. I'm trying to work out what it is about her. Not one of her features is outstanding on its own but the combination … it makes an interesting blend. Those *extreme* features of hers, black hair, firm chin, wide mouth, perhaps she takes plainness to the extreme of becoming attractive.' Eric sipped his bourbon and pondered. 'Or perhaps it's all in her lively personality. Whatever it is, it's nothing other girls can possibly mimic.'

'I've always admired her ever since I've known her,' Casey admitted.

The waitress brought over their dishes. Eric dug into his plate of oysters and resumed his train of thought. 'I was once on the verge of asking Suzanne to marry me. I have to admit, no other woman ever got that far with me.'

Casey stopped with her fork held midway to her mouth. 'What changed your mind?'

Eric leaned across the table and lowered his voice. His green eyes were twinkling. 'I think you'll understand me, because you know them. It was her family.'

Casey found the squid too rubbery for her liking. She swallowed and watched him, waiting for whatever he'd say.

'I went to dinner at their place once. We all know Suzanne hates her mother but I think she wanted to show me off that night. It was a disaster.'

'What happened?'

'As soon as I set my foot in the door, I wanted to bolt straight out again. Even though Suzanne is so attractive, I looked at her dowdy little mother sitting there, chattering away with trivia and trying to be so nice, and had a sudden glimpse of what Suze might look like in twenty or thirty years time. Then, I looked at the wrinkly old grandma and glimpsed what Suzanne would be in *fifty* years time.' Eric threw back his head and laughed. 'No wonder I fled.'

Casey wished she could think of something to say.

'Poor old Suze. Who can blame her for being ashamed of her family? I've never seen a queerer bunch. There's her brother too. What a social outcast loser.'

Although Casey had been furious with Piers a few hours earlier, Eric's harsh words smarted. She found herself shaking her head. 'No, I might've described him that way once, but not anymore. He's a bit weird but not an outcast or a loser. Piers is happy with his life. He *chooses* to keep himself aloof from... well, from most other people, just because he can't be bothered trying to compete on the world's terms.' For the first time that evening, a flash of confidence streaked through her. She'd finally said something that might be construed as discerning. She mustered courage to look Eric in the eye.

'Perhaps you're right. You know the guy better than I do. Casey, you intrigue me. It takes some effort to draw you out but I get the feeling that the harder I try, the more it'll be worth it. I'm looking forward to some really good talks with you.'

'I'd like that too.' Casey lifted her eyes to the glass prisms on the disco ball which hung over the dance floor. As she drew a slow breath, an odd thought shot into her head. The last time she'd felt such light-headed relief was six years earlier when she had just completed her final high-school exam.

Chapter 7

Eric seemed in no hurry on their drive back to the Hills. As they cruised along the dirt road that led home, he slowed to a crawl and placed his left hand on her knee. Casey turned tense and held her breath. He ran his hand higher until it rested halfway up her thigh. By the light of the half moon, Eric's hand looked smooth and cool but felt hot and heavy.

He stopped the car at the end of the pebbly driveway and leaned across to her. Eric's eyes gleamed. He wrapped his fingers around her neck to pull her closer to him and kissed her.

Casey found herself breathless. She didn't know whether she liked the kiss or not. Two impressions crowded other things out. The first was that his lips were wet! The second was that the lingering aroma of oysters and bourbon on his breath was strong. She'd have to take time to work her feelings out once she was alone in her bedroom.

Eric opened his mouth to draw a breath. 'Casey, I've had my eye on you for weeks.' His voice came out in a low breath. 'I know you have a thing for me too.'

It seemed pointless to deny it. 'How ... did you guess?'

He moved closer to her. 'Suzanne told me.'

Although the car interior was dark, Casey's eyelashes flapped apart. 'Did she?'

He gave a low laugh. 'She sure did. I thought I'd better sit back and think it through before I made a new commitment.' His finger traced the outline of her cheek and chin. 'I could tell that you were different to other girls I've dated. You're fresh and sweet. I didn't want to flirt with you if I didn't mean anything. But now I mean something.'

He covered her mouth with his a second time. Casey's forehead broke out in beads of perspiration. *I wonder if Suzanne told him that she put the idea into my head.*

'I suppose I was too proud to immediately take Suzanne's advice.' There was a smile in Eric's voice. 'But I kept you in mind all along. You must've thought I was slow as a wet week-end to make a move. Well you don't have to worry anymore. Things will be different between us from now on.'

At last, a thrill shot through Casey. As Eric released her, she studied his handsome features in the moonlight. If only she'd realised that he'd already made up his mind before he'd even taken her out, she might've felt far more relaxed all evening. As it was, he didn't appear concerned that she hadn't spoken much. Now that he'd settled back in his seat, Casey instinctively opened her door. A gust of cold air blew in. Eric raised one of her hands and pressed a kiss on the back of it. 'I'll see you at work on Monday.' With a wink and a smile, he drove away.

Casey paused by the front door to shake the cobwebs out of her head. She waited until she could no longer hear the rumble of Eric's tyres on the gravel. If the headache wasn't pounding behind her temples, she might be feeling on top of the world. Instead, she felt more like a sleep-walker, swirling through a dream. The thought of dreams reminded her of Eric's greeting earlier that evening.

An angel's dream. That's what he called me. Casey tried to muster another thrill or even a flush of pleasure but she only shivered. Eric's voice had sounded the same as he used with his clients at work.

She opened the door and stepped inside where warmth from the wood fire surrounded her. There were a few glowing logs in the heater. The TV screen flickered and Piers lay on the couch with Jerome stretched over his chest, both sound asleep. Piers' chin rested on top of Jerome's silky hair and the boy gently rose and fell with each breath his father took.

As she tiptoed to the TV and switched it off, Piers stirred. He blinked up at her and yawned. 'Hi. Did you have a good night?'

'Yes, it was fun.' It had been a very long day and Casey suddenly felt more like crying than smiling.

'Good. I've been feeling bad about what I said… because of the way you left. You were right. I had no right to speak the way I did. I'm sorry.'

'Do you mean when you said that if he was looking for a clone of Suzanne, he would have stayed with Suzanne?'

Piers forced an awkward laugh. 'Yes, that!'

'Forget it.' Her anger had been replaced by weariness. 'You were right too. I did ask for your opinion.'

He eased himself to a sitting position, careful not to wake Jerome. 'But I didn't set out to make you unhappy. That was just me being selfish.'

'What do you mean?'

Piers slowly stood. 'Well, I never really liked Eric much when he went out with Suzanne.'

'He didn't think much of you either.' Casey didn't know why she said that. It just slipped out.

'That doesn't surprise me.' Piers cupped the back of Jerome's neck, keeping the little boy's head securely on his shoulder. He hesitated before he stepped into the passage. 'There's just one more thing.'

'What's that?'

'Did you change out of that black dress because you thought I insulted it? That wasn't it at all. I think you looked stunning.'

Now the heat flooded her face. Casey was glad of semi-darkness because even the tips of her ears burned. 'Thanks, but you didn't have to say that.'

Silhouetted in the light of the passage, Piers' shoulders slumped. 'I just wanted you to know. Good night.'

'Good night.' She switched on the kitchen light, ran a glass of water and swallowed a paracetamol. *Why did he have to say it?* If he was trying to make her feel better, it didn't work. His brief comment made her feel more awkward than all of Eric's sweeping tributes because she knew that while Eric gushed compliments for his living, Piers was generally too bashful to bother. She leaned against the sink and gazed out into the inky sky.

Dear God, I should be happy. I want to be happy. I tried so hard for everything to work out right tonight, and things did work out just the way I wanted them to. So why do I feel sad?

Winter set in over the next few days. Mornings in the Adelaide Hills were cold with an intensity that pierced Casey's bones. Jerome liked to visit her in her bedroom and old Sam's paws clicked up the steps behind him. The little boy giggled at the two ribbons of vapour that wafted from the dog's nostrils. Sam couldn't stretch his stiff legs without whimpering but he always cocked his mouth into a smile and nuzzled his nose into the palm of her hand. Then he would heave a sigh, turn around twice and curl in front of Casey's electric heater, taking most of the warmth. She did not have the heart to push him away, even when his damp coat began to steam dry and fill her bedroom with the odour of wet dog.

The following Thursday morning, she knelt by the lounge room fire to wrap a gift in coloured paper. It was Eric's birthday and she had bought him a lovely shirt with chunky stripes of rusty-red and navy blue.

Jerome dashed out of the kitchen. 'Casey, I can't wake Sam up!'

Piers was already outside, warming up his work shed. Casey approached Sam's basket and prodded the old dog with the tip of her shoe. He didn't stir. He was curled up with his nose tucked over his tail but his faded flank did not rise and fall with his normal wheezy breath. Without a word, Casey gripped Jerome's fingers and hurried out in the rain to the work shed.

'Piers, Sam is dead,' she mumbled.

Piers heaved Jerome into his arms. 'I thought it might happen soon. He's been off his food for a few weeks and he's seventeen years old. That's pretty old for a dog.'

They returned to the kitchen where Piers set Jerome on his feet and knelt by the basket. He scratched Sam's ears and stroked his head. Casey flinched as she watched. It was truly terrible not to see Sam's pink tongue shoot out to lap Piers' fingers, as it normally would have. Their affectionate old friend had gone and the shell of a dog remained. Tears prickled the backs of her eyelids. She heard Piers ask Jerome, 'Do you remember when we spoke about this?'

Casey's throat swelled with an overwhelming ache.

Jerome must have seen her sad face. His small hand slipped into hers.

'Sam's gone to heaven.' His voice was mournful. 'He'll be able to run again. He won't be tired and sore.' Jerome bowed his tousled head and began to weep.

Piers turned away for a moment and Casey saw him dash something from his own cheek. He faced her again with a sheepish smile. 'Even *I'm* a bit teary. He's been a big part of my life. I was only six when we got him.'

'I remember Sam from way back too.' Her voice was tight.

'Can I pat him?' Jerome sobbed.

Piers nodded. 'Give him a goodbye pat.'

'Are you going to dig a grave?' Casey asked.

'Yeah. The ground'll be hard and cold but we'll find a spot.' He kissed the top of Jerome's head. 'We'll give the good old fellow a decent funeral. He deserves one.'

Jerome pressed his face into Piers' shabby work jacket. 'I know Sam's happy now.' His voice was muffled. 'But I'll miss him.'

'Do you want to go somewhere when we finish? Maybe we'll visit Nanna and Great-Gran in Victor Harbor.' A gust of wind struck the side of the house as if a giant's hand had hurled it. Rain coursed down the window panes. Piers had to raise his voice to be heard above the deluge on the tin roof. 'On second thoughts, it's a rotten day for it.'

Casey looked at Jerome's soft, sweet profile and longed to think of something to cheer him. 'Jerome, do you like gelati?'

Without turning his head, he nodded against the front of Piers' jacket.

'There's a good café a few doors from where I work. It's called The Hedgehog's Hole and it's your Auntie Suzanne's favourite place for a quick bite to eat. It has thirty different flavours of gelati on Tuesday and Thursday nights. Today is Thursday. Would you like to meet me there after work and have some?'

He turned his face and she detected a pale smile. 'Ess.'

She looked at Piers over his head. 'How about it? It's on the same road as the studio, just a few doors down on the right.'

'Sounds good to me. Okay, it's a date.' He flushed over his choice of words. 'I mean we'll see you there. Gee whiz Casey, you know what I mean.'

She found herself smiling. 'Call it a date if you like. We'll only be there until Jerome decides he's had enough gelati.'

'That could be all night. Have you seen the way he stacks dessert away?'

'He's a growing boy.' She shrugged into her black, woollen coat and buttoned it up over Eric's present to keep it dry for her dash to her car. 'How about six o'clock?'

'Sounds great. We'll look forward to it.'

On her drive into work, Sam's death had time to sink in. Casey had always loved him. She remembered the lopsided way his puppy paws had run behind their bicycles on the way to school. On weekends, Suzanne would send him almost crazy with delight by tying a foil tray behind her bike and peddling circles around the backyard. Sometimes Piers would clip a lead onto his handlebars to take Sam for long runs around the district and the girls would protest, because they wanted Sam to stay with them. Although he hadn't been her dog, Casey had grown fond of him all over again.

Now he wouldn't be there to rest his chin on her knees while she sipped her last cup of tea before work. She wouldn't feel the ripple of his swallow or his light breath on her hand. Casey was surprised to find a tear streak down her cheek followed by another.

In spite of efforts to re-apply her make-up, her misery must have been evident when she stepped into work. Suzanne took one look at her and hurried from behind the counter to pull her to a seat. 'Casey, what's up?'

'Sam died during the night.' Her face crumpled. 'And Jerome found him.'

Suzanne raised a hand to her own mouth. 'Good old Sam was the best! I remember the day we chose him from the pet shop. I'd just turned eight years old. Mum was going to take another dog but I chose Sam because he stared right up into my face with his big brown eyes and licked my fingers.' She fumbled for a tissue herself.

Eric surveyed them with an indulgent smirk. 'Girls, is this a dog we're talking about?'

'Not just any old dog,' Suzanne countered. 'He was better than some people.'

'Anybody would think he was your nearest and dearest relative.'

'He was one of my favourite family members.'

Eric winked at Casey. 'We won't go into that. You'd better both dry your eyes. Our first client is due in fifteen minutes and we don't want her to see two thirds of our staff dissolved in tears. Life goes on.' His tone was not unkind.

'It does indeed.' Suzanne loudly blew her nose and followed him to the back room. Casey joined them. On the little table was a wonderful black forest cake, a small platter of fresh sliced fruit and a strong smelling selection of cheeses.

'This is my birthday present for Eric,' Suzanne grinned. 'Soon we'll have an extra-nice morning tea. There's a bottle of port in the fridge too, to go with the Stilton cheese. Port and stilton are a perfect match, you know?'

The thought of her own gift suddenly seemed drab and mundane alongside Suzanne's extravagant spread. *How can I compete with this? I don't even* know *these things that Suzanne knows.* Casey gave him her parcel anyway.

'Happy birthday, Eric. This is only simple but I liked it when I saw it.'

He shaped his lips into a kiss. Eric tore off the paper and shook out the fabric. He glanced from his new shirt to Casey's face and back again. Finally, Eric sighed and shook his head. 'Casey, sweetie, thanks for the thought but this really isn't me. Take it back and they might give you a credit.'

It was far worse than she'd imagined. 'Sorry, I just thought...' Casey looked down at her knees. There was no point talking. She had to save her breath to keep her face from crumpling again. *I should've guessed. Look at the clothes he wears to work everyday! Idiot!*

'I've hurt your feelings, haven't I?' He raised her chin and peered into her eyes with deep concern. 'I feel like a mongrel. I didn't mean to make you sad. There's nothing wrong with the shirt. I'm just very particular about what I wear. You'd prefer me to be honest, wouldn't you? If I took it, you'd feel even worse when you never saw me wear it.'

Casey managed to nod. 'I do prefer honesty.' She folded the shirt back into its paper and stuffed it in her handbag. She knew she'd have trouble finding the receipt. She wouldn't take it back. She'd save it for Dale's Christmas present.

'Whenever Eric wears casual clothes, he only ever chooses from two

French designers,' Suzanne put in, 'and one of them has no local retail outlets. You need to order from a special catalogue.'

If you know so much about him, why aren't you still his girlfriend?

Eric raised Casey's left hand and caressed each finger at the knuckles. 'Don't take it to heart. I'm flattered that you'd think of buying me a present. Now, I have something that just might cheer you up.' He drew a plastic ticket wallet from his pocket. 'You and I are going to see some live theatre tonight. I've booked the best box seats over the stage. We'll have a bite to eat first and celebrate my birthday in style.'

'That sounds great.'

'I'll make sure it will be.'

The tinkle of the bell over the door announced the arrival of their first client. Eric brushed a kiss down Casey's cheek and stepped out to greet her.

A second later, Casey remembered something. Piers and Jerome.

'I can't go out with Eric tonight. I've organised something else.'

Suzanne shut the fridge door with a thump. 'Can't you cancel it? What could be more important than this? You've been hanging out for weeks for Eric to even notice you.'

Casey hated the position she found herself in. 'It's sort of short notice.'

'That's because Eric wanted to surprise you.'

'Well it sure worked.'

Suzanne's mouth narrowed to a straight line. She folded her arms in front of her. 'What's so important that you'd consider calling off a night on the town with Eric?'

'I felt sorry for Jerome. He was really upset to find Sam lying in his basket. I asked him if he'd like to have gelati at the Hedgehog's Hole tonight. He said he would and Piers agreed to bring him down.'

All at once, the creases smoothed from Suzanne's face. 'You can easily cancel that. One night is the same as any other to them but it's Eric's *birthday*. Those theatre tickets are expensive. They can only be used tonight and they're not refundable. You have to go! Piers'll understand.'

Casey peeled a ragged nail from her left thumb with her teeth. 'I guess he will. But will Jerome?'

'Of course he will. The poor little poppet. I can understand why you want to cheer him up but next week will be better anyway. Jerome will have had time to come to terms with Sam's death.'

'That's true.'

'It'd be a huge mistake to put Eric off. Believe me! He bought those tickets last week and he's crazy about taking you.' Suzanne leaned closer to whisper, 'I've never seen him so besotted with a girl for a long time.'

Casey couldn't help feeling pleased. 'Has he been talking about me?'

'All the time. He's been raving about your sweet personality and your vibrant hair.'

Casey found herself laughing. 'Well I guess it wouldn't be too hard to phone Piers and postpone the café until next week.'

'You have to! Eric'll take it the wrong way if you don't. Don't blow everything you've worked for.'

Casey looked at Suzanne's animated face and felt a rush of gratitude. She hated making choices and now the choice had been made for her.

Chapter 8

She found a phone booth in a shopping mall at lunch time. Casey preferred to do it away from work in case Eric overheard her. She pressed in the number and listened to the dial tone. Finally, somebody picked up the phone.

'Hello, Piers Bowman speaking.'

'Piers, it's Casey.'

'Hi Casey!'

She cringed at the pleasure in his tone of voice. In the background, a small voice distinctly cried, 'Is that Casey? Ask her how long!'

'About five hours now. Okay!' Piers chuckled into the receiver. 'I suppose you heard that. He's been asking every half hour.'

'That's why I phoned. You see I have to… cancel.' Instantly, Casey decided to withhold the reason. The truth would sound too selfish and callous. 'We're snowed under with work at the studio and Eric and Suzanne have asked me to work overtime.'

'What a pain.' Piers sounded sympathetic but she could detect his disappointment. 'Never mind. We'll make it another time.'

'How about next week?' Her own voice rang shrilly in her ears.

'Okay. It's good to hear that work is going so well for Suzanne, anyway.'

'Hey?'

'Because she needs you to work overtime.'

'Oh yeah.' Casey felt uncomfortably hot beneath her collar. 'We *are* busy but I'm really sorry to upset Jerome.'

'Don't give it another thought. He'll be fine. I might even take him somewhere else instead.'

'I hope you do.'

'Well take it easy and don't work too hard.'

Casey forced cheerfulness into her voice but she was glad he couldn't see her face. 'I won't. Bye.'

As soon as she hung up the receiver, she felt a heavy lump sink to the pit of her stomach. She felt heartsick not just because she had told a lie but because she'd let them down. She realised she had let herself down too. Casey had looked forward to a casual bite to eat with them. It would've been more relaxing than going out with Eric. Dates with him were an extreme effort, constantly trying to say and do exactly the right thing.

As she hurried back to work, Casey raised her face to the thin ray of sunshine and made an effort to look on the bright side. *There's no harm done. I'll meet them next week instead.* She filled her lungs with fresh air and tried to muster enthusiasm for her night out with Eric. Dinner and live theatre with such a handsome man would be a treat. *I've handled it the best way I can. Nobody will be upset.* Yet Jerome's eager, 'Ask her how long now,' rang in her ears.

Suzanne stood behind the counter. 'Have you phoned Piers?'

'Yeah. We've agreed to make it next week.'

'See, what did I tell you? I knew Piers wouldn't care. He's pretty good that way.'

'I know.' Casey returned to her job of labelling finished photographs for customers to pick up. Labelling herself a liar left a bitter taste all through her. She never wanted to repeat it.

'I thought we'd try Suzanne's little joint.' Eric set off through the light rain.

'You mean the Hedgehog's Hole?'

'That's it.'

'You're kidding me. I didn't think that place would be...' Casey hesitated. She had been going to say, 'I didn't think that place would be classy enough for you.' She quickly re-phrased the words in her head. 'It's not as stylish as the places you usually take me to.'

Eric raised one eyebrow. If he'd noticed her slip of the tongue he chose to ignore it. 'You're right, I've never been there before. I prefer places a little more up-market but tonight the food isn't such an issue. We just want a quick bite so we can get to the theatre in plenty of time. Suzanne says this place has good croissant fillings so I guess it's as good as any. Come on.'

By now, they were standing by the café door. Although her coat was damp with drizzle, Casey stopped moving. 'But I'd rather go someplace different. I've been here quite a lot.'

'You haven't been here with *me*. Come on. We're getting wet.' He opened the door and stepped inside.

An open-fire blazed in a corner and warm, delicious odours of sizzling meat and hot bread enveloped them. Behind a frosty glass counter, tubs of gelati waited to be scooped into, all the colours of the rainbow. A smiling waitress looked up from wiping a table. 'Find yourselves a good booth near the fire before we get too busy.'

'Over here,' Eric said.

They ordered drinks and croissants. Eric lowered his voice and remarked, 'I know why I don't come often to places like this. They don't even have napkins to spread across our knees.' With a gusty sigh, he settled back to wait for his meal.

'Sometimes they do. Maybe they ran out. The food is delicious, anyway.'

'I can't give you my verdict on that until we leave.'

Their hot croissants had just arrived when Eric's eyes fixed on something behind Casey's shoulder. 'Look who just walked in. Isn't that Suzanne's brother and his kid? You said he was your housemate. What are they doing in this neck of the woods?'

Casey found she couldn't twist her neck to see for herself. All she could move were her shoulders, which slowly hunched in on themselves. She wanted to fill as small a space as possible.

'Daddy, look! It's Casey.'

Her mouthful of croissant turned to sawdust. The rest thumped onto her plate, forgotten.

Jerome tugged Piers to their booth.

'Hello,' Eric said pleasantly. 'It's Pierre, isn't it?'

'No, but that's close. It's Piers.'

Jerome's face glowed. He slipped into the booth beside Casey. 'We thought you wouldn't be here. But you *are!*'

Piers flushed bright red. 'Jerome, we should find another...'

But Eric shrugged good-naturedly. 'You might as well join us. We won't be here for long and then you'll have this booth to yourselves.'

Piers hesitated. Casey guessed that he couldn't come up with a polite way to refuse. 'Okay, thanks.' They went to choose their gelati and returned five minutes later with heaped bowls.

'I decided to take Jerome out after all. I thought we'd eat, then look in and say hello to you and Suzanne at the studio. I haven't seen it since it was only recently set up. Are you having a tea break?'

'Sort of. We're...'

'It's almost six thirty, man!' Eric cut in. 'Work's long over. Suzanne left at five on the dot. Casey and I are off to see some live theatre when we finish here.'

Piers glanced at Casey with a flash of understanding. She saw a flicker of raw hurt and then he looked down at his bowl. 'What are you going to see?'

While Eric told him, Casey grappled to find a way to exonerate herself in Piers' eyes without making Eric aware of her plight. 'Today is Eric's birthday. He bought theatre tickets to surprise me.' She prayed that Piers would think through the nuances of that and understand why she had stood him up.

'Many happy returns. How old are you?'

'Twenty-six, man!'

Jerome chortled into his gelati. 'That's old.'

'Not all that old,' Piers said. 'Have you had a good day?'

'Not bad, for work. Would've preferred to be playing golf.'

'I remember you were a pretty good golfer.'

'You mean when I went out with your sister?' Eric gave a snort. 'I'm a lot better now than I was then.'

'What's your handicap now?'

Casey stopped listening to their chatter. Only Jerome's starry face was serene. He had almost polished off his chocolate gelati and had a dripping brown beard.

Casey's eyes were drawn to Piers' left hand, which fiddled compulsively with the edge of his paper placemat. His fingers were covered with calluses and a few cuts. The nail of his thumb was chipped. She forced her eyes to look higher.

He was wearing a forest green windcheater she had never seen before. It accentuated his dark hair, inky eyes and clear complexion. If she'd ever imagined the two men together, Casey would've expected Eric to show Piers up but in some strange way, the reverse had happened. Most of the other diners who'd filtered in were dressed casually like Piers. In their designer label clothes from work, she and Eric appeared ridiculously overdressed. Casey raised a finger to her perspiring neck. Her tight collar was itchy and not even comfortable.

As soon as Jerome had finished his bowl of gelati, Piers was on his feet. 'We'll see you later. Good to catch up with you, Eric. Have a good night.'

Jerome threw his arms around Casey for a goodbye hug. 'See you at home,' he chirped.

Piers plucked him away. 'Your face is dripping. You'll make her dirty.'

'He already has.' Eric looked at Casey's shoulder.

'It isn't much.' Casey searched her handbag for a tissue. 'I don't mind.'

Piers tugged a clean hanky from his pocket and wiped Jerome's chin. 'Sorry. They should have serviettes here,' he said with a forced grin.

'I said something like that myself,' Eric remarked.

'I'm all clean,' Casey assured them. 'No harm done.'

But Eric still focused on the spoiled clothing with veiled displeasure.

As Piers and Jerome stepped outside, he gave a low chuckle and mumbled in her ear, 'Doesn't the fool realise that it's all-you-can-eat night? His little runt could've had more gelati but I wasn't going to be the one to tell him. Still, I have to admit, he looks startlingly like our Suzanne.' He stood, brushed a crumb from his white linen trousers and took her hand. 'Let's go.'

Casey ducked her head against the driving rain and hurried to keep up with Eric's long strides. Several times Suzanne had lauded Eric's brilliance, but Casey wondered if Suzanne had ever noticed the hard-heartedness that went with it. But was Eric's hard-heartedness any worse than Casey's own duplicity? The duplicity that had been found out! *God is closely watching you and He weighs carefully everything you do.* She recognised the proverb but did not know why it had suddenly popped into her head. Casey couldn't help shuddering.

⸺⸺⸺⸻⸻⸻

The rest of the evening was a blur. At the theatre, Casey lost the thread of the plot and couldn't pick it up again. Eric would have taken her for drinks afterwards but she pleaded a throbbing headache. She wanted to get home before Piers went to bed. She hated thinking that she'd offended anyone and was anxious to apologise properly and hear what he had to say, if indeed he was still willing to talk to her.

The drive up the Freeway was long and cold. Her heart hammered when she saw that the lounge room light was still on. When Casey stepped inside, Piers was in the bathroom cleaning his teeth. She settled down to wait on the couch. In her early days of boarding with him, she would have been delighted to slip upstairs and avoid him. He was taking so long, she wondered if he intended to avoid her. Normally, Sam would have shuffled over to rest his nose on her knees. Casey almost couldn't bear the loneliness of the room without him. At last Piers stepped out, wiping his hands.

'Didn't expect you back so soon. Your mother phoned about an hour ago. I've written the message on the pad but she said to tell you not to drive straight home tomorrow. They're coming to visit you here.'

'Thanks.' Normally, the news would have pleased Casey, but she was too preoccupied to care. Piers was still talking to her. He seemed prepared to let the dismal evening pass without a word but she could not. Her heart ached.

'Piers, about tonight! I really did want to keep our arrangement but when Eric asked me, I just…'

He jerked up his hand to stop her. He did not want to hear. 'Casey, let's just forget it. I know how you feel about Eric. No hard feelings, okay?'

She gulped and nodded. 'I'm sorry.'

'That's alright,' he replied. 'But I wouldn't have minded if you'd told me,' he added with a sigh. He gave her a smile before he went to bed but it appeared sad and forced.

There was no sleep for Casey. She cried hot tears into her pillow but they didn't ease the tightness in her chest. *Dear God, I'm sorry I lied. I thought it was only a white lie. My motives were good.* She blinked up at the dark ceiling, disgusted with herself. Even Eric was more honest than she was. *At least he told me straight away that he wouldn't wear my present.* Casey thumped her pillow hard as she recalled her response. *'I do prefer honesty,'* she'd said. The worst part was that she'd hurt Piers, and she hated hurting other peoples' feelings.

What was it about Piers, anyway? He'd changed. He seemed more confident now than he used to be. He was so timid at school. He used to be too nervous to look anyone straight in the eye. He was just…well a wimp who used to get picked on and beaten up. Other boys treated him as if he wore a 'kick me' sign. *Now he's different. I'm not sure why. It's as if he's learned to be comfortable in his own skin.* Casey knew there was more to it than that. There was a refreshing calmness about Piers that she had come to appreciate. *But he'll never trust me again.*

Staying in bed was futile. Casey switched on her heater, wriggled into her dressing-gown and huddled on her window seat. The half moon was streaked with red. Hazy clouds fairly raced across its face and the leaves on the trees tumbled.

She considered what Piers had said. *'I know how you feel about Eric.'*

Casey rested her forehead against the cold pane. 'I don't know how he thinks he knows. I haven't even worked it out myself.'

Chapter 9

Casey hurried home straight after work to greet her parents. Still miserable after the humiliating encounter in the café, the sight of her father's bristly grey moustache and her mother's round, cheery face was enough to lift her spirits a little.

First, they walked around the grounds. Helen Miller admired two young, smoky grey cats hiding in a lavender bush. That was enough to draw a smile from Jerome.

'Are they your kittens?' she asked him.

'On'y sometimes,' the little boy piped.

'They come from the house down the hill,' Piers added. 'I reckon they spend just as much time up here as they do there.'

'Do you feed them?' Doug asked.

'Ess,' Jerome said.

'Then there's your reason.' Doug Miller paced the length of the verandah with his hands behind his back, looking with interest all around him. 'Those little self-sown pines are too close to your foundation,' he told Piers. 'If I were you I'd pull them up or you'll have trouble with them later. Mark my words.'

Casey knew the way her father's mind worked. He was never lavish with compliments. His sharp eye always honed in on things that could be improved. It had taken Casey most of her life to realise it but mentioning these to people was his way of being friendly and helpful. She hoped Piers would take it the right way.

'Is that your work shed back there? I'd like to look in.'

'Sure.'

The men walked away. Jerome hurried to catch up to Piers. Casey and her mother went into the kitchen where Casey got together the odd assortment of chipped tea cups. She had forgotten to be embarrassed about them until now, while her parents were visiting. But Helen didn't seem to notice or care. She peered through the window at the expanse of rolling green hills.

'This home has a beautiful country feeling.' Helen stepped through to the lounge room and eased herself into an armchair while Casey poured boiling water in the teapot. 'When do we get to meet Eric?'

'I'm not sure.'

'Tell him to hurry up and visit us. I'm getting so excited I can hardly contain myself. My daughter's first boyfriend and I haven't even met him.'

Casey longed to share her mother's excitement but her core of anxiety was too deep to chip away. 'Mum, could I ask you something?'

'Of course.'

'How did you know that you loved Dad?'

Helen Miller pushed her glasses further up on the bridge of her nose. 'That's a sudden question to hit me with. Any reason for asking?'

'Not really. Things have worked out great with Eric. Suzanne is over the moon.'

Now, Helen's brow creased. 'It doesn't matter if *Suzanne's* over the moon. What about you?'

'I want to be but... I don't know. That's why I'm asking. How do you know when you're really in love?'

Helen sipped her tea and thought carefully before she answered. 'We're all unique, of course. I was mad about your dad from the moment I met him. My heart would pound like a drum whenever he walked past. I was jealous of any girl he looked at and if he looked in my direction, I'd turn to mush. I couldn't get him out of my head.'

Casey giggled to hear her mother speak in such a manner about her gruff father with his sparse hair and shiny bald patch. 'Go on.'

'Well, I think the important thing people in love have in common is that you can't wait to be with the other person and every moment apart from each other seems to drag. And when you are together, you feel you come alive. You're truly energised.'

Casey sipped her tea. 'That's my problem. I'm not that way with Eric. Being with him is fun but I'm always relieved when it's over. It doesn't energise me. It drains me.'

A look of concern flashed through Helen's eyes. 'Perhaps you're trying too hard to impress him. Just relax and be yourself. You're a wonderful, warm-hearted, smart girl.'

'Yeah, it might be just lack of confidence.'

'I wish I could tell you what you need to know.'

'Don't worry about me. I'll work things out.'

'Would you feel more comfortable talking to your sister about it? Abby has been married for almost ten years now. She'd love to give you some advice. You know Abby.'

'I've thought about phoning her.'

Helen's face began to shine. 'You won't have to. That's the news we've come to tell you. Abby phoned last night and told me to expect them for a visit next week.'

'That's great!' It was just the news Casey needed. She looked forward to seeing Abby and Jeff and young Sarah.

'I'll cook a family roast to welcome them home next Saturday, if you want to come.'

Her mother's delicious roasts were worth going home for on their own. Seeing Abby and her family after almost two years would be a bonus. 'I'll be there.'

The men returned from the shed and wiped their feet by the back door before stepping into the kitchen. Casey poured black tea into a cup for her father. When Doug came into the lounge room, he sat on the opposite armchair to his wife. That left nowhere for Piers to sit but beside Casey on the couch. He gave the fire a stir with the poker before he did so.

Helen smiled at Jerome and asked, 'Do you like having Casey living here, Sweetie?'

To Casey's relief, he nodded.

Doug looked at the boy with amusement. 'Why? Does she play games with you?'

'Sometimes,' Jerome said.

'Which is your favourite?'

'Mud fights,' Jerome said at once. 'But we've only done that once.'

Casey let out a hoot. 'That started out as a disaster before it turned into a game.' She told them how Ben had stolen Suzanne's dress from the clothesline.

'He was teasing me!' Piers added. 'He saw me chasing him and knew what I wanted but he looked me straight in the eye and took off. Then he'd stop every few minutes to see if I was still coming. I *saw* that dress getting torn but I couldn't do a thing about it. Suzanne called me a dumb idiot when we told her.'

Helen regarded Piers with compassion. 'Did you manage to pay your sister back?'

'Oh yeah.' He was laughing. 'We lived on bread and water that week but it's all paid for.'

Helen's face turned thoughtful. She glanced from Piers to Casey and back again. Her mother's scrutiny made Casey feel uneasy. She had no idea what Helen was thinking but decided she didn't really want to know.

<hr>

The following morning, Jerome was pink-cheeked, runny nosed and refused his breakfast. By evening, his temperature had soared. He was sick for several days. Each evening when Casey returned from work, he lay on the couch too wrung out to raise his head. She flinched each time she heard his hoarse coughs and watched his ribcage heave beneath his pyjamas. It was truly horrible to see him so low. Casey bought Jerome a colouring book to try to arouse his interest but he could not muster the strength to turn the pages.

Moira phoned several times. Once Casey spoke to her while Piers was rocking Jerome in his arms.

'He's still very sick,' she reported.

'I wish I could come to look after him,' Moira cried. 'You tell Jerome that I'll talk to him over the phone as soon as he gets better. Tell Piers that if his grandma was well enough to be left alone for a few hours, I'd be there in a flash.'

When Casey repeated the message, Piers rolled his eyes. 'So what's new?' was all he remarked.

On the fourth morning, Jerome rolled off the couch to trudge across the floor and pick up a toy truck. By evening, he was sitting up, watching a video and clapping his hands. 'Hey Casey, I've coloured four pages of that book!'

She admired his art and breathed a sigh of relief that their ordeal was over.

But the next morning, Piers was clumsy when he tried to fix Jerome's cereal. 'Don't come too close,' he warned Casey. 'I think I've caught Jerome's flu.'

'Keep it to yourself then.'

'I'll try.'

She was glad to hurry out the door.

The next evening was Friday. Although Abby and her family were due home the very next day, Casey offered to stay in Mount Barker to look after Jerome so that Piers could go early to bed. But on Saturday morning while she packed her overnight bag ready to go home, she heard Piers sneeze several times. Then, for some reason, he snapped at Jerome to give him a break. Casey paused for a second. She had never heard Piers speak harshly to Jerome before. She heard nothing else he said because Jerome started to cry and Piers began a coughing fit. Casey knew that one solid day of rest might do him a lot of good.

As she wound the cord around her hair-dryer, other thoughts niggled like mosquitoes. Piers had often been generous to her. He'd driven her into the city to meet her friends the night her car had broken down. He'd immediately come up with the cash to pay for Suzanne's torn dress. And perhaps most importantly, he hadn't held a grudge when she'd stood him up to go out with Eric. At least, he hadn't *seemed* to hold one. Casey had been about to push her hair brush into her bag but she flung it onto her pillow instead. 'Bother! Of all weekends, why did he have to be sick this one?'

She went down to the lounge room. Jerome was playing with his cars while Piers hunched beside the fire, shivering. At first, he protested when she told him her decision. 'You've looked forward to going home.' His dark eyes were shadowed and sunken but still gazed at her with their usual blend of shyness and admiration.

'I'll see Abby and Jeff tomorrow. I've made up my mind. Today, I want to see you in bed while Jerome and I have a good time together.'

Piers felt too wretched to refuse her offer a second time. He paused with his hand on his bedroom door. 'You're my good angel.'

She flushed. 'Well hurry up and get better. Then we'll all be happy.'

'I'll try,' he promised. 'Call me if you or Jerome need anything.'

She phoned home to explain why she would be unable to make it for lunch to welcome Abby and Jeff. Her mother was disappointed but understood. Then Casey turned to the daunting sight of Jerome, waiting behind her with his head cocked. The whole day stretched before her.

She asked, 'If we could do anything you liked today, what would it be?'

Jerome's eyes were luminous. 'Anything?'

'Anything. As long as it's here at home.'

'Let's build a racing track for my cars.'

So Casey spent the first part of the morning on her hands and knees near the fire, pushing Matchbox cars back and forth with 'toot' noises. They played hide and seek behind chairs and curtains. Then she read him two huge piles of story books. When her voice grew strained, Jerome asked her to chase him through the kitchen with a toy lawn mower. Casey tired of the game long before he did. She was glad when Jerome decided to watch a video. While he danced to the music, she sipped a cup of tea. Casey wondered how Piers ever managed to get any of his own work done any time.

She fixed Jerome some melted cheese on toast for lunch, and when he'd eaten it, he came behind her and tugged her sleeve. Her heart skipped a beat when she saw that his bottom lip was trembling. *Oh oh.*

'Casey, I wet my pants.'

She groaned. Indeed he had! He stood with his legs wide apart and his tracksuit bottoms were drenched. There were some tasks Casey had always steered clear of and this was one of them. She hurried to Piers' bedroom. He had told her to call him if she needed anything. He could clean up the accident and then return to bed.

However, he was in such a sound sleep, he didn't notice when his door creaked open. Damp strands of hair clung to his hot face and his breathing was slow and shallow. Casey made a *st st* sound against her teeth just to see what would happen. Piers didn't stir.

Casey paused to peer around the bedroom. It was the only room in the house she was unfamiliar with. On a small shelf that ran along the bare wall above his bed were two framed photographs. The largest must have been of Jerome when he was a newborn. His tiny face looked incredibly precious and soft. Although Piers' face was not in the photograph, Casey could tell that it was he who cradled Jerome against his chest. She recognised his long fingers with their strong knuckles.

In the second photograph, two people stood beneath a weeping willow. There was Piers with his wavy hair cut slightly shorter. His arm was wrapped around a young woman with the willowy figure of a mannequin. Anna Carter! Who else could it have been? The girl who had been an abstract notion in Casey's head now had a face and she was a vision. Her creamy complexion was flawless and shiny black hair flowed carelessly over her shoulders. Casey didn't wonder that Piers had fallen in love with her.

But how could such a beautiful girl have been attracted to him? Casey remembered a time, years earlier, when she'd suspected that Suzanne's brother had a crush on her. Whenever she shared a meal with Suzanne's family, Piers would sit tongue-tied and foolish, just staring at her, until she didn't know where to look. *He was so creepy.* Casey had preferred visiting Suzanne's house when Piers was out, which was not half as often as she would have liked. What could Anna have seen in him?

Something in Piers' expression arrested her attention. Casey pursed her lips and tried to work it out. The answer struck her like a blow. It was the love with which he gazed down at Anna Carter, as if he worshiped the ground she stood on, that made some starving place deep inside Casey ache. *Has Eric looked at me that way?* Perhaps she'd been too preoccupied with herself to notice how he was looking at her.

One more thing caught her attention. On Piers' bedside table was an open Bible. *Since when has he been interested in studying the Bible?* Moira Bowman had attended her parents' church for many years but neither of her children had ever gone with her. Casey saw that Piers had underlined a verse on his open pages. She couldn't resist stepping closer to read it. He had heavily underscored, *He will keep in perfect peace all those who turn to Him, whose thoughts turn often to the Lord.*

Casey studied Piers' slumbering face again. Questions darted through her head but she doubted if she'd ever bring herself to ask him any of them. Spiritual beliefs were a personal matter. Part of her longed to flick through his Bible to see if he'd underlined anything else but Casey would never do such an intrusive thing. She reminded herself that a tired little boy was waiting for her.

As she stepped into the laundry, Jerome darted over to her with a smile on his face. 'Casey, I did an accident but I fixed it myself!'

'Did you really?'

He nodded, with a beam. 'Those wet pants I put in the washing machine.' He pointed to the source of his pride, a pair of damp underpants slung over the rim of the washing machine. Her heart warmed towards him.

'That's excellent, Jerome.'

'You just need to clean the floor.'

She couldn't help laughing. 'If you know the procedure, why didn't you make it to the toilet on time?'

He hung his head. 'I do most times. I was just so 'cited thinking what we could do next.'

She smiled as she followed the trail he'd walked and scrubbed the damp floor. At least *somebody* thought she was exciting.

'What *are* we gonna do next?' he asked.

'Have you run out of ideas?'

'I think so.'

She looked at the clock. It was three thirty in the afternoon. 'How'd you like to watch me cook some tea?'

She perched him on the kitchen counter and he swung his legs against the cupboard beneath them. Casey cooked a quick stew from anything she could lay her hands on. She found several vegetables in a box and a chunk of fresh steak in the fridge. Piers would probably not be hungry but she had to eat herself and Jerome seemed to like watching her chopping and frying.

His eyelids had grown heavy and he yawned. Casey left her meal to simmer on the stove and carried him to bed. To her relief, Jerome snuggled into his pillow for a nap. She lingered to watch him until she was certain he was sleeping soundly. His chin was a firm knob and his mouth was relaxed and slightly open so that she glimpsed his two top teeth. With his magnificent curling eyelashes closed together like butterfly wings, Jerome's beauty made her heart ache. Having seen the photo of his mother,

Casey understood why he was gorgeous, yet the closer she studied him, the more she realised that she couldn't see much of Anna Carter's likeness in him. Jerome's features were most like Piers'.

She rested her head on the foot of the bed and closed her drooping eyelids. One day with Jerome had exhausted her far more than a whole week at work. Casey decided to rest for ten minutes but when she opened her eyes again, the chinks of sky between the curtains were almost dim and Piers was leaning in the doorway.

'Hi, I can see he must've given you the run around.'

'Nothing I couldn't handle.' Casey scrambled to sit up. 'How long have you been watching us?'

'Only a few seconds. I must've slept the whole day away.'

'You almost did.'

'I feel a whole lot better. I'll have a shower then probably stay awake all night.'

Casey tiptoed out of Jerome's bedroom. She stirred her fragrant stew in the kitchen to the gush of running water from the bathroom. Soon Piers came out with his dressing gown tied around his waist. His wet hair was dishevelled.

'I made a stew,' she said. 'You can have some if you like.'

'Why not. I'm game to try anything.'

She looked up sharply and saw that he was teasing her.

They shared their meal across the kitchen table from each other. Casey was close enough to notice his clean scent of shampoo and soap. 'This is delicious,' he said. 'If I had my normal appetite, I'd be able to put away heaps.'

'I made plenty. Jerome can have some when he wakes up and you can have more tomorrow.'

'Thanks.' He coughed into the crook of his elbow. 'Casey, I was sorry to spoil your plans.' He raised his eyes to look at her. 'But I'm glad you stayed.'

Heat flooded her face. 'It was no big deal.' His damp hair shone beneath the ceiling light. She lowered her gaze to his shirt button and watched a pulse twitch in his throat. Looking up again, she saw that he was watching her with a slight smile playing around the corners of his lips. *This is ridiculous! Can't I be at ease with any man?*

Chapter 10

She enjoyed the glorious winter morning on her drive home. Rippling hills looked as if they were covered with green felt. Shafts of sunshine filtered through chinks between gum leaves like golden wine and groups of grubbing galahs alongside the road shimmered to the sky in pink and grey clouds. The entire landscape danced with colour.

The first person Casey saw when she stepped inside was Sarah, her six-year-old niece, kneeling on the floor surrounded by paper dolls. She jumped up and sprang over her cardboard and paper circle. 'Mum, Casey's here!'

Casey lifted Sarah and gave her a whirling hug. Having grown accustomed to carrying Jerome, her niece felt strangely long and lanky.

There was movement from the kitchen door and Casey looked up to see her sister with a hand on her hip, smiling. 'Why couldn't you make it home to welcome us yesterday? Are those Bowmans more important than your own sister?'

Casey took a step forward, laughing. She knew Abby didn't expect an answer. The sisters embraced for a long moment and it still gave Casey a pleasant feeling to be on an eye-level with Abby. For so many years, she had been the baby and Abby had towered over her. When she stood back, she saw that her sister had lost weight and there were lines around the corners of her mouth which had not been there before. Despite her blonde prettiness, Abby's eyes were red and tired and she appeared older than her thirty years.

'It's so great to see you? Where's Jeff?' Casey blurted.

A shadow flitted across Sarah's face and she ducked her head and returned to her dolls. Abby sighed. 'He didn't come. We've left him.'

<hr />

It was nothing like the warm homecoming Casey had expected. When her parents walked through the door, her mother's tired, drawn expression and her father's grim nod told the story. Lunch time was a sober affair. Casey guessed that the previous day when Abby dropped her bombshell had been even worse and she'd probably done well to remain behind with Piers and Jerome.

'Jeff loves his work and friends at the gym more than he loves us,' Abby was saying. 'He's often out of the house from the crack of dawn 'til midnight. He must think his clothes get washed and ironed and his meals cooked by magic. He gets impatient if he does come home at a reasonable hour and I don't have a meal waiting, but if I do, he's sure to phone me and say he won't be home until ten! I don't know what his plans are from one moment to the next and I'm the one who had to uproot myself from all my family and friends in Adelaide just so that *he* can work in his flash firm! If he reads Sarah a two-minute bedtime story he seems to think he's done his fatherly duty for the next two months!'

'Can I go an' roller skate in the back yard?' Sarah asked at last.

Abby drew a deep breath and nodded.

For several moments, the adults sat in silence. Sarah's face passed back and forth across the window as she skated.

'This is all nonsense, my girl,' Doug Miller said at last. 'You ought to make an effort to understand Jeff's point of view. He must be under intense pressure to perform well at work. He doesn't need somebody to heckle and nag him at home.'

Abby bristled. 'So you think I should give one hundred per cent and Jeff can give zilch? Don't you want me and Sarah to stay here? Is that it?'

'Haven't you listened to a word we've said for the past two days?' Doug snapped.

'Of course you can stay,' Helen added. 'This is your home. You can stay for as long as you need to.'

'For as long as it takes for you to come to your senses.' Doug stood up and pushed his chair back. 'I think you and Jeff should both grow up. Look at what you're doing to that little girl.' He opened the sliding door with a jerk and joined Sarah in the back yard. They began to play a game of cricket using Dale's old bat and stumps.

Abby's voice was muffled when she spoke. 'Dad's lucky to have had someone willing to pamper him and put up with whatever he does for the past thirty-two years.'

'We've had our rough patches. No marriage is smooth sailing.'

'I've decided that men stink. All they do is take, take, take. Dad resents me being here! What about Dale? Look at the way he's sponging off you both like a parasite. He's out fishing and enjoying himself this very moment. He's never done a hard day's work in his life. How come Dad thinks that's okay?'

'He doesn't. We don't know what to do with your brother, but that's another problem.'

Casey turned away. Lunch was finished and she'd heard enough.

There's no way I can ask her for advice about me and Eric now. She'll just tell me that he stinks. At a loss for something to do, she decided to join the cricket players. Soon after Casey stepped outside, her father returned to the house. His heart hadn't really been in the game. Sarah played in a listless manner, as if she were doing Casey a favour.

An hour before tea, Casey's brother Dale walked in with a few stunted tommy-ruffs. As the family sat around the dinner table, Casey's mother remarked, 'Poor Moira Bowman looked exhausted in church today. She had a big shock last week. The doctor has told them that her mother probably has only a few months left to live.'

The news was a shock to Casey too. 'Then old Mrs Bowman was sicker than we thought?'

'For several months, it seems she has been. She's had lung cancer that's spread to her lymph nodes.'

Doug added, 'It's just that she's complained so much about every minor ache and pain for the last twenty years, nobody noticed her new symptoms as anything to be concerned about.'

Helen looked across the table at Casey. 'Moira said she hasn't told her children yet. She's going to tell them this week. So don't you mention it. Perhaps I shouldn't have told you.'

'Don't worry, I won't say anything.' Casey had always had better subjects to discuss than Suzanne's grandma.

Abby was glaring at Dale. 'Your fingernails are filthy from gutting and cleaning fish, so I wish you'd just touch the slice of bread you want and not all the others.'

'You've only just come home so don't start bossing me around already.'

Their father said, 'It amazes me that you two haven't seen each other for over a year and already you're bickering after two days.'

Casey couldn't help wondering if bickering between men and women was inevitable. She imagined herself and Eric in the future, sitting and sniping at each other. Casey and Eric were even more different than Abby and Jeff had been. Even now, she knew she did not see eye-to-eye with him on everything. Casey wanted to close her eyes and stop thinking about love affairs that went wrong. She realised she was looking forward to getting back to Piers' place for a bit of peace and quiet.

━━━━━━━━━━━

Casey heard the telephone ring the following evening after Jerome had been asleep for an hour. She went downstairs in case the call was for her, but Piers held the portable phone receiver with one hand while he poked the fire with the other. 'How bad is it?' he was asking. Casey went to wash herself an apple instead.

When she placed her core in the compost bin, she returned to the lounge room and found him sanding the chair back he'd been working on. His lips were pursed tight and he stared at a crack in the wall.

'Bad news on the phone?'

'Yeah. That was my Mum. She reckons Gran has cancer and probably has only a few months left to live.'

'I'm sorry,' she said automatically.

He wrapped his left hand around the back of his neck and sighed. 'Don't waste your pity on me. I'm sure I wasn't thinking what you thought

The Risky Way Home

I was thinking.'

'What were you thinking?'

'You might be shocked. I was trying to think of one good memory about her.'

'Did you come up with anything?'

He rolled his eyes in a comical gesture. 'It was pretty tough. At first I could only think of bad things, like when I was fifteen and she stopped me from learning trumpet.'

'I remember when you were learning trumpet,' Casey cried. 'We all thought you sounded terrible but Mr Anders told you to keep it up.'

She remembered something else. She had been in Suzanne's living room with a crowd of other girls rehearsing for a drama play. Henrietta was in the kitchen and they overheard her fretful voice sniping at Piers.

'Even if you could play like James Morrison, you're wasting your time. Do you really think they'd want a boy like you in the school band? They're looking for someone with good looks or at least a smidgin of personality. You'll get no further than the audition.'

Casey had sniggered along with the other girls as he swept past them with burning cheeks, looking at his toes. But as soon as Henrietta returned upstairs, Suzanne had stopped laughing and scowled after her stooped back. 'I hate her guts.' Her voice had been low and vitriolic. 'She always treats us that way and Mum never stops her.'

Piers' voice brought her back to the present. 'There was nowhere I could practise without Gran hearing me and Mum told me to take up a quieter hobby. It was no big deal.'

Casey watched his hands deftly sanding a graceful curve on the chair back. 'I reckon you're better at woodwork, anyway.'

'I guess I *was* pretty bad at music.'

'So what good memory did you think of?'

'I was about nine years old and she was hassling me to be more like Suzanne. I think Suzanne was her favourite. She was always saying, "At least your sister has a bit of guts and gumption." I'm sure you must've heard her sometimes when you were over. Anyway, on this day I'd forgotten to take my Ventolin to school and wasn't allowed to go swimming. When I got home, she got stuck into me, telling me what a pain in the neck I was with my head always up in the clouds. I already felt upset about not being allowed to swim and I'd had a gutful of her.'

'So what did you do?'

'I packed a bag with my toothbrush and Ventolin, a change of clothes, three of Mum's fudge brownies and two bananas. I decided to run away from home. Do you remember the old lumberyard a few blocks from school?'

She nodded.

'I went there to hide. Sat for hours between a couple of log piles. I was happy for awhile but by the time it grew dark, I'd eaten all my food and started to get hungry. While I was trying to work out what to do next, a policeman found me and said, "Time to come home, son." Mum had been out of her mind and had them searching for me. I was scared stiff when the police car pulled up in our driveway. I expected Gran to skin me alive, but by the time Mum had finished telling me how I'd almost killed her with fright, Gran just squinted at me over the top of her glasses and said, "I never thought you'd have the guts."'

'Then what?'

'Then I had some tea and went to bed.'

'You call that a good memory?'

He grinned at her. 'Not really, but it's the best one I've got.'

'I thought you were going to tell me that she said something nice.'

'That was nice, for Gran.'

Casey was silent for a moment. 'At least you showed her that you had enough guts to take on a new home, new baby and new occupation all at once.'

He was laughing. 'Thanks for the compliment, but she had a different name for all that. She called it "being a loser."'

Casey laughed along with him. She could tell that he wasn't really unhappy. Although she had never liked Henrietta Bowman, Casey's heart was heavy for Piers and Suzanne to think that a person could live for over eighty years and leave behind no good memories for her family.

The Risky Way Home

Chapter 11

'I don't know why Mum even bothered to phone.' Suzanne jerked the iron over a white shirt. It was the first time she'd taken over Casey's task and her eyes flashed as if she were an extension of the iron. Even her black hair seemed charged with electricity and Casey fought an impulse to smooth it down.

'I'll bet Gran told her to tell me she's dying and it's my fault for all the trouble I caused her over my life.' Suzanne mimicked the peevish drone of her grandmother as she whipped the shirt off the board and wrenched it onto a coat hanger. '"*I told you all there was something wrong and nobody believed me.*" Well, she can't expect us to believe she's been slowly dying of cancer for twenty years!' She made a mock whine again. '"*Maybe now she'll be remorseful for the shameful way she's always treated me!*"'

Eric laughed out loud from behind the reception desk and Casey giggled too. Amusing an audience seemed to help Suzanne feel better.

'I said, "Thanks for telling me." What else did they expect me to say? Was I supposed to howl my eyes out over the phone? But then Mum says, "How do you feel?" The cow! I knew she was only phoning to have a dig at me.'

'How do you know that was a dig?' Casey put in. 'Maybe she genuinely wondered how you felt.'

'I could tell from the tone of her voice. And then she hinted that I should go to visit Gran before she dies. But I'm not going to.'

'Might as well just go and have it over with,' Eric advised.

Suzanne snapped another coat hanger off the rack. 'No way! That old bag ruined my childhood! Did I ever tell you we never even had a decent holiday? Whenever we were near a place that had Poker machines, Gran wanted to gamble. Piers and I had to wait out in foyers for hour after hour while she dragged Mum in to play.'

'Sounds boring,' Casey said.

'Boring? You bet it was, but boring is too mild a word. It was torture. We had nothing to do but sit on our butts and watch the hands of a clock turn around.'

'Didn't you complain?' Eric asked.

'Of course we complained! But Gran would snarl at us and tell Mum that after all she'd done for us, she deserved something from Mum in return. Like, what had Gran ever done for us?'

'What did your mother say?'

'I'll tell you! I remember one time when we were in Victoria. Piers and I both gave Mum an earful while Gran was in the shower. We pleaded with her not to leave us in a hotel foyer again. She said, "I know how you must feel. I promise I'll do something about it." And do you know what she did?'

'What?'

'She bought us a lousy deck of cards!'

Eric's lips twitched behind the counter. Casey looked at Suzanne's face and bit back her own urge to laugh. She could tell that this time, they weren't supposed to. She stepped over and placed a hand on Suzanne's shoulder instead. Casey's light touch set off a storm. Suzanne's shoulders slumped and she began to sob.

Eric stood in the doorway. 'Come on, that was years ago.'

Suzanne switched off the iron and fished a crumpled tissue from her pocket.

'Come and sit in the storeroom until you feel better,' Casey said.

Suzanne nodded and followed. 'I'm okay.'

'Of course you are,' Eric said.

Suzanne cleared her throat and drew a slow, shuddering breath. 'How is Piers taking it?'

'Not as hard as you,' Casey replied.

Suzanne's chin shot up. 'I don't want you to get the wrong idea. I'm not crying because Gran is dying!'

'We know you're not.'

Suzanne forced a watery smile. 'I think I was crying because she didn't die years ago.'

Although she seemed to expect a laugh for that, Casey couldn't quite manage one.

'I think you're amazing to have lived with her for all those years.'

Suzanne smoothed her own fly-away hair. 'It was hardest for me because she hated me most. I'm sure Piers was her favourite.'

'Not according to him. He thinks you were.'

Suzanne's lip curled into a sneer. 'He's got to be kidding. She was always nagging me to be more like him.' She managed to mimic Henrietta's croaky voice one last time. '"Why don't you try to be more quiet and reasonable like your brother? He never flies off the handle over such stupid things."'

Casey was too surprised to speak. She suddenly glimpsed how the old woman's mind had worked. Henrietta Bowman had played games with her family, setting one grandchild off against the other.

Did she expect perfection? Maybe making her family sad was the only fun old Mrs Bowman ever had.

Casey's mother phoned that evening.

'Henrietta Bowman will turn eighty-five next Thursday. Moira wants to arrange a little supper party because she knows it'll be her mother's last birthday, but she's having trouble thinking of people to invite. Will you go?'

'I'd rather not,' Casey said.

Helen's voice lowered as if she were telling a secret. 'Dad and I don't want to go either, but it means a lot to Moira. I hoped you'd consider going, if only because you work with Suzanne and live with Piers.'

'Well, are they going?'

'Moira's asked them but I don't know what they told her. Maybe if they refused, you could have a word with each of them.'

'No way,' Casey said at once. 'Why should I try to twist their arms?

It's nothing to do with me and they're the ones who had to put up with her for all those years!'

'I understand that. But she is dying. They won't have her for much longer. Won't you come? You've always liked Moira.'

'I'll think about it.'

When Casey hung up, she went to find Piers. He was working in his shed.

'Are you going to your Grandma's birthday supper?'

He heaved a sigh. 'I s'pose I'd better. But I reckon it's a bad idea of Mum's. Gran hates having people around.'

'I've just been invited too.'

Piers put down his screwdriver. 'Cool. Why don't we drive there together? Then when Jerome gets tired, you'll have an excuse to shoot off because you'll be with us.'

She knew that Jerome usually began to feel sleepy at around eight o'clock. 'Sounds good to me.'

<hr>

'I agreed to go to Gran's supper thing.' Suzanne crossed a letter T with a black slash in her ledger. 'It was a bit of a cop-out for me. I guess I've got to see her some time so I'd rather get it over and done with while other people are there. Then maybe ...,' she trailed off.

'She won't be so reactive?'

'Yeah, that's a kind way of putting it.'

'I'll be there too,' Casey said.

Suzanne looked up with a swift smile. 'Great. Can I catch a lift with you?'

'I won't be driving. I'll be going with Piers and Jerome.'

'That's even better. Tim has refused to come with me. I pleaded with him to support me the *one* time something like this happens. He said he'd rather drink poison.' Suzanne giggled. 'I can't blame him. I'd rather drink poison myself. I refuse to walk in there alone, but now I'll go with you and Piers instead.'

On the night of the birthday, they set off in Suzanne's car. Casey sat in the front passenger's seat beside Suzanne. Piers and Jerome were in the back. On the long drive to Victor Harbor, Jerome sang songs and counted the trucks they passed while Suzanne and Piers shared stories.

'Do you remember the Christmas she gave us each two pairs of school socks and that was it?'

'Yeah, the stingy old bag. And do you remember how she shaved your head when you caught head-lice, before Mum got home from the shops?'

'I thought she was going to have my scalp. I had a cut on the top of my head for weeks. Do you remember how she'd make us sit at the table until we polished off everything on our plates? You stayed there until midnight, once.'

Suzanne's pretty face wrinkled. 'Yeah, it was liver! You'd swallowed yours and I could see you trying not to retch. Still makes me sick to the stomach whenever I think about the smell of that stuff. Do you remember when she insisted that you stop learning trumpet?'

'Yeah, I was just telling Casey about that the other night. Do you remember how there'd be hell to pay if one of us took a biscuit from her special packet?'

'That's right! She counted them every time she took one!'

'I don't know if I believe half of all this!' Casey put in.

'That's just the start!' Suzanne cried. 'I won't even begin to describe the way she behaved the night I brought Eric to meet them.'

When Suzanne parked on the curb near their old home, a silence fell over the car. Jerome broke it. 'Let's go in an' see Nanny.'

Suzanne shuddered. 'I can't *stand* this place. I keep expecting to see Gran's head poke out of the bedroom window to abuse me for messing up the gravel on the path.'

Piers was waiting for Jerome to climb down from his seat. 'We only have to stay for an hour or two.'

Moira answered the door in a cloud of rose-scented perfume. 'Come in! I'm so glad you all came.' She gave them each a peck on the cheek and scooped Jerome up into her arms but her gaze lingered on Suzanne. Casey watched Moira's eyes pool as if she were looking at sunshine itself. 'It's been awhile, Suzanne,' Moira breathed.

Suzanne managed a tight smile. 'I've been very busy.'

Casey greeted her parents and the other guests. They were mostly people from her parents' church. She knew the Smith and Porter families.

Old Pastor Hargreaves and young Pastor Whitelock were talking to Casey's father while Pastor Whitelock's children sat in a corner, running Moira's shagpile rug between their fingers. Emily and Hannah Whitelock, the youngest girls, swooped on Jerome.

'What's your name?'

He hesitated. 'Jewome,' he mumbled.

'Do you want to play with us?'

He blinked at them and hung his head.

'Have a cupcake.' Emily handed him one from the table.

As Jerome took it, he gave her a shy smile. Emily gripped his hand and shot her sister a triumphant beam as if she'd won a contest. 'Let's go and play under the kitchen table.'

Casey saw Henrietta, wearing a stiff, new flannel nightgown, with a crocheted rug draped across her knees.

'Mother, the children have come to see you for your birthday!' Moira cried. 'Look! Suzanne's here.'

The old lady glanced up. 'So I see.'

'Hello, Gran,' Suzanne said.

'I always told your mother it'd take my death to get you back under this roof, young lady. You've proven me right.'

A hush filled the room followed by a burst of soft chatter, as other guests began new conversations all at once.

'No, I haven't. You're not dead yet, Gran.'

Henrietta whipped a hanky from her dressing-gown pocket and coughed into it; a rasping, thick sound. 'I'm as good as dead. Why did you bother coming?'

'Mum just told you. To see you on your birthday.'

'Is the sight of you supposed to make me feel good?'

Suzanne's cheeks appeared hollow as she clamped her jaw. 'No. It never has before.'

'You treat me with contempt all your life but now that I'm almost dead, you expect to breeze in here as if everything's nice and rosy.'

Moira gasped. 'No, Mother. *Please.*'

Suzanne shot her a withering stare. 'Save your breath. I told you I didn't want to come but you laid on the guilt trip. You were blind as a bat, as usual.'

The Risky Way Home

Now the room was genuinely quiet.

Moira sank her face into her hands. Helen Miller placed the teapot on its holder with a clink. Casey had never seen her mother so completely at a loss for something to say. Her father gazed into his coffee as if there was a picture at the bottom of his cup. Piers flexed his fingers, red-faced.

Henrietta tilted her chin. 'At least now she's showing her true colours. I can't stand hypocrisy. Perhaps now that she knows I'm dying, she's come crawling back to see if she can get her hands on any cash I might happen to leave behind.'

A tear streaked down Suzanne's face. 'I'll bet I have made your night! You must feel satisfied to have got that off your chest. I wouldn't take your lousy money if you paid me!'

The oldest Whitelock boy let out a snigger. He pressed a hand over his mouth and looked with horror to see who'd heard him. Casey looked down at her lap, feeling cold and sick inside.

Suzanne swept across the floor to her mother's bedroom door and turned with her hand on the knob. 'You see, she can't be nice to me even when she's dying.'

'Wait.' Moira slipped softly after Suzanne into the room and closed the door without even glancing at her mother. Nobody else knew what to do with the crusty old lady. Henrietta sunk her head between her shoulders like an old tortoise retreating into its shell. She closed her eyes and ignored the muffled sobbing that could be heard from Moira's bedroom.

Most of the guests seemed to think it tactful not to leave immediately but they stood up to hunt for purses and keys as soon as a polite length of time had elapsed. As Henrietta seemed to be genuinely asleep, they said their farewells to Casey's mother, who was Moira's closest friend.

Without his new friends, Jerome yawned, climbed into Casey's lap and ducked his head beneath her chin. Helen disappeared into the kitchen to begin washing supper dishes. Her husband, who rarely lifted a finger to help at home, was quick to follow her. Jerome's breathing turned soft and regular and, with a flicker of surprise, Casey saw that he had fallen asleep. She had never known a person as quick to nod off as Jerome and now it meant that she was stuck in her armchair near the kitchen door.

Piers rose to his feet and took a step toward the kitchen.

'Where do you think you're going?'

The sudden sound of Henrietta's gravely voice made Casey jump. Piers stopped in his tracks and flinched. Casey watched him square his shoulders and turn slowly to face his grandmother.

The Risky Way Home

Chapter 12

'I thought I'd help Mr and Mrs Miller with the dishes.' There was an edge of defensiveness in Piers' voice.

'And leave me all alone?'

Casey realised with relief that although she could see half Henrietta's profile, the old lady could not see where she sat with Jerome unless she craned her neck to peer behind her shoulder. Good!

'Everyone thinks I'm a vicious old dragon, don't they?'

'You can't blame them, Gran. Why do you always have to be so mean?'

'It's my job description. I'll bet every person in this room came to see the show. How horrible can old Henny Bowman be tonight?'

He rolled his eyes. 'Well, you didn't let them down, did you?'

Henrietta cleared her throat. 'You hate my guts, don't you?'

Piers shuffled on his spot. 'Gran, will you just…?'

'Sit down!' she snapped. 'Even though you can't stand the sight of me, at least do me the courtesy of sitting down while I talk to you.'

He sat stiffly on the armchair across from her and folded his arms across his chest.

'I don't want any namby-pamby lies, boyo. The least you can grant a dying woman is an honest answer. You and your sister always hated me! Didn't you?'

The pause which followed grew uncomfortably long and Casey felt the back of her own neck turning hot.

'Did you want us to?' Piers asked at last. 'All our lives, you seemed to try your hardest to make us.'

'That means you do.'

Casey saw the muscles at the side of Henrietta's sinewy throat twitch. 'You listen to me! You don't know half of it, you self-righteous little toad. My life was rotten long before you or your sister came onto the scene. When I was younger, I used to hope things would get better. But I had one disappointment after another. It's a harsh old world so I became a harsh old woman to match it. You and Suzanne were just the last straw that made me see my life was hopeless.'

'What did we do?' Piers didn't seem to realise that his voice had risen. 'What harm did we ever do to you, apart from not being the way you wanted us?'

She heaved a ragged sigh. 'I can't be bothered dredging the sordid story up after all these years. Let me tell you just one thing. Your father was a swine who made your mother's life hell.'

Casey kept her eyes riveted on Jerome's flickering eyelashes.

'If that's true, it wasn't our fault! I don't even remember him.'

'Save your theatrics,' Henrietta said testily. 'I was angry with your mother because she married him against my better judgment. Then, when he showed how depraved he was, she relied on me to help her out of her mess. It all used to mean something to me. I'm telling you this to prove that I couldn't care less anymore.'

Casey saw Piers flex his knuckles in a nervous gesture. 'What did... he do?'

Henrietta's withered fingers plucked the tassels which hung off her armchair. 'I don't want to talk about it. I'm dying! That occupies most of my thoughts. For almost eighty-five years I've felt that I was living in hell. Soon I'll be in the real hell. I suppose you'll be happy!' Her shoulders twitched.

'Why do you think you're going to hell?' he asked curiously.

'Well, why do you think? Use your brains.'

'I don't know. Do you agree with me and Suzanne that you treated us badly?'

She snorted. 'Never! I know I had my reasons for being bitter but nobody else would understand what they were. Why would God be any

The Risky Way Home

different? He's the one who gave me this rotten cancer.'

'Why blame God for that? I reckon it was more to do with forty years of chain smoking.'

'Don't you dare lecture me like your mother. And don't change the subject. Everyone hates me. God hates me too.'

'No, He doesn't,' Piers stated.

'What are you talking about, you fool of a boy? Do you know the mind of God?'

'I know that much.'

'You're talking rubbish!'

Instead of replying, he said, 'Do you know, Gran, I never said that I did hate you before.'

Casey saw the old lady's chin flick up. 'What?'

'I don't hate you,' Piers repeated.

Henrietta blinked at him. 'Why not?'

For the first time, he grinned as he shook his head and shrugged. 'I used to hate you. But ever since Jerome was born, I stopped hating people. It takes too much energy.'

Henrietta's raspy breathing turned quieter.

'I forgive you for the way you treated me,' Piers told her. 'I want you to know that. And if I forgive you, how could God not forgive you, if you ask Him to?'

Henrietta gave a thick sounding cough and rolled her handkerchief into a tight ball.

Piers stood up. He touched her shoulder, then leaned over and kissed her forehead. 'I don't hate you, Gran,' he repeated. 'That's the honest truth. So why would God hate you?'

The old woman said nothing. After a moment, Casey saw a drop of water fall onto the arm of the chair. Shock coursed through her as she realised what it was. Henrietta Bowman was crying. Then, Casey's skin crawled with disbelief. It was like seeing a stone gargoyle give way to tears. A flicker of movement from Moira's bedroom door caught her eye and she looked up to see Moira and Suzanne standing in silence, watching. Moira's face was a study of wondrous amazement but Suzanne's was streaked with hostility. 'I'm ready to go home.'

Henrietta drew a shuddering breath and composed herself. 'Will either of you come back to see me before I die?' Her faded old eyes looked from one of her grandchildren to the other.

'I will.' Piers spoke quietly.

Suzanne shot him a scorching glare. 'I'll never set foot inside this house again.' The hand that gripped the leather strap of her handbag shook. Casey caught sight of a thick, red covered notebook wedged into a side pocket of Suzanne's bag. 'Anyone who's coming home with me had better get in the car now.'

'Suzanne, please don't go yet,' Moira begged. 'Come and have a cup of tea.'

'It's far too late for a cup of tea, Mum.' Casey knew Suzanne didn't mean the hour of the night. It was not yet 8.30.

The drive home was cold and unpleasant.

'You've done it again!' Suzanne's back tyre hit a pot hole and Jerome woke up with a start.

'What have I done now?' Piers asked.

Suzanne spoke over her nephew's whimpering. 'What do you think? You showed me up! You made me look ten times worse than I already did by proving how wonderful you are. Just the way you always used to when we were kids.'

'That's a load of rubbish!' Piers waited until Jerome settled down again before he spoke on. 'I started feeling sorry for her. That's all. She's scared to be dying.'

Suzanne let out a bark of a laugh. 'So she should be. I wouldn't want to be headed where she's going. But that was smooth work of yours.' She put on one of her mimics; a vacant, inane drawl. '"*If I can forgive you for bullying me, tormenting me, stamping out my potential and treating me like dirt all my life, don't worry Gran. God will too.*" Gee Piers, that's the most pathetic piece of drivel I've heard you come up with ever!'

'You've made your point! Now can we please change the subject?'

Her profile was set like granite. 'No, I won't! You showed all the people how much nicer you are than me. I wish they could hear the way you talk to me!'

The Risky Way Home

'Nobody else was there except for me and Jerome,' Casey put in.

Suzanne swung around to face her as if she'd been stung. 'Casey, I can't believe that buttering-up act worked even on you!'

Her cheeks filled with heat. 'I'm just trying to make you feel better. Nobody else heard anything that was said. Mum and Dad were in the kitchen and the other guests had gone.'

'I wasn't buttering Gran up, anyway!' Piers declared from the back seat. 'I never used to do it when we were kids, either. So just drop it!'

'How could you kiss her?' Suzanne made a throw-up noise.

'Just one of those spur-of-the-moment things.' There was a note of embarrassment in his voice.

When they reached home, Suzanne waited long enough for Piers to detach Jerome's booster seat before she sped off with a squeal of her tyres. They stood beneath the clear night sky and Piers peered foolishly at Casey over his armful of Jerome in the chair. 'I agree with Suzanne about one thing.'

'What's that?' Casey was shivering.

'I don't know why I kissed Gran.' He pulled a face. 'What came over me?'

'It was the right thing to do.' Her quiet voice drifted up to the milky sheet of stars.

'Do you think so?'

'Yes. She cried when you did. You wrought some kind of change in her. Did you notice?'

'No. *Did* she? I can't imagine Gran crying. I must've been too stunned by what I did to look at her. I didn't think I was going to say half those things I said to her, either. But Suzanne didn't have to rave on at me like that.'

'Don't worry about Suzanne,' Casey reached out to touch his shoulder and turn him toward the front door. His muscles were taut with the weight he bore. 'She wasn't there to hear the conversation. What you told your Gran... well, it might have been just what she needed to hear. Come on, let's go inside. You put Jerome to bed and I'll set the fire. Then I'm going to have a hot cup of milo. Do you want one?'

'Yes please.' He gave a laugh. 'After all, we didn't get to have a drink at Mum's place.'

Casey flicked the kitchen switch and saw the cheerful room flood with light. As she prised the lid off the milo tin, Piers looked in from the passage. 'Hey, Casey.'

He caught her off-guard. Her heart beat faster as she looked up. 'Yeah?'

'You only need to strike a match to the fire. I already set it before we left.'

'Okay.' She felt slightly let down. She wondered what she hoped he'd been going to say.

As he made his way to Jerome's bedroom, she called, 'Hey, Piers.'

He turned his head to look back. 'Yeah?'

'Did you really believe all that stuff you told your Gran?'

He hesitated. 'Which bit do you mean?'

'About God forgiving her for the way she treated you and Suzanne?'

'Oh, that. Yeah, I believe that. Absolutely.'

Her spirits began to lift. 'Good.' That was what she hoped he'd say. She didn't want to think that he'd been speaking empty platitudes.

Chapter 13

The following morning was Friday. When Casey arrived at work, she found the car-park more crowded than usual. The only empty space was between a mini-bus and Eric's car. As she swung her steering wheel to maneuver her way into it, a grind against her left door made her heart lurch. Casey left her engine running and stepped out to look. The hair on her arms stood on end. *God, look what I've done!* She had scraped the door of Eric's Porsche. Three smudges of paint near its handle looked like a dirty claw mark.

Sick to the stomach, Casey forced her feet upstairs to work. Suzanne had thrown open the doors to let in the fresh breeze.

'I wish there was some way we could screen the ugly ones,' Eric was telling Suzanne. 'I'm fed up with pretending these women are drop-dead gorgeous when it takes all my willpower not to laugh in their faces. That one yesterday walked like this.' He strutted with mincing footsteps across the floor, wriggling his hips.

'Eric, stop!' The giggling Suzanne dabbed her eyes with a tissue.

He turned and caught sight of Casey. 'Hey, why the long face? We weren't talking about you. You are drop-dead gorgeous.'

'Eric, I just did something terrible!' Her mouth tasted like sawdust.

'Come on, nothing could be this…'

'I scraped your car.'

His eyelids sprang apart.

'How bad is it?' Suzanne gasped.

Eric didn't wait to hear Casey's answer. He darted outside and took the balcony steps four at a time. Casey and Suzanne found him standing beside his car. The veins behind Eric's temples throbbed through his skin.

'How could you scrape a parked car?' If his green eyes had been spears, Casey would have been impaled. 'How could you be so stupid?'

She forced words past her numb throat. 'It's only... a few inches and it's... fairly faint. Maybe people will hardly... notice.'

'This is a Porsche! Not a heap of junk on wheels like...' Eric turned and kicked her brown Gemini as hard as he could. 'Of course they'll notice.'

Casey's head spun as she watched her car rock. 'I'm sorry!' She knew that was pathetic but her mouth babbled on of its own accord. 'I can't tell you how sorry I am.' Something light wrapped itself around her shoulders and Casey flinched. It was Suzanne's arm. She drew a jerky breath, grateful for the support.

Eric's expression of dark rage set into one of calm, smouldering resentment. 'You'll be sorry, alright. I know you haven't got the money to pay for this, but you'll have to find it.'

'I will. I promise.'

His mouth twisted as if he'd like to spit. 'You promise? You have no idea how much this car costs. You'll have to borrow it from your folk because you won't be able to afford it from the paltry salary we pay you.'

'It might not be as bad as it looks!' Suzanne's voice rose, clear and calm. 'There are just a few faint inches of paint and not even a dent. Take it to your garage. It might be cheaper to fix than you expect.'

Her words jolted Eric to action. 'I'll do that right now.' He swung open his door and climbed in.

'Remember, you have a client in twenty-five...'

'She'll have to wait.' He reversed sharply and narrowly missed colliding with the back of Suzanne's red Pulsar.

I guess he would have expected me to pay for that too. Casey tried to keep her face from crumpling.

'Take it easy,' Suzanne advised her. 'Things might be better than he expects. I'll make you a cup of tea to calm your nerves.'

Back up in the storeroom, Casey mumbled, 'How much do you think it'll cost?'

Suzanne busied herself with a dash of milk and one teaspoon of sugar.

'Don't think about it yet. Eric will be more lenient when he's had time to cool down. He really loves you. He told me he does.'

Casey took an obligatory sip of hot tea because Suzanne had made it for her, the thought of Eric's 'love' becoming more distasteful by the minute.

'That car has sentimental value,' Suzanne was saying. 'It was a gift from his parents and he's very proud of it. You know how men love their status symbols.'

Casey peered into the depths of her cup. 'Even more than they love people.'

Suzanne made a tch tch sound against her teeth and sat beside her. 'You have to accept him along with his faults. It's how he's made. He wouldn't be Eric if he was any different. Now, you sit there for as long as it takes you to calm down.'

But Casey stood up. 'I might as well start working. I won't calm down until I find out what they say at the garage.'

Suzanne was busy photographing one of Eric's clients when he returned. Casey looked up from tidying the make-up table with a thumping heart.

'They'll be able to shine the paint up without needing to send away for replacement parts from overseas.' Eric bent to brush a kiss across her cheek. 'I regret being forced to say the things I said.'

Is this an apology? Casey realised it was the closest to one she could expect from Eric.

'I'll take you out for drinks after work and we'll put it behind us.'

The thought of acting her usual cheery self late into the night for Eric was more than she could bear thinking about. 'No thanks. Not tonight.'

'Why not tonight? Have you got something else on?'

Her mind spun with acceptable sounding lies but she decided to tell the truth. 'Yes, I want some time to myself.'

He breathed a long sigh from his nostrils. 'Are you huffy over what I said? Casey, get over it. I was pushed to the limit.'

'I understand, but I still need a quiet night.'

'To lick your wounds and feel sorry for yourself? How long will it take you to get over it, have a drink with me and be reasonable?'

The brittle edge in his voice stirred something uptight deep inside of her. 'Maybe never.' It was the truth. She hadn't realised until she heard it from her own lips. Suzanne's friendly voice invited the client in the photography room to follow her out to the till. Eric kept his voice down to a fierce whisper.

'Why the hell not?'

'Because I'm not the sort of girl I think you're looking for.'

'The only sort of girl I'm looking for is one who'll give me love and support. I was mad enough to think you'd be that sort of girl.'

The bell above the door tinkled as the client left. Suzanne poked her head into the make-up room. 'What's going on here?'

Casey bit back the sharp retort on her lips. 'Eric's car is going to be just fine.'

Relief washed over Suzanne's features. 'Well, that's fantastic.' She blew out a great breath and looked from one to the other. 'I thought I heard arguing.'

'You were wrong about how Casey is pining for a handsome, classy career man to sweep her off her feet. She's just as good as told me we're through.'

Suzanne's eyes widened. 'Casey, no! Can't you see that he was just upset about...?'

'About his car! I know! Suzanne, why did you tell him all that stuff?'

'What stuff?' Her bracelets jangled as she raised a hand to scratch her neck. 'You were interested in him! Don't try to tell me you weren't.'

'But you put the idea in my head. You tried to set me up with Eric from the moment I met him.'

'Hey, you didn't have to go along with me. I was doing you a favour. I thought he'd be the making of you.'

A favour? Casey's skin turned hot and prickly. Suzanne's earrings suddenly seemed too bright and brassy and the walls of the small make-up room seemed to spin around in circles. Casey wanted to kick something the way Eric had kicked her car. She longed to seize Suzanne's slim shoulders and shake her. Instead, she said stiffly, 'You needn't have bothered. I didn't need the favour. I was fine the way I was.'

Suzanne stretched her long fingers in an appealing gesture. 'But you weren't! You were unemployed, at a dead-end with your study and told me it'd been a waste of time. You practically pleaded to work with us and we

The Risky Way Home

gave you this job even though you were under-qualified. You told me all this! And I was trying to help you.'

Casey's chest was tight with something she knew was not tears. The thing was too tightly wound and knotted. Suzanne's words were entwining themselves around Casey's heart, crushing the spirit out of her and leaving her with nothing to say.

Eric's nostrils flared. 'My first impressions of Casey were right. She wouldn't know a good offer if it zoomed out of the sky and zapped her like lightning.'

'Eric, don't speak while you're so angry. You need to consider her point of view too. Those were pretty harsh things you...'

'You don't need to help anymore,' Casey cut in. 'Maybe he's right. I was the wrong person to come and work here, if it meant having to be the sort of girl Eric would like.' And although it was mid-morning, she slipped through the door and down the balcony steps to her car. She didn't know if they'd come after her. And she didn't care.

—————————

Casey wandered around the shops feeling shell-shocked. *I'll be fired. That's for sure.* Even if she wasn't, she would have to quit for there was no way she could work for Suzanne and Eric anymore after what she'd said. Casey had taken pains to stay in Suzanne's good graces during their years at school because she'd seen how miserable Suzanne could make the lives of anybody she held a grudge against. Now all her ground work was shattered in one morning. Suzanne would never forgive her. And she'd have to find another job. But she couldn't go back to live with her parents because there was no room for her. Abby and Sarah were using Casey's bed and the couch. Dale was still there too. And their father wouldn't want all of them living under his roof.

There was nothing to do but go home. Casey sat outside in her car and gazed at Piers' old van. It was covered with so many dents and scratches she doubted if he'd even notice another. *Pity it had to be Eric's car I scraped and not this one.*

Jerome heard her car door slam and dashed down the verandah steps to meet her. 'Casey, Daddy and I made a cake but it turned out yucky.'

She stepped inside to a delicious, warm aroma but Piers stood by the stove prodding something that looked like a sunken tuft of dirt in a pan.

'What have we got here?' Casey cried.

'I don't know what you'd call it. I don't understand how it can be scorched black around the edges but still gooey in the middle.'

'What sort of cake is it supposed to be?'

'Mum's double chocolate treacle cake. I phoned her up to ask for the recipe but she wouldn't just read it to me. She had to describe exactly how she makes it from the top of her head, and she kept leaving bits out and adding them later. Took about half an hour to get it out of her.'

'You're crazy to try one of your Mum's cakes. You should've just bought a packet mix from the shop.'

'Yeah, I wish I had. Never mind, Ben'll like this one.'

'No, it smells too good to give it all to Ben.' Casey rummaged through the pantry. 'Cut off the black bits for him and we can use the rest.' She set custard powder on the table and pushed a box of jelly crystals into Piers' hands. 'Here, you make this up and I'll get some custard going. We'll have a trifle. Jerome, how'd you like to break the cake into little bits and cover the bottom of this bowl with them?'

'Okay!' The little boy began tearing the cake into chunks with his fingers.

Casey knew that if she hadn't had such a terrible day, she would enjoy watching him.

'We're going away tomorrow,' Jerome chirped.

'Who's going away?'

'Me an' Daddy.'

A chill shot through Casey. They were two people she thought she could count on to remain predictable. She wasn't sure how she felt about finding out that she couldn't. She carefully measured custard powder into a cup as she asked, 'Where are you going?'

'To Melbourne for a week.' Piers stood by the electric kettle, waiting for water to boil. 'Guess who phoned me this morning? Justin Edwards. You asked about him not long ago and he's getting married day after tomorrow. Gave me a call to invite us to his wedding. And I thought, "Why not?"'

'Who gives their guests just two days notice? They're supposed to send invitations a month or two in advance.'

'I know, but Justin's never been like everyone else. He only proposed to her last week and they can't see any sense in waiting.'

'His fiancé must be either easy-going or stupid.'

'She's great. I've met her. Katie's a gorgeous girl.'

Something in his enthusiastic tone irritated Casey. She shook the powder into her simmering milk and began to stir. She hated the hollow feeling eating her from the inside out. 'Isn't it ironic?' she remarked under her breath. 'Old Giggles can find a perfect woman but Mr Wonderful can't.'

'Who's Mr Wonderful?'

'Eric.'

Piers had just set the jelly into the freezer to set and turned to face her. 'What do you mean Eric can't? He's got you, hasn't he?'

Although tears had been nowhere near the surface all day, Casey's eyes prickled. She blinked hard to make sure they were dry before she spoke. 'I had an accident today and scratched his car.'

Piers' eyes shot wide open. 'Not the Porsche?'

'Yes, and will you get that stunned expression off your face? You look just like Suzanne. It's Okay. After telling me what he thought of me, he drove it off to his mechanic and they told him it only needs a bit of a shine. I hope my insurance company comes to the party.'

Piers exhaled slowly. 'You're lucky it was nothing more serious.'

'I'll say I am. I would've been bankrupt. He threatened to take me to the cleaners for every cent I had.'

'Well it is a Porsche,' Piers looked awkward but also suitably sympathetic.

Jerome had finished pulling the cake to pieces. 'I wanna go and give Ben the burnt bits.'

'Okay, off you go. Mind your fingers.'

As the screen door clanged shut behind Jerome, Piers asked Casey, 'Would you like me to make you a cup of tea?'

'No!' she said, with irritation. 'What is it with you Bowmans? You all seem to think a cup of tea will fix anything.'

He grinned sheepishly. 'You're right. I sounded like Mum.' He pulled up a chair and sat across from her. 'Sorry.'

'I've probably lost my job. I walked out on them after telling them exactly what I thought. Not about the Porsche. About other stuff. I don't know why I said all the things I said. I didn't even realise I thought them until they all came tumbling out. I'm such an idiot.'

Piers wisely held his tongue for a long moment. 'Do you enjoy working in the studio?' he asked at last.

Casey twirled a strand of hair behind her ear. 'It's okay.'

'If you had a choice, is there anything you'd prefer to do?'

'I'm… not sure. My dad was disappointed when I didn't stick with teaching but I hated it.' She began to wish she'd accepted a cup of tea after all. When she was agitated, Casey liked to hide behind something steamy and hot. 'I just wanted to be like Suzanne.'

Piers let out a laugh. 'Why?'

Casey flushed. 'She was always so much fun to be around. She seemed to lead such a perfectly happy life without even trying.'

He shook his head. 'That was what she wanted people to think. It's an illusion. If you knew her as well as I do… she's totally messed up. I've lived with both of you, and I can tell you, you're far easier to live with.' Piers grinned and flexed his knuckles. 'Trust me on that.'

She managed a wan smile. 'Thanks. Suzanne couldn't be more messed up than I am, though. I wouldn't have a clue what I should do now.'

'That sounds like something I used to say. I think I can understand how you feel. You couldn't ever be more messed up than I used to be.'

'Are you talking about when Jerome was born?' Casey probed. 'Suzanne told me a bit about your ex-girlfriend. I asked her. I'm sorry.'

Piers heaved a sigh. 'That's Okay. It's no secret.'

'I saw Anna's photo in your bedroom,' Casey told him. 'She was beautiful.'

He nodded. 'Smart too. And she had heaps of energy. But what attracted me most to her was that she seemed to care so much for others. She stuck up for any person or animal who was hurting and she did it in a far more forceful way than I ever could. I admired her way of telling everybody what she thought straight off, without even needing to think about how she wanted it to sound. I really thought I was in love with Anna.'

'What do you mean you *thought* you were?'

He hesitated for a long moment. 'Maybe this is why I haven't wanted to talk about Anna to you. I've felt so much guilt about my attitude towards her. Even though I always thought I was acting for the best all the time I knew her, I was sure I'd stuffed up both our lives. I told her I loved her and moved in with her. To this day, I don't actually know if I fell out of love or not. It was more as if I found out that I'd never fallen in love with the real Anna at all, but with one I invented in my own head to suit myself.' As he spoke, he raked Casey's face with his eyes as if to gauge if she was following what he was trying to say.

'Anna thought she wasn't addicted to drugs but it was clear to everybody who knew her that she was. She was spending a fortune, frittering both our savings away. Then she went over the edge. She wasn't supposed to get pregnant. Nobody wanted it to happen. She was going to put Jerome up for adoption. But when he was born I went in to see him. They told me I shouldn't, but I wanted to. There he was, sort of squinting at a fold in his sheet. I can still remember exactly how he looked. I was staring down at what was supposed to be my biggest mistake. Everybody told me he was. Anna wouldn't look at him. Her folks were humiliated. Mine were furious. People from the adoption agency were coming for him. Everybody was behaving as if he shouldn't have happened. I don't know how long I stood there for, just watching him and thinking how weird it was that the biggest mistake of my life turned out to be the most perfect thing I'd ever seen.'

Piers paused to wrap his hand around the back of his neck. It was one of his few left-over gestures from school days. He used to look as if he wanted to close into himself like a telescope. Casey waited, saying nothing to interrupt his train of thought.

'Before I took a step away from his crib, I knew I wanted him. I knew that if I never saw him again, I'd find it hard to recover. For the rest of my life I'd keep wondering about what I'd lost. Jerome was trying to twist his head. His hair was all wispy and damp. I couldn't believe that I could turn to mush over someone in just a few seconds.'

'Suzanne told me what a long, hard battle you fought to keep him,' Casey said gently.

Piers gave a ragged laugh. 'That's an understatement. Even though I was only twenty and single, I was amazed by how many people tried to talk me out of keeping him. One social worker lady took me to her office and went into a long spiel about how I was making an emotional decision instead of a realistic one. I felt as if I was back in Primary School. At the end, I told her I still wanted him. Then she got nasty and called me a very selfish young man.'

'But you stood firm and look how great things have turned out for both of you.'

'Not in the beginning. Jerome cried non-stop for the first six weeks. I swear I couldn't get him to sleep for more than twenty minutes at a time. Mum and I took him to a doctor to find out what was wrong. It turns out that he was having withdrawal symptoms from Anna's drugs. By the time he got through it, I was walking around like a zombie. I knew that Gran's eyes were always fixed on me, waiting for me to crack under the pressure so she could say, "I told you so." I kept my mouth shut because I didn't want to give her a chance to say it. If she'd said it, I would've...' Piers searched for words strong enough to express his frame of mind. He shook his head and shrugged. 'I would've needed to think of some way to make her regret it. And I was too exhausted to come up with anything good.'

Casey laughed. 'You got through it with your sense of humour intact.'

'I'm glad you think so. Suzanne said it made my jokes even worse. But after those first few weeks, the change in Jerome was incredible. Three months after he was born, he was like a different baby. He turned as placid as he is now. Sometimes I wonder if the torture I went through during those first eight weeks helped make it easier for me to handle the following three years.'

'Of course it did. Nothing's ever wasted. Did Anna come to see him ever?'

Piers shook his head. 'I never expected her to because she said she wouldn't. Anna always stuck to her guns.' He sighed heavily. 'Did Suzanne tell you that she died?'

Casey nodded. 'Do Anna's parents ever see Jerome?'

'Yeah, they come a couple of times each year to visit him.'

'It's a great story, Piers. And you're fantastic with Jerome. You showed 'em all.'

'But he's been even more fantastic for me. He rescued me from having to live up to everyone else's expectations. Even that social worker spoke to me as if she thought I was a loser. And even though I thought I was a loser, I knew that she was making a snap judgment. She didn't even know me. Jerome showed me that I could find the nerve to stick to an unpopular decision. It was easy when I knew I was doing the right thing. And when he's old enough to understand, I know what I'm going to tell him.'

'What will you say?'

'That we're not supposed to listen when other people say we're not good enough. And that we don't have to do or be anything other than who God made us to be. I know that I've made a difference in Jerome's life. And that's made all the difference in mine.'

Casey wouldn't have believed she could muster a smile on that disastrous day. 'Thanks for telling me that. I think it's just what I needed to hear. It gives me hope that I'll work out what I should do with my own life.'

'Well, maybe it's not as hard as you think. Why don't you stop thinking about what your parents want or what Suzanne wants or what Eric wants? What do you want?'

'I can't work it out.' She felt like a puffy dress which had been pressed flat with a steam iron. There was nothing left. After trying to be what would please everybody, Casey pleased nobody and least of all herself. She had given away her identity in small bits and pieces. 'If I have any talents or skills, I don't know what they are.'

'Are you kidding me? You mean you really have no idea?'

'No.' She looked up. 'Do you think I have some?'

'They stand out a mile.'

'Then what are they?'

He hesitated and shook his head. 'I don't think I should tell you yet. You can work it out for yourself.'

'Come on, Piers! I'm in no mood for playing games. Just tell me.'

'No, I'll bet if I told you now, you'd just deny it.'

'Okay, but if I can't work it out, will you please tell me?'

For some reason, he was blushing. 'Why are you so anxious to know what I think? After all, it's just my own idea.'

'At least you have an idea.'

'How's this, then? I'll give you my opinion in a week's time when we get back from Victoria. That'll give you plenty of time to think about it.'

Too much time! Casey's hollow feeling grew deeper than she imagined she had space to contain. She'd told Eric that she needed time to herself but now the prospect of a whole week alone in the house disturbed her.

'Listen, I don't quite know how to put this, but if Suzanne tries to talk you out of having me here…'

'I've never listened to anything Suzanne says and I wouldn't start.'

'But you've only heard my side of the story. She and Eric must be furious. I scraped his magnificent car and then gave them a mouthful of abuse. Wouldn't you be angry?'

Piers folded his arms across his chest. 'I promise you, Casey, that if I ever own a Porsche, I won't get mad if you run into it.'

She felt her own tense and sore face soften into another genuine laugh.

Chapter 14

When Casey woke, she looked out of her window. Three clear spears of sunlight penetrated the peachy mist which hung over the hills and lit up three patches of ground. It was the time of year in which the air was balmy but the grass retained its verdant winter gloss. She opened her window to inhale the dewy morning scent and spotted Piers running with Ben near the edge of the property. The events of the previous day flooded back into her mind and her good spirits fell with a thump.

Ben's bleat of pure joy reached her ears as he kicked up his hooves. Piers managed to keep up the pace he set. They moved like lightning. *If Ben expects that sort of exercise from me while they're away, he has another think coming.* Casey quickly got dressed and went downstairs to join Jerome, where he sat on the verandah steps.

Piers returned to the house barely panting. He flashed his smile. 'Hi, will you move Ben's picket around during the week?'

'Sure.'

'Are we going *soon?*' Jerome asked with great impatience.

Piers tousled his hair. 'As soon as you finish your breakfast.'

Casey waited around until they left. She sat on the steps and watched their car out of sight. There were just a few more things to do before she could leave. She went upstairs to pack a change of clothes into her overnight bag, then back outside to herd Ben into his enclosure. Casey scratched him around his horns. 'I'll be back tomorrow night,' she promised. 'I know you like a change of scenery, old boy.'

The sound of car tyres rumbled along the driveway behind her. Casey turned and saw Suzanne's small, bright red Pulsar. Suzanne poked her arm out of the window and waved.

Drats! If only I'd left five minutes sooner! If Casey hadn't been seen, she would have considered dashing to the house to hide. She knew she'd have to face Suzanne some time but had hoped to prolong it for as long as possible. She heaved a sigh as she waded back through the long grass to greet her. Casey's tracksuit pants were covered with yellow pollen and small prickles from the knees down.

Suzanne was stepping out of her car. 'I had to come and talk to you. I was going to phone, but I really wanted to speak to you in person.' She was wearing a tight, satiny black dress with a low back and looked chic and lovely. Casey wiped her own sneakers on the doormat and said, 'Come in.'

Suzanne was looking around the empty kitchen. 'Where are Piers and Jerome?'

'They've gone away for a week to a wedding in Melbourne.'

'Who's getting married?'

'Justin Edwards.'

'That goofy guy from school who giggled like a wind-up toy? You're kidding me. How did Justin Edwards manage to get hitched?'

'Don't ask me.'

'Piers had some really weird friends.'

'He sure did.' Casey didn't mind chatting about people they used to know but wondered when Suzanne would cut to the point. 'Coffee?'

'Yes please, my usual black.' Suzanne took a seat, leaned across and flicked on the small kitchen radiator. She rubbed her hands up her upper arms. 'I always feel cold in this house, even on warm days.'

'These are thick walls. It takes a few hours each morning to properly warm up. I didn't set the fire, either. I'll be going to visit my family soon.'

'Then I'm glad I caught you. We really need to talk.'

Suddenly, Casey found herself anxious to jump in first. 'Listen Suzanne, I'm not sorry about what I said, but I *am* sorry for walking out like that.'

'Don't worry. I'm not upset over that. I was just a bit surprised how angry you were. I thought you were besotted with Eric.' Suzanne inspected the backs of her bright red nails. 'Did you really dump him?'

'I didn't come straight out and tell him we were through, if that's what you mean. He jumped to that conclusion himself. And then I realised that he had the right idea, anyway.' She poured boiling water into Suzanne's cup.

'Why?'

Casey sighed as she set the two cups on the table. 'You went out with Eric yourself. Surely you can guess.'

Suzanne looked almost ready to smile. 'I had my reasons. I want to hear yours.'

'Okay. He's self-centred and he can be a bit arrogant.'

Suzanne's white teeth flashed. 'That's our Eric. I'd say more than a bit. But he has plenty of good qualities too. Would you consider giving him another chance?'

'No!' Casey was surprised how adamantly she meant it.

'I see.' Suzanne took a sip of coffee and licked her lips. 'In that case, you should've handled him differently. If only you'd come to me for advice, I could've told you how to figure out a way for him to believe that he dumped you. That's the most pain-free way to deal with Eric. That's how I did it.'

Casey felt her mouth gape open and quickly snapped it shut. 'But he told me…'

'That he dumped me? I know. That's what he was supposed to think. It wasn't difficult. I just had to behave as if I was more interested in other things than I was in him. Then, as a last screw in the coffin lid, I introduced him to my family.'

'That's why he said he…'

'Dumped me? I know.' Suzanne giggled. 'I might've had an advantage over you there. Your family are more normal than mine.'

Casey thought of Dale and Abby, both living back at home with their parents. 'I wouldn't bet on it,' she grinned.

'It was tricky for me to dump Eric,' Suzanne explained. 'I still needed him.'

'You mean for the business?' Casey began to understand.

Suzanne ran a thoughtful finger around the rim of her cup. 'We were living together when we set up the studio. I could never have done it without him. Whatever else he is, Eric's a stunning photographer and his folks are loaded with cash. I even had to ask Mum to lend some to me. And so she should. She owed me some cash to make up for ruining my life. That studio was an incredibly expensive business to start.'

'I'll bet it was.'

'So when I'd had enough of going out with Eric, I didn't want to throw away all we'd worked for.' Suzanne took another sip. 'I'm still fond of him. That's why I went to sit and listen to him ramble on over drinks for hours last night. I know he's a pompous pain in the rear-end and I could never live with him again, but I can't imagine my life without him in there somewhere.'

Casey took the opportunity to ask something which had long puzzled her. 'Why were you so anxious to set me up with Eric? If you couldn't stick with him yourself then why did you think that I…?'

Suzanne blushed. 'Oh Casey, promise you won't hate me for this?'

Suzanne's response took her by surprise. 'Try me.'

'Here goes, then. I suppose if I don't say it, Eric might. When he went out with other girls, I was afraid they'd talk him into quitting the studio and leaving me in the lurch. What self-respecting girl would want her boyfriend working in a partnership with his ex-girlfriend?'

'I see what you mean.'

'With you, it was different. You'd be right there working with us. You wouldn't be luring him away somewhere else. I noticed the way you looked at him from the start, the way all girls do, as if you'd never imagined such a drop-dead gorgeous hunk in real life. And I thought you might be patient enough to put up with his super-ego.' Suzanne rolled her eyes and shook her head. 'It seems nobody is that patient.'

'I can't say I didn't give it a go.'

'And he'll get over it,' Suzanne said. 'I told him not to give you a tough time at work on Monday. He promised he won't.'

'At work? You mean you still want me back?'

It was Suzanne's turn to gape. 'Of course I do! You weren't considering quitting over this, were you?'

Casey twisted her fingers on her lap beneath the table. 'It did cross my mind.'

'No way!' Suzanne leaned across the table to touch Casey's arm. 'I love having you with us. You and I go back a long way. You always listen to me and not everyone does. It'd be a pain to have to break someone else in now, when you're such a good worker. Please stay.'

Casey found Suzanne's friendliness disarming, as usual. 'I hadn't made any other plans.'

Suzanne stood and stepped around the table. She enveloped Casey in a tight hug. 'You're a good friend. I'm sorry for pushing you at Eric, whether you liked it or not.'

Casey found herself enfolded by the sweet scent of Suzanne's perfume. 'I guess it's water under the bridge now.'

Suzanne stood back and smoothed her sleek, black dress. 'I'm really glad I came to see you. Thanks for the coffee. I have to go home and get ready for something that Tim's taking me to. Sometimes I wish I could stay home for just one week-end to catch my breath.' She began to rummage through her handbag. 'But I'd soon be bored to tears if I did. I never know what to do with myself when I'm alone. Aha, found it.' She placed a red covered notebook on the table. Casey knew she'd seen it somewhere before. Then she remembered it was that night at Moira's.

'I'm passing this on to Piers. Will you give it to him when he gets back?'

'Sure. What is it?'

Suzanne let out a groan. 'Mum's old diary. A load of stinking rubbish. Can you believe her? She insisted I take it home that abysmal night at Gran's birthday. It's meant to tell why she left our father and never speaks about him. Now she tells me she thinks she should've let me read it years ago.'

'Have you read it?'

Suzanne flicked her shaggy hair back over her shoulders. 'I glanced at the first few pages but I'm no great reader and her handwriting is so tiny you almost need a magnifying glass. I'm not going to risk ruining my eyesight on a load of twaddle like this.'

'Are you sure you don't want to finish it?' Casey couldn't understand why Suzanne, who always craved to learn more about her father, wouldn't persevere with a book which claimed to do just that.

'I glanced at the first few pages and it was pretty clear what sort of book it'd be. I was in no mood to read a load of one-sided trash about my father.'

Then Casey understood. She remembered what Suzanne had told her mother when Moira pressed her to stay for a cup of tea. *It's too late for that, Mum.* In the same way, Casey guessed that it was also too late for Suzanne to read the diary.

'Piers might persevere for longer,' Suzanne said. 'If there's anything interesting in it, he can tell me. You can read it yourself if you like. You always loved to have your nose in a book. For all we know, Mum might've written the next great Australian novel. Anyway, au revoir for now. I'll see you on Monday morning.'

Casey stood and watched Suzanne's car out of sight. Then she collected her overnight bag, locked the empty house behind her and set off.

The situation at home was more bedlam than Casey had anticipated. With Dale, Abby and Sarah all crammed beneath her parents' roof, the house was stretched to its seams. Both Abby and Dale had belongings jam-packed in their old bedrooms and spilling out into the passage. Dale's drum kit had been joined in the lounge room by two of Sarah's bean bags. The house had never seemed so inadequately small in the days when Casey, Abby and Dale all lived at home. Sarah had been assigned to sleep in Casey's bedroom. Although she didn't mind the idea of sharing with her niece, Casey decided that she'd rather return to her spacious, quiet dormer bedroom. She didn't even bring her overnight bag inside. Her father appeared relieved.

Dale's friends, Steve and Matt, had arrived with their electric guitar and keyboard and the three young men began a loud, heavy metal jam. Casey's parents hurried to take Sarah to a playground for an hour. Abby blocked her ears with a scowl and disappeared with a magazine to her bedroom. While Casey peeled herself an orange in the kitchen, the phone rang.

She picked it up. 'Hello.'

'Hey, is that you, Casey?'

She recognised the hearty tones of Jeff, her brother-in-law. 'Sure is. Hi Jeff.'

'Is that Dale's band I can hear in the background?'

'Yeah, if you can call it a band.'

'They sound pretty good from here.'

She winced as her brother clashed his cymbals. 'I'll bet they sound better from there than they do from here.'

He laughed. 'How've you been? I hear you've started a new job.' Jeff kept her talking for several minutes. Casey knew that he didn't call just to chat with her, yet he seemed genuinely interested. That had always been his way. Casey had fancied herself head-over-heels in love with him the year she was twelve years old, when he had married Abby.

Finally, he got to the reason for his call. 'Casey, tell me the honest truth, how are Abby and Sarah?'

'Both well.' Casey began to feel awkward as she tried to work out the best way to respond. Would he prefer to think that they were happy or sad without him?

'Did Sarah get the little china doll I sent her?'

'I think so.' Casey had no idea. 'You could ask her yourself if she was home, but Mum and Dad have taken her to the playground.'

'Is Abby around?' he asked casually.

'Yes, if you'll wait a moment, I'll get her.'

Casey hurried to her sister's bedroom. Abby waved her hands and shook her head. 'I'm not going to talk to him.'

'You'll have to now, because I told him you're here.'

'That's your fault, Casey! There's no way I'm going to talk to that snake!'

'Well, what am I supposed to tell him?'

Abby raised her *Family Circle* like a shield. 'I don't care what you tell him. Just get him off the phone.'

Casey glared at her sister. She hated the awful thing Abby was forcing her to do. Every nerve protested as she picked up the phone receiver. 'Jeff, I made a mistake. She can't come to the phone right now.'

He let out something that sounded like a grim laugh. 'You mean she won't? Never mind, Casey. Thanks for trying. It was good speaking to you, anyway. See you... sometime maybe.'

Casey dashed back to confront Abby, who sat with her shoulders hunched, the magazine crumpled and forgotten on the floor.

'You could've just listened to what he had to say. Maybe he wants to patch things up with you but how do you expect him to make amends if you won't even speak to him?'

'I've been over the same issues with him one hundred times. Sorry to put you in an embarrassing situation, but you should've had the sense not to tell him I'm home.'

'He sounded so friendly and sad.'

Abby made a scornful noise in the back of her throat. 'I know Jeff always had you and Mum wrapped around his little finger. No wonder he has tickets on himself.'

'He *doesn't!* If you think Jeff has tickets on himself, you should see Eric.'

Abby's blue eyes froze over like ice. 'I don't even know this Eric guy, but your experience of men wouldn't fit on a shopping receipt, so don't try to give me advice.'

Casey was glad when the time came to go. She didn't understand Abby any more than she understood Suzanne.

Back home at Piers' place, she decided it was hardly worth the effort of setting a fire just for herself. After the din at her parents' house, the extreme quiet seemed to ring in her ears. Casey tidied Jerome's toy box, folded Piers' blue jumper that he'd left on the couch and placed it on his bed.

Going to bed seemed the best option but it was too early to sleep and she'd just finished the novel she was reading. Casey consulted the TV guide and found nothing to interest her. She had no new book to begin and her gaze automatically locked onto the spine of Moira's red journal. *I can't read that. She meant it for her children.*

Casey scanned other titles in the shelf instead. She raised her eyebrows as she pulled out a volume entitled, *Empower Yourself.* On the flyleaf, she read attractive feminine handwriting. *Dear Piers, here's something to help you pull your act together. All my love, Anna.*

Casey pulled a face and replaced it on the shelf. Once again, she looked at Moira's journal. Casey wanted to read it. No other book appealed to her while that waited there. She was curious to learn about Suzanne and Piers' father. She had the house to herself for the rest of the week and nobody need ever know.

The Risky Way Home

There are far worse crimes than reading a book. And Suzanne gave me permission to read it. I don't have to read it all, anyway.

The thought made her flush for yielding to temptation but by now, she was resolved in her decision to read it. There was so much she wanted to know about why Suzanne turned out the way she did. Perhaps it would explain Suzanne's anger and what family secret lay behind her mother's behaviour.

Moira's Diary

January 1st

My name is Moira Elizabeth Tyler and I am almost twenty-one. It's a brand new year and Mother and I are living in Paris with some of my father's old friends. Monsieur Dupont and his wife recently found out about Dad's death seven years ago. They discovered that Mother and I lived alone in London for all that time, and invited us to share their home for the time being. Monsieur Dupont is the head of a huge company of financiers. Only they and their two grown-up sons live in this enormous house.

Although I'm happy, Mother still seems sad. I don't think she will ever get over Dad's death. She says he was the only good thing that ever happened to her. Her name is Henrietta Tyler. She was born in Australia but never talks about her family except to say that they neglected her. My father was an English tourist who met her in Australia when they worked together. They became great friends. Eventually he asked her to marry him. Mother said yes, with the condition that they leave Australia and move back to England so she could start a new life. I always longed to visit Australia but she always insisted that she'd never set foot back in the country that caused her so much grief, so I guess we never will.

Mother is always nagging me because she wants me to go out with Monsieur Dupont's older son, Andre. I prefer his brother, Jean.

I can't believe I've known Jean-Michel Dupont for such a short time because it feels as if I've known and loved him forever. He is twenty-seven years old, tall with wavy, dark hair and the most stunning blue eyes. He took me out into the country on his moped. Even though it was freezing, we rugged up and had a fantastic time. That same evening, we went to a nightclub in the city where we danced until the early hours of the morning. A few days later, Jean treated me to a meal at the casino.

He has had a terribly sad life. His parents have always favoured Andre. They'd never intended to have a second child and made sure poor Jean knew that he was a mistake. They sent him to horrible boarding schools to get him out of the way and treated him as a nuisance during the holidays when he had to go home. He used to cry and plead with them not to send him back to school, but they ignored him. Knowing this about Monsieur and Madame Dupont, I no longer like them as much as I did when I first met them.

Andre has a huge private office in their father's firm but Jean has a poky little room with noisy air-conditioning and a dingy view overlooking a back alley. He says he feels like a sewer rat.

He asked me, "Why didn't you want to go out with Andre when he asked you?"

"Because I didn't fancy him."

Jean's eyes began to gleam. "So you like me better?"

He knows the answer to that very well. I just laughed and said, "Do you like chocolate sauce better than gravy on your ice-cream?"

He burst out laughing. "Mama and Papa were very disappointed when you turned up your nose at their precious number one son."

January 18th

We've been out together almost every night. We've walked along the river and over the magnificent bridges of Paris. He took me to the markets and bought me a wonderful silk evening skirt. We usually get home long after the others are in bed. Jean takes me up to his bedroom. At first I felt nervous that somebody would guess I was there, but he said, "So what if they guess?" He stroked my cheek with his finger and said, "You've lived with your cranky old mother for far too long, my sweetheart. I love you with all my heart."

I burn inside whenever he says things like that. I go into Jean's bedroom with him because it's what I want to do most in the world.

The Risky Way Home

However, I always manage to be back in my own bedroom before the crack of dawn, so that nobody will find out. There is no point in making people angry if we can prevent it. He doesn't know my mother as well as I do. She can make life unbearable for anybody she holds a grudge against. And I can't help fearing that if his parents find out, they might make me and Mother leave.

February 16th

Something terrible has happened. Nobody knows but Mother. Jean doesn't know because he's gone away for a shooting trip with some friends. I am counting the days until he comes home. I really need to tell him.

Six days ago I woke up intending to write in my diary but felt too sick. As soon as I climbed out of bed, I had to rush to the bathroom to throw up. I thought I'd caught a stomach virus because I kept being sick at intervals throughout the day. On top of that, I felt so tired and dizzy that I longed to snuggle up in bed and sleep the day away, if only I wasn't feeling so queasy in the stomach. After three days of this, I woke up feeling a bit better. When I got dressed and went downstairs to breakfast, the smell of Andre's egg and bacon sent me reeling right back to the bathroom to cringe over the basin. I was beginning to feel alarmed because no normal bug had ever been so prolonged before. I could barely hold my head up straight when Mother found me there, hunched over and crying. She whisked me off to see a doctor, hoping to get some medicine to settle my stomach. I was happy to oblige, longing for anything to stop the sickness. It was like being on a terrible carousel I couldn't climb off.

Doctor Paget, a middle-aged man, pushed his glasses up on the bridge of his nose, looked me up and down and asked, "Could you possibly be pregnant?"

For a moment, I didn't know how to respond because Mother was sitting there and I didn't want her to know all that I've been up to. But I knew that if I lied to the doctor, he wouldn't be able to get to the bottom of my illness. So I admitted, "Oui, there might be a chance." Then I watched Mother's eyes bore into me like steel. I knew she'd tear strips off me with her tongue as soon as we stepped out of the surgery.

Doctor Paget pottered around his desk, searching for something. "That'll be the first thing we'll test for. If it shows up negative, I'll consider other possibilities." He made me produce a urine sample and tested it with some sort of thin strip. I could read the news in his eyes before he opened his mouth. Although he addressed his words to me, he looked at Mother when he spoke. "I'm afraid you are pregnant."

"Could there be a mistake?" Mother demanded.

"I'm sorry, not likely."

Everything in the room had receded to a blur for me but I clearly remember the doctor's wiry grey hair. He roughly calculated my dates and told me that I must already be six weeks pregnant. For about a month, I've had a tiny baby growing inside of me and never guessed that was why I felt so nauseous and wrung-out.

Mother was furious. She did tear strips off me. "We'll find an abortion clinic. We won't tell Yvette and Philippe. We'll take care of it ourselves and they'll never need to know. You got yourself into this hideous mess and I'll get you out of it." I've tried to steer clear of her since we got home. I haven't even looked her in the eye because I know what I'll see there. Somehow, I can tolerate the sound of her harsh and nagging voice but I can't bear the sight of the resentment and hurt deep in her eyes.

I want Jean to get back. I want to feel him hold me.

February 24th

Jean is back and I told him the news. I so longed for the sight of his comforting smile but it didn't come for a long time. We were walking in his parents' garden and he appeared grim as he admitted that it was a "damn pretty kettle of fish."

He perched on a stone wall to think. "I have to say, it'll be one in the eye for Papa and Andre if I'm the one to have a son and heir for Dupont and Partners." Then a smile did begin to flicker around the corners of his mouth. I was so pleased to see it, I felt encouraged to wrap my arms around him.

Jean returned my hug. "Moira, don't worry your pretty head about a thing. We'll have the baby. Pay no attention to your mother's nonsense. We'll get married, move out of this joint and have our son, oui?" He planted a kiss on my forehead followed by one on each cheek. "What do you say?" By now he was beaming the wide, joyful smile that I love.

"I say that'll be fantastic." I'd been dreading the abortion clinic.

He raised my chin with his thumb to peer into my eyes. "Fantastic, eh? Does that mean absolutely wonderful and altogether marvellous?"

For the first time that dreadful week, I smiled. "Oui."

"Say it," he demanded.

"Absolutely wonderful and altogether marvellous." I found myself actually laughing.

I expect Mother to do her best to talk me out of our plan but I refuse to let her push me around for the rest of my life. I know she doesn't like Jean but there is no way I am going to give him or our baby up.

February 28th

When I told Mother my decision, it was worse than I expected. She stormed out of my bedroom leaving me so shaken that I crawled beneath my covers and burrowed my head under the pillow to try to pull myself together.

She tried to forbid me to go out with Jean any more. She said cruel and disgusting things about him. "Don't even dream of spending the rest of your life with that boy. He's wrong for you!"

That boy, she called him, and he's twenty-seven years old.

"I didn't mind you being polite to him for his parents' sake but you'll marry him over my dead body!"

"Why do you hate Jean so much?"

"He has serious problems. He's mentally unstable. You listen to me, my girl! He doesn't have a steady or reliable bone in his body. He's been a problem to his poor parents from the time he was a youngster. He lets money filter through his fingers like water and he's even threatened his mother with violence when she refused to give him more. He seems to think he's entitled to suck their hard-earned cash out of them like a leech."

I wasn't going to listen to such poisonous lies without trying to defend him. "Now I understand! You've been listening to the Duponts.

They say these things because they never loved him!"

She grabbed my shoulders and shook me. "Listen to sound common sense! They're his parents! They know him better than you do! Yvette says that sometimes she wonders if he's schizophrenic. He has a way of changing his moods with no warning. When he was a youth, he used to hit her! Once he knocked one of her teeth out. Don't get tied up with that!"

"What rubbish! Just because they're his parents, they know nothing. They might've known him longer but I know him better!"

She gave me her tight-lipped look and her nostrils were flaring. "I can't believe you're too stupid to heed a clear warning!"

I wanted to cry but I kept trying to reason with her. "It's obvious to me what's happened. Yvette and Philippe Dupont have talked themselves into believing all that ridiculous junk just to absolve themselves from the guilt of sending him to horrible boarding schools and making his life miserable. They resent Jean because he dares to be his own man. After listening to all this, I can understand why he hates them! What sort of parents would say such horrible things about their own son? They've treated him shamefully."

"They've treated him far better than he deserves! His father has given him a position in the company which he's not even qualified for, after the way he carried on at school, stirring trouble for his teachers and frittering away all the money Philippe and Yvette sent him."

I'd had enough. "Don't say another word. I refuse to listen to any more of this slander about the man I love. I love Jean and I'm going to marry him."

Mother slammed my bed post with the palm of her hand as if she wished it was my face. She had a coughing fit because she keeps smoking her disgusting cigarettes. "If you marry that man, I'll never speak to you again."

"That'll be a nice change." I hadn't meant to say that. It just shot out.

It was then that she stormed out of my room and slammed the door. Although she hadn't lit up a cigarette in my bedroom, she left her stale, smoky odour behind her. I hate it and I'll be glad never to have to put up with it again.

The Risky Way Home

If only I had a supportive mother who understands what love means. I guess I've failed to be the sort of daughter who could give her a reason to keep living after my father died, although I tried. I doubt if anybody could please her. There's no living with her! I rubbed my stomach and promised the little baby in there that I'd be a different sort of mother. I'll encourage my children to confide in me and do my utmost to understand their points of view. Jean is so certain we're having a boy, I've got into the habit of calling the baby "he". When I'm happily settled with Jean and our new baby, I'm certain I won't miss Mother a bit. Good riddance to her!

March 2nd
We'll be married this week-end. Jean has booked a celebrant who'll do it for us. I'm very excited, although I still feel nauseous and tired. It'll be a huge relief not to have to smile and behave as if everything is normal in front of the Dupont family. When I was younger I dreamed of having a wedding with hundreds of guests and wearing a white, flowing gown, but the thought of leaving our families who don't really care about us and eloping is a far more romantic thought. I have a small carpet bag packed with a silky white negligee. I can hardly wait for the moment when it's all over and he can see me in it. I'm glad I haven't grown fat yet. In fact, pregnancy seems to be making me thinner because I've been eating so little.

March 18th
It's all over. I've been Mrs Dupont for just over a week. I almost thought we wouldn't make it because Andre drove past while I was waiting for Jean at our rendezvous spot. I was sitting on the stone wall at the end of the long Dupont driveway next to one of the stone gargoyles, trying to look as innocent as if all I had in my bag was shopping. Andre didn't seem to notice anything amiss.

I waved to him, hoping he'd drive on past, but he parked near the gate, got out and came over to me. "Bonjour, Moira."

"Bonjour." The palms of my hands were sweating.

"Have you been unwell lately?" He was scrutinising my face.

"No. Why?"

"You've seemed a little quiet and you've lost colour. I've been worried."

"Thanks for your concern but I'm fine. I had a bit of stomach virus but I'm getting better."

He breathed in a long breath and fiddled with his watch face as if he wanted to say more. "I've noticed how attached you seem to have become to my brother."

I said nothing.

"Moira, please don't take this the wrong way, but I'm warning you not to go on with it."

I blinked and looked up at him. "Go on with what?"

He was beet red, which did not improve his looks. "What I mean to say is...I love my brother very much but I'd feel very remiss if I didn't warn you that Jean is the last fellow any girl should get tangled up with."

If I hadn't been waiting for Jean I believe I would have run away. "Thank you."

He cleared his throat. "Moira, Jean never truly loved anyone but himself. Nobody can understand him and we've given up trying to."

I was sick to the stomach and this time I knew my pregnancy was not responsible. I didn't want to open my mouth but knew I'd have to think of something to say to make him go away. "I'm sorry Andre."

He still made no move to leave. "Moira, I put my foot in it, didn't I? I've gone about this all wrong but please take a few days to think over what I've just said."

"Okay, I will." I was willing to say whatever would just get rid of him.

"Please talk to my mother - about Jean. It must be hard for you to hear it from me but please hear it from her."

That's when Jean arrived. I was frightened when I looked at him. His face was hard and furious and didn't soften when he glanced at Andre, who was sitting up close to me holding both my hands in his. "You waste no opportunity to try to steal what's mine."

Andre stood up and wiped his hands down the legs of his brown tweed pants. "Jean, I have a right to simply speak to one of our guests."

Jean seized my arm and pulled me against him. "All my life you've got your clutches into everything that's mine but you can't have her." He practically shoved me into his car and slammed the door behind me. I stared down at my knees, determined not to look at Andre again. Jean slid behind the wheel, revved up his engine and took off. All the way to the registry office his profile was grim. I hated his brother for having ruined what should have been the most exciting drive of my life.

"I didn't know he was going to come and sit there. I didn't want him there."

"It seems a good thing that I'm going to marry you without a moment's delay." He was curt.

My eyes stung. I knew that I'd cry if I spoke and that would mess up my face for our wedding ceremony. I tried to convince myself that Jean's brusqueness was a sign of his passionate nature. It was proof that he loved me more than anything else. It was a good thing.

On the way up the steps of the registry office, I squeezed his hand. "I love you," I whispered.

He looked down into my eyes. Although he didn't smile, his blue eyes were shiny and he squeezed my hand back.

The celebrant had a friendly manner but I was busy trying to control my nerves. I wish I'd taken in more of the ceremony so I have something to tell our children. When we arrived at our hotel, Jean was happy again and hummed as if I'd never met Andre. He raised my chin with his thumb and kissed each of my eyelids. "You're the best thing that's ever happened to me. Don't ever forget that. When our son is old enough, we'll tell him about the romantic, unconventional way his parents rushed away to be married."

Whenever Jean says things like that, it makes up for anything else he does.

March 30th

I can hardly believe it but we're living back with the Duponts. After the way we eloped, I had no idea that Jean intended to go back to them. I'd hoped to live in a small apartment, just the two of us, but he says that Parisian apartments are dumps compared to his parents' mansion. He said they owe it to him to have us back because he's their son. I thought I'd be far too embarrassed to face his parents again but they made it easy for me. They were kinder than I'd expected. Madame Dupont seemed to feel sorry for me.

"Your mother has moved out," she said. "She's leased a small apartment near the river. I don't know her address but I'm sure she'll want to know if we've heard what's become of you."

"Merci," I didn't press her for details. If Mother railed at the Duponts and made a scene after we left, I didn't want to know. In spite of what Jean says about city apartments, I'll bet she's living in a comfortable one. I know my father's death made her a wealthy widow. I pushed prawn cocktail around on my plate with my fork, trying not to catch Andre's eye across the table. I wish we didn't have to live with them.

After dinner, Madame Dupont beckoned me to the kitchen and rubbed my arm in a motherly sort of way. "You poor girl. You made a huge mistake by running away to marry Jean."

I looked into her kind eyes and read genuine warmth. "I know," I mumbled. "We shouldn't have done it like that. I'm sorry."

She held me at arm's length then pulled me close again. "Oh Moira. I hope you won't live to be sorrier than you ever dreamed. You should have come to Philippe and me and told us about your pregnancy. We would have taken good care of you. Philippe and I aren't ogres."

I hardly knew what to say to that. I mumbled, "I'm sorry," again.

"Jean knows we would have done our best to talk you out of such a rash move, but it would've been with your best interests at heart. Jean will not be an easy husband. You haven't known him for long, my poor dear, but he can be very...difficile."

Her words left me with a creepy, crawly sensation. Why do people keep saying that?

April 1st
The horrible nausea has gone and Jean is no longer tetchy with me. He's so virile and active I can understand why he felt annoyed.

April 21st
Yesterday morning, Andre knocked on my door with an armload of English books he'd bought at a market stall. I felt flattered that he'd

think of me and thanked him for the books, although I could see that they were nothing more than a bundle of old medical journals. Andre was not to know that.

Mother visited me just once since Jean and I were married. I'm trying to convince myself that I don't care but deep down, I can't help feeling sorry about our rift. Although I never felt close to Mother, she's the only blood relation I have left. It hurts to think that she might shun her new grandchild when the time comes.

June 6th

Jean is so certain this child will be a boy, I guess I've got into the habit of referring to the baby as "he."

Mother sent an invitation to visit her in her apartment. When I waddled up her steps I could tell that she was trying hard not to look at the bulk beneath my maternity dress. She offered me fruit juice and petite fours without mentioning my condition. Eventually she told me that she never wants to see Jean's face beneath her roof.

October 11th

The baby was born last night at eleven o'clock. She has black downy fuzz all over the top of her head and her eyes have a smoky quality that I could lose myself in. She is sublime.

Jean's initial reaction to her birth made me miserable. I didn't expect the news of her gender to hit him quite so hard. I know he had his heart set on a son but how could he look at her velvety face and sulk for so long?

"Duponts have always had boys," he shot at me.

"Not this time. She must be extra special."

I tried to come up with a way to make him warm to her. Reasoning with him and asking him to hold her hadn't worked. The solution I found was quite by accident. I simply thought of a name for the baby and he disagreed with my choice.

"I'd like to call her Julia." My best friend was Julia and I always liked her name. But Jean positively bristled when I suggested it.

"She's my daughter too."

My heart leaped. "What would you call her, then?"

"I'll think on it," he promised.

By the time I'd finished my next meal, he'd decided. "Suzanne Marie. It sounds feminine and chic." The case was closed. He wouldn't hear a word of discussion. It took me awhile to get used to the name. My initial feeling was that Suzanne sounded too mature and womanly for such a tiny infant but she'll grow into it.

Later that evening,, Madame Dupont let slip the origin of the name. It seems Suzanne had been the name of an old flame of Jean's from school. Monsieur Dupont told me she had the sultriest voice he'd ever heard for a young girl. Suzanne Marie Dupont it is. I like it more each time I say it.

I'm glad she's a girl. I'll have the privilege of seeing her blossom into a lovely young woman.

March 20th

Suzanne is five months old and has a sharp pair of pearly teeth poking through her bottom gum. We all love her. She's a sunny baby who fills the house with the sound of her chuckles. I think she knows she's the darling of the family. She grins whenever anybody looks at her. Andre dangles rattles over her crib and plays peek-a-boo whenever he has a spare moment. Then, when she gives so much as a grimace of wind, he laughs as if he's the world's funniest comedian.

Jean hates it when Andre holds or plays with Suzanne.

"She's my daughter! Not yours!" He snatches her away and glowers at his brother.

I find the situation embarrassing. Andre is merely a fond uncle and to his credit, he never seems to take Jean's behaviour to heart. He says, "Oui, oui, I'm leaving," and rolls his eyes at me as he walks out of the room.

Mother visited last week. She didn't hold Suzanne but looked at her for a long time while Suzanne sat propped up with cushions.

"Look at all the dark hair and her mawkish pallor," Mother said, "There's more than a dash of Dupont there, mark my words."

I hope there is. Jean likes to think she looks like him. Suzanne has stolen her father's heart and that's all I could have hoped for.

July 30th

Suzanne now walks everywhere and she's only nine months old. She takes dainty steps on tiptoe like a tiny ballerina. I have to keep a close eye on her because if I turn away for one second, she scurries off.

I've received many compliments about her silky hair and cheeky, elfin face. When Jean is home he likes to bounce her on his knees and pretend he's a helicopter. Her curls fly around her face and she screams with laughter but he always tires of the game before she does. When he walks off she cries after him until he snaps at me to keep her quiet.

Jean's been been away with two of his friends all week. They've taken their hunting rifles into the country looking for venison and poultry. I don't know how long he'll be gone. I'll never forget the first time he didn't come home the night I expected him. I was almost beside myself with fear that he'd accidentally shot himself. Suzanne was fresh and active in the morning but I was a mess. Jean breezed home before lunch and scolded me for worrying about him. So now I stay calm, even when he's away for three or four days at a time.

I worry now for a different reason. I wonder why he likes to spend so much time away from me. Although he still makes a fuss of Suzanne, he often snaps at me when I ask him about his plans. "I'm not accountable to you!" he says. "You'll see me when I get back." I'm finding it hard to fill our days with interesting things for Suzanne to do because she's so familiar with all her toys. She gets restless if we stay in our own part of the house for hours on end. I always long for Jean's return but then, when he comes home, the only change is that I have to keep Suzanne out of his way while he sleeps.

August 12th

Something terrible has happened. It was four thirty in the afternoon and Jean had been out since dawn. Suzanne was ignoring all of her toys and standing beside the door to the rest of the house, grunting at me. I took her by the hand and wandered down to the big kitchen to borrow some tea because my tin was empty. Although Mama and Papa Dupont were out, Andre was sitting in the lounge room watching T.V. and chuckling.

"Bonjour, Moira. Come and watch this. It's funny."

I saw that it was just an old Laurel and Hardy comedy routine. I wasn't really interested but Suzanne was scrambling onto one of the armchairs so I sat down on the opposite one. She bounced on the cushions, then slid to the floor and scooted to Andre with her tiny mincing footsteps. He held out his finger and she wrapped her fist around it, beaming all over her face.

Andre straightened her small palm and began to play "Round and Round the Garden." After the fourth time, Suzanne squealed with laughter, anticipating the tickle that was coming. A tremendous CRASH made us all jump. I thought a meteor had hurtled into the side of the house. Then I realised the French doors behind us had been slammed so fiercely, their panes still rattled. Jean was standing there, glaring at us.

"Bonjour," I cried.

He jerked his chin at Suzanne. "Get her out of here."

"We were just..."

"I said GET HER OUT OF HERE!"

As I rose, he seized my shirt front and hurled me into the passage. Andre was on his feet protesting. Jean dumped Suzanne at my feet and slammed that door behind us too. Her face crumpled and she wailed.

I heard Jean yell, "You rotten, sneaking son of a bastard!"

"You should be ashamed of yourself to treat a lovely young woman like trash, Jean-Michel."

"The way I treat my wife is my own business!"

"She was just watching TV. You expect her to stay all day behind closed doors in your part of the house like a trophy on a shelf? You're off this planet, Jean!"

Suzanne's wail had developed into a scream. I scooped her up and hurried upstairs. She'd just settled into her playpen when Jean marched in. He looked like he could breathe fire.

"What the hell were you playing at?"

"Nothing! I'd gone to borrow some tea and I was watching T.V."

"We have a perfectly good television set up here!" I could smell bitter, heavy fumes of alcohol on his breath. "You just didn't expect me home. Admit it! This'll teach you to flirt with Andre behind my back!" He stepped back and swung the back of his hand so hard against my mouth that I tasted blood.

"I wasn't flirting with Andre! That's ridiculous! He's Suzanne's uncle, for heaven's sake. He was just being friendly."

"Shut your mouth!" Jean's fingers dug into my collar bone until I gasped for breath. "Femme fatale. Now I know your games! If you weren't so damn easy, you'd never have got into the fix with me in the first place."

He dragged me to our bed and flung me onto it. I could hear Suzanne cooing in her pen and silently thanked God that she was content. My throat was burning. Jean pinned my shoulders onto the mattress and breathed his bitter breath into my face. "I just came back to get changed. I'm going to meet my friends. You'd better be here when I get back!"

I lay there on the bed until Suzanne began to fret. Then I bathed her, fed her and rocked her until she fell asleep. After a warm shower, I rubbed ointment into the sore, red marks around my throat. I could see the shape of every one of Jean's fingers imprinted on my skin. I started to cry and couldn't stop. By the time he got back, I'd stopped crying and was in bed again.

He opened the top two buttons of my nightie and looked at the finger marks around my neck. "Wear high collars for the next couple of days." Then he stretched out beside me and quickly fell asleep.

August 2nd

I've found out that what I've suspected for a few weeks is definitely true. I'm expecting another baby.

My queasiness and dizziness is familiar but not this bone-aching weariness. I don't want to bear another child for Jean. My hands are more than full with the one I already have. I know Jean so much better than I did before. He drinks almost every night. I smell it on his breath and in his clothes whenever he steps inside and my stomach instantly churns. I try hard not to let him see me flinch because it infuriates him when he suspects that I'm not delighted to see him. He says that my impudent face is asking for a slap and it's my own fault when I get them.

He used to love me not so long ago. If I'd been able to consistently give him what he wanted, our lives might still be wonderful. Perhaps there is some fault in me that makes him feel the need to strike out at me. I don't dare tell a soul in case there is a grain of truth in what he so often says. I know he'll never listen to me but sometimes I beg him not to go out and drink. He usually has the same reply.

"If you behaved like a proper wife, I wouldn't! Anyone whose wife hates him as much as you hate me deserves to drink as much as he likes."

Is there any truth in that? I honestly don't know. It seems to be a vicious circle. The more he drinks, the more I dread what's coming and the more he belts me when he reads the fear in my eyes.

Whenever I look at myself in the mirror, I see a gaunt, washed-out, undesirable figure. To think that not so long ago, I thought myself pretty. I make an effort to put make-up on for him and also for his parents and brother for they must never suspect what Jean does to me. If they ever mentioned it to him, I'm afraid he might go completely berserk and kill me.

This pregnancy is taking its toll on me. I pray that God will forgive me but many times I've prayed that this baby would be miscarried. I have no room in my heart for it. I have no strength to worry for the safety of yet another life. But my prayers are not answered so I guess it has to be this way. Each day is the same as the last and I know that I have no choice but to face them.

August 3rd

I've told Jean the news. I didn't expect him to be delighted but I was relieved when he wasn't annoyed either. "It'd better be a boy this time," he said, as if I have any control at this stage. I don't want to face another of his fits if it turns out to be another girl. I feel certain in my heart that this baby will be a girl. At least Suzanne still holds a firm place in Jean's heart and I pray that nothing will change that.

December 12th

This baby is not as much of a wriggler as Suzanne was but I swear that it responds to my emotions like a barometer. Whenever Jean's voice booms suddenly, the baby jumps inside of me as if it knows the sound. Last night Jean came home and shoved me hard against the wall. His fingers burned my wrists. "You're still wearing the filthy dress you were in this morning! Why don't you ever wear the red one I bought you? Not good enough for you?"

"It's too tight just now!"

He slapped a hand over my mouth. "Shut up! Do you want to have Ma and Pa rushing up here to tick me off? They'd blame me for making you upset. They wouldn't know that you provoke me just to get a rise out of me! Everything bad that happens around here has always been my fault, according to them. And that's just what you'd want them to think, you cow!"

He gripped my shoulders hard and shook me. Jean always takes care not to touch my stomach and hurt the baby but my head crashed against the wall and I pleaded with him to stop. For once, he let go and stalked away. The baby threshed and jerked inside me as if I was still being shaken.

I just read over what I wrote back in August. I didn't want the baby then but now I've changed my mind. Affection for it flooded my heart as soon as I felt those first flickers of movement. I don't know if I look forward to its birth next March or dread it. I long to hold another little bundle in my arms, yet I fear what Jean might do to me when I have no medical condition to keep him from pounding me in one of his tempers. Then I get frightened that the baby will be another girl and he'll beat her too.

I love Suzanne with all my heart but when I look at her prettiness, I doubt that our second little girl could possibly be so beautiful and then he'll compare them and hate the new one even more.

January 1st

My legs have been cramping as they did before at this stage of my pregnancy.

Mother joined us for lunch on Christmas Day. We had it with the Dupont family downstairs in the dining room. At the end of the day, I walked with Mother to her train station.

"I just can't take to that kid of yours," she said.

"Suzanne?" I felt stung.

"Look at the way she fawns over that idiot of a father. In all the time I sat at that table, she ignored you."

I explained, "She doesn't see Jean much and she loves him."

Mother turned to study me. "Why doesn't she see him much? Doesn't he take good care of you? Does he have a mistress? Has he grown tired of you?"

For one moment, I longed to tell her about the way he treats me but had enough sense to know it would be a waste of time. For all her mental energy, Mother is so slight and thin, there is nothing much she could do for us even if she wanted to help. I don't know if she'd care anymore and, I admit, a small, proud part inside of me doesn't want to hear her tell me that I should have listened to her before I ran away and married him.

"I only meant that he works hard."

Mother snorted. "Works hard at being a jerk."

I'm actually relieved that Suzanne loves Jean so much because it makes her life safe. He likes to feel loved. I've come to think of Suzanne as my own little safety shield. If she preferred me over him, I hate to think of how he'd take it out on her in his drunken tempers.

Suzanne runs so fast, I find myself grunting to keep up with her, slow and heavy as I've become. She laughs to see me try. I glimpse her merry little face hiding behind trees and bushes, calling, "Mama, boo!" She thinks I can't see her sparkly eyes looking at me.

I love her and don't blame her for preferring Jean. He's a very handsome man and to her baby heart, he's a dashing hero.

March 11th

I'm a mother again. After another long, harrowing labour I was exhausted. I've heard people say that each successive birth gets easier. In my opinion, that is not the case.

The midwife, a lovely woman who spoke English to me, handed me my tiny baby wrapped in a soft, white blanket. The feathery soft sheet of dark hair and delicate profile were like Suzanne's but this baby was slightly smaller. Only eight pounds. I stroked the fine, almost transparent little eyebrows and managed to croak, "She's gorgeous!"

"He," the midwife corrected.

I believe I must have gaped at her like a mad woman. "Pardon?"

She gave me a wide beam. "Madame Dupont, you have a beautiful little son."

A tear rolled down my cheek and fell on his velvet cheek. He turned his face and gave a muffled sneeze. The sight of a boy so tiny made my heart ache. The woman must've thought me completely daft but I opened the blanket to see for myself. And guess what! He is a boy!

March 29th

Jean is overjoyed about his son. He holds him all the time without being asked and doesn't pass him back until the poor little mite gets a tummy ache. The baby suffers from colic. Suzanne never had it so I have no experience to draw from and hardly know what to do for him. There seems to be nothing I can do but cuddle him and wait it out while he arches his back and screams. It brings out the worst in all of us.

"Do something, you stupid woman! You can't leave him in such pain! What sort of mother are you?" Jean's eyes flash sparks at me.

"I'm doing the best I can." I've tried feeding our son slower but my milk streams out and he gulps when he drinks. I've tried burping him for longer, rubbing his wee tummy and putting him to sleep with his front pressed into me. Whenever he's hungry, I groan. I know I have to feed him but I steel myself for what I know will happen. He will soon be writhing and screaming again.

"What's wrong with your foul milk?" Jean snaps.

"If only I knew!" I've been eating a bland diet, chewing my food slowly and trying to think positive thoughts, but whenever Jean steps near us, I feel myself turn tense. The baby's agony is heart-rending to watch. His legs stiffen. His face turns different shades of red and I worry that he'll swallow his own quivering tongue. He can screech for a whole hour. When I think neither he nor the rest of us can bear any more, his eyes close and he slumps against my chest with his nose and forehead covered in tiny sweat beads.

The midwife said, "Don't worry, this rarely lasts beyond the first six months."

She was trying to comfort me but I wanted to scream. How can we bear this four times daily for six months?

For the second time, I had no say in the naming of our baby. I would have liked to have called him Jerome, after my father, but Jean has insisted on Piers Philippe Dupont. "Philippe" is a tribute to his own father which surprised me because Jean usually has nothing but a mouthful of invective for the old man. Perhaps blood runs thicker than water. I'm not sure why he chose the name "Piers." I'll get used to it.

Piers is a lovely, cuddly baby when he doesn't have colic. He likes nothing more than being held close to my heart. His eyes are the same translucent grey as Suzanne's yet there is a wistful quality in their depths as if he's lived through his share of trouble and turmoil, although he's not even three weeks old. Must be all that colic. If ever there was a baby I'd want to wrap in cotton wool, this would be the one.

I dare to hope that Piers may be the turning point in my relationship with Jean. Jean so wanted a son from the start. If our children could have arrived in the opposite sequence, first boy, then girl, things might have been easier for a few years. Now that Jean has the boy he wanted, I am praying that he'll give up drinking binges with his rough friends.

May 18th

At two a.m. last night, Piers had just woken me for a feed. Suzanne was sound asleep in her cot and while I was sitting up in bed nursing Piers, the bedroom door swung open and Jean lurched in. I was sorry he had to come home while the baby was awake. Jean never leaves Piers alone. He bumped twice into the wall before he made it to our bed and a sour odour enveloped him. He blinked his bloodshot eyes at us and slurred, "I see my son and heir is awake."

"Not for long," I whispered. "I'm about to put him down for sleep."

But Jean's huge hands plucked the baby off my breast. Piers' face immediately crumpled and he screamed.

"No. You have him all day and he's going to play with his papa now." Jean's common sense seems to evaporate when he's drunk and he forgets how to handle a baby. He held Piers at arm's length and shook him, trying to stop the crying. Piers' head flopped and his howling mouth opened even wider.

I pleaded, "Give him back. You'll drop him."

But Jean gave me a back-handed slap across my mouth. "Shut up, woman! You've done this to him! You've taught him to hate me. He's a mollycoddle."

"He's only nine weeks old! He's not old enough to play games yet. He needs me most of all now."

"Like hell!" Jean stood up with Piers' head slumped over his elbow and made his uncertain way across the floor to Suzanne's room. I saw him shake her awake. "Would Papa's princess like to come for a drive?"

Her foggy eyes brightened when she saw him. I'm not certain she understood his question but she said, "Oh, oui."

I wrapped my hand around his elbow. "Please don't be crazy."

He stiffened and I knew I'd chosen the wrong tactics. I tried to change them. "You look tired and I know you've been working hard. You and the children all need a good sleep. Then you can play tomorrow."

He brushed me off and shifted Piers to one arm so that he could help Suzanne up. Jean could barely manage to stroke her hair straight. "Your mama thinks she has sole right to you and your brother, ma petite, but we'll show her." He tickled her nose with a tress of her hair and Suzanne giggled.

Jean turned to look at me on their way out and said, "If you wake Papa or Andre, I promise I'll take les enfants away and you'll never see them again. You know I never make empty threats. I'm doing you a favour. Have a few hours of sleep and we'll be back before you know it."

I heard Piers' crying all the way down the stairs and then the front door slammed shut. My heart was being torn apart. I have learned to take Jean at his word. If I tried to seek help from the rest of the household, he'd keep his promise to take the children away from me. However, I was petrified that he'd have a drunken accident and hurt them. I knelt at a chair beside the window and the hours passed like weeks. I even tried to pray but I'm sure God doesn't listen to me anymore. Maybe He's letting me suffer the consequences of my choice to marry Jean. My breasts swelled like over-inflated footballs and milk streamed down and drenched my nightie.

At dawn, the car finally returned. My trembling legs could barely carry me downstairs. The air was crisp and cold. My bare feet were burning on the frosty gravel and Jean strode past me into the house without saying a word.

I flung open the car door and there were my two angels blinking at me. Suzanne was no longer smiling. She rubbed a hand across her face and babbled, "Cold! Cold! Bubby cwy!" I took her face between my hands and kissed her icy cheek, then snatched Piers out of his infant seat. He'd stopped crying now. He was gasping mouthfuls of air as if he were choking on it. His body shivered as I pressed him against my warmth. His grow-suit was drenched and bitterly cold.

I hurried the children inside to sit beside the radiator and nurse Piers. Suzanne tiptoed to our bedroom to stand beside Jean and watch his snoring slumber. She touched his cheek and cocked her head with an expression of grave concern.

Piers' tiny, icy fingers slowly turned warm but he was too overwrought to respond to me. He didn't stop shivering for over half an hour. He kept turning his face away from my breast and gasping. After a very long time, he began to suckle. It gave me an intense feeling of relief.

At that moment, I knew I hated Jean. It's written down in ink. I can't believe I even considered falling back in love with him. He'll never change. I don't even want to love him anymore. I just want him to stay away from me and the children but I know that's too much to hope for.

February 24th

Piers is eleven months old and Jean snipes at him continuously because he can't walk yet. Suzanne walked at nine months, so Jean believes that Piers must be very slow and backward because he still crawls. Even his mother tries to assure him, "Suzanne was just remarkably early," but he listens to no-one.

This evening, he jerked Piers up by the shoulders and said, "Two steps is all I ask of you! Take two steps for your Papa or I'll smack your hand."

Piers swayed on his feet and whimpered. The poor baby knows that his father is always cross with him. Whenever he hears Jean's

The Risky Way Home

heavy tread on the landing, his knees thump the floorboards as he crawls as fast as he can to me. I can't protect him, though. Jean is enraged whenever he sees Piers fleeing to me for refuge.

I had to sit there, helpless, again. When Jean let go of him, Piers fell into a heap on the floor and howled. He stretched his little arms out in my direction but Jean picked him up and smacked both hands, hard. "You don't need her! She's already turned you into a sap and a milksop. Now, just walk!"

By the end of the session, Piers had hit the floor five more times and already sported the beginnings of at least three new bruises because he is simply not ready to walk. I'm no child expert but I think that Jean's efforts are just setting Piers back. You don't teach a child to walk. Once I would have tried to reason with Jean but now I know that he will not be reasoned with. Nothing will make him understand that Piers' temperament is simply different from Suzanne's. She was restless, adventurous and eager to explore. Piers is not like that at all. I've brought out all the baby toys that Suzanne was never interested in. Piers is content to sit with them for an hour, feeling the different textured fabrics and shaking the rattles. I'm sure his attention span must be long for his age but Jean brushes me off when I tell him so. "You're turning that boy into a girl," he says.

It is hard to watch something so wrong taking place right before my eyes, knowing there is nothing I can do about it.

September 8th

Suzanne has been sulking all day.

"Come and read a story with Mama," I coaxed her.

She pouted and pushed me away. "I don't want you. I want Papa!"

In the morning, she'd been hovering around Jean's elbow while he was trying to make Piers catch a ball.

"I can do it, Papa."

He brushed her aside. "I know you can but I want to see your brother do it."

Her face crumpled and she retreated to a corner. Yet she still loves him devotedly.

Jean's thinking is completely warped where Piers is concerned. When the baby finally took his first four steps just after his first birthday,

I allowed myself to draw a breath of relief hoping that now Jean would get off his back. But things have become worse. Jean has gone far beyond expecting Piers to do whatever Suzanne could do at the same age. He expects him to perform feats that no normal eighteen-month-old baby could possibly do, such as reciting poems and handling tennis racquets like a junior athlete. He's totally forgotten that Suzanne had been several months older than Piers before he had her memorising little rhymes. He has made that boy so traumatised and uptight, it's a wonder he opens his mouth ever.

Perhaps if Suzanne had been the quiet, reflective baby and Piers the outgoing, talkative one, Jean would have been happy. I've given up trying to guess that man's thoughts.

December 27th

All week long, Suzanne and Piers have had a croupy chest virus. Suzanne started to mend but Piers grew steadily worse. I wanted to take him to a doctor but Jean wouldn't allow it. He'd been belting the baby and I'm sure he wouldn't want any doctor to see Piers' bruises.

"Do just what you did for Suzanne and he'll be fine." Jean shot a glare at Piers. "He needs to toughen up."

Then, three nights before Christmas, Jean was at the pub and the rest of the Dupont family were out at a work break-up party. The children and I were alone in the house when Piers took a sudden, shocking turn for the worse. His breathing became loud and rattly. I dashed to his cot. I'd seen or heard nothing like it before. He was sitting up, gazing up at me with big, frightened eyes. His chest heaved for every gasp he took.

I snatched him up and dashed to the bathroom but holding him over a steamy sink as I'd done when he had croup didn't help. In fact, it made the wheezing sound worse. My own eyes filled with steam so I could hardly see. I turned him over my knees and thumped his back. He kept making choking sounds as if some giant hand was squeezing his windpipe.

I don't know how my rubbery legs managed to take me to the phone. Holding Piers in my arms, I dialled for an ambulance. Then I tried to let the family know. I had no idea where Jean and his friends were carousing but I knew where Papa Dupont's break-up party was.

Papa could not be found but Andre came to the phone. I spoke to him while Suzanne wandered out of her bedroom and plucked my arm to be lifted up too. Piers' head drooped on my shoulder, wheezing that horrible rattly noise into my ear.

"I don't know what's happening to him. He's choking!"

"Moira, the ambulance will be there in a flash." Andre's voice was steady and calm. "You keep that little man wrapped up warm. I'm leaving now. I'll see you at the hospital. I'll be there pronto."

The ambulance arrived. Piers clung to me when the men tried to prise him away. If he hadn't been so choked up, I know he would have howled his protest. They tried to reassure him but he threshed and kicked when they placed a rubber mask over his nose. It covered his whole face except for his wide eyes which darted back and forth above its rim. Every vein and sinew in his neck bulged as he strained for air. I had to sit with him on my knees and Suzanne was sobbing by now, "Is he going to die?"

"No, no, no!" How could I reassure her when tears dripped down my own nose? She huddled beside me with a wretched expression on her face.

We were almost at the hospital. I saw the great "Emergency" sign beaming like a beacon through the foggy night. As soon as we got inside, a thickset doctor took over. Without saying a word to me, he began barking orders to his staff. "Bring an adrenaline injection...We need aminophyllin and cortisone." The intimidating sound of those long words made my flesh crawl. Piers struggled and moaned when he saw the needle but nobody seemed to care about his state of mind. They were too busy trying to save his life. He looked so tiny when they took him away to connect to another breathing apparatus. At last, a female nurse addressed me. "You need to fill out admission forms."

I tried, but my hand was shaking horribly. That was when Andre came striding down the long, grey corridor. He sat beside me and touched my arm, reassuring me with all the words he could find.

"Everything passes. I'm sure God has plans for you all. Just think He already knows the grown man Piers will be some day." He tried to ruffle Suzanne's hair but she shied away from him and ducked her head beneath my chin. Jean has taught her how to shun her uncle.

"Madame Dupont," the doctor called. He glanced at Andre. "Is this your husband?"

"No. I'm her brother-in-law."

The doctor turned back to me. "Where's your husband?"

My heart was almost bursting. "I don't know! How's my son?"

"We've stabilised him. You can come through."

I came after him, carrying Suzanne. The doctor hadn't said that Andre couldn't follow, so he did. I saw instantly that Piers' breathing was deeper and more even. Two spots of pink had returned to his cheeks and when he saw me, he stretched his arms to me.

I turned giddy as I sank beside the stretcher bed and hugged him. "Merci, Doctor Rousseau, merci."

"Now, what's all this?" The doctor's tone was stern. He raised Piers' little pyjama shirt and there was a great ugly bruise on his rib-cage, purple in the centre and greeny-yellow around the edges. My heart jolted.

The doctor's eyes probed into mine. "How did this happen?"

Suzanne was tugging my face and I remember trying to pull her hands away while my mind whirled to think of something to say. "I don't know. I think he had an accident outside with his father last week."

The doctor watched my face for several moments longer, then curtly nodded. "He appears to be a very frail, anxious little boy."

"He is." I should have kept quiet because I don't think he'd expected a reply. I wanted to hide my face and never look up again. How could this strange doctor know that my silence protects the children? If I told the truth, Jean would kill me.

Andre was also gaping at the bruise on Piers' rib cage. When he looked at me, I knew that he knew. I shouldn't have called Andre from his party.

"Your son's attack was asthma," Doctor Rousseau told me.

"I didn't know asthma could be so..." I couldn't find words to express my shock. I'd known asthmatics but I'd never imagined anything like the frightening ordeal Piers had just gone through.

"It can be a life threatening condition. That was quite a severe attack," the doctor explained. "You need to make an appointment to visit a clinic with your husband. The staff will explain to you both, step by step, what must be done for Piers. It's not just a matter of treating him when he has an attack. You must learn preventative measures, to lessen the chances of this happening again."

When the doctor left us, Andre mumbled, "Jean will pay for what he does to you and those children. He's no man. He's a fiend from hell. He always had a fiery temper when we were young. I wanted to believe that he'd grown wiser. I'm furious with myself for giving him the benefit of the doubt." He smashed his hand into his fist softly so that Suzanne and Piers couldn't see him.

"Moira, I'm so sorry," Andre went on. "My hiding from the truth has caused you and the children so much pain."

"Please don't say a word to Jean," I pleaded in a whisper. "He'll murder us! You have to believe me. You won't be helping us if you tell him. We can bear it if he doesn't know, but if you try to stop him, you'll make things worse.'

I saw that his eyes were shiny. "Moira, things can't go on this way. He will kill you anyway, all three of you, over time. We have to get you and Suzanne and Piers away from him."

"We can't leave him! Andre, don't you have any idea? That'd be the worst thing we could do. He'd chase us. He wouldn't let me leave him for one hour!"

At last we were given the all clear to go home and Andre drove us in his car. All the way, I thought about what he'd said. Piers was sleeping soundly by the time we arrived. I lifted him out of the car and felt the warmth of his precious head and the tickle of his hair beneath my chin. He still had the antiseptic hospital smell. I would have died if anything had happened to him. The sight of the elegant mausoleum I've been slowly dying in for three years made me so unhappy, I could barely force myself to go inside and face Jean.

Before I entered, Andre touched my elbow.

"I've been thinking hard. I'll look out for somewhere safe for you and the children to go. I know I haven't been much assistance so far and that will always weigh on my mind, but you can count on me from now on."

I shook my head. "Nowhere will ever be safe enough." Why won't that penetrate his thick head?

Andre placed a finger over his lips and disappeared to his wing of the house. Now I am uptight and confused. The slightest noise makes me jump. Whenever I hear a step on the stair, I imagine that Jean is coming to belt me. Whenever I hear Piers cough or draw a sharp breath in his sleep, I rush to him, imagining that it might be another asthma attack. Whenever I see Andre, I tremble with fear that he's going to do something rash. And whenever I consider that nothing will happen and that we'll go on as before, I want to die anyway.

December 31st

Jean did fly into a raging fury a few nights later when he received an account in the post for our emergency visit to the hospital. He was pacing the length of the room with flashing eyes and barely waited for me to put the children to bed before he pitched into me.

"I told you not to see a doctor!"

"I had to, or Piers would have died of asthma."

Jean's mouth twisted as if he wanted to spit. "Asthma? I can tell you why he has asthma! You breathed in your mother's foul-smelling cigarette smoke while you were pregnant with him!"

I stayed quiet. Once I might have replied that I'd barely seen my mother during either pregnancy but one thing I've learned about Jean is that he does not listen to reason.

"Why did Andre need to stick his beak in?" Jean's fingers dug into my shoulders. "Why did you call him?"

"I would've called you, if I'd known where you were."

"Don't give me that hogwash! You're a sneak and a filthy stirrer!" He swung his hand and belted me across the side of the head. "I'll bet you told him rotten stories about me. You told him how Piers got those bruises. Didn't you? You want my name to be mud. You want to see my family hate me even more than they always have."

My right ear was buzzing. My voice might have been loud but it sounded hazy. "I never told him a...'

I got no further. Jean shoved me against the wall and boxed my other ear to make me "own up." In the past, he's beaten me until I've agreed with anything he accused me of, just to make him stop, but there was no way I was going to admit to such a preposterous lie.

The Risky Way Home

"Tell me it's the truth!" he was growling. "Tell me it's the truth and I'll stop!"

"Never!" I'd sunk down on my haunches against the wall. The inside of my mouth had filled with blood and my head was full of the hum of a hive of wasps. The most frightening thing about Jean is that he always believes he's the only person who's ever right. I cannot recall that he's ever shown a twinge of compunction over anything he's done, even when I still loved him. I'm now certain he was born without a conscience. I fully expected him to murder me but suddenly he released my arms. I huddled there blinking at him, hardly daring to believe that he'd stopped.

"I know how to make you admit it." He stalked into Piers' room and bent down over the cot. Then I could hardly breathe.

"NO!" I screamed.

But Jean had hauled Piers out of bed. The little boy blinked groggily and when his eyes focused on his father, he began to whimper.

"Stop that squalling!" Jean smacked him fiercely across the legs.

"Leave him alone!" I pleaded.

When Piers heard my voice, he stretched out his arms to me but Jean flung him savagely on the floor and kicked him. Piers let out a cry. I got down on my knees and tried to wedge myself between them. I was hovering over Piers, trying to shield him from the blows. I felt his breath and tears on my face but Jean wrenched me back by the hair, shoved me out in the sitting room and locked Piers' bedroom door.

"You're the one who won't admit the truth so you can listen to me punish your son instead."

I'll die if I ever have to live through anything like that again. Every vicious strike of hand on flesh, every sharp cry from Piers, tore another shred from my heart. I pounded the door with all of my strength, although I knew full well that it would achieve nothing. I knew that Mama and Papa Dupont were out at another party. Andre wasn't home either and we have no nearby neighbours. I dashed to the phone to dial the emergency number but then Jean lurched out of Piers' room and snatched my arm. He ripped the phone out of its socket and flung it against the wall.

"I'm going out! If you tell a soul, I'll kill both of you. I could do it so that nobody would ever know." He slammed the door behind him.

I hurried in to Piers. Jean usually avoids our faces when he belts us but this time he was not so careful. Piers was bleeding profusely from his nose. He squinted at me as if it hurt him to open his eyes any wider and gasped, "Mama." There was a swelling around his eye and a cut on his bottom lip.

I gathered him as gently as I could in my arms, kissed his forehead and caressed his face. A pulse behind his eyelid pounded against my fingertips. Another one hammered hard within his neck. Nobody could ever find a sweeter baby and Piers' life struck me suddenly as more fragile than a flower in a storm. It would take just one extra wrench of Jean's hand in a fit of rage to snuff the life out of the little boy. I knew then that Andre is right. My silence is not protecting us from being murdered by Jean.

I heard a mournful, muffled noise from behind Suzanne's closed door. I fetched her out and we all went to the sitting room couch. Piers rested his face against my neck and Suzanne knelt on the floor, huddled against my knees. It was she who finally broke the silence.

"Mama, I wish you and Piers would stop making Papa angry."

I could not even think of an answer. What would I say? I was too choked-up to talk anyway. There I sat, rocking Piers and stroking Suzanne's hair for hour after hour when we were startled by a rap on the French door panes. My blood turned to ice. I imagined that Jean had returned and that if I made the slightest move, he'd kill us. I drew the children closer and forced myself to turn and look. It was Mother. Although she's never hiked up the steep hill to knock on our French door before, her expression was impatient, as if I was foolish to be surprised.

"Moira, let me in!"

Without setting Piers down, I hastened to do so. She breezed over the threshold and looked me up and down.

"Your brother-in-law sent me. Now, tell me why..." She broke off at the sight of Piers' bloodied shirt and face. I'd never seen Mother lost for words before but it lasted only a moment. "Open your dressing gown!" she demanded.

I instinctively refused. "No, let me get dressed instead. I've just been lazing around..."

"I'm your mother!" she cut me off. "Just do it!"

I found myself obeying. It was like revisiting the past which I used to hate, but certainly preferable to facing the near future, when Jean would return home. I was too sad and tired and completely heartbroken to resist. So I unbuttoned my top three buttons. It was enough to reveal dark bruising around my collar bone. Mother tugged loose the shoulders so she could see my upper arms, which were just as mottled. Her mouth was a familiar straight, tight line.

"So this is the way that animal you married treats you and his children?"

Instead of answering, I found myself sobbing. I hitched the dressing gown back over my shoulders and buried my face in Piers' hair.

She said, "You can't stay with him for another moment." Then I raised my eyes to see if she was serious.

Mother went to fetch a damp cloth from the kitchen to clean Piers' bloodied face. I just sat there while she snapped at Suzanne to get herself dressed. Suzanne shot her a saucy glare on her way out. She dislikes her grandmother's harsh tone, but I barely mustered the strength to care if Mother noticed Suzanne's expression. Piers nestled his head beneath my chin and his eyelids began to droop. I can't remember how I got started, but there I was telling Mother all that I'd kept to myself for the past four years. I guess the relief of finally getting it all off my chest was greater than the pride which had kept me silent for so long.

At the start, Mother sat still and kept her eyes riveted on my face but soon began pacing back and forth across the rug.

"Don't Philippe and Yvette have any idea what goes on beneath their own roof?"

I wearily shook my head. "Not the full extent of it, I'm sure."

"What sort of idiots are they? I'm going to see that the fiend they call their son gets what he deserves and nobody is going to stop me! Moira, why have you put up with this, you foolish, foolish girl? Damn the Duponts. I'm going to call the police."

I had to shake off my apathy for the children's sake. I shook my head and my teeth began to chatter. "Please don't. If you do, he'll kill us. Even if they went so far as to put him in prison, he'd sit there brooding about it, getting more and more furious. He'd be back to murder us. I'm certain of it. Please Mother, if you want to see us live, don't tell anybody, let alone the police."

She uttered a swear word. "Andre Dupont was right. I need to take you and the children as far from that swine as I can, where he would never dream of looking for you. Then I'll tell the French police."

The idea of being able to escape from Jean made me light-headed. Anywhere away from him would be heaven on earth. My stomach began to churn. I felt an urge to hunch over the toilet bowl and knew that if I did, I would almost certainly be sick.

"If we go back to England, he'll find us there." As I spoke, the nausea swelled higher again, to my throat. "I need more than the Channel between us and Jean. Nowhere would be far enough away." Dimly in the background, I heard Suzanne clattering away in her toy box and singing a little French tune.

Mother sat down and leaned close to me. "How about Australia?"

A wild hope ignited in my heart.

"Tell me, does he know that I come from Australia?"

Although Piers is quite light, he suddenly felt like a lead blanket draped across my knees. I wanted to be up pacing the rug. "I don't think so. I might've told him before we were married but I'm sure he would've forgotten."

"I've never mentioned my background to Yvette and Philippe," she was muttering. "It'll be the safest place for you and the children. There's no doubt about that."

"Mother, what a wonderful idea!"

"Don't breathe a word of it to the children." I saw her scrutinise Piers to be certain he was sound asleep. Mother is a tiny person but her expression was fixed like granite. "If either of them lets it slip, our game will be up."

"I'd never tell them," I promised. How I admire Mother for this. Her cool thinking head is amazing. "I don't know how to thank you."

"I don't want to hear this now. I ordered you not to marry that man and you defied me. This is the cost of going against my better judgment."

Once I would have resented her words but not anymore. If this plan of hers comes off, I'll owe her a huger debt than I could ever possibly repay.

The Risky Way Home

January 5th

Today was our escape day.

We had breakfast down at the big table. Mama Dupont went out with her bridge group and the three men left for work. I could not bear to look at Jean lest he read my secret in my eyes. I glanced at the sandy, thinning hair on the back of Andre's head as he stepped out of the door, knowing that I will never see him again. I feel bad about not giving Andre a clue where we'll be because I know he genuinely cares. I won't dare send him a line when we settle down. I know that he'd tear up or burn my letter but it wouldn't be worth the risk. Andre might have turned out to be quite a good friend.

Suzanne and Piers loitered over their oatmeal when everyone else had left. I could not swallow a mouthful. It took all my energy and focus to keep my voice calm and cheerful. I helped them to get dressed quicker than usual. "Make haste, my sweethearts, it's going to be a good day. We're going out for a surprise."

I kept my eyes glued to the front windows. At last a black taxi-cab arrived with Mother seated beside the driver. My insides lurched as if I were already airsick. I was glad I'd eaten nothing. Clutching our two bags, I hustled the children out to the taxi. Despite my efforts to appear calm, they both began to cry.

Suzanne grumbled, "You didn't tell us we were going with Grandma!"

Piers sobbed, "I want Jacques."

My heart skipped a beat. How could I have forgotten? Jacques is a fuzzy brown teddy bear, shabby and squashed, but Piers loves him. When he's frightened or upset, he often cuddles Jacques. The sight of his grandmother's grim face in the front seat might have made him want his bear. I asked the driver to please wait so that I could rush back into the house. I had to retrieve the key I'd just slid beneath the doormat and my hand trembled so hard, I could barely turn it. To my utmost relief, Jacques was not difficult to find. Piers had tucked him beneath the sheet at the foot of his cot.

I couldn't blame Piers for needing comfort. Mother's scathing glare almost scorched me as I slid in beside the children. "Moira, sometimes I swear I could slap you! How dare you hold us up for something so stupid!"

Piers clutched the bear to his chest and sucked his thumb. I was as annoyed with myself as Mother was, for a different reason. How could I have forgotten to pack Jacques in the first place? Piers has little enough to love without depriving him of his favourite toy. We could buy him another teddy but it would not be Jacques.

Suzanne's face magically cleared when I told her we'd be going to the airport to catch a plane to London. She thoroughly enjoyed the flight across the Channel and even at Heathrow Airport, hopped from one foot to the other, fairly bursting with excitement. She did not stop chattering about everything she saw. I could not concentrate on a word she said but I was glad she was happy, because Mother had been snapping at the children for every little thing and Piers was pouting and dragging his feet.

We'd been on our next flight for several hours and I was still tightly wound like a yo-yo when the sun began to sink and we could see nothing but inky sea beneath us. Suzanne plucked my sleeve and looked up at me with her big shiny eyes. "I'm bored with this plane now. I want to go home to Papa."

Taking her hand, I began to search for words to explain that we were not going back. Mother beat me to it. She'd grown irritable with Suzanne's incessant chatter.

"We aren't going back. Your father is a bad man. We're going to live in Australia and the sooner we arrive, the better. Now, keep your lip buttoned for just ten minutes!"

The colour drained from Suzanne's face. When she opened her mouth I thought she was going to be sick but she let out a screech. Mother smacked her legs and Suzanne screamed louder. She kicked the back of the chair in front of us. When I tried to stop her, she rolled her hands into little fists and began to punch me. Every head in the plane must have turned to look but I was too embarrassed to glance up. Suzanne had set Piers off too but at least we couldn't hear his whimpering over her shrieking. It took the combined strength of Mother and me to grasp Suzanne's arms and legs and hold them down. After a tremendous struggle, she slumped in her seat.

I ventured to wrap my arm around her. "I'm certain you'll have an

The Risky Way Home

even better time in Australia than you ever did at home."

She shoved my hand off her shoulder. "I want Papa. He's going to be very mad. You're the bad one. You and her!"

Mother ordered us all to keep quiet. Suzanne tilted her pointy chin and Piers crawled onto my lap with Jacques clutched tightly against his chest. Both children nodded off to sleep with sheer exhaustion. Suzanne's pixie face wore a scowl even in slumber and I was able to trace my finger down the dried tear tracks on her face.

After a long stop-over in Bangkok, we boarded another plane. The increasing distance between me and Jean helped unravel the tight knot in my stomach. I leaned my head back to relax. The sky was streaked with light and soft, golden sunshine poured over my face. I closed my eyes and allowed myself to relish the warmth. I'd not experienced such refreshing peace for more than four years.

The pilot's voice over the speakers told us to peer down for a good, clear view of Australia. I gazed out at powdery looking wasteland, rolling in red waves for as far as my eye could see. There were occasional narrow tracks like thin threads in a bright blanket. They seemed to begin and end nowhere. I didn't allow myself to think about trying to live in such a bleak country. For now, the sheer monotony soothed my soul.

The passengers behind us commented about the barrenness of the land to one of the stewardesses. She laughed and assured them, "It's different in the large cities. Most Australians live around the coasts. It's beautiful and full of colour." I might try to work up a bit of excitement tomorrow.

Suzanne began to stir. I nudged her to take a look at the land. After a quick glance, she bowed her head and wept afresh.

"I want my park. I want my house and my pretty dresses. I want Papa."

I spoke across the children's heads to Mother. "Do you think she'll ever come 'round and forgive me?"

When Mother turned her face to look at me, I saw that her cheeks were wet with tears. She dashed one from her cheek and grumbled, "To be perfectly honest, I couldn't care less. I'll never come 'round. I never wanted to set eyes on this country again. Look what you've done to me. You've broken my heart."

I feel so bad I can't find words to speak. I can hardly even find words to write how guilty I feel about causing Mother and Suzanne to live somewhere they'll hate.

March 14th

We've been settled here in Australia for two months and I've begun to overcome my fear that Jean will find us. As Mother reasoned, how could he? We've covered our tracks so well. Although she used to live in Sydney, we've chosen a large coastal town an hour's drive from Adelaide, way down in South Australia. It has a good sized shopping centre with many of the conveniences Mother loves, such as theatres and book stores. We've paid a deposit on a lovely old house with a deep verandah on a wide, shady street. I can hear the soothing rumble of the ocean from the back window. Mother would have preferred a larger, grander house but we both agreed that we feel safer in a modest-sized one. Surely no crazy Frenchman could possibly find us here. The more I think about it, the safer I feel. I wonder if I will ever feel totally sure of our safety, beyond a doubt.

We've taken the precaution of changing our surname to one I'm sure Jean has never even heard. We can't possibly remain Duponts or become Tylers. He knows both those names. It was Mother who decided that we ought to adopt her long-forgotten maiden name, Bowman. Moira Bowman. It still sounds very strange but the more I write it or repeat it to myself, the quicker I'll get used to it.

For the first time since our arrival, I had three solid sleeps last week. I still dash into the children's bedrooms to check on them the moment I wake up. I always breathe a sigh of relief to see their peaceful, sleeping little faces.

The time will soon come when Suzanne will begin school. I can only hope and pray that being around other children will settle her down. At the moment, she tilts her pointy chin and refuses to speak any of the English she's learned. Mother snaps, "Let the little wretch speak French. She'll soon be anxious to change when other children make fun of her." Sometimes I wonder why they persist in resenting each other so doggedly, this sixty-five-year-old woman and four-year-old

The Risky Way Home

girl, who actually have so much in common, not the least, their hatred of this new country.

If I praise the warm climate, Mother is sure to complain that it dries out her skin. There are beautiful, brightly coloured birds here. Rosellas and galahs and cockatoos. That stewardess was spot-on about the vivid colour of Australia. I've never seen such brilliant plumage but Mother says their raucous squawks make her head ache and Suzanne stares at the ground and refuses to even look at them.

To my surprise, little Piers has latched onto using English beautifully. I love to hear to him prattle. He still wakes up in the night once or twice a week screaming with nightmares, as he used to back in Paris. I rush in to find his forehead and nose covered with tiny beads of sweat and his eyes bright with terror. That alone is enough to convince me that leaving Jean was the right thing to do.

I wonder if Piers will ever entirely forget his traumatic infancy. He is painfully shy. Whenever people speak to him, he ducks his head and avoids eye contact. Mother scolds him for it and he always scrambles onto my lap for a cuddle. I cannot seem to hug or kiss the sad expression from those big, dark eyes. He looks like a small refugee, filling in time waiting for some calamity to occur.

I know that Piers loves me but sometimes feel that he does not trust me. I try to assure him that nothing will hurt him, yet he cringes and turns pale whenever he hears footsteps on our porch or a knock at the door. I can't blame the poor lamb. I failed so dismally at protecting him from his father for so long. Now that we managed to escape from Jean so easily, I wish with all my heart that I'd removed Piers from him several long months ago.

Last Sunday morning, I stood on the back steps and heard the sweet peal of church bells. I had a sudden yearning to attend a church service but Mother has forbidden it. "God didn't help you escape from your pig of a husband. I did!" At one time, I might have argued with her but I don't have the heart to disobey now. I'm well aware that my refusal to obey her four years ago, when she ordered me not to marry Jean, has cost her dearly. Under the circumstances, I'm reluctant to argue with her. A rift with Mother is the last thing I want now.

Chapter 15

Casey turned a page and found the rest of the journal blank. Moira's diary was finished. For whatever reason, she had decided not to continue recording the story of their new life in Australia.

Casey went down to the bathroom to dash cold water over her face. She was a sticky mess. Earlier tears had dried up and fresh ones streamed down to take their place. Her face was a blotchy mask that creased into wrinkles when she pulled a face at herself. She washed it, patted it dry and returned upstairs to curl in her window seat.

The book she had expected to fill the whole week was over in one sitting. *Moira must've tucked it away somewhere because she couldn't stand the sight of it anymore. It probably brought back too many memories of Jean.* Starlight stung Casey's eyes.

Now she saw why old Henrietta Bowman was so mean to her grandchildren. It wasn't because of anything they'd done. They just reminded her of Jean Dupont! Casey now understood why Moira had been so careful to toe the line all those years. And why she hadn't let Suzanne join the student exchange to France.

Casey's restless mind would not allow her to sit still. She returned downstairs, flung open the front door and paced the moonlit verandah. Moira's story had a happy ending. *So why do I feel so sad?* She hoped walking would drive the lingering impression of gloom from her head but it didn't. Whenever Casey paused to lean over the rails and drink in the stillness, sorrow draped over her like a shroud.

Henrietta Bowman had never forgiven her daughter or grown fond of Moira's children. She was soon to die, as bitter as she'd been the day she'd turned to her daughter on the plane and told Moira that she'd broken her heart. And Suzanne still resented Moira too much to want anything to do with her. Poor Moira, who had so longed to make her family happy, had failed. Casey pressed her eyes into her pyjama sleeve. This was no fictional story but the real life of people she knew. It was *not* a happy ending.

But Piers is happy. Casey clutched at any bright spot to Moira's story. She took the stairs to her bedroom three at a time and huddled beneath her quilt. Piers was undoubtedly the happiest person in the whole mess. That didn't make much sense because he'd had as many negative experiences as any of the others. He had borne the brunt of his grandmother's aversion as much as Suzanne. He'd been teased and shunned at school and fathered a child from a broken relationship. And he'd been treated appallingly by his own father when he was far too young to understand why. Casey couldn't figure Piers out. He had every right to be as mixed-up and embittered as the rest of his family. But for some reason, he wasn't. It was all part of his weirdness, she thought.

Each day at work seemed a whole month long. Eric was making an obvious effort to snub her and for that, Casey was relieved. It suited her to be able to do her work without talking to him. However, by Friday afternoon he showed signs of wondering why she didn't care.

Casey was kneeling by the shoe racks, sorting footwear into their proper pairs after the day of photo shoots when somebody tapped her shoulder. She looked up to find Eric looming over her, grim and handsome.

'When do I get my second chance?'

Casey silently reproached herself for not taking time to think what she would say should he ask. Her mind had been preoccupied with Moira's story. 'I'm sorry Eric. I don't want to try again.'

A muscle in the left side of his jaw twitched hard. It gave her a split second to prepare herself for a terse reply.

'You didn't go out with me for anywhere *near* long enough to make up your mind so soon.'

She set a pair of stiletto heels neatly in place on the rack. 'I wouldn't be so blunt if I didn't feel certain.'

Eric's lips pursed tight. 'Oh well, some people just don't know what's good for them.' He strode out of the wardrobe room and closed the door behind him with a firm click. She surprised herself by not even caring. Eric seemed to have more than enough love for himself to make up for the loss of her love, anyway.

Casey glanced at her watch. It was a quarter to five. In another fifteen minutes she would be free to drive home to her parents' house. Her overnight bag was already packed and in the car. She used the time to straighten the make-up table and left on the stroke of five o'clock. Suzanne was nowhere to be seen and Casey didn't wait to find out where she was.

On the country road, the knot of tension at the back of her neck began to unwind. But at the end of her drive, Casey stepped into another room full of gloom.

Her mother told her, 'I just came back from Moira's. Her mother is so snappy and spiteful to her and Moira does everything she can to make her comfortable. It makes my blood boil. If that old lady wasn't dying I'd give her a piece of my mind. I just don't understand how Henrietta can be so nasty.'

But now I know why she is. Casey pursed her lips tight because she knew that if she hinted even that much, Moira's whole awful story would pour out. She longed to tell her family but she was not supposed to know about it herself. Her mother would certainly not approve of her reading the journal. Even Suzanne and Piers didn't know the story yet.

The telephone began to ring. 'I'll get it.' Doug heaved himself out of his armchair. He returned with a grim smile. 'Speaking about the Bowman family, this'll make Casey happy.' His eyes gave a slight twinkle. 'It's the Bowman person.'

Casey rushed out to the kitchen phone with one name on her mind. *Piers!* Had he phoned to let her know he'd arrived home a night early? Her pulse quickened and she could barely stand the suspense of a few seconds as she lifted the receiver and breathed, 'Hello.'

'You sound puffed,' Suzanne's voice answered. 'There was no need to run.'

Casey's eyes prickled with the bitterest tears.

'You dashed away quickly after work. I meant to catch up with you before you made it all the way back to Victor Harbor. Never mind. There's a cocktail party on tomorrow night. I thought you'd like to come.'

'No thanks. I have other plans, Suzanne. But thanks for thinking of me.'

'What other plans?'

'Just something I've planned for a long time.' *What business is it of hers?*

'Well, can't you put it off? I have a friend I'd like to introduce you to. He's a male nurse. You might like the nurturing, caring type.'

'No thanks. Listen Suzanne, I'd rather not be introduced to any new men at the moment.'

Suzanne's silence was decidedly prickly. 'I'll bet you have no other plans for tomorrow night at all. Casey, you need to be adventurous with men. Just because you didn't hit the jackpot with Eric is no reason to just give up!'

'I'm not giving up. I'd like to move in my own time.'

'So be it. You can sit home and twiddle your thumbs all week-end if you like, but that's your problem.' The receiver clicked in Casey's ear. She paused for a few seconds to compose herself.

I didn't even ask for her help. Who does she think she is?

Her parents glanced up when Casey returned. Her annoyance flared unreasonably at her father. 'Dad, why didn't you just say it was Suzanne?'

Doug Miller's jaw dropped. 'I assumed you'd know. Whenever she calls, you always race to the phone like an Olympic sprinter. I always call her "that Bowman person."' His brow furrowed. 'Who else did you think it'd be?'

Casey shook her head and turned away. 'It doesn't matter.'

Her mother's bright voice followed her along the passage, teasing her father. 'She obviously hoped it'd be another Bowman person. And I doubt if she was anxious to hear from Moira or Henrietta. Don't worry, dear. You've always missed what was right under your nose.'

Casey's ears burned. *Great!* She knew that if she went back into that room and demanded to know what her mother meant, she would burst into tears. She could hear Dale's teasing hoots, Sarah's cheery laughter and the bounce of the basketball. Casey longed for total silence. She closed her bedroom door, flung herself face down on her bed and pounded her pillow. Then she burst into tears.

Chapter 16

Casey left when her family went shopping the following afternoon. She hoped Piers and Jerome had returned early but the house was empty. She almost wished she'd stayed in Victor Harbor. Casey filled her time with cooking. There were plenty of vegetables in the pantry and some minced beef in the freezer. She set about making her mother's favourite meat loaf, with cauliflower au gratin, scalloped potatoes and honeyed carrots. When she stepped outside to feed Ben the scraps, the delicious aroma wafted from the kitchen window.

Casey scratched the wiry white hair around Ben's horns. 'What if they don't come home, old boy? What if they decide to stay in Melbourne for another day, or even another *week*, without bothering to let me know? You and I'll have all this food on our hands.'

Ben made a whickering noise and poked his nose back between her hands when she stopped scratching. Casey giggled and caressed his head again. The sinking sun was a glowing ball when she heard the familiar rattle of Piers' old van on the dirt road. Casey stood on the verandah and waited.

Jerome scrambled out as soon as the van stopped. He ran to her with his arms raised high but stopped a foot short. He ducked his head with a coy smile and dashed away. 'Too shy, Cay-seee,' he called over his shoulder, but she could see his eyes sparkling. Jerome threw his arms around Ben's furry neck instead.

'Hello.' Piers was smiling too. 'I didn't expect to see you tonight. Thought you'd be home with your folks.'

'I left early.'

He appeared bleary-eyed and tired. On his chin was a shadowy growth that made him appear exotic rather than sloppy. Combined with his bright red T-shirt and the black waves of hair falling onto the back on his neck, he looked like a gypsy.

Casey managed to scoop up the giggling Jerome for a hug. 'I've cooked some tea. Are you both hungry?'

'You bet. I didn't know what we'd have.' Piers rubbed his hands down his grubby jeans. 'Thank you, Casey. We'll just tidy ourselves up a bit.'

She dished up while they quickly showered. Jerome kept up a constant spiel of chatter during tea, about towns they'd visited on their way to Melbourne and playgrounds they'd stopped at. Piers put in a few words about his old school friend and his new wife. Casey studied him stealthily across the table, the thought of his mother's diary foremost in her mind. She now knew more about Piers' background than he knew himself. She felt a twinge of contrition for reading the journal.

'But Daddy got sick,' Jerome was saying.

'Nothing too bad,' Piers put in quickly. 'Just a bit of asthma. It was pretty dusty on the road.'

Concern swept through her. 'Are you okay now?'

'Sure. I never get it as bad as I used to when I was a kid.'

Jerome gave a great yawn and his head began to nod. Piers stood up to heave him over his shoulder. 'Let's get you into your own bed. You'll sleep well tonight.'

Casey began to wash dishes and when Piers returned, he dried them. She gazed at him sideways and brought up another topic that had been on her mind all week. 'You said that when you get back, you'd tell me what you think my strengths are.'

Piers grinned as he wiped his hands and hung up the damp tea towel. 'Yes, I remember. But I sort of hoped you'd forgotten. I've been feeling a bit embarrassed about saying that. I reckon if I tell you, you'll think I'm being corny.'

They adjourned to the lounge room where he sank into an armchair and gazed down at his knees.

The Risky Way Home

'I promise I won't think you're corny. C'mon, tell me.'

'Okay, it's just that you're always so kind-hearted.'

'What?' She wondered what he would have thought if he'd seen her the previous night at her parents' house, arguing over the phone with Suzanne and then snapping at her father.

His face flamed. 'There, I told you you'd think I was corny. I'd better explain what I mean. You've always seemed to have compassion. You make people feel cheerful. You have a knack of seeing the best in people and situations and not even looking for the worst. And in my opinion, that's the best gift a person can have.'

'Well … thanks. I'd never have come up with that.' Casey tried to match his words with the picture in her mind. She sadly shook her head. 'But do you know what I think you've done? You've just described yourself. That compassion stuff is your thing. Not mine. Maybe some of it rubbed off on me while I was here.'

He was staring at her. 'If it's my thing, it's only because I learned it from you.'

'What? I mean, how?'

His eyes were deep and clear. 'Do you remember at school, when I accidentally smashed that ceramic vase you were working on?'

'I'll say I do. I could've throttled you.'

'It didn't show,' he said quietly. 'I tried to apologise and I could see you were shaking and trying not to cry. I wanted to curl up and die. But then you said, "It's Okay, Piers. I know it was an accident. We can't change what happened so I might as well get over it and be happy."'

Casey stared. She clearly remembered the occasion but had long forgotten whatever she'd said. While he'd been trying to apologise she'd clenched her teeth and fists tight, convinced that as he was Suzanne Bowman's brother, she must keep a lid on her fury. She hadn't forgotten the unflattering names she'd called him to her friends after school.

'Was it really that simple? You changed your outlook on life because of what I said back then?'

'Yeah, well that's what started me thinking. I always remembered that advice. It helped me through lots of … well, lots of stuff. And it's not just that time with the ceramic vase. It's all the time. You always make time to play with Jerome. You never fob him off the way I've seen others do. You didn't even think of that, did you? That's because being kind comes so naturally to you, like I said.'

A bubble, warm like milk, surged in her chest. 'I'm glad you told me. I didn't think you'd say anything like that.'

He was blushing again. 'Well, what goes around comes around.'

'I have something else to show you.' She leaned across to pull Moira's journal from the shelf. 'Suzanne brought this for you to read. It's your mum's diary from twenty years ago.'

Piers flicked through the pages and whistled. 'I can't believe she wrote all this without ever showing us before.'

'You'll understand why when you read it. Suzanne told me I could read it so I did but perhaps I shouldn't have.'

'You've already read all this tiny writing? It looks as if a little beetle stood in ink and walked across all the pages in her book.'

'You get used to it quickly. It was a compelling story. Very sad.'

He gave his crooked grin. 'Do you reckon I should take some tissues?'

'I definitely think you, of all people, should.'

Piers appeared at breakfast time with rumpled hair and shadows beneath his eyes. 'I finished it. I was reading until past two o'clock.'

'What did you think?'

'Pretty freaky. All the time I was reading, I couldn't remember one single detail. Except being afraid of my father, that is.'

'That's a *good* thing!' She couldn't suppress a shudder.

'Suzanne and I didn't know a fraction of what happened, did we?'

Casey drew a breath to ask more but the telephone rang. Piers stepped into the hall to take the call. He returned a few moments later and blew out his breath in a long puff. 'That was Mum. Gran died last night.'

Although everyone had expected it soon, Casey still felt a ripple of surprise.

'She must've died in her sleep. Mum found her this morning. She knew something must be wrong when Gran didn't call out for her morning coffee and paper. She's been yelling from her bedroom every morning for years. I remember it well.' Piers put on a shrill mimic. '"Moira, are those kids reading the paper? I'm supposed to have it first!"'

He didn't appear the least bothered so it seemed inappropriate to offer condolences. 'Oh well,' she said. 'That's a big part of your life over and done with.'

He grinned as if she'd made a joke. 'I'll say it is.'

'How's your mum?'

Piers turned sober. 'It's hard to tell. She sounded a bit numb. Like a prisoner out on parole. I mean, looking after Gran was a hard job but it's been her whole life for twenty years.'

'Are you going to see her today?'

'She'd like me to. She's already thinking about funeral arrangements.' Piers glanced toward Jerome's bedroom door. The little boy, usually up at the crack of dawn, hadn't stirred yet. 'It won't be much fun for him.'

'Would you like to leave him here with me?'

Piers' face brightened. 'I wasn't hinting.'

'I'd love to look after him. I'm home one day earlier than normal so you might as well make the most of it. You're right, Jerome would have no fun at your mum's house today.'

'I accept, then. Thank you. Don't know how long I'll be there but I'll try not to make it too long.' As Piers went off to shave, she heard him mumble, 'Won't be much fun for me, either.'

------*------*------*---*------*------

Casey indulged Jerome for an hour of hide-and-seek. Her challenge was in pretending not to notice the obvious. If she couldn't glimpse his pixie face shining behind cushions or curtains, she was bound to hear his muffled giggling. Casey tired of the game first.

'Jerome, how'd you like to go to the playground?'

'Yes, *yes,* YES!' He'd only recently learned to enunciate the word properly and jumped higher with each 'yes.'

'It's no wonder you crash at night, after using up so much energy every moment you're awake.' Casey set up his booster seat in her car and Jerome prattled all the way to the playground. When they arrived he ran across to a small slide while she took a seat on one of the benches.

I wonder if anyone would think I'm Jerome's mother. Casey thought he was by far the most beautiful child there. His delicate features topped by masses of wavy, dark hair made her heart melt. She found herself hoping others would assume she was his parent, and settled back to enjoy the fantasy.

This was a good idea of mine. He could burn his excess energy while she relaxed. Casey wondered if Henrietta Bowman had ever been content to spend a pleasant morning with a beloved child. She could not imagine it. Casey felt a pang of regret for the old lady's miserable life.

Somebody tapped her shoulder and Casey whirled around. Eric Adams stood behind her bench, immaculate in a Lacoste shirt and fawn trousers.

'What are you doing here?'

His expression was dark. 'We need to talk. You took off so fast after work on Friday. I know you wanted to avoid me. So I've been to your house and found nobody home. Luckily I spotted your car over there as I drove past.' He jerked his chin back at the playground carpark.

'Hey Casey, look what I made!' Jerome had found himself a spot in the outermost corner of the sand pit. The sunshine burnished his hair like copper. He pointed to a small sandcastle decorated with twigs and pebbles.

'Wow! That's a beauty!' Her expansive mood closed like a telescope beneath Eric's scrutiny.

Jerome beamed, showing his dimples.

Eric checked the bench for bird droppings before sitting beside her. 'Why are you stuck looking after the kid? Where's what's-his-face? Pierre?'

'With his mother, because his grandmother just died. Eric, what did you want to talk about?'

'I deserve to know why you won't give me a second chance.'

'No particular reason. We don't have much in common. I'm a fairly simple person and I felt like you wanted me to try and change my habits.'

His green eyes were fixed on her like lasers. 'You don't have to change. Stay as simple as you please. I don't expect you to be glamorous like Suzanne. I just appreciate your affection and support.'

She lifted her gaze from Eric's probing eyes to check on Jerome. He'd left the sandpit and stood with his head cocked to one side, watching a girl ride a small spring horse. Casey turned back to Eric.

'I think our plans, and even the ways we prefer to spend our leisure time are far too different to support each other.'

He leaned closer. 'You could make an effort to stretch your mind to my level.'

She bit back the peal of laughter before it left her lips. Eric was deadly serious. Casey didn't really feel like laughing, anyway. 'I don't feel the need to stretch my mind. I'm happy with the level it's at.'

He muttered a swear word. 'This is too much! I'm trying to understand how you feel but I can't see that I've ever done anything wrong, except for showing my frustration when you scraped my car. Anyone who wouldn't be annoyed by that would be a jellyfish, not a man! Casey, I don't know what you're looking for! Some fairy-tale Prince Charming who never loses his cool? Guys like that don't exist. You think you're so smart to have landed the job with us but it was nothing to do with your merit. I'll tell you why you're with us. Suzanne wanted you. And do you know why? She didn't want to hire an assistant who'd show her up.'

Something ripped Casey's heart raw. 'If that's how you feel, I don't know why you bothered to come looking for me.'

'Casey, look! I'm right up here!'

Jerome was standing high at the top of the largest metal slide. Her heart lurched. He wasn't steady or coordinated enough to be up there with older children. Casey was on her feet.

'Jerome, wait!' He was still smiling, so she tried to sound calm. 'That is high! You're a quick climber. I'll help you slide down.'

She was close enough to hear the boy on the ladder behind Jerome grumble, 'C'mon, little kid. Are you just gonna stand there?'

Jerome turned to face him and lost his balance. His arms shot out to grasp something solid but clutched only air. He hurtled backwards over the edge and appeared to hit the ground head first. Casey's lungs were too frozen to even scream. Trance-like, she took the remaining steps needed to sink down beside Jerome. If only he'd opened his mouth to cry, her terror wouldn't have been so thick. His silence was sickening. Jerome's eyes were closed with his beautiful lashes poised like butterflies above his cheeks.

'I'll call an ambulance,' a woman told her. 'Don't move him until they get here.'

Casey heard an anguished sob and realised that it came from her.

Another mother cried, 'Jaydon, keep away from the little boy. He needs to stay still.'

The first woman gripped Casey's shoulder. 'I'm a nurse. Are you his mother?'

She tearfully shook her head. That dream collapsed too. 'I'm his... babysitter.'

The nurse clucked her tongue. 'Where are his parents?'

'There's only his father. He's in Victor Harbor.'

The butterflies flickered. Jerome groaned softly.

'Don't move!' the nurse told him. 'There's a good boy.'

Jerome's throat worked as his eyeballs wildly scanned the surrounding faces.

'Jerome, it's me, Casey. You had a fall but we'll soon make you better. Don't be frightened.'

His grey eyes focused on her, then pooled up. The remaining colour drained from his face and his bottom lip quivered. Casey knew that she was being no help at all. Her encouraging words were cancelled out by the tears streaming down her cheeks.

Chapter 17

Casey's nerves were ready to snap. Whenever anybody entered the waiting room her pulse sky-rocketed, but so far, the hospital staff had swept past her to talk to other people. She had no idea of what was happening to Jerome and the longer she waited the more likely it seemed that the news must be terrible. The thought of Jerome's happy smile moments before his accident plagued her like a nightmare.

Piers had arrived earlier than she'd expected from Victor Harbor. He'd rushed past her to the nurse's station and she was unsure if he'd even seen her. That might have been as short as twenty minutes or as long as an hour earlier. Casey had lost track of time and every minute dragged like a day. She shuffled her feet and let the chain of events whirl through her tired mind again. Trying to stop it was futile.

When the ambulance staff had arrived at the playground, Eric came and wrapped his arm around her. His face was ash grey. 'It wasn't our fault. We were just talking. Who would've expected him to climb right up there?'

Casey heard herself mumble something about what a fearless climber Jerome was. Her arms were covered with goose-flesh and she felt chilled to the bone. Eric's arm had been the warmest thing in her cold world and she'd appreciated his support.

'It was just a freaky thing,' Eric said. 'He won't be able to charge you with anything.'

Casey's mind was blank until she realised that by 'he', Eric meant Piers.

'He left you in charge of his kid,' Eric rambled on, 'and that was his responsibility. He took the chance. If he tries to pin you with a lawsuit, I'll back you up. I'll tell them you only took your eyes off the boy for a moment and that I only just arrived before it happened.'

'Can't you think about anything but lawsuits?' Casey snapped. 'Jerome is far more important than...' She bit off the rest of her retort when she looked at Eric. He raised a shaking hand to cover his ghostly white face.

'I didn't mean that,' he mumbled. 'I was just saying the first thing that came into my head. That slide wasn't all *that* high! The little guy will be alright, don't you think? He was looking around after he fell. That has to be a good sign.'

Everything had turned even chillier. Casey just nodded because she didn't trust herself to reply without crumbling. She wondered if this was the first time in Eric's perfect life that he'd ever been in the thick of a tragedy.

One of the ambulance crew asked her to step into the ambulance to help calm Jerome and they were taken to hospital. For Jerome's sake, she'd tried to keep her tears locked behind her eyelids.

'Dear God, please don't let Jerome be seriously hurt. Please don't let him be crippled or...' she almost gagged on the next word, even in her thoughts. *'I'll do anything you want me to and never complain about anything again if only you'll let him be safe.'*

A hazy sense of *deja vu* filtered into the waiting room. Casey felt sure she'd lived through the whole ordeal not so long ago then remembered that it was not her but Moira, who had rushed Piers into hospital with an asthma attack. It had been over twenty years earlier but Casey had read about it less than a week ago. Her exhausted brain compressed the two incidents together in time. Surely she'd been sitting there waiting for news of Jerome for over twenty years.

'Casey.'

Her heart lurched as she rose from her chair. It was Piers. She couldn't force herself to meet his eye.

'He'll be okay,' Piers said.

Casey's legs turned to rubber. The room whirled around her but before she could stumble back to her chair, he caught her in his arms. 'Casey, I'm sorry. It didn't cross my mind that you'd be waiting out here for so long.

The Risky Way Home

Everything was a blur when I got here. I could only think about Jerome. Will you forgive me?'

'No… I mean, no I'm sorry!' She could hold back her tears no longer. They spilled down her cheeks and dripped off her chin. 'It was all my fault. He climbed up there so fast but if I'd been looking after him properly…'

Piers cut in quickly. 'I know what he's like. His sense of adventure overtakes his common sense. I don't blame you. I don't keep my eye on him every single minute of the day. But this might be a lesson for him. They'll let him come home tomorrow. He has a slight concussion but no fractured bones showed up on the X-Ray. They told me kids Jerome's age bounce back like rubber balls. But he has the biggest lump on his head I've ever seen. He'll be impressed when he's able to see himself in a mirror.'

It was a long speech for Piers. Casey knew that he was chattering on to make her feel better. It was beginning to work. Her dizziness had receded and she realised her cheek had been pressed against the front of Piers' T-shirt. With her ear against his chest she could hear his heartbeat. She could feel the rising of his chest with each breath he drew. She didn't want him to let her go.

'Come with me,' Piers said.

They walked to the paediatric ward. Huge pictures of smiling ocean creatures lined the corridor but the thick odour of antiseptic and hospital dinners trapped between the walls made her shudder. They entered a small room with two beds. One was empty and Jerome lay in the other with a white sheet folded over his chest. One small hand rested on top of the other and his eyes were closed. Casey saw the great purple-black lump high on his forehead, just beneath his hairline. She winced.

'Piers, I really love Jerome.'

'I know.'

'Are you going to stay with him tonight?'

He nodded. 'It'll make him feel better. But will you be okay at home by yourself?'

'Yeah, I think so.'

He carefully studied her face. 'Will you promise not to keep thinking about what happened?'

'I'll try not to.'

'Is your car still at the playground?' he asked.

She'd given it no thought. 'I suppose it must be.'

'I'll give you a lift back. Jerome won't wake up for awhile. They've sedated him so he'll have a good rest.'

'Okay, thanks.' When Casey stepped into warm twilight, she drew a slow breath. Every cell of her body seemed to dance for as long as she sat beside Piers. But when she slid behind the wheel of her own car, her head sank onto the steering wheel. Her spirits had been springing from happiness to sadness and back again all week and at last she felt limp and wrung out.

Casey ran a warm bubble bath and sank into it. The bathroom window was opened wide so she could gaze up at the creamy belt of the Milky Way. She remembered to thank God for answering her prayer for Jerome. *But what can I do to make Piers put his arms around me like that again?*

Casey smiled sheepishly. Trying to deny the wish was not worth the effort and she was too tired to try. After all, she'd promised not to think about Jerome's fall so she needed something to fill the vacuum.

Did I hug him back? The question vaguely disturbed her because she couldn't remember. She did not think she had.

<hr />

Casey sat beside her mother at Henrietta Bowman's funeral. Attendants were spaced out in the small parlour. Henrietta had refused to allow Moira to have the funeral at church but the people who came were all Moira's church friends anyway. Henrietta's glossy walnut coffin was very small. Her overbearing personality had been enclosed in such a tiny body. Casey shuddered to think of the gruff old face lying in there and drew her eyes back to the living people.

Moira sat with slumped shoulders between her children in the front row. She looked like a small abandoned orphan. Casey squirmed, concerned by the regret etched on Moira's pale face. *What'll she do without her?* Looking after Henrietta was Moira's reason for living. Casey did not think she would recover for a long time.

Her mother gently nudged her. Casey hadn't heard the celebrant tell the assembly to rise for the final song. The service had been short and matter-of-fact, as Henrietta would have wanted it.

Now that they were standing, Moira appeared dwarfed by her children. Casey guessed that they had inherited their height from the formidable Jean-Michel Dupont. Suzanne scowled with distaste at the whole business. She hadn't wanted to be there and made her feelings clear but it was harder to guess what Piers was thinking. His expression was solemn and respectful.

Casey made the most of her opportunity to study him while he wasn't watching her. He inclined his head to speak to his mother and Casey wondered what he had said. She watched him fold the crease of his flyer and bow his head for the final prayer. She lowered her own head and found it hard to draw her eyes away from the soft, dark waves of hair that brushed the back of his neck. By now, she was willing to admit to herself that she would never tire of watching Piers, whatever he did.

Chapter 18

On Father's Day morning, Casey quickly wrapped a parcel in her bedroom. She already had a gift for her own father but it had occurred to her late the previous night that Piers needed a present too and Jerome was too small to go out and buy one. In a flash she knew what they could give him. The rejected T-shirt she'd offered Eric for his birthday. The bold stripes of red and blue would suit Piers wonderfully.

Casey bit off the last bit of tape and wondered when to ask Jerome to give him the gift. They'd be together all day. Casey's mother had invited Moira and her family to share their Father's Day lunch. 'She's been so low-spirited since Henrietta's death and I hate to think of her spending a holiday alone in that house.'

As Casey had expected, Moira and Piers had accepted the invitation but Suzanne had declined. 'I've nothing against your family but I couldn't bear watching Mum pretend to celebrate Father's Day. Thanks to her, we don't even *have* a father.'

Casey tied a red ribbon around the parcel and decided not to wait. She found Jerome lying on his stomach surrounded by crayons, colouring a picture of a racing car. When she whispered her plan his dimples popped out. Hugging the gift to his chest, he pattered out to the work shed in his fluffy slippers. Casey followed.

She relished Piers' astonishment. He spun Jerome off his feet and peered over his head to where she stood in the doorway. 'Thank you both.

I'll wear it this afternoon. I have nothing else this smart.'

That's a different reaction to the first time I gave that present. Casey hurried to the kitchen before she laughed aloud. It was shaping up to be a good day. She was upstairs humming in her bedroom when she heard Suzanne's car cruise along the driveway. Casey hurried down to meet her at the kitchen door. 'Hello, have you changed your mind about coming with us?'

Suzanne stared. 'Coming where?'

'Father's Day.'

Suzanne remembered in a rush. 'I'd completely forgotten about Father's Day. No, I just popped in for a chat. You aren't going yet, are you?'

Casey peered surreptitiously at the hands of the clock. It was already 10.30 but her parents would understand if they were a little late. 'No. Would you like a coffee?'

Suzanne had already settled onto a chair and flicked the heater fan to warm her ankles. 'Yes please, my usual black.' Over piping hot sips, she tried to put her restless thoughts into words. 'Casey, I don't know what's the matter with me. The fun seems to have drained out of everything. Ever since Gran's funeral, I've had to drag myself out of bed. But when I'm there, I can hardly sleep.'

Casey noticed the evidence of this in the heaviness of Suzanne's eyelids. She hardly needed her purple eye-shadow for its effect.

'I'm glad to be rid of her,' Suzanne went on. 'I'm just feeling empty. I don't quite know how to explain it. All my life I've been trying to prove to Gran that I could shine without her. I can't remember a time when I didn't want to rub her nose in my success. The studio, the cameras, all those wonderful clothes.' She forced a laugh. 'Now that the old bag is dead, they all seem a bit pointless. She's got the better of me after all.'

'But you're doing it for yourself!' Casey cried. 'And for your clients. You built that fantastic business. It's a credit to your creativity and vision. You *still* shine, whether she's here to know it or not.'

Suzanne's smile lacked some of its usual sparkle. 'I knew you'd try to cheer me up. That's why I came.' She looked up as Piers stepped into the kitchen. 'Hi, you look nice. Is that T-shirt new?'

'Yeah, it's a Father's Day present.' He explained how Casey and Jerome had given it to him and recognition dawned in Suzanne's eyes.

'I thought I'd seen it before. It's the same one you tried to give Eric on his birthday, isn't it Casey?'

Casey caught sight of Piers' crestfallen expression and turned cold inside.

'Didn't he like it?' Piers asked. 'Not good enough for him?'

'It's a little too casual for Eric,' Suzanne said, 'but Casey didn't realise.'

Casey's cold insides boiled to intense heat in a flash. She knitted her brows and scowled in Suzanne's direction.

Suzanne turned an innocent face toward her. 'What's eating you?'

Piers let out a laugh. 'Talk about not realising.' He turned to Casey. 'Don't worry, I'm still gonna wear it.' He breezed out to his bedroom.

Casey knew that if she opened her mouth some of her steam would seethe out but she opened it anyway. 'Why did you have to tell him?'

Once again, Suzanne's face registered surprise. 'Does it matter?'

'Well how'd you like to think you got a present just because someone else dumped it?'

'Is that all? Don't give it another thought. It's only Piers. He doesn't care about things like that.'

Casey drew a breath but had no reply. All she could do was hope that the day would improve.

Father's Day grew steadily worse. Casey had always been sensitive to other people's moods and gloom hung over her parents' backyard like a shroud. She found herself watching Moira Bowman's fluttering hands. They reminded Casey of a pair of white, ragged moths. When Moira was not chattering feverishly to Helen Miller, her eyes would well with unexpected tears. They were circled with dark shadows, not unlike Suzanne's.

Helen spoke in her hearty tone to boost Moira's spirits but Casey recognised the note of strain in her mother's voice. Abby stayed slumped in a deck chair, dour and quiet. She sipped a wine cooler and stared at her red painted toe nails. Sarah and Jerome were drawing pictures with sticks in the dirt around Abby's chair, but Abby didn't spare a glance for them.

Helen tapped Casey's shoulder and nodded toward Abby. 'Treat her with kid gloves today. She's woken up in a mood. I'm sure it's because it's their first Father's Day without Jeff, even though she says she doesn't care.'

Casey nodded. She didn't need to be warned.

Only her father and brother seemed oblivious to the heaviness that hung in the air. Doug Miller stirred red-hot coals in his ancient brick barbeque while Dale turned sausages and chops. Piers approached them to ask if he could lend a hand. She heard her father reply that they had it under control, thanks.

Dale glanced at Piers, then pointedly turned his back and began to discuss family friends with his father. Indignation stirred beneath Casey's skin. Her brother had perfected his manner of communicating rudeness with as little effort as possible. He slurped a bottle of beer without offering one to their guest. Piers got the message and backed away. Only then did Dale grin in his direction. He leaned across to whisper some furtive comment to their father.

By now, the pit of Casey's stomach was clenched like a fist. *That rotten Dale spoils everything. Why does he have to be so mean?* She wondered what she could say to Piers to excuse Dale's behaviour but whatever it was would have to wait until her eyes stopped burning or she would look like a bigger fool than her brother.

To her astonishment, instead of staying put, Piers drew a deck chair close to Abby's. Casey was close enough to overhear what he said to her.

'Hey Abby, I wondered if you could give me some advice about Jerome. You've had plenty more experience with Sarah.'

What happened next was truly astounding. As Abby looked up, her face brightened as if a light bulb had been switched on inside her. 'I'm sure I can help. What would you like to know?'

'He still wakes up twice during the night, and then it's really hard to settle him down again. I was hoping he'd be too old for this by now.'

'That could be for any number of reasons. Perhaps he needs less stimulation before bed. Why don't you start quieting him down an hour earlier and giving him a hot drink? Another thing you could try is...'

Casey's mother beckoned her inside to help with the salads. Abby's voice was still as animated twenty minutes later when Casey stepped out again. Piers leaned forward with his wrists resting on his knees, seemingly hanging onto her every word. 'You need to establish a firm structure, even when you're exhausted. I know that can be tough but believe me, it'll be worth it. When Sarah was Jerome's age she went through a very stubborn phase when she refused to hop into bed at all and I tried…'

Helen nudged Casey and raised her eyebrows in Abby's direction. 'They have a lot to talk about.'

Casey leaned closer to her mother to whisper, 'I think I've worked out the secret to keeping her happy. We need to keep asking her for advice from time to time.' Casey almost giggled at the simplicity of it. The truth was as clear as Abby's shining face. Nobody had realised that along with grief over her marriage break-up, Abby had mourned the loss of her role as family counsellor.

Helen gaped at her. 'I think you're right. You're a genius.'

'I can't take all the credit,' Casey admitted. 'You need to thank Piers too.'

When lunch had been eaten and the table cleared, Abby and Piers still leaned close together, deep in conversation. Although it had been good to see Abby turn happy again, her sister's exuberant babble began to grate on Casey's nerves. She sat with Helen and Moira sipping tea and trying not to appear grouchy. The women spoke about sewing and washing detergents. Casey swirled her cup and decided she'd made the wrong decision. She should have joined Sarah and Jerome where they knelt on all fours in the garden studying ant hills. Abby and Piers frequently glanced over at their children, smiling. *At least then I'd be noticed! Surely she's had time to tell him her whole life story by now!*

'Abby's such a pretty young woman,' Moira was saying. Casey almost ground her teeth. She was certain she'd never had such a lengthy conversation with Piers herself after months of sharing a house with him! But she didn't have Abby's fluency with words. Neither did she have her sister's flashy smile and sunny blonde hair that had swept Jeff off his feet. Casey's last cold inch of tea tasted like mud.

The long conversation ended while she testily thumped greasy meat trays in the sink. Abby placed a pile of dirty plates beside Casey's elbow. 'Will you let me give you some advice?'

Casey didn't turn to look at her. 'I'm sure you will, whether I like it or not.'

'Forget this Eric fellow,' Abby counselled. 'I've never even met him but he sounds like a bore. If I were you, I'd set my sights on Piers.'

The tips of Casey's ears burned. 'I thought you might fancy him yourself, the time you spent talking to him.' She hoped she sounded as if she were making a joke.

'If I was seven or eight years younger I think I would.'

'But I thought you don't like men anymore.'

Abby began covering left-overs with cling film. 'He's an exception. He's polite to his mother and very sensible, but I like him in spite of all that.' She laughed at her own joke. 'I admire him for bringing Jerome up all by himself. He's interesting to talk to and has a sense of humour. Not bad looking either. Casey, sometimes I think you must be blind.'

Casey dunked a tea cup into the water with a thump. She longed to gaze straight into Abby's eyes and reply, 'If you think I'm blind, that makes you the blind one!' But that would be revealing far more than she wanted to. She glared into the sink with a mood the same colour as the murky dish water.

When Casey fetched her jacket to leave, she found her brother trying to carry their father's huge sack of coal back to the garden shed. His veins were bulging as he heaved it two inches off the ground and let it fall with a thud. 'Dad, for cryin' out loud! You cram this too full. You'd have to be flamin' Hercules to lift this. I'd like to see *you* take it.'

'I'll take it,' Piers said. He heaved the sack over his shoulder and asked, 'Does it go in the shed?'

Dale's mouth hung slack as he stared.

'Yes thanks, Piers.' Doug's eyes twinkled.

Dale scowled as he brushed coal dust onto his jeans. 'I have better things to do than working out at a gym or whatever nerdy thing he does in his spare time.'

'Such as sitting on your backside watching T.V. and guzzling beer?' their father grinned.

Piers emerged from the shed and saw Casey grinning at him. He flushed when he realised she'd witnessed his action.

'Nice work, Hercules,' she said slyly. 'I saw Dad and Dale dragging that sack out between them when we got here. What made you so confident you could take it single-handedly?'

Piers brushed off her question with a laugh. 'I know I must be stronger than I used to be. When I first set up my business, I couldn't carry three planks across the yard without making a couple of trips but now I can do it easily.'

'Well, you showed him good.'

His smile flickered. 'I thought so too.'

———————————

That night in bed, Casey flipped through Moira's diary again. Even though she now knew what the pages contained, the descriptions of Jean's cruelty to Moira and Piers still made her wince.

When she finally fell asleep, Casey dreamed that while she was driving to work, a strange beast began a loud volley of thumps from inside her car bonnet to escape. Breathless with terror, Casey screeched into the nearest car park, left the car and raced along the pavement before the monster had a chance to emerge. However, the incessant knocking pursued her no matter how fast or far she ran. Her legs became sluggish and heavy to move while hot breath warmed the back of her neck. When she twisted her head, she saw that it was no monster but a tall, dark-haired man with the gleam of a maniac in his eye. Although she'd never met him, she sensed with certainty from Moira's description that this must be Jean-Michel Dupont. With a hammering heart, Casey jerked awake.

She drew three long, slow breaths. *I'd better stop thinking about that diary!* Yet something was still wrong. Her skin prickled as the knocking from her dream persisted. It took a few seconds to work out that somebody was standing outside in the dark, pounding on the front door.

Casey rolled out of bed, snapped on her light and stumbled downstairs. Piers was emerging from his own bedroom, bleary-eyed and tousle-haired. As he switched on the lounge room light, Casey heard a sob behind the door.

Still groggy, Piers fumbled with the lock and Suzanne almost fell inside. 'You took your time.'

He squinted at the hands of the clock. 'It's a quarter past two. I was asleep.'

'Me too.' Casey's eyes had become accustomed to the light. Suzanne wore a beautifully tailored cherry coloured dress from the studio but her face was a blotchy mess. 'Suzanne, what happened? Are you okay?'

'No, I'm terrible! I'm through with Tim!'

Intense relief that it was nothing worse flooded through Casey. 'I'm sorry to hear that.' She hoped her tone matched her words.

'Don't be sorry. Do you know what he's been up to? He's been having an affair with Ingrid behind my back!'

'Ingrid's your other flatmate?' Piers asked. 'Right?'

'Right! I went out with some other friends but got home earlier than they expected me. I found Tim and Ingrid rolling around on the couch together, kissing!' Suzanne covered her face and wept.

Casey caught Piers' eye. Neither of them knew what to say.

'She was supposed to be one of my best friends. Some friend. To think I was so grateful to Tim for letting her board with us. He always had the nerve to expect me to thank him, as if he were doing me a big favour. Now I feel sick to my stomach.' She wiped her hand across her streaky face. 'Sorry, I'll try not to wake Jerome.'

'Did they try to excuse themselves?' Casey demanded.

Suzanne snorted. 'You should've heard the carry-on! Tim started bellowing at me. He reckons it's my fault he started an affair with Ingrid. I'll tell you his story. When Gran died, I started getting on his nerves. I kept wanting to talk about my troubled childhood and after the first five hundred times, he couldn't take any more. Ingrid was trying to talk him into having more compassion for me, and somehow their feelings for each other snowballed from there. Have you ever heard a bigger load of stinking...?' Suzanne paused to gasp a breath. She rolled the tip of a matted strand of hair between her fingers. 'I'll bet they're cuddling up laughing at me right now. Either that or telling each other what a dope I am.'

'Suzanne, I'm really, really sorry.' Casey cringed but she could think of nothing different to say.

It seemed to be enough. Suzanne was in her arms, sobbing on her shoulder. 'Casey, I knew you'd be sympathetic. That's why I came here. I couldn't think of anywhere else to go. I'll look for a new apartment as soon as I can but I need to stay here for now.'

'You know, Mum would be glad to have you,' Piers said. 'She's all alone in that empty house now.'

Suzanne jerked herself from Casey's embrace. 'I wouldn't crawl back to Mum in a fit. I'd rather die! I only wanted to stay here for a few days! If you don't want me I'll book into a hotel, but…'

'Calm down,' he interjected. 'I didn't mean you aren't welcome to stay here.'

Suzanne's head drooped and she sank onto the couch. 'It'll just be a stop-gap. I'll start looking for a new place first thing tomorrow. I'll sleep here on the couch. I stripped the duvet off the bed.' She gave a sniffling giggle. 'I left them with nothing but Ingrid's single bed one. That was my way of getting back at them. Pathetic, I know.'

'I'll make us a cup of tea,' Casey said. It occurred to her that she sounded just like Moira Bowman.

'Make mine coffee,' Suzanne mumbled.

When Casey came out of the kitchen with the hot drinks, Piers had returned to bed and Suzanne was already huddled on the couch with her king-sized duvet flowing onto the floor.

'Do you know what? I'll get over this. I've just been thinking it might be a blessing in disguise. I'm going to make my life even better! I'll do it just to show them. Do you remember how I said that I've lost heart for work since Gran died? That doesn't matter anymore. I can shove my success down Tim's and Ingrid's throats instead. Casey, maybe it's the best thing that could've happened to me.'

When Casey got back to bed she felt too wound-up to fall asleep again. She knew that downstairs, Suzanne was not sleeping. The kitchen door thumped, the television blared for ten or fifteen minutes, the toilet flushed and finally, the kitchen floorboards creaked as Suzanne paced. Casey rolled onto her side. Having Suzanne's volatile personality beneath the roof charged the atmosphere of the house with tension, even when she was in a different room.

Chapter 19

True to her word, Suzanne searched the classified advertisements of several newspapers each morning for flats and apartments to rent, but two weeks later had found nothing. 'This is a nightmare.' In her opinion, the places within her price range were all in dismal suburbs. Meanwhile, her continual presence in Piers' household was wreaking havoc.

Suzanne rejected the couch after her first night of trying to sleep on it and claimed Piers' bedroom while he set up a stretcher-bed for himself in Jerome's room. Never before had his bedroom bulged with such a mass of clothes, cosmetics and accessories that spilled its guts out into the rest of the house like a living creature. Suzanne, who groomed herself impeccably, left a trail of shoes, stockings, jewellery and screwed-up tissues in her wake. By the time she finished her shower each morning, there was barely enough water for anyone else for the rest of the day.

She had played a quick game of Snap with Jerome on her second night with them but quickly tired of it and refused to play any more games with him, no matter how he pleaded. 'I have serious things on my mind, little poppet. You'll understand when you grow up.' Then she commandeered the T.V. set to watch soap operas and shoved his kids' videos behind the T.V. to make room for some of hers. For the first time ever, Jerome began to pout and was less than satisfied with his zany 'Auntie Suze.'

She sniped at Piers continuously. Her list of complaints seemed to be endless. She said he'd lost one of her best earrings when he searched in his bedroom for his Walkman, because she couldn't find it anywhere! He used the last bit of milk she'd been keeping for her breakfast, and it had been her bottle. She'd paid for it. He expected her to take messages from his clients over the phone, but she had enough problems of her own. How was she supposed to remember when he didn't even keep a pen handy? He let Jerome have too much of his own way with the T.V., and now they were all suffering for it! He didn't remember to keep the toilet seat down and that enamel was freezing in the middle of the night! She was too nervous to hang anything on the clothesline in case Ben got hold of them. She didn't know how Casey had managed to share the house with him for so long without turning crazy!

At first Piers tried to turn a deaf ear but late one evening his control snapped. Casey heard him tell Suzanne that if she hated living with him so much, the flats she rejected could hardly be any worse. He found Casey alone in the kitchen and fumed, 'I told you what it's like living with her.'

'At least you don't have to work with her too.' Casey gasped as soon as the words left her mouth. She had only meant to think them. When his bitter expression changed to a grin, she whispered, 'Don't tell her I said so.'

'I wouldn't do that. She doesn't know how carefully we've all been tiptoeing around, trying not to upset her.'

On Friday morning, Suzanne crunched her toast and pored over the Real Estate section of the *Advertiser*. She looked up with a smile as Casey entered the kitchen.

'Hey, I've just had a fantastic idea. I don't know why neither of us thought of it before. The flats I like are too expensive for just me but we could manage if you and I shared. There are a few here that sound perfect for us. What do you say?'

Casey swallowed her first mouthful of muesli. 'No thanks. I already have somewhere to live.'

'But why would you want to stay here?' Suzanne waved her crimson-painted finger tips to take in the rustic kitchen, untidy with her own pile of coffee cups and late night supper dishes. 'It's always freezing cold and nothing even matches! We'd make the new place gorgeous! There'd be far more life there, too. We'd always have people coming and going and we'll keep dividing the cost of petrol to work.'

Casey set down her spoon, trying to choose the best words to refuse.

The Risky Way Home

'It's not so bad here. I'm well set-up now. And remember, you're the one who brought me here.'

'That was just because you had nowhere else at the time. Are you worried about leaving Piers in the lurch?'

'That's part of it.' Casey felt she'd be wise to say no more.

'Don't give it another thought. He can't expect you to stay if a better offer comes up. He doesn't even have a decent hot water service.' Suzanne flung open the back door and hollered, 'Piers, come here!'

When he left his work shed, she told him, 'Casey and I would like to share a flat but she's worried about leaving you with no boarder. I told her of course you wouldn't mind. You never expected her to stay forever, did you?'

'Of course not. Casey is free to live wherever she chooses.'

They were running late for work. Nothing more could be said just then. Casey went out to wait in Suzanne's car while Suzanne fetched her bag and keys. *How could this have happened? I haven't even committed myself but they're talking as if it's all settled. And he isn't upset. He's so eager to be rid of Suzanne he doesn't even care if it means I go too.* Casey had to press her stinging eyes into her coat sleeve so that when Suzanne breezed out, she wouldn't see how close she was to tears.

⁕⸻⸻⸻⁕

She decided to spend the week-end with her parents. Driving to Victor Harbor was the only way she could think to escape from Suzanne and Piers. She wanted to hear no more of Suzanne's plans for sharing a flat, and she certainly didn't want to listen to Piers telling them how wonderful it would be. So instead of spending an evening at home as she'd planned, Casey sat at her mother's kitchen table shelling peas with Abby and Sarah.

'You'll have to make room for tea in a minute,' their mother told them.

'That's easier said than done,' Abby remarked. Empty pods, escaped peas and tufts of green stringy stuff were everywhere. Casey and Sarah pushed it all across to one side of the table.

'Come and get it, everyone.' Helen had prepared a lazy meal of cocktail frankfurts with bread, butter and tomato sauce. She told them she'd spent the day helping Moira Bowman sort through some of Henrietta's personal papers and it had exhausted her.

'Dale, you could've had a shower before tea,' Abby was complaining.

He'd recently returned from a fishing trip and his jeans were plastered with mud to the knees. He'd been sitting outside scaling and filleting the dozen small mullet and garfish he'd caught and brought the odour inside with him. 'What's the point of having a shower until I've finished, Princess Perfect?'

'It's just that you're putting the rest of us off our…'

Their father hurried into the kitchen, straightening the collar of his flannel shirt. 'A bloke in a Porsche just came. Casey, he must be your friend.' A loud knock followed.

'The house is a mess!' Helen began a mad dash to retrieve dirty dishes from all corners of the kitchen.

Eric pushed past as soon as Casey opened the door. 'We still haven't had that talk. Suzanne told me I'd probably find you here. We're going to thrash it out. You can't put me off forever.'

Her cheeks were burning. 'Come through to the kitchen. We were just about to have tea.'

Eric moved his chair a few feet back from the table as if to surround himself with an area of clean space. His aroma of spicy aftershave blended with Dale's odour of fish gut.

'Eric, I'm afraid you've caught us on a lazy night.' Poor Helen hardly knew where to look. 'I would've loved to cook you a proper meal. Perhaps one day soon? But you're welcome to join us for hotdogs.'

He glanced at the table. 'No thank you.'

Casey could sense her mother's poise leaking out of her.

'At least let me get you a drink. We have apple juice or beer if you'd prefer.'

'I'm fine, thank you.' For once he knew better than to request his usual glass of bourbon.

Only Casey's father could be relied upon to engage Eric in small talk as if he often entertained men in lavish suits. He began a spiel of chatter about the sea breeze and all the work he'd done on the house over the years. Although Casey knew Eric wouldn't be the least interested, she could have hugged her father.

Dale drew a deep swig from his beer bottle, began one of his loud

The Risky Way Home

belches, remembered their guest and tried to smother it mid-stream.

Abby sat demurely buttering a slice of bread but regarded Eric with dancing blue eyes. She looked across at Casey. The glint of apologetic amusement in Abby's eyes brought a surge of something unexpected rolling up Casey's throat. She took a moment to work out that it was a giggle and not the sort that could easily be swallowed. Casey quickly excused herself. She dashed to her bedroom, clicked the door behind her, sat on the bed and laughed out loud.

'Maybe they think I'm so ashamed of them, I've gone off to cry,' she mused. 'I'd better go and rescue them.'

When Casey returned, Eric was on his feet. He barely glanced at her on his way to the front door. 'I have other things to do. I'll see you at work on Monday.'

Then Dale astounded everybody. He pushed back his chair and followed them. 'Nice to meet you, mate.' He extended one of his stained hands with its chipped, grimy nails.

Casey watched Eric's eyes flicker to Dale's hand and up again. His lip curled as he turned away. 'I'm glad to have met you, too.' His tone was frosty, but polite.

Her subdued family waited until he'd driven away before they all began to speak at once. Helen buried her face in her hands. 'I've never felt so embarrassed. I've been so anxious to meet him too. Oh Casey, he barely even spoke to you.'

'He smelled like a perfume factory.' Sarah's nose was still twitching.

Abby turned to her brother. 'Tell me one thing. Why were you suddenly so well-mannered? You never give any of my visitors the time of day.'

'Because he was looking at me as if I was a slug. It's my house. Who does he think he is? I just wanted to see what he'd do if I offered to shake hands. Casey, you're not serious about him, are you? Please say you're not. He says he was glad to meet me. I've never heard such tripe. He's a stuck up…'

'Dale!' their mother interjected. 'That's enough! Look at this pig sty. I can hardly blame him.'

'Thanks, everyone,' Casey said when she could fit a word in.

'We tried our best to make him feel at home. There's no need to be sarcastic,' Doug told her.

'Wait a minute, Dad.' Abby was laughing. 'She's serious. Why are you thanking us?'

'For helping me get rid of him at last. Dale, he was telling the truth. He was glad to meet you. Notice he didn't say it was nice to meet you.'

'You're not making sense,' Doug said. 'What difference does his choice of words make? Glad to meet him? Nice to meet him? It means the same.'

Casey shook her head. 'No it doesn't, Dad. He didn't think it was nice to meet Dale. But he was glad to meet him because now he thinks he knows what sort of family I come from. You all did for me what the Bowmans did for Suzanne.'

'I still don't understand what you're talking about.'

Casey wished she could share the joke with somebody who already understood and didn't need it to be explained. She thought of Piers. He knew both Dale and Eric well enough to relish the story. She could hardly wait to get home and tell him. Then she remembered why she was with her family in the first place. Casey stopped smiling. Things wouldn't be the same with Piers before too long. He expected her to move out and live with Suzanne. Pretty soon they would become like strangers yet again.

⁎——⁎——⁎——⁎——⁎

She went to church with her parents on Sunday morning but Casey's mind wandered so she barely heard a word. *Wish I could've concentrated.* Although he had to be well over eighty years old, Pastor Hargreaves would always be Casey's favourite preacher. His sermons were encouraging and straight to the point.

The old man approached her after church in the hall where people were having refreshments. 'Will you explain your worried frown, young lady? I can see peoples' faces very clearly from the podium. I hope it wasn't something I said.'

'To tell you the truth, I didn't have my mind on the service at all,' she admitted. 'I *was* thinking of other things. I'm sure you were excellent and I'm sorry I missed most of what you said.' She couldn't remember Pastor Hargreaves without his halo of wispy-white hair. As a child, Casey had drawn him a special picture of himself with glued-on cotton-wool hair. For as long as she could remember, he had spoken to her after church. When she was very small, he'd stooped down and called her his 'little bright-haired doll.'

'I haven't spoken to you for a long time. Come through to my office for a chat.'

The sympathy in the pastor's faded blue eyes attracted her and she remembered that she was free to speak more candidly to him than to anyone else. He didn't know the people in her story. Although she followed Pastor Hargreaves to his cosy office tucked behind the kitchen, Casey had no idea what she was going to say.

'It must be a matter of the heart,' he began.

She found herself smiling. 'What makes you think so?'

He gave a knowing wink and drew his radiator close to their knees. 'It's just that you've grown so pretty, it was my first guess. I hope it's not too stuffy in here. I know the weather's been warm but I still get chilly.'

'No, that's fine.' She hadn't been in the elderly pastor's office for years and basked in the warmth. The walls felt saturated with his years of prayers and God's presence seemed to fill the little room like a comforting blanket.

'So I've established that your thoughts must be with a young man?'

'Two young men.' Casey wanted to see the pastor's reaction and she wasn't disappointed. His eyelids sprang wider apart.

'Please tell me more.'

'I don't want to mention any names.'

'I promise they can remain anonymous. Tell me about the first.'

Casey decided that if she was going to tell the story, she might as well have some fun. 'Okay. I've just broken up with him. At least, I hope he'll leave me alone now. A friend of mine talked me into going out with him a few times. But I found out I didn't want to keep seeing him.'

'May I call that one, Young Man Number One?'

'Yeah, sure. When I tried to tell him, he wouldn't give up.'

'I can't say I blame him. Who'd want to let you go?'

Casey forced a polite smile. 'But I can't understand him. He wants to change me. I don't know why he wouldn't stop chasing me. I think it must've been just as Suz...., my friend said. His pride was bruised to think that anyone would want to break up with him.'

'Some predicaments we get ourselves into quickly can take far longer to wriggle out of.' Pastor Hargreaves had sympathy in his voice. 'If you had been listening, that's what I preached about. Now how about Young Man Number Two?'

Casey had almost made one blunder already. She chose her words extra carefully. 'He's somebody I've known for quite a long time and never thought highly of. But now things have changed.'

'And you've fallen in love with him?'

She instinctively ducked her head. 'I've never actually used those words out in the open like this. I asked my mum to describe what being in love felt like. I guess if it's anything like what she said, then I *might* be.'

'What was her description?'

Casey gave a sheepish laugh and rattled it off. 'She said that your heart pounds like a drum whenever he walks past, and when he glances in your direction, it turns to mush. I know that sounds so corny but...' Casey looked up. 'I can't put him out of my head. If I turn up at..., well, somewhere I expect to find him and he's not there, I'll be grouchy until I see him. And when we are together I feel as if I'm dancing inside even though he barely looks at me.'

The pastor's eyes were shining. 'Helen said all that about Doug?'

'Yeah. I thought it was pretty hilarious when she first said it.'

'It's beautiful.'

'Beautiful for her that she got her man,' Casey muttered.

'And you're certain that Young Man Number Two doesn't share your feelings?'

'I doubt it. But the most annoying part is that once I used to think he did. But back then I wasn't interested in him.'

Pastor Hargreaves hunched forward to pat her shoulder. 'It's clear to me what you need to do.'

Casey had always liked his clear-cut manner. 'What's that?'

'Tell Number Two how you feel.'

She was shaking her head before he'd even finished speaking. 'I can't. I've left it too late.'

'But imagine if he feels the same way. You'd be doing both of you a grave injustice not to mention it.'

'Then why can't he tell me?' she asked with some bitterness. 'I wish we lived back in your youth. Wasn't it the man's role to tell the woman then?'

'Yes, but that might not happen in your case even if you lived sixty years ago.'

It was Casey's turn to raise her eyebrows. 'Why not?'

'It seems to me he might possibly think you're still in love with Number One.'

Casey wished she could think of a sanctified oath to vent her feelings. 'You're right. That's just what he'd think.'

"Mistakes follow us.' The pastor's eyes were twinkling. 'But never mind. They can be fixed. You just tell him you love him. What's the worst that could happen?'

'He could laugh at me and tell me I'm a dunce. No, that's not his style. He'd try to let me down as gently as he could. And that'd make me feel like a squashed beetle.'

'If he'd do either of those things, it'd be clear that he wasn't the right one for you, after all. And then your problem would be solved, because at least you'd know.'

'But it wouldn't be solved. Because I'd still love him!'

Pastor Hargreaves raised a knobbly finger. 'Aha! That's what you needed to hear yourself say.'

Casey gazed a long moment at the knees of her skirt. 'You're right. I have to tell him.'

'And I hope it goes well for you.'

'Well, if he tells me I've made a huge mistake, I'll probably be too busy dying of embarrassment to come here again for months. And then you'll guess what must've happened.'

Pastor Hargreaves' voice followed her to the door. 'Before you go, will you answer one more question?'

She turned. 'Sure.'

'It's about Young Man Number Two. Is he Moira's son?'

She almost choked on her gasp. 'Who told you that?'

Pastor Hargreaves smiled impishly. 'I'm sorry, Casey. It was just a hunch. I've met that young man and his little nipper at his mother's place a few times and had some good chats with him. I know you're staying with him. I like him. I really like him. That boy reminds me of a modern day Brother Lawrence.'

Casey sank her red face into her hands. 'Great. Brother Lawrence was a monk.'

Pastor Hargreaves threw back his head and gave one of his hearty laughs. 'Well, there's where the similarity ends. Piers is definitely no monk. And you're one of the only girls I think would be good enough for him.'

'If I'd known you knew, I'd never have said all that stuff I said,' Casey mumbled. 'I wish you hadn't let me ramble on.'

'If I hadn't guessed who he was, I wouldn't have said the things I said either. You're a treasure, Casey. Do you think I'd advise you to go and tell just anyone you love him? But I didn't ask you just to make sport with you. I asked because I think I can tell you something that you might find encouraging.'

'What's that?'

'I have a sneaking suspicion that he might feel the same about you. I saw him watching you at his grandmother's funeral while you were busy talking to his mother. Believe me, I've lived long enough to know that a man doesn't watch a woman for that long, and with that expression, for no reason.'

Chapter 20

Casey parked beneath the carport and caught sight of Piers and Jerome up the slope of the hill near Ben's enclosure. She took a few moments to watch them unobserved. Piers swung Jerome onto Ben's back and held him steady for a short ride. When Jerome began to slide over to one side, Piers caught him up and spun him through the air. Casey heard Jerome's peals of laughter through her closed car windows. Slowly she climbed out, knowing that Piers would stop his clowning act as soon as he saw her. Then she'd have to find a way to tell him what she'd resolved to say.

She was right. As he saw her crest the hill, Piers shook off his silliness. 'Hi. You're back early.'

'There was nothing to do with my family.' *I'm so dense!* That was not the reason she'd returned. Instead of saying that she'd come back to see him, she was already making up fabrications. *How on earth am I supposed to tell him how I feel about him out of the blue?* She'd anticipated that the job would be difficult but now that she stood before him, it seemed impossible. The sea air near her parents' home had been clear and crisp but now that she was back in the Hills, a few spots of rain hit her face. Casey glanced up at smudgy clouds that matched her state of mind.

'Where's Suzanne?'

He shrugged. 'I think she went to look at one of those flats. If you'd been half an hour earlier, you could've gone with her.'

It was worse than impossible!

'I don't even want to go and live with Suzanne in one of those stupid flats! Nobody even thought to ask me. You both just assumed I'd fall in with Suzanne's plans, as usual.'

'I thought she had asked you, and that you'd agreed.'

'Fat lot you know, then! If you'd even bothered to look at me you might've seen me shaking my head. But no, I'm just 'Dumb Ole Casey', who always jumps whenever Suzanne clicks her fingers.' She winced as she spoke. Not only was she not telling him how she felt, she was slashing their friendship to shreds and couldn't seem to help it.

The tiny ball of a sun behind her shone into Piers' face. He gave her a puzzled squint. 'I never thought that at all. Why are you so mad?'

She drew a shuddering breath, wondering what was going to pour out next. 'Because you once told me you wouldn't listen if Suzanne tried to talk you out of having me here.' Casey didn't know if the drops on her face were tears or rain. 'And now look what's happened. The very first time she tried to get me away from here, you totally broke your promise.'

Jerome gave a nervous intake of breath. He was watching her with wide eyes. *Great! Now I'm a monster, just like when I first came!* Guilt was slathered onto her irritation but instead of extinguishing it, it kindled the flame. 'So thanks for nothing!'

'Hey, hold on a minute!' Piers protested. 'It's only because I thought you wanted to go! I wasn't kicking you out or anything. That promise still stands. If you want to stay, I'll back you up.'

That knocked the fight out of her. Casey had no more words to say. *And I still haven't told him.* She heaved a sigh and mumbled, 'I do want to stay.'

'Then stay! You've grown to love this place, like me, haven't you? I can understand that.' Piers raised his eyes. 'All this wide empty green space and fresh air grows on you, I know.'

'Those aren't the things I'd miss most.' It exasperated her even more that he was behaving so reasonably after her tirade.

'What then?'

Casey knew that at least one of the drops on her face must have been a tear because it was too warm to be rain. 'I'd miss you, you dope.' At last she'd said it, but found she couldn't look him in the eye.

'What did you say?' She heard the incredulity in Piers' voice.

The Risky Way Home

'I think you heard me.' The rain began falling steadier. Jerome dashed to the shelter of the verandah and Casey turned to follow.

'Casey, hold up a minute!' Piers cried.

She quickened her pace and pretended not to hear him. What a mess she'd made of the whole thing. But of course his speed was more than a match for hers. Piers caught hold of her hand.

'Hold on!' he repeated. He sounded as if he was laughing and she resented it.

'I don't want to say it again!' she almost yelled.

'Okay, I'm not asking you to. I must've heard you right. I'd never have imagined you said that. I just have a question for you.'

She kept her burning eyes open because if she closed them, they'd surely drip. 'What is it?'

He hesitated and moistened his lips. Piers' throat rippled as he swallowed. He didn't seem to notice the rain and when he spoke, his voice was low. 'Haven't you any idea of the way I've always felt about you?'

Water teemed down in earnest now. Casey slowly shook her head. 'No. How do you feel about me? You never, ever told me. I couldn't guess. How come you never told me?'

He quirked one eyebrow. 'At school? You'd never have gone out with me.'

'I mean more recently. Since I lived here.'

Jerome's piping voice was calling to them from the shelter of the verandah but neither of them cared about the rain.

'Why would I? That would've been dumb. You were crazy for Eric!'

Casey groaned. 'There's one talent I have that you didn't mention the time I asked you. I have a genius for completely stuffing things up.'

Piers' crooked grin was firmly in place. 'I think we've both got that talent.'

'How long have you felt anything for me?' she asked.

He was still holding her hand but let go to gently raise her chin. 'Since we were both about thirteen. You always looked so calm and happy. There was something translucent about you. I used to hear Suzanne and her friends talking when you all came over, and you were never mean or vicious, like some of the others. The place would light up whenever you came. If you ever glanced in my direction, I wouldn't know where to look. I was always trying to think of ways to impress you but when you were there, they seemed pathetic. I just turned into this speechless idiot with mush for brains.' He chuckled at her expression. 'You look surprised. Don't forget, I've had ten years to think of all this.'

Now she felt as if the streaming rain on her cheeks should have been burning.

'Is it really over with Eric?' Piers was asking.

Casey nodded. Words bubbled up and she still didn't know what they were going to be but now she wanted to talk. 'I told him it was because we were too different from each other but that was really only part of it. I could've forced myself to put up with his arrogance for longer if I'd really wanted to. It was something else. I couldn't very well keep going out with him while I was falling for you.'

Heavy drops stung her arms through the sleeves of her shirt but Casey didn't care. The wonderment on Piers' face was all the warmth she needed.

'Now I have a question for you,' she said.

'What is it?' He sounded excited.

'Remember that time at the hospital when you hugged me? Did I hug you back? I couldn't remember.'

He instantly shook his head. 'No. I would've remembered that for sure.'

'I thought not. Can I make up for it?'

He opened his soaking arms wide. 'Please do.'

Then she was rubbing her cheek against his chest, feeling his wet hair drip down her neck. His flannel shirt squelched as she wrung it out to draw him closer. He lifted her off her feet and spun her around. Casey was laughing. Piers was laughing too. Being soaking wet with him was better than being dry with anyone else. Another, far smaller hand slipped into Casey's. She gazed down into Jerome's damp, smiling face.

'Are you playin'?' he asked. 'Can I play too? Is this gonna be like that mud fight?'

Piers swung his son up high on his shoulders. 'Much, much better than that.'

The Risky Way Home

Casey never would have believed that doing mundane activities could be so exciting. When they'd changed into dry clothes, she and Piers played several games of Snakes and Ladders with Jerome. They kept gazing shyly at each other and smiling. Casey's hand would brush against Piers' while she shook the dice and moved her counter. Before Jerome went to bed, she made some cinnamon toast while Piers fixed hot chocolate. Although they'd worked in the kitchen together many times before, they'd never stood so close with their shoulders touching. Her pulse raced with the thrill of what was being postponed until Jerome was asleep. Casey stretched out on the rug and listened while Piers read Jerome his bedtime story. Finally the little boy's eyelids drooped and they were able to tuck him into bed and return to the couch.

'Were you pleased that day Suzanne phoned and asked if I could be your boarder?' Asking the question set her face on fire but that didn't matter. Casey knew she could easily make Piers blush too.

'I was stunned. I would've dropped the phone except that I was holding it so tight.'

'Do you mean you already had plans to steal my heart?'

He was blushing already. She knew it would be easy.

'No, I knew you wouldn't have had very fond memories of me. But I did wonder if there'd be any way I could change your mind. I knew I'd probably be setting myself up for a kick in the teeth but thought I'd take the chance. Just in case it was a divine appointment, you know. God had already been good to me in other ways.' He laughed self-consciously. 'Once I almost gave myself away.'

'When was that?'

'After the mud fight Jerome enjoyed so much. When Ben tore that dress, I thought you'd never speak to me again. But then you laughed and we all had so much fun. I admit I started trying to plan my next move. You don't know how close I came to speaking up and asking you out.'

She entwined her fingers through his. 'What stopped you?'

'The very next night was your first date with Eric. And when I found out he was coming, I was so annoyed with myself.'

'You were a bit snappy that night.'

'So you remember how I stuck my big foot in my mouth and made you cry? It was just that I felt so dumb. After convincing myself that I wouldn't get any wild ideas about you, I'd come so close to making the biggest mistake ever. There I was, sitting and wondering how I could apologise to you when his Porsche rolled up. I can tell you, right on the spot I vowed to never, ever let my imagination run away with me again.'

'And all the time, the biggest fool was me,' Casey sighed.

'No, you weren't. It seemed perfectly reasonable to see how you'd prefer him over me.' Piers looked at her curiously. 'I want to know when you did start thinking about me like that. Not to mention why.'

'It might've even been the night of that mud fight. I'd definitely started the day Sam died and I invited you and Jerome to meet me for gelati. Hey, what's up?' He'd relinquished her hand to cover his face.

'You have a way of remembering my dopiest moments. When I walked into that café and saw you and Eric…' Piers' shoulders stiffened. 'Aaargh! I was ready to grab Jerome's hand and dash out but then he saw you. And you saw us. I just wanted to crawl under the nearest table.'

'But you weren't dopey at all. I felt so terrible for making it seem as though I'd stood you up.'

He was peeping at her from between his fingers. 'What do you mean "making it seem?" You did stand us up!' Casey could tell from his voice that Piers was laughing.

'You might not believe this but I would've far rather been there with you, even way back then. When I got home, I cried. I would've done anything I could to make it up to you.'

He wrapped his arm around her shoulder. 'Do you still want to?'

'Of course. That was one of my worst nights ever.'

'Then why not invite us there again? It was pretty good gelati but I wasn't in the frame of mind to enjoy it.'

'It's a date! How about this Thursday night?'

'Sounds good.'

Casey nestled close enough to feel his hair brushing her cheek. 'To think I asked my mother how it feels to be in love,' she mumbled.

'Did you? What did she say?'

'She said I'd know when it hit me. And I did. With Eric I kept trying to gauge my feelings about him but with you they just bubbled up and overwhelmed me. I just wanted to shake you! I was screaming inside, "What can I ever do to make Piers pay attention to me?"'

'And all that time I was trying my hardest not to pay attention to you.' He brushed a kiss against her hair. 'I was trying to be so careful to hide how I felt about you.'

She felt her insides warm in a way they never had for Eric. 'And I was afraid to show how I felt about you. So do you think it was a divine appointment, that day Suzanne phoned you?'

He raised her knuckles to his lips. 'The divinest appointment ever.'

'But there's just one thing,' she murmured.

'What's that?'

Casey hid her face against his shoulder. Her cheeks burned so hot she imagined she must look an unflattering shade of scarlet. 'Now that things have taken a different turn, I need to reassess where I'll be living. Staying here with you could be fraught with difficulties now. I don't believe in living together outside of marriage.'

'I hadn't even begun to think that far.' He sounded crestfallen. 'But I know you're right. I'll really miss you. So will Jerome.'

'Don't worry, you're bound to see far more of me than you ever did when I first moved in.'

'Do you promise?'

'Yes. There's nowhere else I'd rather be.'

Casey was tilting her face for a proper kiss and Piers was bowing his head closer when the front door swung open and Suzanne snapped on the bright ceiling light. While she stood blinking at them Casey almost laughed at Suzanne's slack jaw. *This must remind her of when she found Tim and Ingrid on the couch! It's terrible!* Casey turned a giggle into a cough.

'How long has *this* been going on?'

Piers pretended to misunderstand the broader scope of Suzanne's question. 'About five minutes.'

Then Casey couldn't help it. She let out a strangled noise that couldn't be disguised. Suzanne glared at each of them in turn but her gaze lingered on Casey. 'So this is why you seemed so reluctant to move out with me! You might've told me! I don't need to be kept in the dark like a child!'

'I will share the flat with you,' Casey said quickly.

Now two sets of inky grey Bowman eyes were staring at her.

'I'm not sure I'd even want you to, now! Why would you even think of leaving? I can't figure you out, Casey. That's about the weirdest thing I've ever heard.' Suzanne swept out to the kitchen.

Piers tightened his grip around Casey's hand. 'Don't worry about her. We've done well. I didn't think we'd get rid of her that quickly tonight.'

Casey laughed. Even though Suzanne was cross, she didn't care. Her spirit was soaring. *I love Piers and he loves me!* Who would've believed anything that fit so perfectly would ever happen to her?

Casey hadn't expected to catch a wink of sleep. When she finally opened her eyes, spring sunshine shone through the chinks in her curtain. She squinted at her clock and was surprised to find she'd slept in. Outside, she heard Piers letting Ben out of his enclosure to take him for his morning run.

Despite her happiness, Casey went downstairs with some trepidation. If Suzanne was still vexed with her, it would be a long, hard day at work. Suzanne's was the first voice she heard, chattering brightly with Jerome in the kitchen. Casey dared to hope that was a good sign. As she entered, Suzanne turned to greet her with the wide, bright Bowman beam. An even better sign.

'Morning, Sleepyhead. I was beginning to think I'd need to wake you up. Sorry about my reaction last night. I was just surprised. You understand, don't you?'

Before Casey could respond, Suzanne rushed on. 'I wasn't mad because you fell for Piers. It was just that I wanted to be the one to set you up with a man. I suppose it would've made me feel useful.'

Jerome piped up, 'This strawberry one, Auntie Suze.' He waved a sachet of instant cooking oats beneath her nose.

Suzanne eyed it dubiously. 'Sorry Poppet, I've never cooked one of these before.'

'I'll do it.' Casey was glad to busy herself fixing Jerome's breakfast.

'You see what I mean,' Suzanne said. 'You don't mind doing boring, everyday things. I can't be bothered but sometimes it bothers me that I can't be bothered. But I was talking about you and Piers. The more I thought about it, the more annoyed I got with myself for not thinking of it first. Even the things I'm supposed to be good at, like setting up matches, I'm bad at.'

'I'm glad you didn't try. It's been hard enough these last few months, pussyfooting around each other trying to hide how we felt. If you'd tried to stir anything up between us, it would've made things really awkward.' Casey turned aside her glowing face and poured milk on Jerome's porridge.

'But I can't believe I was so eager to see you with Eric that I missed what was right under my nose. And the most infuriating thing is that this is so much better.'

Casey shyly scrutinised her. 'Better in what way?'

'Well just think, if you two ever tie the knot, I won't just be keeping you as a good friend. I'll be getting you for a sister.'

'Gee... thanks.' Casey could have hugged her. She had never met Suzanne's equal for irritating her one moment, then winning her right back over again the next.

'Hey, in a way I did help set you up with Piers. I'm the one who got you living here.'

'I know. I owe you a huger debt than I can ever repay. That is, unless you'd like me to set you up with my brother.'

Suzanne threw back her head and laughed long and loud. 'You're hilarious, do you know that?'

Casey grinned too.

'I have just one more question,' Suzanne said. 'You had a chance with Eric. So why choose Piers? He's so eccentric.'

'That's the easiest question ever. I can understand him and be myself with him.' Casey was up, rinsing her bowl and stroking Jerome's curls. 'When I first started working for you, I wanted to make myself extraordinary. But hanging out with Piers has shown me what a real extraordinary person is like. They value the ordinary things in life. It's the only real way to live.'

Suzanne didn't speak for a moment. 'Casey, the only person who'd equal you is Piers himself.' She slowly sipped her last inch of black coffee. 'Don't ever tell him I said so, but I might even mean that in a good way.'

Chapter 21

Casey sat alone behind the studio's counter just after lunch break. Suzanne was taking an inventory of the wardrobes while Eric kept himself busy in the viewing room. He'd not spoken a word to Casey since his visit to her parents' house but she'd seen him glower in her direction. Casey surprised herself by caring even less than she'd expected. A man in a dark suit stooped beneath the low door frame to step into the studio.

'Can I help you, sir?'

He stared fixedly at her.

'How can I help you?' Casey repeated.

The stranger's probing blue eyes scrutinised her from head to waist. 'Forgive me. You can't be the person I'm looking for.' His voice was thick with a foreign accent.

Being examined so closely unnerved Casey. This customer was suave and smartly dressed. She hoped her discomposure didn't show on her face.

'Are you Suzanne Dupont?' he asked.

'No, but she's here. I'll call her for you.' Casey was relieved to move away from him.

Suzanne swept in with her charming smile that displayed most of her teeth. 'Good afternoon, sir. How can we help you?' Her graceful confidence was disarming, as usual. Wisps of hair escaped from her clasp in the seemingly careless manner which Casey now knew took an hour each morning to achieve.

The man's jaw turned slack at the sight of her. 'Great heavens above! I think it might be you!'

Suzanne frowned. 'Do I know you?'

He cleared his throat. 'Not anymore. Allow me to re-introduce myself. You might find my story hard to believe but please hear me out. My name is Jean-Michel Dupont.'

The room spun around Casey. For an instant, she forgot to breathe.

Suzanne's self-assurance was gone as she stretched a hand toward the man. 'Papa?'

'It is you!' With two strides he clutched her slender hands. His face was flushed and fierce. 'It's And I was just about to walk out. I'm so glad I asked! After all these years, I've found you. I didn't know if you were living or dead. My Suzanne! My petite belle.'

Casey couldn't draw her eyes from him. Jean Dupont's hair was highly coiffured and remarkably thick and black, with only a few patches of silver around his temples. He appeared younger than Moira, although Casey knew he was six years her senior. His gold rings and highly polished shoes were almost dazzling. Casey breathed slowly, to calm her thumping heart.

'You've grown so incredibly beautiful,' Jean turned his head to take in the premises without relinquishing Suzanne's hands. 'And such a successful business woman. Look at you. You used to be my prattling little dancing girl.'

Suzanne's mascara had started to run. 'I've always remembered you. And I never stopped wanting to see you even after all these years. I wanted to return to you from the moment we arrived in Australia. I can't believe this is happening.' She ducked her glowing face and blinked hard.

Jean's eyes flashed sparks. 'What your mother did was criminal!'

'How did you find me after all this time?' she cried.

He dug into his breast pocket and extracted one of their business cards. It was crumpled and worn around the edges but the name 'Suzanne Dupont' still glittered in bright gold letters. 'I was in the city with the big bridge. What's it called? Sydney! The woman beside me on the ferry had this card in her purse and your name leaped out at my senses. My petite Suzanne, I did not believe it would be you for one moment, but I asked the lady if she could spare the card. I couldn't leave any leads unchecked, even after all this time. I once combed every inch of Britain and the United

States searching for you. I never dreamed Moira would shanghai you to the other side of the world?' His face turned grim. 'If only I'd known long ago, I would've been here like a bullet from a gun. I never dreamed she'd let you keep your name intact.'

'She didn't!' Suzanne was laughing and crying. 'I changed it back to Suzanne Dupont just for my business. I loved the sound of it. It just rolled off my tongue. Mum and Gran had changed our name to Bowman.'

'Bowman?' Jean pronounced the name with its two distinct syllables. It sounded odd and foreign on his tongue.

Icy fingers of foreboding tickled the back of Casey's neck. She stared at Suzanne, trying to catch her eye, willing her to reveal nothing else. She was witnessing the opening of a Pandora's Box that should have stayed tightly sealed. If things hadn't already gone so far, she might've considered butting in to tell Jean Dupont that he'd chosen the wrong Suzanne after all.

'Bowman was Gran's maiden name,' Suzanne told him.

'Do your mother and grandmother live in this city too?' Jean's accent made the words sound like 'muzzer' and 'gran'muzzer.'

'Gran died a few months ago.'

'I'm sorry to hear that.'

I'll bet he is! He had begun to appear his age to Casey. The frown lines around Jean's mouth and eyes were etched deep. 'I would have liked to have renewed your grandmother's acquaintance.'

'You're not missing much, believe me. The rest of us still live around Adelaide. Piers has a little boy. You didn't know it but you're a grandfather.' Suzanne let loose one of her loud giggles.

Jean closed his eyes and shook his head. 'That news is enough to set my head spinning. I confess it's even harder for me to imagine Piers grown up than it was to imagine you. He was so much the little enfant.'

Casey fought an urge to creep out of the studio and begin running. But Suzanne chose that moment to remember her.

'He's all grown up alright, and this is his new girlfriend, Casey. But she was one of my very best friends long before she was ever his girlfriend.'

Jean Dupont studied Casey's face with renewed interest. 'Nice rosy little piece,' he mumbled. 'How do you do?'

She watched her own hand grasp his. Jean's hand was strong and smooth. His rings pressed into Casey's fingers.

The Risky Way Home

The viewing room door swung open and Eric stepped out. Suzanne pounced on him and tugged him forward. 'You won't believe who this is in a million years. He's my father from Paris who I haven't seen for twenty years. You always thought he was a figment of my imagination, didn't you? Papa, this is my partner, Eric Adams.'

Eric's gaze took in the older man's tailored clothes and elegant bearing. Casey knew Eric well enough to see that Jean Dupont had made a favourable impression. He extended his hand. 'I'm pleased to meet you, sir.'

For several awkward moments, Jean did not return the salute. He raised his eyebrows and turned back to Suzanne with a glint of suspicion. 'Partner?'

Her merry giggle tinkled through the room. *'Business* partner, that is.'

Only then did Jean Dupont give Eric's hand a stiff shake.

'Suzanne, where can we meet tonight? We have twenty years of catching up to do.'

'Let me take you out to dinner. I'll show you my new flat first. I'm going to move into it next week. Why don't we go now? No way can I work for three more hours now that you're here! Eric, you'll have to hold down the fort yourself. Papa's here.'

Casey quickly asked permission to leave too, hoping that Suzanne would agree.

'Okay! You go and tell Piers that our father is here. On second thoughts, don't tell him yet. I'd love to see his face when he hears the news. But it might be too hard to keep to yourself. Tell him if you like, Casey.'

The glimpse of her own dormer window through the trees seemed to wink at her, as if surprised to see her home so early. Piers and Jerome were nowhere inside. They weren't in the work shed or near Ben's enclosure. Casey discovered them lying on their backs beneath the shade of a large pine tree at the top of the hill near the fence. They hadn't heard her soft approach.

'That one's a horse with a flowing mane.' Piers pointed up into the sky.

'Yeah, horsie.' Jerome's little shoes thudded the carpet of pine needles beneath him.

They were searching for cloud pictures. Piers saw Casey and scrambled to sit up. 'Here's more sunshine. Why are you home already?'

She sank down beside him. Casey longed to simply enjoy the October warmth. The air was balmy like medicine after the recent rainfall and the ground springy. Casey gazed out over the blue and green panorama. A brilliant canopy of sky melded into the blanket of billowing grass. Casey loved that time of year when heat began to soak into the ground while the countryside was still vibrant after its winter rain. Despite the wide open space, she pressed close to Piers as if they were enclosed in a tight spot.

Casey didn't want to be the person to break the news to him, but if she didn't tell Piers, it would hang over her. She knew that if she *did* tell him, it would hang just as heavily over him. And then the gloom would stretch to cover them both. Whether or not she opened her mouth, it had spread too far already.

'Piers, your father came today!'

She wished she hadn't been so blunt. He turned rigid and although the sky was bright, Piers' pupils dilated.

'You mean Jean Dupont?'

Casey flinched. Although they'd both read Moira's diary, neither of them had ever spoken that name aloud. The sound of it from Piers' lips made her stomach churn. She didn't want to echo the name, so Casey just nodded.

'He came into the studio?' Piers prompted.

Casey nodded again. 'He found one of Suzanne's silly business cards in Sydney and came to Adelaide to check it out.' She nestled close to Piers and told him the whole story while Jerome poked pine needles between the straps of her sandals. When Casey finished, the great silence buzzed in her eardrums. Then Piers wrapped his arm around her.

'Don't worry about him. We're all grown up now. He won't be able to hurt us anymore. And he might have changed.'

'Maybe,' she said, though she doubted it.

'What was he like?'

Casey stroked the back of his hand with her thumb. Piers' hand, with its long fingers and strong knuckles, bore some resemblance to the one she'd shaken that afternoon in the studio. But his hand was younger and leaner with calluses and grazes. She gripped it tighter.

The Risky Way Home

'Very foreign. Tall and dark. He talks fast. His eyes are really bright. And he didn't sound friendly when he mentioned your mother.'

'I suppose that'd be natural, even if he has changed. Listen, even if he is still as bad as he used to be, he's outnumbered. There's only one of him, and we're a family.'

Casey allowed Piers' words to soak into her and warm her through. But when she glanced up at his face, she saw that it was not as reassuring as his voice. Piers was staring at Jerome's busy hands without really seeing them and he looked chilled to the bone.

Chapter 22

'You should've worn something smarter.' Suzanne straightened Piers' shirt collar with her eyebrows knotted in a frown. 'Papa always dresses immaculately.'

Piers looked down at his neat blue shirt and clean jeans. 'What's wrong with this? I don't think I have anything smarter.'

'You look fine,' Casey assured him as she stirred a pot of bubbling pumpkin soup. 'You know Suzanne. She likes everyone to be ultra-glamorous. She's used to seeing people dressed up all day.'

'And so is Papa,' Suzanne said.

Jean Dupont was to meet Piers and Jerome for the first time that evening. Casey had helped Suzanne prepare a special meal for him. Suzanne had been out with her father for the last three nights. After taking him to a restaurant the evening she'd met him, he had treated her to even more lavish dinners twice. Each time, she'd woken Casey in the early hours of the morning, brimming over with chatter about her father's charming conversation, good looks and fine taste in restaurants.

Suzanne swooped on Jerome to give his already shining face a vigorous polish with the dishcloth. She told Piers, 'I should've brought you a suit from the studio just for tonight.'

'I hope you're joking. Isn't this a simple home-cooked dinner? Does he expect it to be a suit and tie affair? He can take me as I am and if he's disappointed, that's his problem.'

'You're so determined to be difficult. You've set your mind to dislike him before you've even met him. Whatever you say, Mum has poisoned your mind against him and she's done a thorough job.'

Piers peered into the wall mirror to fiddle with his collar. 'I hope I will like him. I was only warning you that we ought to be cautious. Casey and I have read Mum's diary and you haven't.'

'Well I've met him, and you haven't!'

'All the more reason you should read the diary. Why don't you read it? It's not too late.'

Suzanne was back in the kitchen, re-arranging her platter of hors d'oeuvres. 'Never. I'm strong enough to choose not to be influenced by Mum's brainwashing.'

Casey checked the table setting. Suzanne's silver cutlery and candle holders were still immaculate. The silver spoon that Jerome clashed against a saucepan lid was from another set. The food was simmering nicely. There was nothing left to do, so she sank down onto the couch to calm her fluttering nerves.

'Please don't make it hard for us tonight,' Suzanne pleaded with Piers.

'What do you expect me to do? Throw my soup at him?'

'No, but I know how weird people can find you. I don't want you to make a bad first impression on Papa.'

Casey squeezed Piers' hand as he sat on the couch beside her. 'Don't listen to her. You aren't weird at all.'

'Of course he is!' Suzanne cried. 'Don't try to pretend you never found him weird.'

Casey blushed. 'Maybe I did once, but I've decided I prefer his weirdness to other people's normality.'

They all laughed. It lightened the mood. Piers wrapped his arm around Casey. 'I'll be on my best behaviour, Suzanne. I'll do everything but call him Papa.'

She appeared in the kitchen doorway, wiping her hands on a tea towel. 'You have to call him Papa!'

'No, I don't.'

Casey heaved a sigh and decided to give up trying to keep the peace. Perhaps their usual bickering helped Piers and Suzanne to deal with their own cases of nerves.

'I call him Papa,' Suzanne cried.

'I know. That's your business.'

'Well, what else can you call him?'

'Sir, Jean or Monsieur Dupont. Whichever he prefers.'

Suzanne scowled. 'It might be best if you call him nothing at all, then.'

'That suits me fine.'

'You're impossible.'

Jerome's voice piped up, 'I need to wash my hands.'

Casey saw his outstretched hands coming toward her, smeared with melted chocolate. 'Whoa, you sure do. Don't wipe them on my skirt.'

Suzanne pursued Jerome with the rag. 'You've been into my after-dinner mints. I thought you were being a bit too quiet. They're around your mouth, too.'

A brisk volley of raps on the door startled Jerome. Piers and Suzanne both stopped smiling at once. Casey stood up, dry in the mouth and faint in the head.

Jean-Michel Dupont regarded Piers wordlessly. It reminded Casey of the day she met him, when he looked her up and down in the studio. This time, even though she was not his object of scrutiny, she felt more ill-at-ease than before. Jean's steely blue eyes devoured every part of Piers; his height, clothing, hair and features. He was like an alien who feasted on people with his eyes.

Piers offered his hand. 'I'm pleased to meet you, Sir.' He sounded steady.

Only then did Jean's mouth quirk up at the corners. Without looking away from Piers' face, he gave what Casey could see was a bone-crunching handshake. Piers set his jaw and returned the pressure.

'Who would've believed this could be little Piers. You have a bit of the Dupont look. I never could imagine you fully grown, but now that I've seen you, I believe I could pick you out of a crowd of thousands.' Jean's eyes flashed as they focused on something closer to the floor and his face filled with wonder. There stood Jerome with his arm wrapped around Piers' leg. Jean Dupont stooped down to extend his hand.

'How do you do, my lad? I am your grandfather.'

Jerome behaved as characteristically as he usually did when directly addressed by a strange adult. His eyes squeezed shut as he buried his face in his father's pants. Jean straightened with a slight frown. 'What's the matter?'

'He's shy to start with,' Piers explained. 'He'll warm up.'

'A carbon copy of his father at the same age? Now I feel as if the clock has been wound back twenty years. You were so backward I could do nothing with you. You must be careful not to raise a milksop.' Jean took a pinch of Jerome's soft cheek between his fingers. 'Has your grandmother been telling you tales about me, my fine boy?'

Casey couldn't help flinching.

Piers answered for his son again. 'No, she never said a word about you.'

It turned out to be the wrong thing to say. Jean's bristly eyebrows drew together, casting a shadow across his face. 'Not ever? I might've expected that from Moira.'

Piers glanced at Casey. *I should've kept my mouth shut,* his expression told her. Casey tried to convey her heartfelt sympathy in a glance. It was going to be a long evening.

***

Dinner progressed smoothly for some time. Jean complimented Suzanne and Casey on their cooking. Being assigned a set spot behind the table helped to loosen Casey's tongue. She even exchanged a few pleasantries with Jean. Things were going better than she had anticipated, although she'd eaten her hot soup and Beef Wellington without tasting a bite. Piers' plate was still three quarters full. He bolted mouthfuls between telling Jean about his furniture business. The older man ran his hand across the smooth top of the hand- crafted table, evidently impressed.

'You ought to expand your business. You need to hire other men to work for you. You could find yourself head of a huge furniture empire.'

Piers shook his head with a grin. 'Maybe that's true in Paris where you come from, but not here in Adelaide. There are plenty of furniture makers as good as I am but not room for many empires.'

'Be positive!' Jean speared his fork through a wedge of potato. 'I have no time for talk of limitation. Do you like confining yourself to a mediocre lifestyle and a paltry income?'

Casey began to feel drained by his effervescence. Jean Dupont seemed to have only one manner of talking and that was loud and earnest.

Piers drew a slow breath before he replied. Casey guessed that thinking of polite and neutral replies to Jean's pointed observations was wearing on him too. 'I actually am doing pretty well. I can work at my own pace and keep an eye on Jerome at the same time.'

Jean turned his attention back to the little boy. Jerome sat beside Casey and he'd grown accustomed enough to the stranger's presence to relax. He watched the guttering flame from one of Suzanne's candles catch the draught near the kitchen door and laughed each time a wax drop hit the tray beneath it. He touched Casey's hand and beamed at her. 'Hey look, there's another candle growing.'

She ruffled his silky hair. 'That's because we've been sitting here for a long time.'

'Will you let me take your boy out for a day while you work?' Jean asked Piers. 'I imagine you'd welcome a chance to get him out of your hair.'

Piers placed his cutlery down. Jean's questions were growing steadily harder to answer. 'You're welcome to take him out but I'd rather go too.'

'Are you afraid to let him out of your sight or something?'

Piers decided that one didn't need to be answered. He took a sip of water and stared over the rim at his father, waiting with a vague hint of defiance for whatever might come next.

'You must try to understand me.' Jean spoke without unclenching his teeth. 'I had my two children stolen away from me. I need the opportunity to build a relationship with my grandson while he's young enough to get to know me.'

'Of course he must understand!' Suzanne shot Piers an imploring glance while her own carefully crafted eyebrows squirmed into a strange shape.

Piers ignored his sister. 'Please try to understand me. He's my son and you've only just come here. I know nothing about you. For all I know, you could whisk him back to France.'

His words hung in the air for a few moments. Casey could hardly

The Risky Way Home

breathe in the silence. At last Jean spoke. 'Perhaps you haven't changed as much as I first thought.'

Piers kept eye contact. 'Perhaps not.'

Jean's animation returned in a deluge. 'You have no idea of the pain!' His hands waved in spirals above the table. 'The infuriating, agonising frustration of having your own flesh and blood ripped out of your life without so much as goodbye.'

'No.' Piers was quiet and steady. 'And I don't intend to.'

Jean threw his crumpled napkin beside his plate. 'For twenty years I've been desperate to track down you and Suzanne. I could barely speak English when your mother snatched you from me. I guessed that she'd take you to some English speaking nation so I set about learning it. For year after year it seemed that my efforts would be a total waste of time.'

'You speak it very well.' At least that was easy for Piers to say.

'Merci,' Jean said with sarcasm in his voice.

'What Mum did was disgusting.' It seemed Suzanne couldn't bear to keep out of it. 'There's no excuse for ruining our lives as well as her own.'

'Ruined your lives?' Jean's nostrils flared. 'What do you mean? Hasn't Moira been a good mother?'

Piers cried, 'Yes!' and Suzanne blurted, 'No,' simultaneously. They flashed each other glances of annoyance. Suzanne had the grace to flush. 'I suppose she tried to be good in her wishy-washy way but Gran ruled the roost and we always had to play second fiddle. Don't deny that, Piers.' She glared at him as if half expecting him to try. 'I daresay Mum had her reasons for the things she's done, but she's one screwed-up lady. She had to be crazy, to take us from you.'

'It's high time I paid your mother a visit. Suzanne, will you write me down her address?'

For a split second, Suzanne hesitated. 'I know she's a nutcase, but you won't be too hard on her, will you?'

'No harder than she deserves.' Jean spoke in the heartfelt tone Casey noticed he always used for Suzanne. 'I simply want to have a talk. I deserve that much, hey?'

Suzanne seemed satisfied. Her favourite pen scratched Moira's address in her attractive, looping handwriting. Jean scanned the address and nodded. Casey watched his hand tuck it securely into his breast pocket. She'd eaten her meal without the senses of taste or smell, but these faculties returned in a rush and the odour of leftover dinner made her feel queasy. Piers took hold of her hand and squeezed it beneath the table. His hand felt cool.

⭑━━⭒━━⭑━━⭒━━⭑

Piers wasted no time. As soon as Suzanne walked out to Jean's car with him, he snatched Jerome's jacket and warm hat which buttoned beneath his chin. 'We're going for a drive, little fellow.'

Jerome's eyes widened. 'At night?'

Piers nodded as he buttoned up Jerome's jacket. 'Yeah. We'll go to see Nanna. You, me and Casey.'

Jerome jumped on the spot. 'Wow! She'll be surprised.'

'She sure will,' Piers looked up at Casey and quietly added, 'I'm glad Gran's not around to meet him.'

Suzanne stepped back inside. 'Are you going somewhere?'

'Yeah. To Mum's place.'

'Are you mental? It's after eleven o'clock!'

'We've got to beat him there.'

'Now I know you're nuts. Do you think he'll go there tonight?'

'Didn't you see how fast he left when you gave him her address? I'm sure he will. He's been trying to track her down for twenty years. Now that he knows where she lives, he doesn't seem like the type to wait until morning.'

'Listen to yourself. You've completely lost the plot. You're behaving as bad as Mum and Gran ever did. And you totally blew it tonight. You promised you wouldn't stir him.'

Piers cast her a scathing glance. 'What dinner party were you at? In case you didn't notice, he was the one stirring me.'

Suzanne turned an imploring face to Casey. 'Can't you make him see sense?'

But Casey followed Piers and Jerome out the door. 'I think he's doing absolutely right. You ought to read the diary.'

Suzanne's voice trailed after them. 'Then you're already just as prejudiced as he is! Papa has treated me with nothing but kindness and charm. I like him.'

Casey slammed her door shut and let Suzanne have the last word.

Chapter 23

The silence of her car was enough to make her ears buzz after all the talking but Casey soaked it in. The previous night's tension had left her head and stomach whirling, driving coherent thoughts from her head. It had been a relief to leave the uptight Moira alone with Piers and Jerome and get away to visit her own family.

Moira had been terrified almost beyond belief when they told her about Jean. She had crumpled onto the couch, grasped her son's hand and pleaded, 'Please don't leave me. I'll die if I see him.' And she had turned as white as if she already had.

Piers had knelt beside her, reassuring her. 'I promise I won't let him hurt you.'

Moira raised big limpid eyes to his face and spoke words that chilled Casey to the core. 'The thing I've feared most for all these years has happened. This will be the end of me.'

'He's only a man!' Piers cried. 'I didn't find him scary, Mum. He was more of a pain in the neck than anything.'

'Is seeing him what I deserve?' Moira rasped. 'Am I reaping what I sowed all those years ago?' Her teeth began to rattle so her words were hard to discern. 'Perhaps God's judgment has caught up with me and now He's going to let me die.'

Casey had felt useless as a source of support. She still couldn't think of a word she could've said. She had hung back letting Piers do all the talking.

However, she did try to contribute by keeping Jerome happy in the kitchen with biscuits and colouring books. He had dozed off in the car but perked up as soon as they reached his grandmother's house.

'I don't like to hear you say that,' Piers had told Moira. 'Because it's nothing like that other stuff you told me when we were trying to reason with Anna and still didn't know what would become of Jerome.'

'What did I say?' Moira mumbled between grey lips.

'You told me that God protects His people. You said He directs their paths when they don't know where to turn. And you showed me evidence in the Bible to back it up. Do you remember now? You said you find it easy to rely on what's written there because it's full of God's promises to us and He never breaks them. You said it was the only thing we could do. And do you remember what I said?'

Moira shook her head.

'I said I'd choose to believe you because I'd come to the end of my rope. I'd never given God much thought until then, but I could see then that He was all I had left. And since then, I've had reason to agree with you over and over that He keep His promises.'

Moira's hands fluttered to her mouth. 'Piers, I meant every word I spoke at the time. I thought it was true. I thought saying it would help me to convince myself that it's true. But now that Jean's back, I don't know what to think.' She bowed her head and her strands of silvery hair stood out in the dim light like cobwebs.

'Mum, I'll tell you what to think. You got to keep believing God's promises. That's what you said you'd always done while we were growing up. So don't stop believing it just because Jean Dupont has come. If God's Word is the truth, then it's *still* true, whether he's here or not.'

Moira raised her face and clutched his wrist. 'I've got to come home with you. I hate to ask such a big favour but I'm desperate now. I'll try believing what you say. But it'll be so hard now. I'll only have a chance if I'm with you and you keep telling me. Your...,' she bit off the next word, '*Jean* might be here any minute and I'll die if I see him.'

'Of course you'll be coming with us. That's why we came.'

So they all spent a few minutes putting into a bag the bare minimum of things for Moira to take with her. Moira refused to waste precious seconds loitering. They'd driven Casey's car to Moira's, making it possible for all

The Risky Way Home

of them to travel home together. Piers would never have been able to fit an extra person into his van.

'What about Suzanne?' Moira cried. 'She's playing with fire, trying to get close to him. He'll kill her.'

It had been the only time Casey tried to interject a word of her own. 'I'm sure he won't harm her. He was so overjoyed to discover her. He can see she thinks the world of him and he's flattered.'

'That'll only last a little while,' Moira predicted. 'You don't know Jean well enough, Casey. The tiniest imagined grievance will change him in a flash. I once idolised him too.'

At the kitchen table, Casey told her mother and Abby some of what had happened. She couldn't hold it in without bursting, although they'd be able to do nothing to help. They listened and nobody spoke for a few moments after she finished.

'What will happen now that Moira is with Piers?' Helen asked at last. 'That Dupont man will surely guess where she is. Is she going to stick to Piers like glue wherever he goes?'

'I don't think they've thought it through that far but probably yes. Moira can't bear the thought of facing Jean Dupont alone by any chance.'

'That'll smash poor Piers' chance of having any sort of love life.' Abby shot a sly glance at Casey whose cheeks burned in response. After many years of being teased by her family, she wished she'd found a way to control her own thermostat. Abby and their mother had probably been speculating about her and Piers all week, ever since Casey had left after church so abruptly the previous Sunday.

'It might improve his chances. It would've smashed 'em if he didn't bother about looking out for his mother.' She couldn't hold back a sheepish smile. Abby broke out in wolf whistles.

'Good for you! It's about time you started opening your eyes and taking my advice. I told you he was cute. But you'll have your work cut out to find time alone together. Suzanne's still there too, isn't she? That place must be almost as jam-packed as here.'

'Suzanne's moving to her new flat today. She was pretty grouchy with

Piers and poor old Moira this morning. Thinks they're both making fools of themselves. And I'm supposed to be moving in with her later this week. She'd better not try taking her grumpiness out on me.'

Helen had not joined with Abby in teasing Casey. Her forehead was puckered with concern for her friend's plight. 'What if that Dupont person does come to hurt Moira? What can Piers do? Ever since I've known him, he's been a quiet, polite boy. Not the sort I'd imagine would stand up to someone as aggressive as his father.'

'He's stronger than you think.'

Abby turned serious too. 'The person who concerns me most is Jerome.'

'Surely Jean Dupont wouldn't hurt Jerome. He's such a cutie and he's the man's own grandson.'

'But don't forget, Mum, Piers was his own son and we just heard how the brute treated him when he was the same age as Jerome.'

'Yeah, Piers was even younger!' Casey winced when she remembered shaking, not once but twice, the hand that had treated somebody Jerome's size with such cruelty.

'Have they considered calling the police?' Helen asked.

Casey shook her head. 'He hasn't done anything yet. They can't expect the police to take action just because Moira tells them the way he used to behave twenty years ago.'

The ringing of the telephone startled them. Their conversation had made them more keyed-up than they'd thought. Helen leaned back to answer it.

'Hello, Jeff.' She caught Abby's eye across the table. 'Yes, she's here but I still don't know if she wants to talk.'

Abby pulled a face and reached out for the receiver. 'I might as well. He's not going to stop bothering me until I do.'

Casey went to sit in the lounge room. She could hear Abby's sardonic voice saying, 'Don't give me that spiel of blarney. You haven't won me over just because I've come to the phone. You can thank your lucky timing that I'm even listening to you now. We just finished talking about another man whose wife and kids left him but he was even worse than you.'

Casey found herself shuddering at the comparison. She suddenly longed to be home with Piers and Jerome. Rather than cheering her up, visiting her own family left her even more unsettled than she'd been before she left.

The Risky Way Home

Chapter 24

Jean Dupont burst into the studio while Casey was cleaning the front window.

'Where's Suzanne?'

'She's in the make-up room, busy with a…'

With no further ceremony, Jean threw open the dividing door and stood confronting them. Suzanne and her bewildered client blinked up at him.

'Papa, is anything wrong?' Suzanne clutched a strand of the woman's long hair in her hand.

'I need to talk to you. How long will you be with this lady?'

'Well … not much longer. Eric is going to photograph Miss Crichton soon.'

For the next quarter of an hour, Jean paced the carpet like a caged beast, as if Casey was not even there. She dragged out her task of washing windows for the sake of having something to do, trying to ignore his huffs of impatience. At last the women appeared. Suzanne must have hurried poor Miss Crichton through at record speed. As soon as the client was safely in Eric's hands, Suzanne drew her father to one of the plush lounges and sank down beside him.

'Papa, what's the matter?'

'I don't want you to continue this business the way it is.'

Whatever she'd expected, that was not it. 'Why not? We're doing better business than we've done for months.'

'I want you to get rid of him in there.' Jean jerked his chin at the door of the photography room where they heard traces of Eric's flattering directions.

Suzanne's lips still formed a wide smile while her eyes filled with perplexity. 'But I can't. I need him.'

'You told me you have no relationship with him. Was that a lie?'

She suddenly seemed to find herself ill-at-ease so close beside her father and squirmed back a few inches. 'Of course it wasn't!'

'Then you can easily dispense with him. I've seen his type before. He's after anything he can get from you. Believe me. I refuse to sit back and watch my daughter being taken advantage of. You don't need some fancy playboy to boost your image. Your work should be good enough to stand alone.'

Suzanne attempted a giggle to allay his concern. It evaporated in the air like bubbles bursting. 'Papa, my work can't stand alone. Eric is the expert. He has far more technical know-how with cameras than I ever will. He's a professional photographer. We're only friends, as I've told you, but I need him for the business.'

Jean's cheeks grew more blotched with each word she spoke. Casey wondered if he had even tried to follow what she said.

'I thought you'd listen to me, after the way we'd instantly struck it off! I never thought you'd defy me.'

'Papa, I'm not defying you. I'm just trying to explain.'

All at once, Jean acknowledged Casey's presence with a scowl. 'We'll finish our conversation in that room.' He grasped Suzanne's elbow to herd her back into the make-up room. Suzanne's pale face telegraphed urgent messages of surprise and fear to Casey over Jean's shoulder before the door clicked shut. Casey sank onto the couch herself, to think of an excuse to rescue Suzanne. She'd have to wait for a few moments, to make it believable.

Eric and the client stepped out. Eric waited while Casey completed the paper work. As soon as Miss Crichton left, he hissed, 'What's going on? We hadn't finished but we could hear his ranting and raving through the walls. The lady was getting nervous.'

'He's got some bee in his bonnet.'

The door flew open and Jean strode out. 'You're here. Good! We've decided Suzanne doesn't need your services anymore. You can pack your things and leave!'

At first, Eric seemed to think he was addressing Casey, then realised that Jean's eyes were fixed upon him. He gave a rough laugh.

'Suzanne, what's he talking about? If I packed my things and left, you'd have only a room full of clothes.'

'I know.' Her eyes were swimming. 'I haven't decided anything. Don't worry, Eric. Papa and I haven't finished talking yet.'

'Indeed we have!' the older man interjected.

'Listen, Mister, she can't fire me, anyway. She's not my boss. We set up this business together.'

'I'll buy you out. I'll help Suzanne set up an even better studio somewhere else.'

Eric appealed to his partner again. 'Suzanne, don't let him talk you into this. You know you don't have a clue about cameras.'

'I know.' She seemed to have resolved to take a firm stand. 'Papa, I've tried to explain, there's no way I can agree with you. We're doing very well and there's no reason to break up a good going-concern. I love it here.'

Jean Dupont balled his hands into fists against his sides. 'I thought you were different to your mother and brother. I thought you were on my side, but you'd choose some cocky young upstart before your own father.' The intensity in his voice thickened his accent.

'Papa!' Suzanne's voice was like glass shattering.

Eric was incensed enough to grasp Jean's shoulder and spin him around to face him. 'Who do you think you are? I was Suzanne's friend long before you came onto the scene, Mister, and I won't stand back and watch you ruin our business. You're her father, not her keeper!'

Jean swiped Eric's hand away with murder in his eyes. 'How dare you lay a hand on me? I promise you'll regret that!'

Eric stepped back, only slightly abashed. 'My friendship with Suzanne has nothing to do with you. What do you have against me, anyway? I don't even know you and when I met you I was more than willing to be friends.'

'The day I befriend a gold digger will be the day hell freezes over.' Jean turned back to Suzanne. 'I haven't finished discussing this. I'll pick you up from your flat at seven thirty sharp.' He made it clear that he was not asking her. He was telling her. Jean turned on his heel and strode out.

That night was Casey's first in her new flat and she was already homesick for her attic bedroom at Piers' house. Suzanne had dressed as carefully as usual for dinner with her father, but all the make-up and eye-shadow she applied could not disguise the swollen shadiness around her eyes. Jean came to pick her up at seven thirty, as he'd arranged. It was the first time Suzanne had joined him with a downcast expression, although she tried to smile.

There was nothing for Casey to do but try to settle into her new home. After the tranquillity of her last home, she wondered how she'd ever get used to traffic streaming along the street past their windows, not to mention residents of other flats coming and going at all hours. She fixed herself a cup of tea with a twinge of melancholy that seemed to belong to a former time. Casey couldn't account for it until she heard a door slam and the cheerful voices of two strangers laughing together before they went into another flat. Then she remembered. It was lonesomeness. Somehow, without her even being aware, that familiar old shadow had completely lifted during her last few months boarding with Piers.

Casey was about to switch on the T.V. when somebody knocked at the door. It sounded quite low to the ground and something about the lightness of it kindled a spark of anticipation. When she threw the door open, there stood Piers and Jerome. Jerome's small knuckles had been poised to knock again. At once, Casey's dreary night turned into a bright one.

'Thought you could do with some visitors,' Piers said.

'I sure can. Come in! But where's your mum?'

'Good old Pastor Hargreaves took her out to dinner.' Piers looked around the bare sitting room. 'He offered to take us too, but I think he understood when we told him we'd rather see someone else.'

'And he guessed that it was you!' Jerome's eyes widened like saucers.

'That was amazing.' Casey winked at Piers. She lifted Jerome and spun him around until he couldn't stop laughing. Then she set him on the couch and said, 'Auntie Suzanne and I have left a basket of surprises for you to find in the kitchen. You can go and see when you stop being dizzy.'

'I stopped now!' Jerome scampered through to the kitchen, still slightly

The Risky Way Home

unsteady on his feet. 'Can I play with 'em already?'

'You sure can.'

The clatter and crash as the wicker basket full of toy cars, building blocks, crayons and skittles was tipped over the floor instantly made the place feel more like home. Piers winced. 'We'll help you tidy that up before we go.'

She wrapped her arms around his neck. 'Don't you dare talk about going.' Then she raised her face to kiss him. 'You have to stay for ages.'

'We'll stay for as long as you make us.' He kissed her again and settled onto the couch beside her. When Piers wrapped his arm around Casey's shoulders, the empty spot inside her was comfortably filled. After the events of her day, it relieved her to see him looking happy. His smiling face made a change from the anxious, tense and troubled ones that had filled her mind.

'Has Jean been to see your mother yet?' She decided to get that name out of the way fast.

'No, we still can't work out what game he's playing. But do you know what? I'm not even bothered about him anymore. All the things I've been trying to convince Mum over the last few days have been sinking into my own head.'

'You mean that God's looking out for her?' Casey realised that she badly longed for Piers to speak those words to her too.

He nodded. 'When he first found us, I guess you saw how shocked I was. I'd always guessed that my father wasn't very nice. Else why would she never speak about him? But just the same, it was hard to come to terms with what I read in Mum's diary. Now that he's here, I think we're just supposed to deal with it. God's done some really wonderful things in my life, which I thanked Him for. So I started thinking that if I turned all scared and panicky like Mum, it'd take me right back to where I started from. And I never want to be back there.'

'Do you mean before you started trusting Him?'

'That's right. I clearly remember admitting that my life was one colossal mess with me in charge and I told God that if He wanted it any better, He'd have to take over. I promised Him that if He arranged it so I could keep my son, I'd trust Him for absolutely everything after that. It was that simple. It was like a pact. And it did work out. So I'm treating this business with Jean Dupont as a bit of a test. If I do take back my side of the bargain and don't trust God to work this out for me too, then why should I expect Him to keep His part?'

'I follow what you're saying,' Casey said slowly. 'God kept His side of it so now you're keeping yours.'

Piers snuggled closer to her and kissed her hair. 'That's about right. Running around scared instead of keeping on trusting Him seems crazy to me, like darting out of shelter into the enemy's firing lines. God said that He'll protect me if I trust Him to. So if I don't trust Him to and He still protects me, it'd be like making Him out to be a liar? Does that make sense or do I sound like a raving lunatic?'

'It makes sense.' She couldn't work out why he was chuckling to himself.

'That wasn't my only prayer that was answered,' Piers said. 'There's another one that might be even more of a miracle than getting to keep Jerome.'

'What was it?'

He leaned back on the couch while his eyes danced. 'About ten years ago, before I was even really on speaking terms with God, I threw another wild prayer up to heaven.'

'What was it?' His teasing expression made her giggle.

'I prayed that Casey Miller would look at me just the way you're looking at me right now.'

Chapter 25

Somebody else knocked at the door. Casey opened it to find Eric standing there with the irritated expression she had come to recognise. He stepped inside and grunted when he saw Piers and Jerome.

'I haven't come to interrupt anything. I'm looking for Suzanne.'

'She isn't home yet.'

Eric's shoulders slumped. 'For crying out loud, don't tell me she's still out listening to that crackpot.' Beneath the soft light of the bare ceiling bulb, he appeared more haggard than Casey had imagined Eric could look. The eyes he turned to Piers were streaked with red.

'Your old man is a nutcase,' he pronounced with a shake of the head.

It was time to put personal differences aside. 'I know,' Piers said soberly.

Although Suzanne was not home, Eric seemed in no hurry to leave. He sat on the edge of an armchair and demanded, 'What can be done about him? I don't mind telling you that I'm concerned about our business. I'm worried about Suzanne too. We've been through a lot together and I don't want to see her hurt.'

'We're worried too, Eric,' Piers said. 'I don't think there's any way to reason with him. He's just as you said. A nutcase from way back.'

Eric asked Casey, 'Have you told him what happened in the studio today?'

She flushed. 'I was just about to.'

Eric rolled his eyes and told Piers himself. Casey added a few extra details about the way Jean had behaved while Eric was busy with the client. At the end of the story, the three of them looked at each other, lost for more words. Jerome's chirpy voice was the only one to be heard. He glanced up when he realised that no adults were speaking, smiled a little and lowered his voice to a whisper.

'I thought using "Suzanne Dupont" on her business cards was a bit silly,' Eric remarked at last.

'Yeah, me too,' Piers said.

The door swung open and Suzanne herself entered, followed by her father. Jean's eyes narrowed when he saw them together.

'Look what we've walked into. A cosy little conspiracy to plot how to get rid of me.'

Eric's dumbfounded expression might have been humorous at any other time. 'Of all the nerve! Who do you think you are?'

'And what makes you think we want to be rid of you?' Piers asked, remaining cool.

Jean snorted. 'Don't play innocent with me. Do you really think I'm so naïve or you're so inscrutable as that? Where's your mother, Mummy's Boy? Hanging from the ceiling at your place?'

Suzanne raised a hand to her mouth and groaned.

Jean studied her for a moment. 'I see now why you're so resistant to my sound judgment. It's not entirely your fault. Everywhere you turn, there are numbskulls waiting to fill your head with their nonsense. As soon as I leave, they'll try to undo all of my hard work and make you listen to their backbiting. I guess I cannot prevent that. But I won't give you up without a fight. I've searched for you for far too long to ever give up on you.' He stroked her hair. Suzanne stiffened.

'I'm going back to my hotel but I want you to promise to consider what I've said.'

'I will,' she said, though she jerked a little.

'You're not welcome here,' Eric scowled.

'I certainly have more right in my daughter's flat than you do. Suzanne, I have high hopes for you. Only you were strong enough to resist your mother's devious mind-games for all these years, unlike someone else.' He flashed a scathing glance at Piers. 'I know that must've taken some character. It pains me right here to see you wavering.' He pressed a hand against his chest. 'If only you'll stand firm and give me a chance to undo all of that confounded mess.'

Suzanne's head drooped. The gesture said clearer than words, *'I've had enough.'*

Jean raised her face and planted a loud kiss on each of her cheeks. 'Goodbye, my sweet girl. I'll see you tomorrow. I know you'll come to your senses.' Without a glance at anybody else, he strode out. Casey drew a deep breath. Only the cloying aroma of his aftershave remained.

'That arrogant French...' Eric was too flustered to come up with a suitable epithet.

Now that the heaviness had lifted, Suzanne switched back to her usual talkative self. 'Not only does he want me to quit working with you, Eric, he doesn't even want me to keep living in the country! He wants to take me to live in Europe somewhere to keep house for him.'

Piers let out a laugh of disbelief.

'What sort of lifestyle does he think that'd be?' Eric scowled.

'He thinks it'd be the pinnacle of all my dreams. He's completely serious. He says I live too close to the rest of my family to please him. When I tried to explain that I couldn't just drop my life for a whim, he was furious.' At last, Suzanne sank into a chair.

'I don't know what got into me in the restaurant tonight. He kept browbeating me for so long and he was so vicious in the way he spoke about Mum. When he tried to demand that I pack my bags straight away to go with him...,' her cheeks burned as she looked at each of their faces. 'I got a bit teary. It was just that he latched onto the idea like a pit bull terrier and wouldn't let go.' Suzanne's chin was not quite steady so she hid her face in her hands.

Eric sat on the arm of her chair. 'Do you agree with me now, that he's a total jerk?'

Suzanne's head made a motion that could have been a nod.

'Well then, don't worry about him anymore. Don't even give him the time of day!'

'Do you know what he did next?' Her voice was steady enough to speak again. 'He bellowed at me, in front of everyone. Called me a snivelling sook. He said we have to finish talking in the car because I'm obviously too hysterical to take out in public.' Now Suzanne looked up, no longer seeming to care that her eyes were pooling with tears. 'He grabbed my elbow and forced me out with him.'

Eric was on his feet again, pacing the floor. 'Surely that's abuse! He can't get away with laying a hand on you. There must be some sort of restraining order we can get.'

'I don't like to think of these two girls staying here alone once we've gone,' Piers mused. 'If he were to come back, who knows what he might do?'

'Suzanne could share my flat, but that might make the monster even more ropable.' Eric stopped in his tracks, self-disgust spreading across his face. 'What am I saying? Who cares what he thinks? She can come back with me anyway.'

'And Casey can come with us,' Piers said. 'Most of her clothes are still there, anyway. Suzanne's welcome too, but I don't know if she'd want to live under the same roof with Mum.' He turned enquiringly to his sister but she remained quiet, letting the plans drift over her head.

Casey sat beside her and whispered, 'Are you okay?'

Jerome had stopped playing and bounded over from the kitchen. 'What's wrong with Auntie Suze?'

Suzanne rested her hand on his soft hair and looked up. 'I can't believe we're having this conversation. How could he behave this way? I don't get it. He's my own father but tonight he carried on as if I hate him. And I've always loved him! It makes no sense.'

Eric had sunk beside her again. 'Suzanne, even though he's your father, he's practically a stranger. You owe him nothing.'

'That's easy for you to say, but I've never thought of my father as a stranger. I imagined him as a fantastic person. My greatest dream has been to find him, to escape from Mum and Gran. He was my holy grail. You think that sounds stupid, don't you? So do I. I feel like the prize idiot. But I can't expect you to understand. Can you try to imagine how it feels to find out that your father is totally unhinged?'

Piers stood behind the couch and squeezed her shoulder. 'Well I know

The Risky Way Home

how that feels. It's been the same for me, you know. Except for the holy grail thing, maybe.'

Suzanne said nothing for a long moment. Then she raised her hand to cover her brother's. 'For once in our lives, you were right!'

'You don't have to say that,' he told her. 'You weren't stupid to hope that he'd be decent.'

'But you don't get it. I probably made things far worse than they would've been. Did you hear what he said to you, about Mum hanging from your ceiling? I'm the one who told him how you rushed off to fetch her after the dinner we had for him. I made a real story of it. I thought we were going to have a good laugh at your expense. If I'd known how bitter and aggressive he'd turn, I would never have said it.' She twisted her neck to look around at him. 'Sorry, Piers.'

'It's okay,' he mumbled.

'There's more. While he was lecturing me in the car, I had a sudden flashback from years ago.' With her free hand, Suzanne scooped Jerome onto her lap. 'I remembered him making you stand two inches in front of him so he could hit you. You knew what was coming and you were crying. But whenever you flinched, he said he'd do it harder.' She buried her face in Jerome's hair. 'And he did.'

'I never remembered any of those things until I read about them in the diary.'

'Any of what things?' Eric demanded. 'What else did the swine used to do?'

'Have you still got that old diary?' Suzanne asked.

Piers nodded. 'I'd given it back to her. But now that she's living with me, she brought it with her. She didn't want to leave it around her place for him to find.'

'I reckon I'd like to read it now.'

'Yeah, sure.'

'But don't tell her you're getting it for me. Just say you want another look at it.'

He sighed. 'Okay, whatever you say.'

Casey returned home with Piers. Suzanne decided to spend a few days at Eric's flat while she worked out what to do about her father. Casey moved straight back into her attic room. Moira preferred to use Piers' bedroom, which now smelled like rosy perfume. Piers still slept on Jerome's bedroom floor as he'd been doing while Suzanne was living with them. It suited Casey to be back, although she hated to think about the rent she and Suzanne were paying between them for a flat neither of them were living in.

Having her there suited Moira and Piers too. It meant that Casey was often available to drive Moira places in her own car so that Piers no longer had to take his mother everywhere he went. On Saturday morning he needed to deliver some cupboards to clients and Casey had agreed to drive Moira and Jerome to fly Jerome's new kite in a busy city park. Moira felt safe from Jean Dupont where there were crowds of people around, and he wouldn't know where they'd be.

'I was hoping we might be able to call on Suzanne too,' she suggested. 'I haven't seen her since Gran's funeral but I've been thinking about her so often.'

'I know she'll be in the studio putting together a few portfolios because she's fallen behind with her deadlines.'

Moira's face brightened and immediately shadowed again, like sunshine flickering on a leaf. 'Would it be too much for me to ask you to drive me there to see her before we go to the park?'

'Of course it's not too much to ask.' Casey found it easy to be generous where Piers' family was concerned. 'We have all day at our disposal.'

A glow settled on Moira's features again. 'Bless you, Sweetie.'

'But we got to be quick,' Jerome insisted. 'I got to fly my kite. Daddy says today is a good day.' They had owned the kite for a week. Each morning Jerome had been anxious to hurry outside with it but there had not been enough wind.

Casey peered out the window at the swaying tips of the poplars along the driveway. 'There'll be plenty of time to fly your kite.'

Piers stooped to kiss Jerome's head on his way to rinse his breakfast dishes in the sink. 'Tell me how it goes. Wish I was coming too.' He left the house first.

Not long after that, the others set off. Strong gusts shook the sides of Casey's car on the Freeway and thin clouds stretched across the sky

The Risky Way Home

like wisps of cotton being sucked into a vacuum nozzle. Although windy days were not her favourites, they made Casey feel restless to be moving. Jerome's feet caught the mood and kicked the back of Casey's chair while he chanted, 'Fly a kite! Fly a kite!'

Casey parked in her usual spot at work. As it was Saturday, the other shops along the balcony were closed up. Suzanne had left the studio door open to welcome the fragrance of yellow jonquils that now grew in the flower barrels along the balcony. She sat behind the desk with her shoulders hunched over the portfolio she worked on. Moira squeezed Jerome's hand tight and mumbled a brief prayer.

Suzanne's face lit up with a smile when she saw Casey but darkened when she saw who stood behind her. Casey wondered whether either Moira or Suzanne realised how similar their mercurial expressions were. She guessed that neither of them studied their own faces while they were animated. Suzanne seemed to mask hers.

Moira took one step inside the door and stretched her hand to her daughter. 'Suzanne, how are you?' Her voice quivered. 'I know what you've been through with your ... with Jean. I can't tell you how sorry I am to have brought it upon you.'

Suzanne fixed her gaze on the collar of Moira's old-fashioned sun dress. 'Are you trying a guilt trip on me? You know I brought his visit upon myself.'

'I don't know what you mean.' Moira's face was puzzled.

'Piers must've told you about my business cards. Suzanne Dupont!' Moira shook her head with wonderment.

'No, he didn't tell her,' Casey said 'He said he wouldn't.'

'Oh.' Suzanne muttered a personal imprecation. 'Forget about that, then. Anyway, I've read your diary! Mum, why on earth didn't you show us years ago? Perhaps it was your fault he came. Piers and I deserved to know what he was like but you kept us in the dark. You watched me waste my life longing for my father when you could've ended it by telling me what a brute he was.'

'Would you have believed her if she'd told you?' Casey couldn't help trying to make it easier for Moira.

Suzanne tilted her chin. 'Perhaps I would've believed her when I was small.'

'It was wrong of me, I know,' Moira cried. 'I always thought I was probably at fault. But I was only thinking of you. I didn't want to burden you or Piers with more than I thought you needed to know. Can you find it in your heart to forgive me for withholding it from you?'

Jerome tugged Casey's hand and mouthed the word, 'Kite!'

She grinned at him and just as silently returned the word, 'Soon!'

'Will you stop it?' Suzanne groaned. 'Mum, please listen to yourself! That's the way you used to behave with Gran. I'd get fed-up listening to you demean yourself. The wicked witch is dead but she crushed any inch of backbone you ever had. I can't tell you how sick that makes me feel.'

Moira began to stammer an apology. She paused to consider what her daughter had said and changed her mind. 'It was because I defied her by marrying your father.'

'So she helped you out of a tight spot! Isn't that what people are supposed to do for each other? It gave her no right to treat you like dirt and use you as her personal slave from then on. Not to mention the way you let her treat us! That's the only thing I think you needed to apologise for, but you never did. You just kept apologising to all sorts of other people for everything else. She should have apologised to you. I wish she was still alive now that I've read that journal of yours. I would've made her apologise. At least I would've told her a few home truths.'

Moira could find no words but simply watched Suzanne with her limpid grey eyes.

'When I read that diary, I wanted to fling it against the wall. I felt so furious by the way everyone behaved. Not just you but her! And him! They used you badly. They should've both been sorry. Instead, they left you feeling personally responsible for every bad thing that ever happened.'

Casey kept her eye on Jerome, who marched around the studio with his hands behind his back, staring up at each photo with his head cocked to the side.

Suzanne moistened her lips. 'I decided not to be like them, even though you've antagonised me as much as anyone else.'

Moira seemed to notice that she was still standing just one step inside the doorway. She quietly moved in closer.

'So here goes. Mum, I'm sorry for any extra grief I've caused you over the years because of my attitude. There, now I've done it! I've proven that

I'm better than they were.'

Casey couldn't help laughing at Suzanne's dubious apology.

Moira took the last couple of steps to Suzanne and pulled her into her arms. 'It means the world to me to hear you say that.'

Suzanne did not embrace Moira back but she did not resist either.

Jerome bounced over beside them. He'd given up on Casey and decided to question somebody else. 'Nanny, can we fly the kite now? Auntie Suze, you want to come?'

It was good to see Moira and Suzanne smile together at the same thing. Suzanne lifted Jerome off his feet to give him a spin. His dimpled face giggled over Suzanne's shoulder once, twice, but the third time his eyes fixed on something behind Casey. Jerome's eyebrows drew together into his wary expression. Casey instinctively whirled around to see what he saw.

Jean Dupont stepped over the threshold rubbing his large hands together. A smile spread across his stern, handsome features. 'I'm sorry to break up this touching little reunion.'

Casey's heart thumped against her ribs. He sounded anything but sorry.

Chapter 26

She rushed past him to lean over the balcony and scan the footpath below for people. Not a soul was in sight. As Casey opened her mouth to shout, a hot hand clamped over it. She winced as one of Jean's gold rings sent a twinge up her front tooth. He dragged her back into the studio, closed the door behind him and locked it from the inside.

Moira made a small noise in her throat that conveyed her terror.

Jean Dupont bared his teeth in a grin as he looked his ex-wife up and down. 'You look even worse than I'd expected. And believe me, I had no high hopes. I'll gladly leave you alone when I finish with you.' He spat a great, wet circle at her feet then turned his smile to Suzanne. 'Sorry about your floor but I couldn't hold back.'

Jerome tucked his face into Suzanne's shoulder and began to cry. Bitter self-reproach hit Casey like a slap in the face. *This is my fault! We shouldn't have come here.*

Jean approached Suzanne and thrust his face close to hers. 'It's you I came to see. I didn't know these others would be here. It must be my lucky day. You're the only one I thought worth saving but you've proven yourself to be as bad as the others. You'd try to avoid me, would you?'

'I haven't been avoiding you!'

He gave a rough laugh. 'I've come to your flat several times for the last three nights and found nobody home. I knew you were with either this old hag or your flash playboy friend. Put this boy down.' He plucked

The Risky Way Home

Jerome from Suzanne's arms, seized her throat and shoved her hard against the wall behind her. Moira screamed and Jerome flung himself into Casey's arms.

'You said you wouldn't listen to her sneaky brain-washing. You were supposed to be on my side. That's what you said!' He kept pushing her against the wall with each sentence.

Casey edged backwards, closer to the door. Without turning his head, Jean's voice lashed out at her like a whip. 'If either of you sets a finger on that door, your beloved Suzanne will be history.'

Casey froze on the spot and saw Suzanne's eyeballs roll in their sockets. Jerome's arms wrapped so tightly around Casey's neck, her own eyes watered. With his hands still circling Suzanne's throat, Jean stared back.

'Do you think I don't mean it? I dare you to test me. She means nothing to me now. She's shown her true colours and I'd kill her in a flash.'

'Dear God, no! Jean, she's your own daughter!' Moira cried.

His face twisted as if he were chewing a lemon. 'Nobody as two-faced as she is worthy of the title of daughter. She's the most sickening of all. At least her brother had the guts to make it clear whose side he's on.'

Suzanne found her voice. 'I'm not two-faced. I know you can't see how insane you are! There's no point trying to tell you. But you'll never get away with harassing us. Eric will be back soon. We were working here together.'

A ray of hope spread through Casey. It burst like a bubble when she looked into Suzanne's eyes. She'd known her friend long enough to read the truth. Eric had not been near the studio all morning. Casey felt all the more hopeless for Suzanne's valiant attempt to lie. She could only pray that Jean would believe her story.

Even if he believed it, he didn't seem to care. 'I'll act quickly, then.' With a savage shove he released Suzanne and unexpectedly wrested Jerome from Casey's arms. He strode through to the make-up room, bellowing over the boy's terrified shrieks.

'I'm sure none of you will try to run for help while I have this kid. I could wring his neck in a flash. I don't want to but if you force my hand ...'

He upended the make-up table with a flick of his foot. Casey's hand shot out to clutch Moira's during the terrific smash. Creams and lotions from broken bottles merged into a dirty brown pool on the floorboards. Jean passed through the wardrobe room like a tornado, tearing dresses and suits from their hangers. By now, Jerome's face was crimson with howls of despair.

'Keep quiet, boy!'

At first it seemed Jerome was going to obey. But he had merely lapsed into one of his breathless silences between screams and his lips turned blue. When he gasped the air he needed, the screech that came must have blasted Jean Dupont's eardrums.

'SHUT-UP!' the man bawled in his face.

He marched into Eric's photography room, heaved a camera from its tripod and flung it against the wall. Jean cursed when the camera did not shatter into as many pieces as he'd obviously expected. Jerome's face was swollen red and blue. Casey, Moira and Suzanne all set themselves upon Jean, but he moved back to the make-up room as if they were no more than flies on his hide. He slammed Moira against the doorway with a lunge of his shoulder and used his free hand to wrest Casey from his other side. Suzanne still seemed to be the focus of Jean's energy. He grasped the front of her dress and pushed her into the wreckage on the floor.

Suzanne's head struck a corner of the upended make-up cabinet with a crack. Her eyelashes flickered once as she gave a soft moan and lay still. Casey tried to scream but a band like steel restricted her chest. Her eyes were riveted on Suzanne's body, lying in the mess with her black wavy hair soaking up the spilled creams. Casey lurched forward to reach Jerome, although she could do nothing for him. She stepped close enough to Jean Dupont to seize the small hand that flopped over his shoulder.

Somebody else was doing all the screaming that Casey wished she could muster. It was Moira, who had sunk down beside Suzanne to pat her cheeks and shake her shoulders.

Repositioning Jerome over his shoulder, Jean seized Moira by the mouth. 'You're going to follow us outside,' he snapped at Casey. 'We're leaving this place and if you try to run away or attract attention, these two die right where we stand, I promise I won't hesitate, so if you want them to survive, you'd better cooperate with me. My car is down below and if any of you try to make a sound, I'll throttle you on the spot.'

Casey saw Jerome twist his neck to stare down at the inert form of his aunt. Although a pulse raced in his throat and he had every reason to scream louder than before, the little boy seemed to have decided he'd be wise obey his grandfather's command. The studio door slammed shut behind them.

What about Suzanne? Casey knew better than anyone that the door automatically locked when it was closed. Without releasing Moira's mouth, Jean Dupont looked at the handle and then at Casey as if he'd read her mind.

'I know it's locked,' he growled. 'I've seen her close it often enough when I've come to fetch her at closing time.' He muttered a savage word that Casey guessed was a foreign oath. 'I'll have to leave her behind. She has what she deserved. I have bigger plans for the three of you, anyway.'

She might die in there, if she's not dead already! Jean's stern face shimmered through a watery screen as Casey's eyes filled. A magpie perched on the balcony rail was the only living creature in sight. Jean Dupont seemed to have everything going right for him. When Moira stumbled, he jerked her to her feet.

His hire car had doors that locked from a central switch in the front. Jean shoved his three captives in the back and deftly bound their hands against their sides. When he had finished, he tied their feet.

'You were planning something like this!' Moira's voice was thick like sticky syrup.

'I am prepared for anything.'

Jerome drew a shuddering breath. 'Auntie Suze! Auntie Suze!' His thin treble was the saddest dirge Casey had ever heard.

'What are you going to do with us?' She had to know the worst.

The blue eyes of the Frenchman shot her an appraising look through his rear-vision mirror. 'You have nothing to fear, my russet-haired gem, if you play your cards right. I've nothing against you except for your taste in men. I've always fancied your looks and I've come to save you from a fate worse than death. Some day you'll thank me.'

Fear rippled from her solar plexus to her spine. Casey felt it spread to every part of her body, leaving nausea in its wake. As Jean drove, she stared at the thick car windows and wondered if she could break one with her feet. The wave of despair that followed was enough to make her gag. Even if she could, there'd be no way she could wriggle out of a moving car with manacled hands and feet. And she could not possibly desert Moira and Jerome.

Jerome slumped across the seat so that his head was on Moira's lap and his chest on Casey's. She felt his heart pound a rhythm against her knees and couldn't even raise a finger to stroke his hair.

Jean rambled on, 'You and my grandson will live. We'll leave this burning hell-hole they call Australia. My grandson is still young enough not to have been tainted by that old witch's lies.' His eyes narrowed as they shifted to Moira. 'And I'll make him forget his father.'

Jerome pressed his eyelids against Moira's skirt. Casey could tell from his shuddering shoulders that he was quietly sobbing. *Whatever happens, I'd die before I let him hurt you, Jerome!*

'First, I'll take care of the dragon lady.' Jean said with cheerful gusto.

'You can't!' Casey could keep silent no longer. Jean meant to kill Moira, probably before their eyes, and neither she nor Jerome could live through it.

His good-humour vanished in a flash. 'Shut your mouth or you'll go the same way. As I said, I fancy you and I'll treat you well but you're not indispensable. If you stir up trouble I'll kill you too, in the blink of an eye.'

Casey slumped back against her seat. *I can't break down. I've got to stay strong for Jerome and Moira. Where's he taking us? Is Suzanne dead? If only I could do something! Lord, we need you like never before. You can do something. Piers says he trusts you completely. If he knew what was happening, he'd be praying for us with all his might.*

The thought of Piers made her catch her breath with an ache that almost split her in two. *Please save us, Lord. Answer my prayer not just for our sake but for Piers too. He has so much faith in you but if he loses his mother, me and Jerome all at once he'll have lost everything and I don't see how he'll ever recover.*

Jerome was watching her. Casey managed to force her lips into something like a reassuring smile although it felt ghastly. It wasn't true that she could do nothing. All at once, she knew what she had to do.

I might never see him again but at least I'll be able to behave the way he'd behave!

Chapter 27

Jean Dupont followed a familiar route along the freeway and through Mount Barker. He was taking them home to Piers' house. As the car rolled along the driveway Casey stared at the back of his head, trying to figure him out. *Why on earth would he bring us here?* There was no accounting for the moves of a person who was surely demented.

Jean parked in front of the little gabled house. 'You've come home to stay, my fine lady,' he directed his comment to Moira. 'But the rest of us won't linger for long.'

'Why here?' Moira asked through ghostly white lips.

His lips turned up into a grim smile. 'Let's just say I'd like to leave a calling card for our son too.' Jean swung open his door and stepped out.

A flash of movement caught Casey's attention but she groaned when it turned out to be only Ben, who had managed to break free from his tether. With a joyful bleat, he gambolled over to greet them.

Jean caught his breath. 'Heavens above! I thought that was a blasted *guard dog!'* With the heel of his boot he kicked Ben squarely in the ribs. The goat let out a startled cry and lay on the ground with his flank heaving.

Jerome screamed his pet's name.

'Did you think I'd be afraid of an old billy goat?' Jean sounded as if he thought Casey had somehow summoned him.

He pulled each of his captives roughly from the car and produced a couple of course rags. 'Now there'll be no passing motorists to see us. I'll be free of the sounds of your pesky voices.' He savagely tied Moira's and Casey's gags then paused while he considered Jerome.

'If you'll give me a kiss and be my friend, I'll not tie your mouth.'

'No! Let us go!'

'Have it your way, little runt!' Jean brought the back of his hand hard across Jerome's cheek. The little boy yelped with pain. Casey's scream stung the back of her throat, even with the gag muffling its sound. With her legs so tightly bound, she could no longer take a step without plummeting to the ground. She might as well have been two miles from Jerome instead of two feet, for all the good she could do.

When Jean Dupont had tied Jerome's gag, he raised his foot again, to smash through the glass of the front window pane. He eased himself through the jagged hole and unlocked the door from the inside.

'Welcome home.'

One by one, he carried his prisoners inside and placed them together in a heap on the floor. At least now Casey could feel Jerome's warmth against her skin.

This is the worst place he could bring us. Now she guessed the method behind his apparent madness. Being in the cosy room surrounded by familiar comforts but unable to move was like being held captive in hell and tantalised with glimpses of paradise. *Please help us, Lord!* Her eyes scanned the room. A few feet from her on the floor was one of her own embroidered cushions. Jerome had used it as a hill for his matchbox cars that morning. They were still spilled in disarray around it, just where his precious fingers had left them.

Casey gazed through to the kitchen where some sandwich workings still lay spread across the bench. Moira had cut two ham and salad sandwiches for Piers to take with him. The telephone began to ring and that was the hardest torture to bear. Jean perched on the edge of an armchair, watching them smugly until it stopped.

'This is where Moira will stay when I finish with her. That'll be part of Piers' surprise. Won't he feel like a naughty boy for neglecting his mummy?'

His words were grenades that exploded Casey's self-control. She forced herself to cling to the last shreds of it, reminding herself for what felt like the hundredth time that giving way to hysteria would get them nowhere. But another, more sinister voice was whispering to her heart that staying in control was doing them no good either. She swallowed down a rising sour taste at the back of her throat. Casey's whole body seemed to be screaming at her to begin panicking. *No!* Perhaps keeping calm was all that was buying them time.

Jean was up on his feet, striding across the carpet. 'I'll take care of the first part of Piers' surprise.'

They heard him kick the work shed door once, twice, and the third time it burst open. Casey heard thunderous crashes as circular band-saw, drill press and power sander all hit the floorboards. *Keep going,* she urged in her head. *Even this is buying us time!*

Smaller metal tools tinkled like Christmas bells as Jean's arm swept them off shelves and hooks. Tinnier clangs must have been cans of paint and lacquer flying across the room and bursting open. Casey looked at Moira, whose eyes flooded with tears as she watched Jerome. Then the phone began to ring again. The frustration of being unable to answer it made Casey want to fly apart.

He'd finished out there. She heard Jean puttering around in the kitchen until the telephone stopped again. When he appeared, he was chewing a rough sandwich he'd thrown together.

'Hard work makes me hungry,' Jean remarked. 'Moira, I suppose you know I'm going to kill you. Surely you must've realised all these years that it was just a matter of time.'

Moira resigned her head.

'Then perhaps you can understand why I've dragged this out a little. I could've left you lying in the studio with Suzanne but after what you did to me, you don't deserve a quick, humane end. Pity I can't drag out your suffering for twenty years, as you did mine. So I guess you won, really.' He crammed the last wedge of sandwich into his mouth. 'But I'll have the last word. Perhaps I'll strangle you right now.'

Casey's heart lurched as he rose to his feet. The time for staying calm was over. Action was needed now. When he stepped toward Moira, Casey kicked him with her bound feet as hard as she could.

A rush of air escaped from Jean but he took only two steps back. Casey wasted no time on thoughts of dread or fear. They would sap energy that she badly needed for fighting him off. Deep inside, she knew she was ultimately bound to lose, tied up as she was, but she spent no time thinking about that either. Hot tears trickled from her eyes but tears seemed to sap no strength. Although she could hardly see through them, Casey guessed that it would use more vital energy to try to stop them.

The shrill telephone bell pealed again. By now, she wondered if it was the same caller each time. *Why couldn't they come to visit instead?* Through the noise, there was a faint sound that she could scarcely bring herself to believe. Casey dared to pause and listen. Then her pulse sky rocketed. There was no doubt about it. It was Piers' old van, rumbling over the pebbly driveway.

Jean heard it too. He whipped his head around to peer out the window and without a word, stalked to hide behind the door. Casey heard a moan from Moira. Her own initial relief turned to the sickliest surge of fear.

Piers' car door slammed shut and she heard his sprinting footsteps. Of course the sight of Jean's car and the smashed window would have alerted him. Piers flung open the front door and rushed in. In the split second it took for his eyes to adjust to the dimmer inside light, Jean sprang from his hiding place and pounded Piers across the side of his head. Piers struck blindly back and caught his adversary with a clip on the shoulder that almost sent Jean spinning. Casey saw a glint of Jean's teeth as he sprang at Piers again. But Piers' attention was momentarily diverted by his first sight of the captives on the floor. Horror flooded his features.

Forget about us! Look out for yourself!

As if he heard Casey's silent scream through her skull, Piers turned back to face his father. In the split second it had taken him to look away, Jean had made a move to shove him against the wall.

Piers raised his knee, aiming for Jean's groin and stomach. He knew he'd found his mark when the man sucked in his breath and screamed a string of French obscenities. Piers used his sudden advantage to push forward and take another swing at Jean's head. The older man ducked but not before his ear was grazed. He retaliated by thumping Piers' cheekbone.

Hot moistness from the rag grated the corners of Casey's mouth as she tried to scream. Similar sounds of muffled dread came from Moira and Jerome. She was close enough to wriggle the little finger of her right hand out of its bind to touch Jerome's hand. Casey found it rigid with terror and ice cold.

The Risky Way Home

Jean Dupont kicked Piers savagely across the knees. Piers stumbled but didn't fall down. He aimed a blow at Jean's chest but Jean saw it coming and twisted to dodge its full force. He managed to grasp Piers' left wrist in one of his iron hands. Jean's mouth was set in a grimace and sweat dripped down his temples. With a hard chopping motion from his free hand, Piers managed to loosen Jean's grip and wrest his hand free.

Casey suddenly saw something she could do. One of Jerome's toy trucks was about eight inches from her elbow. It was slightly larger than the matchbox cars. Jean Dupont would surely notice if a prisoner humped her body into the fray to try to trip him over but there was a slight chance that he might overlook a small truck.

She glanced at Jean. Perhaps it was almost too much to hope. Casey wriggled close enough to nudge the truck with her chin. Trying desperately to keep her movements small, she used her shoulder to bring the small vehicle down closer to her legs. There was no way he could fail to notice what Casey was doing if he did happen to glance around, but Piers was taking every ounce of his concentration.

The strenuous effort to keep her moves tiny took all the strength Casey could muster. She found herself gasping and her gag had turned sodden. At first she thought she'd been breathing too fast but realised that the wetness was from perspiration that oozed from her forehead and every pore in her face.

Now that the truck was beneath her feet, she eyed it. It was surely too small to trip a person up and she had to wait until Jean's boots were in a perfect position to send the truck careening in a straight line. Her eardrums swirled with blood that seemed too thick to move anywhere else in her body.

This is close enough! She wasn't at all sure that it was but knew a better chance might not come. With the truck beneath the soles of her shoes, she drew her knees back and pushed with all her strength.

Casey could have cried. Wrinkles in the carpet made the truck's progress more awkward than she'd anticipated and it stopped a few inches short of Jean's feet. He glanced down briefly and kicked it aside.

But before Jean looked up again, Piers had knocked him off his feet with one enormous blow. In a flash, he was upon him. Piers pinned Jean's arms to the ground behind his head and leaned over them with all his weight. Even Casey could see that Jean Dupont was in no position to break free, though he threshed on the floor, cursing and trying to escape as hard as he could.

At last Jean lowered his head back on the carpet. The blue eyes that gazed at the ceiling were bright with undisguised fear.

'You won't last much longer, idiot boy! You'll tire and I'll break free.'

'I'll last as long as it takes, Papa,' Piers replied tersely.

'In no time you'll be exhausted.' Jean's accent was growing thicker and harder to understand. 'You're wasting all your strength to hold me down. When you show the slightest sign of fatigue, I'll be up and grind you to pulp.'

'But you're forgetting one thing.'

'What's zat?' Jean spat.

'I'm not three years old anymore.'

Piers released one of Jean's hands to slam his arm hard beneath Jean's jaw. The cracking sound filled the room like a pistol shot. At the same time, he brought his knee beneath the man's groin again. Casey could see that the Frenchman was in serious pain. He writhed on the floor with his face in his hands, groaning.

Piers was kneeling beside her. The poise he'd kept so wonderfully from the moment he'd rushed inside was gone and he didn't try to control his weeping. The eye that Jean had belted was swelling and Piers seemed confused to know what to do first. He tried to fiddle with Jerome's hand cord and untie Casey's gag at the same time.

'Your mother first,' she breathed when she could.

'What?'

'Help Jerome and Moira. No, tie him up first. Do it quick.'

'Yeah! I'd better.' He managed a watery smile. 'I'll be back.'

Casey sat with her head between her knees, battling tidal waves of nausea and dizziness so severe she almost fainted. *Suzanne!* She guessed by Moira's jerking shoulders that she had the same name on her mind. *What's happened to Suzanne?*

The Risky Way Home

It seemed to Casey that a whole twenty four hours worth of activity was crammed to fit into the one that followed. Everything happened in fragments because her shot nerves kept phasing out, yet ironically enough, the details of whatever she did manage to watch had never been clearer.

The telephone rang again and it turned out to be Eric. It turned out he'd gone to the studio, found Suzanne and she'd regained consciousness. Suzanne tried to talk to Moira, who broke down and sobbed so hard she couldn't talk coherently. She passed the phone back to Piers and he was barely comprehensible himself. Although he hadn't broken down like Moira, he rambled on in jumbled sentences. Casey could tell that Suzanne's shrill voice was just as wound-up from the other end.

'Everyone's okay!' Piers kept repeating. 'Nobody's badly hurt.' It seemed he had to say it more than twenty times before Suzanne would believe him.

After that call, he made a few others. In no time the front yard was filled with police cars, two ambulances and even some news crew. Casey had heard the phone calls and knew Piers hadn't called the reporters. Moira was still sobbing while Jerome sat on her knee and stroked her cheek.

'Don't cwy anymore, Nanny. He's all tied up now.'

Casey gaped at him. 'How can you be so calm?'

One of the medical officers remarked, 'Kids of his age are often the most resilient people of all. They seem so vulnerable but they take things in their stride better than many adults. It's probably a credit to the way you've raised him.'

Casey realised the young man assumed she was Jerome's mother. She didn't bother correcting him.

The policeman in charge turned out to be a consummate joker. 'That was slick work, son,' he told Piers. 'Are you sure you didn't choose the wrong vocation? Forget about carpentry. We could use you in the force with us.'

Piers had recovered his composure enough to grin. 'No thanks. You blokes can keep your jobs and I take my hat off to you.' Although he sounded as upbeat as Jerome, he didn't quite look it.

The officer pretended to be disappointed. 'You're kidding! You handled yourself so well.'

'I had to.' Piers couldn't hold back a shudder.

The family had their last glimpse of Jean-Michel Dupont, who glared at Moira on his way out. One of the other police officers had snapped a pair of handcuffs over his wrist. On their way out the door, he said, 'You're coming with us and you won't escape justice as swiftly as you did in your own country.'

Casey looked at Piers and he shrugged. They would find out what that remark meant later.

'Daddy, he hurt Ben too. Ben fell over.'

Piers rested his face in Jerome's hair. 'Don't worry, he's okay. He was racing around the yard when I first got back.'

'Why did you come?' Casey cried.

Her question made him start trembling again. 'I almost didn't. I was so close to not coming. Thank God I did.'

'Thank God,' Casey echoed. 'But why did you? You said you'd be gone all day.'

'Jerome's kite,' Piers replied simply.

'What?'

'When I made my first stop, I found the kite wedged behind the driver's seat in my van. You assumed that I'd put it in your car boot, but I forgot. I'd accidentally left it in my van when we took it to the park that day there wasn't enough wind. I never got around to taking it out again.'

'So you thought you'd bring it back for him?' Moira was stunned out of her tears.

Piers nodded. 'I had to back-track and I knew I'd be putting myself behind all day. That's why I almost didn't come. But then I remembered how much he'd been hanging out to fly it today, so I came back. I was hoping you would've all realised you didn't have it and come back too. You should've heard me grumbling all the way back up to the hills.'

Nobody spoke for a long moment. Casey wanted to but her throat was too tight. Piers broke the silence himself.

'If I'd just kept on with my work the way I wanted to, he would've…'

'But you didn't! You came!' she said quickly.

He responded by pulling her into his arms. She could feel his heart hammering. 'I can't stop thinking what might've happened. I never want to lose you. I want to marry you.'

Casey made a movement to crane her neck and look up at him. 'What did you say?'

Piers pulled a face. 'Sorry. I shouldn't have said it yet. Not here. I'm a total mess, aren't I?'

'Yes to both those things.'

He paused to consider what she'd said. 'What do you mean to both?'

'Yes, you're a total mess. And yes, I'll marry you.'

Moira suddenly began laughing and crying all over again. She turned aside with Jerome on her lap to whisper something in his ear.

'You don't need… more time then?' Piers breathed.

'Listen to me, I was frightened out of my wits today. I'm not going to bother mucking around and pretending to be shy. Life's too short for that. I don't need any time at all to tell you I'll marry you. You ought to know that.'

Piers was laughing as he rested his cheek against her head and Casey let herself turn limp in his arms. She raised her hand to stroke his hair.

'You know what you've just done, don't you?' she whispered. 'You've turned the worst day of my life into the best.'

He kissed her cheek and looked down at her with his lopsided smile. 'I reckon you'll always remember the day I proposed, anyway.'

Chapter 28

Not until the following day did they learn the full story about Jean-Michel Dupont. Casey and the others had been taken to hospital and were soon discharged. She had spent some time with her own family, lying on the couch and enjoying Helen's and Abby's care. Even Dale and her father hung onto every word she spoke about their ordeal. But she didn't want to stay away from the Bowman family for long. She found them all crowded into the flat she shared with Suzanne. Moira, Piers and Jerome were sleeping on mattresses on the lounge room floor. Nobody wanted to return to Piers' house for a few days. Eric was there with them.

After they'd shared a take-away tea, the same good-humoured policeman who had been at Piers' house the previous day knocked on the door.

'I just wanted to be sure you're all doing well. Dupont told us that he wasn't really intending to kill you, Mrs Bowman.' He inclined his head respectfully to Moira. 'According to him, he just wanted to give you a big scare, and tried his hardest to convince us you deserved it. Little did he know, he only convinced us what a dangerous felon he is.'

'What a pathetic story!' Eric burst out. 'Does he think he can get away with terrorising three defenceless women and a little boy without having to face some serious charges?'

'If he did think that, we soon set him straight.' The police officer's mouth was a grim line. 'I'd say he's grown used to dodging the law. That's

The Risky Way Home

the other news I have for you all. Jean-Michel Dupont is wanted in his own country for the attempted murder of his brother, Andre.'

Piers and Suzanne swung around to stare at each other. Moira buried her face in her hands and burst into tears. Casey was sitting on the couch beside Moira and grasped her hand. Casey's own throat was aching with the bombshell.

'I could tell Jean Dupont exhibits all the classic traits of the typical psychopath. He's violent and aggressive, deceitful, with no sign of any empathy for others whatsoever and no remorse. And to think you were married to him, ma'am.'

Casey nodded because Moira couldn't talk.

'Well I can promise you he won't be giving you any more trouble.'

'We all spoke about watching our backs in case he did something this despicable,' Eric said, 'but we still can't believe he really did it. We thought we were just being extra cautious.'

'He's not the sort you'd ever want to under-estimate.'

Then Suzanne broke down. She wept as Casey had never seen anybody weep before, brushing away her tears with the palms of her hands. 'I'm sorry … I've learned something I had to learn, but it's been so hard.' She stopped trying to fumble for words. Piers, who stood closest, wrapped his arms around her. Suzanne bowed her head on his shoulder and kept crying.

Eric looked at Casey and jerked his chin toward the door. Casey stood up and followed him outside the flat. They both knew the Bowmans needed time together.

'Hey, Eric, I haven't heard how you came to be at the studio after he took us away.'

Sighing, he leaned against the wall. 'It was one of the few times in my life I ever decided to quit a golf game after just two rounds. It was such a windy day, I decided I'd rather be at the beach taking photos of crashing waves. I needed to stop at the studio to pick up a lens I needed.'

She could hardly imagine his reaction to what he would have found. 'I guess you got far more than you bargained for.'

'That's got to be the understatement of the century. I didn't even see Suzanne to start with. I couldn't believe the trashed dump I was stepping into, or the clump of mangled metal that used to be my camera. Then I went into the make-up room and saw her.' He covered his face with his hands. 'I honestly thought she was dead. There I was, almost in tears, trying to listen for her heartbeat. When she started to moan, my knees turned to jelly.'

'It was scary for you, but so good for her that you happened to be there right at that moment.'

His mouth quirked into a grim smile. 'It sure was, but she was still the same old Suzanne. I told her to stay put while I phoned an ambulance and the police but she wouldn't listen. She was up trying to wipe cold cream and glass shards off herself, trying to convince me that he was going to kill you all. She wanted to grapple my phone out of my hands so she could call Piers. I told her that if she'd just sit down and stay calm, I'd try to phone him. I called his number time and time again.'

A realisation dawned on Casey. 'Those must've been the calls we kept hearing.'

Eric nodded. 'When there was no answer, Suzanne went into hysterics. She was convinced that Dupont must have murdered all of you, Piers included. She was crying out that it was all her fault for attracting that mongrel into the country and making him feel welcome. All I could do was keep reminding her that we didn't know for sure that anybody was dead. I tell you, Casey, it was such a relief when somebody answered that phone at last.'

'Thank God it all ended well. I feel terrible that poor Suzanne still feels so broken-hearted.'

'Don't worry, I'll look after her. She'll be fine. I'm just glad to see the crackpot out of the country.'

'Eric, thanks for all your help. You've been great.'

He gave a grim nod.

'I'm sorry for the way things were between us,' Casey added.

Eric's brow furrowed as he considered what to say. 'So am I. You might find this odd, Casey, but it was only after you dumped me that I began to take a more thorough study of you. I suppose you could say that I really did fall for you then, in a way. You might be the sort of girl a guy wouldn't take a second glance at to start with but I like hearing you talk. Your warm heart and perspicacity are really something very special.'

She found herself smiling. 'Well, thank you.'

'Don't mention it. I hope Piers realises what a gem he's won.'

'You'll have to ask him. Do you know, Eric, I was sincere in wanting

The Risky Way Home

to go out with you when you first invited me. But I was falling in love with Piers all along. Nobody was more surprised than I was when I worked it out. You see, I'd known him for years and he was the last person I ever thought I'd fall for.'

'I've revised my opinion of him,' Eric said. 'I used to think he was a complete moron. But he's okay when you bother taking the time to talk to him. And of course he was fantastic when he rescued you all from that idiot. I've started thinking I'd better start trying to like Suzanne's family, anyway.'

'Why might that be?' Casey felt a grin spread from ear to ear.

'When I took her in my arms in the studio, she was shaking with tears and her shoulders felt so slender and frail. I couldn't bear to think of that Dupont trying to hurt her. You know, I could still smell the scent of her normal shampoo through all that mess in her hair. I hadn't smelled that for a long time. It brought back memories. Don't say anything to her yet because I still haven't worked out how to tell her. I wouldn't want to let her down. But Suzanne is a person I can relate to and understand. We're both strong characters and I won't pretend to hope things will always run smoothly between us from now on. Still, we've probably given too much to each other over the years to be able to give much to anyone else.'

'I think you're absolutely right. Can I just tell Piers what you're thinking about?'

'Only if he promises to keep his mouth shut until I'm ready to make my move.'

***

'Moira, how are you feeling?' Helen asked. 'You're looking remarkably well but after all you went through, I can't help asking.'

'I'm feeling much better.' Indeed, Moira Bowman had never appeared so relaxed at the Millers' kitchen table. There was lightness to her movements and a glow in her eyes that were completely new and made her appear ten years younger.

'I'm still spinning with relief. For twenty years I've lived with the fear that Jean might come. Now that he has come and I know he won't be back, the difference that it makes to everything is incredible. I've been waking up the last few mornings wondering why the sun seems to be shining so much brighter than usual. Then I remember that it's all over.'

'I'm thanking God each day that all of you were spared,' Helen said. 'I felt sick to my stomach just hearing what had happened. What you both went through was incredible.' She grasped one of Moira's hands and one of Casey's.

Moira seemed to be shuffling in her chair. 'I hope you won't think I'm speaking ill of the dead but I feel like I need to tell somebody something else that's been on my mind. I'm not feeling at all sorry that Mother is dead.' She lowered her voice as if she feared that Henrietta might really be listening. 'I feel guilty about that after all she's done for us. But she used to say things that caused such a weight in my heart. I didn't even realise how burdened I felt until she was gone. Perhaps that was because she would repeat it all so often.'

'What would she say?' Helen asked gently.

Moira took a sip of her tea. 'She'd say, "You need to keep an eye on those two children because they have their father's blood in them. They'll turn bad."'

'What a load of rubbish that was!' Casey didn't care whether or not she was speaking ill of the dead.

'Absolute nonsense,' Helen agreed. 'Suzanne has always been such fun and everyone who meets her loves her. And Piers always lights up the place whenever he comes to visit. Moira, you've raised a thorough gentleman.'

'And we're not the least bit biased in this house,' Abby added.

In the general laugh that followed, Moira raised a crisply ironed handkerchief to dab her eyes. 'Thank you. You've all done me so much good today.'

'Just remember,' Helen told her, 'Whatever happened in those few years between you and that dreadful man, it wasn't a total disaster. You have two beautiful children and one gorgeous grandson to show for it.'

'It seems more than ever that God's hand has been on our move to Australia all along,' Moira beamed. 'We had to come here so that Piers could meet Casey.'

Chapter 29

'Casey, that cloth isn't good enough,' Suzanne said.

'What's wrong with it?' Casey had just draped her favourite lacy tablecloth over the trestle table that had been set up in the work shed for the punchbowl and glasses.

'Can't you tell it's a slightly different shade of cream to the little stripes in these pink and cream lanterns?'

'Yes, but the lanterns will be up so high, I didn't think it'd matter.'

'Of course it matters. We need your engagement party to be perfect. Eric will be here to take photos and you know he doesn't do that for just anyone. Leave it to me. There's a tablecloth folded up in the cupboard at the studio. I'll phone him to bring it when he comes.'

'Suzanne, I know you have my best interests at heart but I'm happy just as it is.'

Piers nodded his approval from the ladder where he'd been hanging some of Suzanne's lanterns around the eaves. 'It looks okay to me.'

'I guess I'm overruled then,' Suzanne said, slapping the back of her hand with a mock frown. Her lips turned down as though about to cry but then she laughed. 'I'm sorry Casey. Just tell me to pull my head in next time I'm overbearing.'

'Yes, I will,' Casey grinned.

Suzanne was looking sideways at her. 'Do you know I've always envied you?'

That was enough to make Casey gape up at her. 'You envied me? Why?'

Suzanne sighed. 'When we were at school, you seemed to have such a great, stable relationship with your family. And you find it so easy to be quiet and content. I've never said this to you before but you used to make me feel sort of shallow.'

'I envied you, for being so outgoing and so much fun.'

Suzanne merely laughed. She'd heard that same compliment over the years from many people. 'I want to ask your opinion on something.'

Casey found her interest piqued by the mysterious lowering of Suzanne's voice. 'What is it?'

'Do you think I ought to give Eric another chance?'

'So he's come out and asked you, has he?'

Suzanne stared. 'No, he hasn't said a word. What makes you think he would?'

'I just assumed that would be the only reason you'd start talking about second chances.' Casey turned so Suzanne could not see her face. She'd almost put her foot in it.

'It's just that after all that happened with...' Suzanne's jawbone tightened for a moment. 'Eric was so great and caring. I started wondering if I still have feelings buried for him. Maybe that's why I tried so hard earlier this year to set him up with you. So I wouldn't have to completely let go.'

'I think you should give it a go.'

Suzanne shook her head and giggled. 'Okay, you don't beat around the bush.'

'It's just that I really believe you'd be great together.'

'I don't know. I suppose if I didn't think there was a possibility, I wouldn't be thinking about him so much.' Suzanne frowned as she stood back to survey the party arrangements with the eye of an artist. 'Do you think we should tie a fuchsia pink crepe ribbon around Ben's neck, to match the lanterns?'

'Do you think it'd stay on for longer than five minutes without him eating it?' Piers hooted.

'Okay, okay. I forgot the dumb animal would do that. I'm just going to get the party chocolates to put on the table.' When Suzanne stepped out

The Risky Way Home

of the shed, Piers climbed down the ladder and wrapped his arm around Casey's shoulders. 'She'll be even worse when it comes time to plan our wedding, you know.'

'Don't remind me. I can't bear to think about that yet.'

'But you still want to go through with it?' he teased.

'Absolutely.' She rested her head on his shoulder. 'Doesn't that show how highly I think of you?'

With a laugh, he raised her hand to kiss her knuckles. 'It really does.'

More from Paula Vince

If you've enjoyed "The Risky Way Home" you'll also love these other stunning romance/drama novels by Paula Vince.

Best Forgotten

A young accident victim wakes up in hospital and can't remember who he is. Why does he have nothing in common with his family? Why does he despise the person he was supposed to be? Why has his best friend disappeared without a trace? Is somebody after him?

His family can offer no solutions. His girlfriend is strangely aloof and he cannot shake off a feeling that the answers will prove more unpleasant than his amnesia. Somehow he must find out as it seems time is running out.

Picking up the Pieces

Two families – two tragedies.

The Parker family and the Quinlan family find out what it means to be in total despair. But there is just a small ray of hope.

Without warning, Claire Parker's world shatters. She must find a source of strength to help her recover or she will never again be the warm and happy person she once was.

In a moment of reckless despair, Blake Quinlan makes a truly terrible mistake. The bitter consequences of his impulse will reverberate through the rest of his life unless he learns to deal with his past.

A Design of Gold

After a traumatic experience, Nicola recovers by taking refuge in Casey and Piers Bowman's spare room.

Jerome, Piers' son, is learning to be a young man, struggling in his quest to make a difference, with ideals of mission life from his childhood hero.

Michael, a teenager who's been down all the wrong roads, is trying to follow the straight and narrow.

As their lives intertwine they grow, learning about themselves and that true discipleship starts at home.

Romance and drama combine in this new book from the author who brought you Picking up the Pieces and The Risky Way Home.

www.ingramcontent.com/pod-product-compliance
Lightning Source LLC
Chambersburg PA
CBHW031211260626
47169CB00007B/2016